THE
DRAGONTAIL
BUTTONHOLE

THE
DRAGONTAIL
BUTTONHOLE

PETER CURTIS

Published by
Sordelet Ink

The Dragontail Buttonhole

Copyright © 2016 by Peter Curtis

First Edition by Sordelet Ink

Cover Design by Marlin Greene / 3Hats Design / Seattle
www.3hats.com

ISBN-13: 978-1944540142
ISBN-10: 1944540148

www.petercurtisauthor.com

Published by Sordelet Ink
www.sordeletink.com

To Carolyn, best friend and partner of fifty years, who has patiently and lovingly helped me on this writing journey, unafraid to comment, edit and improve.

To my parents and grandparents, for leaving me so many tangible memories of their lives, and for making sure I survived the war in 1939.

OTHER THAN MY OWN research, major sources for this work of fiction come from family artifacts, stories, and a memoir dictated by my mother. References to historical events, real people, or real places are used fictitiously. The characters in this novel, except for the toddler Pavel, are either fictitious or deceased. Real people, places, and events have been depicted as accurately as possible in the time frame of 1938 to 1940—always an imprecise venture. Other names, characters, places and events are products of the author's imagination and any resemblance to actual events, places or persons, living or dead, is coincidental.

— Peter Curtis

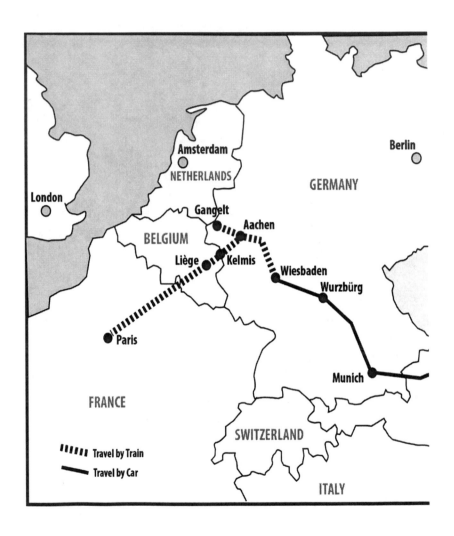

POLAND   Warsaw

Protectorate of Bohemia and Moravia
Nazi controlled in 1939

Prague

Brno

Košice

SLOVAKIA

Bratislava

Vienna   Esztergom

AUSTRIA   Budapest

HUNGARY

ROMANIA

"You shall be forced to leave behind those things you love most dearly, and this is the first arrow the bow of your exile will shoot."

—*Paradiso*, Canto XVII
Dante Alighieri

"There is no such thing as escape after all, only an exchange of one set of difficulties for another."

—*The Dirty Life*
Kristin Kimba

1

PRAGUE
MARCH 15, 1939

WILLY KOHUT, breathing hard, stepped gratefully into the warmth of his store at 19 Masná Street. He stamped his feet and brushed off the snow. *Thank God, I'm still in one piece.*

Unbuttoning his galoshes, he hung up his homburg and overcoat and looked around. The cutting tabletop glistened like a mirror, the club armchairs were in their proper places, and the bolts of English suiting stacked along the wall were perfectly aligned. He mopped the sweat off his face. *Looks fine, but what's going to happen now?*

An hour earlier, at nine, he had reached the Dresdner Bank to find its regular customers, many of whom he knew well enough to nod to, fighting like wild dogs, pushing and punching to get to the tellers' counters. Arguing and elbowing his way through the crowd, Willy had managed to get to the front and withdraw 70,000 korun from his account. Back outside on the bank's marble steps, clutching his briefcase, he'd stopped short. *So it's true.* Not more than a few hundred meters away, columns of German soldiers, armored cars, growling half-tracks, and motorcycles were moving steadily along Na Příkopě Street.

Panicked, he'd dodged his way home through the back streets and alleys of the Old Town district, his mind focused on what to do next. *Money in the safe, hunker down with the family, wait.*

❧ ∂ ❧

Three hours earlier, in the middle of Willy's standard breakfast of coffee, hot rolls, and Duerr's English marmalade, Rádio Praha had announced the devastating news: German army units had crossed the Czech border and were driving unopposed toward the capital. Advance Panzer units were expected in Prague by mid-morning.

Astonished and cursing himself for attempting to wait out Czechoslovakia's repeated crises over the previous months, Willy had woken Sophie and sat on their bed, doing his best to wind down her panic with kisses and reassuring words. Afterwards, as he shaved and dressed, the implications of the radio announcement whirled through his head. With the Nazis taking control of the country, his half-formed plans to sell his store, Anglotex, and leave Czechoslovakia hung by a thread. If recent history was anything to go by, everything would change for Jewish families like his. How bad that change would be in Prague or how it would happen was anyone's guess.

While 18 month-old Pavel slept in his crib, Willy and Sophie gathered the domestics around the dining table. Elena the maid and Nanny Ludmila were uneducated village girls who shared a rented room in the city during the week. Elise, the part-time cook, usually arrived at eleven. Willy's report of the radio broadcast was met by the women with shocked silence, tears, fearful looks, and questions: "What shall we do?" "What will happen to us?" "Please, can we go home?"

"We have two hours before the Germans get to Prague." Willy tried to convey calm and authority, though he could not stop an uncontrollable jiggle of his right foot. "Elena, you will go to Zoryk's grocery on Železná Street. Buy canned food and anything else you think we might need for the next two weeks. Take Pavel's perambulator and fill it up. Madám will give you the money. Everyone else stays indoors, especially Pavel."

"Elena shouldn't go out by herself," countermanded Sophie, her eyes flashing. The soft skin of her cheeks flushed. "The girl is only eighteen. Who knows what the streets are like? Zoryk's opens at half past eight. I'm the one to go. I'll decide what we need. Elena and Ludmila will look after everything here until the master's cousins arrive."

Willy looked at Sophie in surprise. "Good for you, strudel." She was being more forceful than he was used to, unexpectedly pragmatic for the decorative affectionate woman who shared their bourgeois life of servants, fashions, and Prague's social whirl. He slid his hand over hers and gave her a complimentary, admiring smile before rising from his chair. "That's settled, then. As well as food, we need a reserve of money... for..." He shrugged. "For... I don't know what eventualities. I'll go to the Dresdner Bank and be there for when it opens. Janko and Laci are supposed to be here at nine. Tell them to keep the store closed."

A few minutes later, bundled up in warm clothes and furs, Willy and Sophie stood outside the lobby of their apartment building. Fine snowflakes billowed into their faces. "For God's sake, make sure you're back before ten," said Willy, pulling back the soft fox fur of Sophie's hood to kiss her cold cheek. He wanted to appear calm but his pulse was racing. His neck and shoulders muscles tensed as tight as ropes.

Comforted at returning from the bank without incident, Willy lay his briefcase on the cutting table, dried off his spectacles, and frowned. He recognized the spicy stink of Laci's Memphis brand cigarettes. Only customers could smoke in his store, and there were no customers. "Laci," he shouted, "you damned Slovak chimney, where the hell are you?"

As he picked up his briefcase, he noticed wet footprints on the carpet. *Laci again.* He had left his cousins strict instructions to keep Anglotex closed. "Laci, for God's sake," he shouted again, "get your backside in here!" The lazybones *potz* should have been unpacking the latest shipment in the yard instead of smoking in the store.

Employing cousins in the family business had its drawbacks, especially if they were only a couple of years younger than the 26 year-old cousin-boss. Hefty, emotional Laci, and thin indecisive Janko were good-hearted fellows, but they had recently shown some reluctance to obey orders. A year working in Prague had changed the once respectful town Slovaks into habitués of pubs, chasers of women, and frequent requesters of cash advances.

As Willy strode past the stacked shelves, heading for the office, he ran his fingers along the bolts of cheviot tweed, cashmere, worsted, and herringbone. He loved the feel of finely spun British wool: his merchandise.

Hearing clicking footsteps in the apartment above, he smiled; Sophie was back from Zoryk's grocery? He wondered if she had experienced any trouble buying the food—probably the same kind of unpleasantness he had encountered at the bank: people panicking, pushing and shoving to get what they needed. His heart jolted. *God, I hope she didn't see any damned Nazis.*

Hearing the radio playing in his back office, Willy's anger surged. *Laci again!* He swung the office door open, ready to blast his cousin with a mouthful of curses.

It took a few seconds to absorb what he saw: cigarette haze, filing cabinet drawers awry, and half-opened files strewn across the floor.

A shorthaired, lanky man in *feldgrau* uniform, a swastika band on his left upper arm, sat behind Willy's desk. Two heavily built German soldiers in steel helmets stood beside him, taciturn and menacing. They carried Mauser machine pistols. A Czech voice burbled on the shelf radio, but Willy was not listening. Like horses breaking loose from a burning shed, his thoughts raced in all directions. *Here already? What the hell? Why? Have they been up to the apartment?*

"You are Kohut?" asked the officer in a calm but grating voice.

Willy nodded, unable to say anything but he could not help appreciating the precise, form-fitting cut of the man's uniform. He was in the cloth trade, after all

"I sent your employees upstairs to be with your wife. They said you speak German. *Das ist ganz gut.* We won't have to waste time."

Willy's skin turned cold, his stomach churned. He took a deep breath. *What do the bastards want?* He did not dare ask about Sophie, not yet. He paused for a moment to clear his head. In excellent German, he replied, "I am Kohut, Wilhelm. Those employees, they are my cousins. We are a family business. Please, what is happening here?"

"Hauptmann Kreutz, Section two, Gestapo," said the officer with a crisp nod. "The German army is in Prague to protect the civilian population from unrest. From now on, I ask the questions and you give me answers. Understand?"

Willy tried to bottle up his fear. *They're looking for something, but what?* Seconds passed as his mouth turned dry and his hands began to shake. *For God's sake, don't show the bastards you're afraid.* He wetted his lips and swallowed. "I'm a respectable Prague businessman. I've done nothing wrong. What are you looking for in my files?"

The officer checked the document in front of him with a forefinger. Smoke curled from the cigarette tucked into the corner of his mouth, making him blink. "You are a Jew, *ja?* A Slovak from Košice in the south, age twenty-six, married to a Hungarian woman with an eighteen-month-old male child. You have owned this store, Anglotex, since one year? Correct? "

Willy blinked assent, his pulse galloping. *How do they know all this?* The pale, sharp-featured officer noted down something with a silver pencil. "You sell English fabrics for making men's suits and overcoats? Again, correct?"

A wave of outrage destroyed Willy's effort to stay calm. His office was sacrosanct. "Herr Hauptmann, why are you here? What are you doing with my files?" He was unable to keep himself from accentuating the 'you'.

Hauptmann Kreutz glanced pointedly at the corner of the desk where his Luger lay nestled in a holster. "This is my last warning, stupid. Do not ask me questions." With a knowing smile, he lifted a blue folder and waved it at Willy. "This is a list of Czech citizens the Gestapo has designated dangerous and destabilizing elements. You and your fine British store, *mein Herr*, are on the list. That is why we are here."

Fear washed away Willy's temper. He felt sweat under his arms. "*Aber...*"

The officer leaned forward, his eyes glittering with contempt. "You do business with the British, and you also spy for them. We know this from an informant."

A spy! An informant? This is madness. Willy was silent for a moment, shattered by how confidently Kreutz had made the accusation. His heart skittered. Spies were routinely tortured, even executed. *What to say?* His brain stalled; his usual quick thinking deserted him. "I'm not a spy," he said, racking his brain for who the informant might be.

Kreutz came around the desk, slid his hand into the inside pocket of Willy's jacket, and removed the wallet.

Willy was tight as a bowstring. He wanted to smash his fist in the officer's face, but he knew what the consequence would be.

After a cursory examination, Kreutz passed the wallet to one of the soldiers. "Just a temporary confiscation, Herr Kohut, for more detailed study" His cold eyes probed Willy's face, finally coming to rest on his chest. He bent forward to finger the lapel of Willy's jacket. "*Merkwürdig, interessant.* This is a very unusual buttonhole."

Momentarily confused, Willy looked down at his jacket. "It's a dragontail buttonhole, a trademark—the signature of a famous tailor here in Prague." He held his breath at more sounds of footsteps in the apartment above. The pattering ones he knew belonged to Pavel, but he could only guess at the others. *Is Sophie back? Have the Nazis already been up there?* He was afraid to ask.

Curling his lip as if he did not believe a word, Kreutz signaled for the soldiers to come and look for themselves. He grabbed the lapel, jerking Willy forward. "A clever idea; a way for British spies to recognize each other without speaking, a contact signal. This tailor's trademark story is laughable."

The soldiers nodded their understanding. "No, you're wrong," said Willy swallowing his anger. "Check with Moshe Lemberger, a tailor in Old Town. All his best suits have this buttonhole design."

Kreutz shrugged, and glancing down at Willy's briefcase pried it from his grasp. He clicked it open, peered inside, and pulled out a thick bundle of banknotes. A smile broke across his face as he riffled through the notes. "*Ah, wunderschön.* You are most thoughtful, Herr Kohut. The Third Reich is happy to accept such charitable donations."

"That's mine," spluttered Willy, instinctively grabbing at the officer's hand. Out of the corner of his eye, he noticed a sudden movement, and almost instantaneously his right shoulder exploded in agony. Staggering sideways, he felt a cold gun-barrel pressed hard against his temple. His wire-rimmed spectacles slipped sideways. A thick arm held his neck in a suffocating lock.

With his head agonizingly twisted, Willy watched Kreutz stuff the money inside his field jacket. The pressure on his windpipe increased, and he felt the rasping breaths vibrating in his chest. He gagged, tried to cough and pulled ineffectually at the immovable arm. His knees felt like rubber, and the room began to sway and go dim. *I'm going to die.*

"Let the Jew go," said Kreutz, turning to the other soldier.

"You—bring empty boxes from the staff car and fill them with the papers from this desk. The Gestapo will sift through the rest of this mess when they come for a more thorough search."

"What about this Czech filth?" grunted the soldier who had applied the arm-lock. He moved the Mauser from Willy's head to his midriff.

"Blindfold him and stick something in his mouth. He comes with us."

Willy's insides twisted. Feeling the urge to urinate, he tightened his bladder muscles, determined not to show weakness. Someone behind him pulled off his glasses, tied a cloth over his eyes, and stuffed a large ball of crumpled paper into his mouth. His hands were tied behind his back. His crazy thought— that this was what a trussed goose at the Holešovice market felt like— vanished under the salvo of unanswerable questions exploding in his brain. *Have they been upstairs? Where is Sophie? What are the bastards going to do with me?*

In the back of the car, squeezed between two soldiers and his own whirling thoughts, Willy listened to his captors boasting about how easy it had been driving in convoy from the German border, watched by peasants and the pathetic fragments of the Czech army, and how many more victims they had to pick up before lunch.

Twenty minutes later, they pulled Willy out, still blind-folded. He stumbled, trying to keep pace as they dragged him along the pavement. *Is this the end? Arrested for nothing, killed for nothing.*

He heard the creak of a door, barked orders, and echoing footsteps. They were inside now. After a few more steps, he was pushed up a flight of stairs and along a corridor. A loud click, a shove in the back. Someone released his hands and pulled off the blindfold.

Willy spat out the sodden paper as the door slammed shut behind him. He stood blinking in a large, dimly lit room that held a conference table that could have seated 30 or more, if there had been any chairs. Several men stood around the table, hands in pockets. Others sat on the floor, faces turned toward him as he stumbled further into the room. Everything was blurred. *Glasses, where are they?* He patted his jacket pockets hopefully and, with a surge of relief, discovered them. He felt less helpless. More than that, he felt lucky to be alive.

A curly-bearded, pug-nosed man, a couple of inches shorter than Willy's five foot six, approached him. "Hullo, my new friend," he said with a sardonic look, grabbing Willy's arm.

Willy noticed his badly cut suit and lack of a tie. A workman.

"Welcome to the Novotný Legal Chambers." He jerked his head toward the shelves lined with gilded tomes and then pointed at the portraits of serious-faced men in high collars and legal robes. "Consider the irony of our situation, my friend: undesirables like you and me, held prisoner illegally in the offices of a famous Czech law firm. I've been here an hour. The guard said we can expect many more arrivals."

"What is this? What's happening?"

The man shrugged, spreading his hands and then running fingers through a halo of wiry hair. "It seems we are here for processing—detailed interviews: the Nazis ask who we are, what we do, where we live, what possessions we own. The bastards come for us one at a time. My name is Ožtek, Otto, electrician extraordinaire and trade union official. And you are..?"

Willy was impressed by Ožtek's articulate words. *So, an intelligent, possibly well-educated, poorly dressed electrician.*

"Kohut Willy, I sell wool fabric for men's suits." They shook hands. "Do you think we'll be here long?"

Ožtek indicated the galvanized steel buckets lining the back wall. A man was noisily urinating into one of them. "As you can see, this is no hotel. No one is allowed to leave the room unless called."

Panic overtook Willy again. *How will Sophie and Pavel manage?* Laci and Janko would offer practical help and muscle, but only Sophie knew about the money hidden behind the stove and the counterfeit passports in the flour bin—part of his recent clandestine preparations for leaving the country. Now that the Third Reich was in Prague, something Willy never expected would happen, Czech citizens, his family, and especially all the Jews in the city were in uncharted territory. He knew what monstrous things the Germans were doing to their own people.

God forbid they might do the same here.

2

ZORYK'S GROCERY
MARCH 15, 1939

AS WILLY was turning toward Truhlářská Street on his way
to the Dresdner Bank, Sophie pushed an empty perambulator
across Old Town Square toward Zoryk's grocery. Her galoshes
slipped on the slick cobbles as she hurried along. She noticed
that the square was much quieter than usual. Only two of the
grilled-sausage-and-ham stalls were open. Small knots of people
were talking; arguing, gesticulating, and their faces reminded
her of startled deer, uncertain and afraid. A group of unarmed,
grim-faced Czech soldiers sat on the steps of the Jan Hus monu-
ment, heads drooped over cigarettes and beer bottles.

Zoryk's was tucked into a side street one hundred meters
or so from Old Town Square, and Sophie joined the queue
outside the store. She guessed there were perhaps forty other
red-nosed, frightened women stamping their boots in the snow.
No one talked much, except to complain about the cold. A few
were forecasting, with some relish, the horrible things Czech
women might expect from the Nazi soldiers.

After nearly an hour's wait, Sophie lost patience. Knowing
how urgent it was to get home before the Germans arrived, she
forced her way through the crowd, banging the perambulator
against people's legs, repeating "Excuse me, please, my child is
sick." Ashamed of the lie but determined, she disregarded other
women's furious looks. Two of them grabbed her arm, trying to

hold her back. One of them spat in her face. "Go home, stinking Jew." It was like an electric shock. *I've never seen this woman before! How does she know what I am?* Sophie shoved the pram through the doorway with all her might.

Inside, apart from the large crowd of noisy women, the small store was the same as always: walls and ceiling of varnished fir planking covered by shelves stacked with cans, jars of preserves, and staples. On the blackboard behind the service counter, *pan* Zoryk had chalked up his daily specials: DUCK EGGS, ŠPEK, TURNIPS. Underneath was written, ALWAYS BE NICE TO ZORYK.

Halfway to the counter, Sophie's progress was blocked by arguing, angry women. Hands punched and pulled at her. She tried to control herself, desperate to get through and afraid of being hurt. She stuck out her elbows and hips to retaliate and make room, determined to accomplish her task.

"Let the poor lady through!" yelled Zoryk, slamming a rolling pin down on his counter. The crack of wood on wood stilled the crowd. "She has a sick child at home," he said loudly, giving her a wink; Sophie was one of his best customers.

She smiled gratefully, taking his cue. "Whooping cough," she shouted above the renewed hubbub. "I have to get back. The doctor's coming." Like ewes driven by a sheepdog, the patterned headscarves parted for her. The stocky, aproned grocer took her shopping list and helped fill the carriage with potatoes, root vegetables, butter, jam, eggs, and cans of soup.

He shook his head as he took the koruna notes and gave Sophie her change. "Bad news for Prague is good news for me, *paní* Kohutová. I'll be sold out by noon." He nodded toward the back room where a radio blared. "Did you hear the latest? The main German forces have passed through Kladno and Zdiby—tanks, artillery, machine guns, thousands of soldiers. Supposedly, some units are already in Prague. You'd better get home." He pushed three one-liter bottles of milk, five pounds of rice, two loaves of bread, and several wrapped packets of sausage and ham toward her.

Sophie tried to hurry on the way home, but the overloaded pram kept sliding sideways on the cobblestones. Her arms ached, but she was too afraid to stop and rest. Fine snowflakes had covered her purchases. Her watch said 10:15. Close to the tram stop by the *Tabák* booth, several cans fell to the ground. Tears threatened to overcome her, but an elderly gentleman in a fur-trimmed overcoat and homburg stopped to help her pick the cans out of the snow.

"Thank you so much," she said hesitantly. "I'm trying to get home. Have you seen any German soldiers?"

He lifted his hat courteously. "No, *paní*, for the time being it is safe. We have met before, you know. Your husband has the fabric store on Masná Street—a lively young fellow, I must say, always smiling. You sometimes accompany him when he comes to buy sheet music from me. I am František Mulič."

"Oh, yes, yes. The music store. I remember." She pushed the pram forward." I must get home."

The gentleman gave an old-fashioned bow from the waist and tipped his hat again. "With Nazi soldiers coming, you are much too pretty to be in Prague. Take my advice, leave as soon as you can." He turned and limped away.

Sophie hurried on, sloshing through wet snow and puddles. She shivered, afraid of bumping into a band of Germans or being attacked in some dark doorway by rough hands tearing at her clothes. The pram kept veering to the left, and the string bags banged painfully against her shins. She strained her ears for sounds of gunfire. *What if I see soldiers? What will they do? Shoot, rape me on the street?*

She turned the corner onto Masná Street and gasped. A motorcycle and sidecar in camouflage colors crouched like some malevolent insect in the center of the cobblestoned street, only twenty meters from Anglotex. A helmeted German soldier with a snub-nosed gun hanging from one shoulder lounged in the saddle, smoking a cigarette. Another soldier, bareheaded, bent over the sidecar doing something to what looked like a mounted machine gun. Her mind froze on one thought: *What should I do if they stop me?*

With her head down, Sophie pushed the perambulator steadily, hoping not to attract attention. "Can I walk with you, dear?" said a trembly voice behind her. She turned. It was *paní* Pasáková from three doors down. "I'm afraid those soldiers will attack me." The old woman leaned on her cane. "I'm too old for war; I want to die in my own bed."

Sophie put her arm round the old lady's shoulders and

they moved forward. It made pushing her pram all the more difficult, but she felt braver now that she was protecting someone more vulnerable.

The soldiers ignored the two women. Breathless, sweaty, and relieved, Sophie waited until the old woman had entered her house and then pushed the pram to the front door of Anglotex. It was locked. She pressed the bell, and Janko appeared. Looking pale, he pulled the pram over the threshold; several cans bounced out again. Janko's long, serious face seemed even more gaunt than usual as he bent to pick them up.

"Did you see the horrible soldiers in our street?" Sophie blurted. "Is Willy back from the bank?"

Laci appeared from the back with an ashen expression, not at all his ebullient self. "I'm so sorry, Sophie." He put down the bolt of cloth he was carrying and fumbled as he helped take off her coat and hat. "They...they came for Willy, the Sicherheitsdienst—soldiers and a security officer."

Sophie knew the word—she had grown up in Berlin—and fear wrapped itself round her heart. Trembling, she tried to stay upright by holding the table's edge. "Oh, my God. Sicherheitsdienst—security service? Why?" She looked around, wild-eyed, not quite registering the faces around her. "Where is Pavel?"

Janko hung his head. "Pavel is upstairs, he's fine. They wouldn't say why they were taking Willy. His name was on some list."

Laci chimed in. "The officer told us they were Abwehr, military intelligence, arresting people of special interest."

"Special interest? They've taken him?" She felt confused and overwhelmed. Willy was gone; everything was moving too fast to make sense.

Janko and Laci glanced at each other. "We didn't ask anything else, I mean...why," said Janko miserably.

"You mean you didn't even find out where they were taking him?" Sophie felt tears pricking her eyes as she pictured Willy in manacles being beaten and dragged along Masná Street. She felt empty, hollowed out. She rubbed ineffectually at the wet spots her tears were making on the front of her blouse.

The cousins shifted their feet, embarrassed by her fear and their own inaction. "I apologize," Janko said, looking down at his shoes. "We were too afraid."

"*Mami, Maminko!*" shouted Pavel from the staircase. His blue eyes sparkled with pleasure. Nanny Ludmila, looking sad, made her way down with him and set him on the floor. He walked unsteadily toward Sophie, who tried to smile. She wrapped her arms around him and stroked his blond curls. He pulled back, wiping her wet cheeks with his fingers, and looked around at everyone. "*Mami* cry?" he asked in a puzzled voice. For a long minute, no one spoke or moved. Tears began to trickle down Pavel's cheeks.

"Now we've made you cry too," said Sophie, kissing his wet face. "It's all right. We're just very sad at the moment."

"I watched them search upstairs," said Ludmila, blowing her nose and then patting her cheeks dry with a handkerchief. "They ruined your writing desk and pushed the books off the shelves. The brutes broke locked drawers—wood splinters everywhere."

Sophie put Pavel down and hurried toward the staircase, terrified that the Germans might have found the false Hungarian passports hidden in the flour bin and the money taped behind the stove. "I'd better see what damage those swine have done."

As she started up the stairs, she thought about all the precious things the family owned: their beloved Biedermeier desk, her Lötz Witwe glass vases, the Janák cubist easy chairs, and the three Czech impressionist paintings Willy had bought recently. *If the Germans have damaged or taken them, he will go crazy.*

With a firm grip, Laci pulled her back. "What about down here?" he said, frowning. "They made a God-awful mess of the filing cabinets, but it looks like they only took papers that were on the desk and a few files. Is there anything in Willy's office that might be construed as dangerous? I'm sure the Abwehr haven't finished - they'll come back."

Sophie was not sure which way to turn. She went into the store office and Pavel and the cousins followed her. The radio was playing band music, and she silenced it. "Oh God, the mess. What were they looking for?"

"You must burn all the papers in the stove," Laci said with assurance "What if Willy has anti-Nazi materials in the files? Ashes can't incriminate anyone."

"Wait a minute." Janko peered over Laci's shoulder at the mess. "If the Abwehr come back and find we've burned all the business files, they'll presume we actually had something to hide. Don't do it, Sophie. *Oy vey*, what a trouble we're in." He lit a cigarette and inhaled deeply. "Sophie, you must decide."

Under the cousins' expectant gaze, Sophie tried not to show how her hands were shaking. She was used to making decisions about the household, clothes and food, but nothing like this. If Willy came home later to find all the files burned, he would be furious. The cousins did not know it yet but he had made plans to sell Anglotex so they could join Willy's parents in London. She could almost hear his voice bellowing from the office: "How the hell can I sell this damned business with no account ledgers or documents to show the buyer?" Nevertheless, if she did nothing about the files, and the Abwehr discovered incriminating material, she was afraid they would do terrible things to him.

Sophie sat down at the desk, pressing fists against her temples trying to get her thoughts in order. She looked up hopefully at Janko. "All right," she sighed, "a compromise: we'll only burn the correspondence. Both of you must help me. We take out anything remotely anti-German from the files and burn that as well. Willy often cuts out anti-Nazi articles, cartoons from his Ulk and Simplicissimus magazines, and then sends them to friends. He keeps them down here."

"Shouldn't we keep the store closed all day while we do this?" asked Laci.

Sophie nodded, absentmindedly watching Pavel build a small mountain of loose paper on the carpet. If only she could be alone for a while, she could marshal her thoughts and think of a way to help Willy. All she wanted was for him to be back and in charge again, but the task of finding him seemed insurmountable.

"He would want us to keep an eye on the store tonight," said Laci. "You need protection, Sophie, especially if the Abwehr come back—and besides, we don't want to risk getting arrested on our way home. I heard on the radio there's a curfew after eight."

"There's no more Czechoslovakia," said Elena, taking off her maid's pinafore as she came down the spiral staircase. Her nose and eyelids were almost crimson from sobbing. "The radio says we're citizens of the Protectorate of Bohemia and Moravia. What does that mean?"

Laci gave a brittle laugh. "We've turned into ersatz Germans."

Janko took an oval cigarette from his pack and snapped open his lighter. "I slipped out earlier to get a newspaper," he said after a third and successful flick. "*V Praze, je klid*—that's *Lidové noviny*'s headline today. Prague is calm—calm except for the rumble of tanks and Willy gone. And there will be a victory parade." He blew a stream of smoke up into the air.

Sophie jerked her head. "A parade? What for?"

"To gloat. A Nazi parade. Hitler is coming to Hradčany Castle."

Her stomach cramped, acid surging up into her throat. Hitler in Prague signified only one thing: the Germans meant to be here forever.

ℭ∂ℭ

After checking that the passports and money were still in their hiding places, Sophie fed Pavel leftover tangy beef *szoljanka* soup and black bread, Afterwards, she spent a long time in the store office cleaning up the mess left by the Abwehr and working through the store files. She tried to record the dates and origin of the letters and merchandise orders in a notebook, though her mind kept wandering as if she were in a dream—or a nightmare, as if some wizard had waved an evil wand over Prague and made Willy disappear. *What if Willy never comes home?* She yearned for the feel of his arms around her, the solidity of his broad chest against her breasts, his warm hand between her thighs. She was so glad they had seen Rusalka at the opera house the night before and made love afterwards. It was a reminder of their closeness and need for each other.

At times throughout the afternoon, Sophie stopped her work to sing songs and play with Pavel. Nanny Ludmila was almost useless; she slumped in the easy chair in Pavel's room, worrying what the invaders might do to her family in Chodov on the outskirts of Prague. The telephone was silent, and the Ekco radio kept spouting assurances that the Germans would respect the Czech population. Sophie played some of Willy's records on the gramophone, especially his latest purchase, the Ink Spots' hit *'If I Didn't Care'*. Her husband loved to sing along, imitating the American accents. Though she did not understand the words, the slow guitar riffs and the melancholic voices suited her mood.

By sundown, Janko and Laci had finished burning the papers. Fine ash and paper fragments lay scattered on the floor, and the odor of charred paper hung in the air. Sophie did not know what to feel: guilty that she had destroyed part of her husband's dream, or satisfied that she had completed a record of everything they had burned so he would have some idea of what she had done.

That evening, Ruth Eisner, Sophie's author friend from the third floor, brought down some strudel. Ruth was a voluptuous red-haired divorcée who wore art deco clothes in the manner of Alphonse Mucha's posters and wrote erotic novels, one thousand words a day. From the day the Kohuts had moved into the Masná Street apartment, Ruth had appointed herself to the post of Sophie's social mentor in Prague. She was not the most suitable person for this crisis, Sophie realized, but being close at hand, she was better than no one. Tonight, Ruth made coffee and kept Sophie company while the cousins drank beer and listened to the radio. The atmosphere was subdued and tense as they waited for some event, some sign, some hope from somewhere that would bring Willy back.

Shortly after ten, the telephone rang. Everyone sat up. Janko rushed to switch off the radio. Sophie picked up the phone, heart pounding. Her friends never called this late.

"*Pani* Kohut?" A man's voice she did not recognize, soft and silvery. Her fingers tightened on the receiver.

"Yes."

"Your husband is in protectorate custody," he said in Czech. "Tomorrow, you bring him food and clean clothes. Bring also two thousand korun."

She shivered as if she had just stepped into an ice-cold shower; the words making her skin crawl, tensing her muscles. *Willy is alive!* "Who are you, please? Is my husband safe?" She tried to swallow the sob in her throat.

"You want the address, yes or no?"

"Yes please, where is he?" Sophie searched for a pencil.

"In the Václavské náměstí neighborhood, 14 Prilovna Street, the Novotný Legal Offices. Be there at noon sharp. Come alone."

"Prilovna, 14? Yes, I'll be there." As she wrote the address on the back of an envelope, Sophie heard Pavel start to cry in his room.

"At the entrance, you give the password to the guard: *Schreklich*. Come alone, understand."

Schrecklich—German for 'terrible'. That was exactly how she felt: terrible, vulnerable, and frightened. She forced herself to pay attention. "The two thousand korun. What is it for?"

She heard a click. The line went dead.

3

DETENTION
MARCH 15, 1939

FOUR HOURS after being dumped in the Novotný conference room, Willy counted forty-two detainees, some asleep,
many slumped on the floor, their backs against the walls, gazing
blankly into the air. Others conversed in muted tones. Every so
often, someone would get up and relieve himself in one of the
buckets. The air was thick with cigarette haze and the smells
of sweat and urine. Willy felt nauseated yet hungry at the same
time.

He squeezed his eyes shut to block out the sight of so
much despair and thought about home. He put his head in his
hands, his gut churning at how useless he felt. *What the hell is
going on at home? Has everyone been whisked away? If not, then
at least Laci and Janko will take care of Sophie.* After relieving himself in one of the buckets, Willy found his old place
on the floor had been taken and, apologizing, squeezed himself
between two older men. He turned his mind back to Pavel and
Sophie, cursing himself for the haste with which he had left for
the bank—he'd not even taken the time to say goodbye properly: run his fingers through Pavel's curls, hug his sturdy body
and given him a kiss on his plump cheek. *Will I ever see my boy
again?*

He closed his eyes, imagining Sophie's head on his shoulder, the scent of her hair, and her lips on his. He saw her smiling in the kitchen doorway, holding his midmorning coffee. Usually, when she came to the table and poured it for him, he would encircle her hips with his arms and rub his head against her belly, telling her she made the best coffee in Prague. God, how he wished he could turn the clock back. A year ago, their future in Prague had been set until the German aggression started and they planned to leave. He stared at his own fingers, cupped round his knees. Only yesterday, these pianist's hands had controlled and engineered his family's future. Could he ever twist this god-awful situation back into his favor?

The door opened and soldiers bundled in three more men. It was clear to Willy from the fine suits and the rounds of handshakes and introductions that many of the detainees held important positions in the city's institutions: security, administration, business, and the university. Two or three wore Czech army uniforms. The others were apparently "undesirables" with anti-Nazi views—communists, union leaders, priests, and journalists—like Ožtek, the man Willy had met upon arriving. Although Willy saw tall jugs of water and a handful of glasses on the table, there was no food. He accepted Ožtek's offer of a cigarette. Everyone was smoking; it seemed to be the only way to deal with hunger.

For a while, Willy participated in the heated discussions going on around him. Why had they been detained? Why was there no resistance to the Nazis? Why had President Hácha given the country away? No doubt about it, someone said authoritatively, the well-trained Czech military, with the most modern armaments in Europe, could have defeated the Germans.

Eventually, a stalwart, white-haired army officer in uniform banged his fist on the table, making the tumblers jump. The other detainees drew back to give him some space. "You want to know what really happened?" he asked in a voice choked with emotion. "You wish to know why we are here, gentlemen. Well. President Hácha and Foreign Minister Chvalkovský traveled to Berlin yesterday to meet with Hitler, Goering, and von Ribbentrop."

The crowd pressed closer to hear more clearly. "How do you know this?" someone asked.

"I am Colonel Hruček. I was at headquarters when the

message came through." His voice faltered. Willy saw immense sadness in the set of the old man's face, as if all hope had been sucked out of him.

"At the Berlin chancellery, our president protested in the strongest terms that Hitler was promoting Slovak independence from Czechoslovakia by instigating riots through provocateurs and propaganda."

"Quite right!" someone called out. Heads nodded.

"I was told that instead of issuing an apology for interfering in our affairs, Hitler had the gall to accuse Czechoslovakia of destabilizing the whole of Central Europe. He said the Germans would be coming to enforce peace, and if Hácha wanted to avoid the slaughter of the Czech people and the destruction of Prague by the Luftwaffe, he had to sign a surrender document. Hácha resisted. For three more hours, those Nazi swine harangued the old man at the chancellery. At four in the morning, Hácha collapsed."

There was a sudden murmur of astonishment. Willy got to his feet, his temper rising.

The colonel took a drink of water and continued. "The old man was revived by injections from Hitler's doctor. He was handed a previously written surrender statement, forced to sign it and then make a telephone call to military headquarters in Prague. Gentlemen, this is how we laid down our arms without a fight. It was shameful." Tears rolled down the colonel's veined cheeks.

The room was suddenly silent. Willy was appalled. This story was unbelievable; not a shred of human decency had been shown to the Czech president—just ruthless, primitive force applied at the highest level of government.

At nine in the evening, a guard called out Willy's name. He was the fifteenth detainee to be called; only eight had come back, and they looked relieved, even smiled a little. Apparently, they had been asked ordinary questions about their professional and family lives—just a simple interview, no threats, no brutality. But the unspoken question floating in the Novotný conference room was whether this meant that the seven other men who had not returned had been sent home or moved to a different, perhaps more harsh situation. Feeling nervous, Willy left for his interview with pats on the back and words of good luck. It reminded him of the encouraging feel of his father's hand as he walked nervously on to the stage to play in his first piano recital.

A guard escorted him along a corridor to a windowless room lined with metal shelves—an old storage space for legal files, he suspected. Willy sat in a metal armchair across from a man, possibly in his fifties, wearing slacks and an overtight double-breasted blazer, replete with gold buttons. The man had slick hair parted down the middle and his eyes were sleepy and heavy-lidded. Willy noticed two cups and a teapot on the desk in front of him. Fear had dried his mouth; but he could smell the tea's delectable aroma and licked his lips. *Pretentious jacket,* Willy mused. *Self-important. Be careful... no point in trying to humor this fellow.*

"I am Pressburg Mirko, from Bratislava," the man said in perfect Slovak. He pointed to a chubby-faced, bespectacled Nazi officer sitting nearby in a leather armchair. "This is Oberleutnant Grussman—he is an Abwehr observer. If you cooperate with us, you will not be harmed."

The Czech interviewer's face did not seem hostile. *He might even be sympathetic.* Willy straightened in his chair. "Excuse me, *pane* Pressburg. Before we start, I have a question. Does my family know where I am?"

Pressburg nodded as he opened a two-page form and unscrewed his fountain pen. "Your wife has agreed to come tomorrow with fresh clothes and food."

Willy caught his breath—suddenly there was hope. Sophie was willing to risk facing these wolves for him; that showed her courage and love. *But...what if this is a trap for her? Why did he say she was bringing clothes? Damn, they're going to keep me overnight.*

Willy nodded. "That's good news, but why have we been held so long here without food?"

Pressburg glanced at the German officer, who at first glared and then nodded. The Czech reached across to a shelf and produced a plate of small, chocolate-covered honey cakes. "Perhaps you would like some *medové řezy* and a cup of tea? My daughter made them. You can eat and answer questions at the same time." Smiling graciously, he lifted the teapot and poured. "You see? Our German occupiers are quite friendly."

Willy guessed this was a softening-up gesture to show how mild and reasonable the interview was going to be. What was the point in refusing? It would not change anything, and he was ravenous. "Thank you." He leaned forward, picking up the cup with one hand and two small cakes with the other.

Pressburg looked up from his notes. "So, over a year ago, you came from Košice to start a fabric business. Why was that?"

Willy decided to stick to facts that could be verified and avoid opinions. "I ran a fabric store there for my father, called Kohut Sukno. As you may know, just a couple of days ago, Slovakia declared independence from Czechoslovakia." He paused to drink the lukewarm tea. "This time a year ago, there were independence riots, demonstrations, and looting all across Slovakia. In Košice, my store was vandalized three times. So we moved to Prague." Unconsciously, he touched a coin-shaped scar above his left eyebrow, recalling the splintered shards of glass and burning wood, the white slogan splattered across his Košice storefront:

FILTHY JEWS PISS OUT OF SLOVAKIA

"You are one of the Chosen, obviously," said Pressburg with a sneer, writing on his form.

Willy tried not to show his irritation at being stereotyped. He was not thin or shabby, with a hooknose and shifty eyes; he was a muscular sharp dresser, and his nose was short and straight. "Yes, I'm Jewish, but we don't keep the traditions. I'm a Czech citizen, a patriot."

Pressburg gave him a warning frown. "I must remind you, Kohut, Czech citizens no longer exist. We are subjects of the Protectorate of Bohemia and Moravia." He consulted his notes. "You import fabrics from England? How long has this been going on?"

"My father has imported English cloth for fifteen years, mainly from a firm called Kindell & Renfrew. He was their representative for the whole of Eastern Europe. I joined the business after two years of commercial training in Paris and Vienna."

"And your father, his store is also in Prague?"

"No, in Lučenec, but he's not there anymore. After the Munich crisis last October, my parents lost their business. When Prime Minister Beran gave a speech saying that Jews should leave Czechoslovakia, they left. They're in London."

That's what I should have done. Willy bitterly recalled his parent's visit to Prague nine months earlier. They had come all the way from Lučenec to celebrate Pavel's first birthday. Sharing a bottle of Becherovka in the Anglotex office, Father had pressed him to drop everything and leave Czechoslovakia. It was the usual I-know-better-than-you struggle that had started between them in Willy's teenage years, first over the endless hours of piano practice and edicts against playing sports and then, later on, the best way to expand the Kohut business.

He remembered losing his temper, swearing at his father. "*Kurva drát,* bloody hell!" he'd shouted, slamming his glass down on the desk. "I don't want to be a pathetic refugee. For the first time in my life, I'm a success. Anyway, you can probably guess what it has cost me to put Anglotex together. Do you expect me to drop everything and run off with my tail between my legs, owing one hundred seventy-five thousand korun? That would be worse than dishonorable."

Willy watched as Pressburg picked up a dossier and went over to the German officer. While they were speaking in low tones, Willy recalled how the argument with his father had ended: on a sour note. "You always see things through rose-colored glasses," his father said, glaring through thick-lensed spectacles. "And you're extravagant. How much did you spend on that monstrous Bechstein upstairs? Forty, fifty thousand korun? Purchased with money you borrowed from me, I expect."

"There's nothing rose-colored about our modern army, Father—and we have strong allies in the West who will have no problem standing up to the Nazis. I'm not giving up all I've worked for."

His father had grunted, seemingly unimpressed. He waved a finger in Willy's face. "Remember Schiller's words when you think of Czechoslovakia. *Auch das schöne muss sterben*—even beautiful things must die. Don't be an ostrich; get out and save your family."

Willy now regretted his slick reply. "There are fifty thousand other Jewish ostriches in Prague, Father, including most of the rabbis. Are they all stupid? No. I'll stay an ostrich."

"You have visited England?" demanded Pressburg, interrupting Willy's reverie.

Willy jolted upright; the question did not seem relevant. "Yes, to inspect wool factories in the north and talk with our suppliers."

"The name of your suppliers, please." Pressburg readied his fountain pen over the paper.

Willy hesitated. *Is this a trap? Or a way of checking my truthfulness? They must know my suppliers; they went through my office.* "Kindell & Renfrew in London, Saltaire Ltd. in York, and Liddel and Brierly in Huddersfield. Why do you need to know all this?"

"Did you meet with other people in England? Not connected with business."

"I met only people in the wool trade." Willy bit his lip, wondering why Pressburg did not answer his question. "I also visited men's luxury stores in London to get an idea of how to set up a man's clothing business in Prague: Harrods, Burberry, other places in Jermyn Street."

"You had no contact with the police or anyone in the British government?"

Willy stared in surprise. "I was with my father on a buying trip, that's all."

Pressburg glanced at the German almost every time he asked a question. He seemed unsure of himself in the presence of Oberleutnant Grussman. "Your store in Masná Street, Anglotex. It has been profitable?"

Willy nodded. "I'm sure your people have that information."

Pressburg flipped through the pages of a document. "I see you changed the name of your store from Anglotex to Kohut Stoffe. Why and when?"

"It was a business decision. At the end of October last year, when we lost Sudetenland, everything shifted. Our government was bending over backward to please the Germans, and there was plenty of anti-Western propaganda. Customers stayed away, so I switched to a German name, Kohut Stoffe. I thought that might help stabilize our income."

Pressburg glanced back at Oberleutnant Grussman again.

"Our informant indicates that you speak several languages other than your native Slovak: Hungarian, German, English, French, and passable Polish. This is unusual."

Willy took a deep breath. Pressburg's questions were disturbing, but he was not going to give his captors an excuse to prolong his detention. He decided that his attitude would be middle of the road—no anger and no groveling. "I studied commerce in various European countries. My father believed languages would be useful in expanding our business. I have a gift for picking up languages."

Pressburg rolled a blotter over his writing and looked up, lifting a skeptical eyebrow. "You must understand, Kohut, certain things add up here: your visits to Britain, your training in languages, your father's recent move to England, and the name change of your store from British to German. We also know that an Englishwoman involved with the evacuation of Jewish children came to your apartment for lunch last December. Her name was Rowntree. All these pieces of information suggest a possible hypothesis: you might be spying for the British."

Willy slowly shook his head. "I'm a merchant, not a spy." He leaned back in his chair and tried to appear calm, even though his heart was pounding. "As for the Englishwoman, you are asking me to remember one person among the hundred or so people who, over several months, came to lunch at our apartment." Willy had begun to feel uneasy. Being accused as a spy raised the possibility of being detained for God knows how long. He had to plead his case, put up some resistance. "Could you show me the evidence on which you base your accusation?"

The German officer rose from his seat, walked to the desk, and whispered in the interviewer's ear. "Are you familiar with radio transmitters?" asked Pressburg, appearing to ignore Willy's request.

Willy shifted in his chair. "I have two house radios, a Tesla and an Ecko. I know nothing about transmitters." He stopped in surprise as Oberleutnant Grussman strode quickly toward him.

"*To není pravda*, not true," the officer spat out in German-accented Czech, scowling at Willy and tapping a swagger stick against one palm. "According to our informant, you are a reservist in the State Defense Force and you were mobilized last October during the Sudeten handover, manning a machine gun

post on Křížovnická Street. Your unit had a radio transmitter.
You are a *verdammte* liar."

The blow came fast, and even though Willy jerked his head
back to avoid it, daggers of pain shot through his left cheek. He
felt a warm trickle and touched his face: blood.

"I'm sorry, you are correct," he said, pulling out his handkerchief to stanch the flow. He was breathing quickly, afraid
of more of the same. Anger and hate flowed inside him, but he
clamped down on the stupid urge to retaliate. "My defense unit
did have a transmitter. I thought you were asking if I had a radio
transmitter at my apartment. I don't."

Willy carefully readjusted his spectacles. Both these men
were twisting his answers to make him seem guilty of spying
for the British. A small voice in his head kept asking insis-
tently, *who the hell is the informant?* Willy knew many people
in Prague: tailors, customs agents and city officials, local store-
owners, musicians he had accompanied on the piano at parties,
hundreds of Anglotex customers, and neighbors from his own
building and along Masná Street. *Which one?*

Willy doubted that Sophie's servants—Nanny Ludmila,
Elena, and Elise —would dare inform on their employer. The
informant had to be someone who was constantly aware of the
ebb and flow of Willy's business and social activities—perhaps
one of the regular guests at their Sunday lunches, an event that
Willy had dreamed up just after he and Sophie arrived in Prague.

"You keep mentioning an informant," he said as firmly
as he could. He wanted to be cautious, but he had to know...
so he could marshal his defense. "May I ask the identity of this
person? I want to understand the basis for my arrest."

Pressburg brushed food crumbs from his lapels and shook
his head as if he pitied Willy's naïveté. "You think I would tell
you?"

Willy dabbed at his bleeding face, warily observing the
German officer and ready to defend himself physically; the man
was not only vicious but also unpredictable. Pressburg looked at
his watch. "This will be all, for the moment. You will be taken
back to the detention room."

Willy, relieved, rose from his chair. His face ached. "When
will you release me? I want to go home."

"That depends on many things." Pressburg curled a

disdainful lip. "Be patient. Your wife comes tomorrow."

The Oberleutnant smacked the back of Willy's chair with his swagger stick. It sounded like a gunshot, and the chair fell on its side. "*Zurück mit ihm*, take him back," he growled at the guard.

The guard held Willy's arm as if in a vise as they walked along the corridor. The so-called interview had been neither routine nor benign. It had been an interrogation, and Willy knew he was not going home.

4

THE NOVOTNÝ LEGAL OFFICES
MARCH 16, 1939

THE MORNING AFTER Willy's arrest, Sophie and the cousins clustered round the dining table, listening to the newly named Prager Volkssender radio station. Pavel was building walls of wooden bricks in the space under the Bechstein, which he had commandeered as his playhouse. Ruth Eisner had joined them, wearing the multicolored lamé flapper gown she used as a "writing coat," flaming hair cascading over her shoulders. Overwrought by Willy's arrest, she had insisted on "dropping in." Sophie knew Ruth meant well, but she could tell that the romance novelist was enjoying the process of creating a new role for herself: the passionately attentive woman who would do anything to alleviate her friend's distress at losing a dashing husband.

It was still below freezing outside, and the apartment radiators clanked so energetically that Janko had to turn up the radio volume so they could hear the rebroadcast of von Ribbentrop's proclamation: Czechoslovakia was now called the Protectorate of Bohemia and Moravia. A German Reichsprotektor would be responsible for the protectorate's foreign policy and defense, while the revised Czech leadership would be autonomous and run day-to-day affairs. Consequently, life would proceed much as before, only this time under the benign supervision of the Third Reich.

"Filthy lies." Laci circled the piano and paced the room, frowning. Sophie could see from his twitching face that he was struggling to control an outburst. "I don't believe a word of this shit. I heard they picked up several thousand people and sent them to a camp at Milovice." He suddenly turned to Sophie. "All right, Madame Boss, now that Willy has been taken from us, what are your orders for the day?" The way he folded his arms and gazed at her with insolent eyes, she thought, was typical of a man expecting a woman to falter or fail.

She stared at Laci, momentarily speechless. *I'm supposed to know what Willy would do?* She had been awake for hours during the night worrying about Kohut Stoffe and her husband—and now, just like that, Laci was expecting her to make decisions about everything. Didn't he understand? She had been handed a crisis: manage the household, be a mother, run the store, and look for Willy at the same time.

"It's damned cold outside but we should at least open the front and back doors," said Janko. "Even up here, I can still smell the smoke from burning all that paper. It was so bad last night I was wheezing."

"Good idea," said Sophie, relieved that at least one of the cousins was willing to play his part. "We should air out the store. After that, it's business as usual, like the other merchants. We need the sales. It's what Willy would want—and you must be the one to see to the customers, Janko." She gave Laci what she hoped was a schoolmistress expression, punishment for his bellicosity. "Sometimes Laci can be too abrupt with our customers. Now I must get things ready for Willy."

Janko shook a warning finger at his scowling brother, wrinkling his nose in amusement.

In the bedroom, Sophie packed a small suitcase for Willy: clean underpants, pajamas, two shirts, a bar of soap, a shaving brush, a razor, and a towel. She slipped a note of love carefully inside the underwear, hoping that only Willy would find it. She took 2,000 korun from the wallet behind the stove and taped the rest into a recess between the underside of the white marble sculpture and its wooden plinth. The meter-high nude by Gutfreund was all cubist angles and curves, Willy's most recent extravagance.

Then she sat down with Ruth at the dining table, and they

ate a very early lunch of goulash with chunks of black bread and drank glasses of Willy's best *Tokaji*. "You need plenty of energy inside you," said Ruth with a persuasive smile, tossing her hair as she raised her glass to study the clear honey liquid against the chandelier's light. "You have no idea how long you will have to wait at this place you are going to, and this *Tokaji* is the world's best insurance against fear. Here, let me have a look at you." Gently, Ruth pulled Sophie to her feet and stepped back for a critical inspection. "Mmm, that's good: no earrings, discreet makeup, black silk blouse, and unpolished shoes—almost in mourning. Quite appropriate for visiting a Nazi lair. Though you forgot something: your gorgeous hairdo makes you seem rather sophisticated. You need to look like an ordinary *hausfrau*. Put on a beret or a hat. By the way, did you pack enough food for Willy?"

"More than enough: a stack of salami and cheese sandwiches, gherkins, apples, and squares of cake—enough for two meals at least."

"Do you have the money they asked for?" asked Janko, looking more pained than usual. "I hate the idea of giving those bastards our hard-earned koruny."

Sophie nodded. Too bad for the cousins who always seemed short of ready cash; she was ready to spend whatever was needed, even hocking her jewelry and more, to get Willy back.

By the front door, she picked up Pavel and covered him with kisses before slipping on her old serge coat and looking around the apartment one more time. It felt like a crucial moment, the transition from a life of ease and promise to one of fear and uncertainty. She had grown up in Berlin, loved and pampered by her father, a well-paid senior engineer at Siemens, and then married Willy, had a baby boy, and enjoyed a good life. Over the past 24 hours, her comfortable Prague cocoon had unraveled. This was no shopping spree, but a dangerous expedition to get her husband out of the clutches of the Nazis—a frightening prospect but also inexplicably exciting.

Ruth wound her arms round Sophie's neck. "I'm terribly worried, darling. Why don't I dress quickly and come with you? Together we will charm the Germans into giving Willy back."

Sophie shook her head. Her good-hearted friend had a way of dramatizing situations that might antagonize Willy's jailers.

Sophie could not take that risk. "The man on the telephone said come alone. I can't put anyone else in danger. Willy's my responsibility. Besides, I know how to talk to Germans." Sophie put a hand on Ruth's shoulder. "You can help me most by staying here and supervising the servants and Pavel—and keeping the cousins cheerful."

ร ∂ ร

Outside in a fine drizzle, Sophie carried the suitcase to the tram stop. She halted to read one of the red-edged public declarations posted all over the city—a bland proclamation, signed by General Blaskowitz, Kommandant of German Army Group 3, that daily life in Prague would continue normally and quietly under the watchful eye of protectorate authorities.

After a 20-minute tram ride and a few wrong turns and requests for directions, Sophie arrived at the Novotný Legal Chambers, the two lower floors of a four-story, baroque-style building with an elaborate stone portico. Two German soldiers in steel helmets stood guard at the front door, bayonets fixed on their rifles. Her throat tight with fear, Sophie blurted out the password: "*Schrecklich.*" One of the guards opened the door, jerking his head toward the dimly lit hallway behind him. She approached an Abwehr officer seated in front of the staircase, his booted legs stretched out underneath a small desk. He wore a *Schirmmütze* peaked cap, and the word *Feldengendarmerie*— military police—was stitched on one arm, a swastika band on the other. He looked at her with the glittering eyes of a predator, and she knew not to expect any sympathy. Her courage drained away. *Maybe Willy isn't here—and I'm in a trap?*

"Name?"

She put the suitcase down. "Kohut Sophie—my husband is Kohut Willy. I was told to come."

The officer ran a yellow-stained finger down a list clipped to a board on his desk. The hallway light flickered. He glanced up at it and cursed.

"Kohut, Kohut. *Ach*, so. You come to recognize him, yes?"

When Sophie heard "recognize him," excitement and hope pulsed through her body. *Perhaps they will release him.*

"You have the money?"

She hesitated. "Yes. What is it for?" She tried to follow

Willy's head-of-the-family dictum: *Don't take anything for granted. Always ask why.*

The officer sneered. "You think keeping him here costs nothing?"

"When I pay, you will release him—yes?"

The officer nodded, rose from his chair, and held out his hand. "The money."

Sophie opened her purse and handed him the bundle of notes. He licked the tips of his fingers and counted. "I would like a receipt, please." She had also learned Willy's habit of documenting every transaction—family, business, or domestic.

He gave a short laugh and shook his head. *"Nicht möglich.* Not possible." He crooked a finger. *"Komm mit."*

Annoyed by his refusal, she picked up the suitcase, and they walked at a brisk pace along one corridor and then up a dark stairway. On the landing, they stopped at a carved double door with polished brass handles, guarded by a soldier carrying a machine pistol. The officer pushed him aside and cracked open the door. He motioned for Sophie to peer in. "See if your husband is here."

She pushed forward into the room, but he pulled her back by the collar. *"Nein,"* he snarled, *"eintritt verboten*—forbidden. You can only look."

Furious at the rough handling, Sophie wanted to scream and kick at him. She leaned forward again, enough to see that the room, about three times larger than her sitting room, was packed with men of all sizes and shapes dressed in torn and rumpled clothes, some still wearing their hats. Weary, hopeless, unshaven faces turned to look at her. The officer kept a firm grip on her coat but this time did not pull her back.

Because the ceiling pendants were dim, it took a few seconds for her eyes to adjust to the haze of cigarette and cigar smoke. She shuddered at the overpowering smell of stale sweat, urine, and soiled clothes. One group of men stood or leaned against the long, polished table. Others were curled up or sprawled on the floor, smoking or just staring into space. A few rose expectantly to their feet; others wearily shook their heads at her.

Willy was wedged into a corner, head down, arms clasped around his knees. She recognized his spectacles, the pattern of his suit, and the expensive, hand-stitched leather shoes he had so recently bought.

A wave of relief swept her fear away. Even though the officer held her fast, she strained against his hold and raised her voice. "Willy! It's me."

He looked up, recognition kindling in his eyes. She noticed other men looking at her hungrily. It was not the usual sexual admiration she was used to, but nostalgia and sorrow, as though she represented love, food, and home. She felt sad for them.

With some difficulty, Willy eased himself off the floor. Sophie was shocked by his haggard look. He had a cut on his left cheek, his tie was gone, and his shirt collar was undone—perhaps even torn, she was not sure. *Why is he moving so slowly? They've hurt him.* She felt faint; her skin tingled.

"That's enough!" shouted the officer in her ear. He jerked her back, slamming the door shut. "You've seen your husband. Come with me."

She struggled to fight off the iron grip. "He needs the suitcase. I've got clothes for him."

Grasping Sophie roughly by the elbow, the officer marched her with the suitcase to another door and knocked. A faint "Herein" came from within. In a moment, she was inside a small, drab room furnished with a large desk fronted by two metal chairs. Oil portraits of solemn, bewhiskered men in high collars and waistcoats hung on the walls. A breakfront bookcase stood in one corner.

"Stand still."

An officer with close-cropped hair glanced at her from behind the desk, a chilling inspection by pale blue eyes. Without a word, he looked down, opened a file, and began to write. She remained silent, anger roiling at his indifference. A few moments ago, Willy's flashing smile had brought her confidence back, but the longer she stood in front of this man, the more uncertain and vulnerable she felt. She heard the door close behind her and felt unsteady, as if her knees and ankles were disconnected. After a long, unbearable silence, she checked her watch. She had been on her feet for twenty minutes.

Without looking up, the officer spoke. His thin lips hardly moved. "Put your suitcase on this table and then stand back."

After complying, Sophie spoke in precise German, trying to keep her voice steady. "Please, Obersturmführer, why is my

husband here?" She had no idea of the officer's true rank, but
having noted the well-cut black uniform with wide lapels and
generous silver piping on the edging, she thought it would not
hurt to assign him an important rank.

He rose from his chair, put on a pair of leather gloves,
opened the suitcase, and turned the contents over. With a grunt,
he closed the case and sat down again. Except for the scratching
of his pen and the buzzing of the electrolier fixture suspended
from the ceiling, the room was silent. Sophie drew in a deep,
tense breath. "Please, my husband has done nothing wrong. We
are law-abiding Czech citizens. You must let him go. I paid the
requested two thousand korun to the man who brought me in
here."

The Obersturmführer raised his head. She recoiled at his
sardonic smile, a mixture of amusement and disgust. She was
suddenly afraid of the easy power he wielded over her.

He laughed, cocking an eyebrow. "I must let him go? Oh,
no, *meine Frau*. Your husband is still under interrogation. But
if you would like to help us, we might be able to arrange for his
early release."

She nodded and he pointed at one of the metal chairs for
her to sit down.

"*Also, gut.* I want to find out if your husband knows
British people in Prague?" He looked down at something on
his desk. "These names, for example: Anthony Grenville or
Fräulein Doreen Warriner. They work at the British Committee
for Refugees on Slezská Street?"

Sophie shook her head slowly. "Not to my knowledge.
I've never heard of them. I don't know any British people." Her
pulse raced, and she felt her cheeks flush. *Is he going to keep
asking questions, detain me? Is Willy guilty of something?* She
wanted to go home. Pavel needed her and she needed him.

"Not correct, Frau Kohut. Our informant reports a British
guest visited your apartment last November, a woman called
Rowntree."

Sophie fought to stay calm. Who was this informant he
was talking about? "Last year Willy invited guests for lunch
every week. It was a way to build social contacts and market our
business. So many people. I don't recall her." Nevertheless, she
did remember: Tessa Rowntree, a calm English girl Willy had

met at the Customs Administration in the Karlín district—a Quaker and a courier and escort for Jewish children being sent by their parents to safety in Britain.

The officer hitched a sardonic eyebrow as he made a note. "I'm sure you would have remembered an Englishwoman among your usual swarm of Czechs and Jews."

Sophie gulped at the subtle insult but took the plunge. "Please, why have you detained my husband? I'm absolutely sure he's done nothing wrong. Can't you let him go? I would like to accompany him home."

The officer frowned. "For the moment, I cannot give out information, but you can come back tomorrow at the same time with more food and, again, two thousand korun. Perhaps then, you can talk to your husband. Now go home and keep your mouth shut."

Sophie left the building, her heart pounding. It had been terrible, but she was still free and Willy was alive. The idea that people could have so much power over the lives of others was new and frightening. Growing up, her parents had taught her that civility and trust were part of everyday life. Not anymore, apparently. And how could the Germans behave so abominably? It hadn't been so when she was a young girl growing up in Berlin, though it was true even back then that Jews were discreetly despised by many people. When she was an apprentice milliner at Lola Paschal Hats on the Kurfürstendamm, she would often hear customers' disparaging remarks about Jews. She had never told her parents; they disapproved of discussing such things.

Shivering in the cold, Sophie took the tram home, replaying what had happened. Gazing through the smeared panes of the tram, her resentment swelled. The city was awash with the occupiers: helmeted soldiers, military motorcycles, and trucks. Tanks with swastikas painted on their turrets sat like invincible dinosaurs at the main intersections. The visit to the Novotný Legal Offices had sickened her, and dark thoughts circled in her mind.

What if they're lying? I'm afraid to go back there, but I have to do it.

5

VANISHED
MARCH 17, 1939

A GUARD CAME through the double doors of the Novotný conference room and, without a word, handed Willy the suitcase Sophie had brought. His breathing tightened in the smoky haze as he looked for a space in which to open it. The conference room had filled with even more detainees. Most were squeezed together on the floor like damaged pieces of a jigsaw puzzle.

Willy managed to find room under the table. He found Sophie's note and read it avidly. Pulling out a clean shirt, and not caring who was watching, he struggled to exchange it for the bloodstained one he was wearing. Someone helped him put his arms through the sleeves—Otto Ožtek. Willy offered him a sandwich and an apple. They ate slowly, side by side on the floor, savoring the food.

The electrician bit into his apple. "Where is your store, comrade?"

Willy smiled. "Masná Street. I hope it's still open for business. I specialize in selling fabrics for men's suiting. High quality stuff only."

"I've never been in a fancy place like that. In fact, I never got round to having a proper suit made. I always bought second-hand. So tell me, what's so special about your store?"

Willy released a wistful sigh for the familiarity of his shop. "I opened it a year ago. Interior walls in green velveteen, a mahogany cutting counter, red pile carpet, leather armchairs, a button-back settee for customers, and a wood stove. I have a mannequin in the window dressed as a British businessman: pinstripe suit, bowler hat, and a Union Jack on his shoulders. I wanted Anglotex to have style like the stores I visited in London and Paris. There is nothing like it in Prague."

Ožtek laughed. "So does your mannequin display the symbol of British capitalism - a tightly rolled, black umbrella?"

Half-smiling at the memory, Willy nudged his companion. "Not just that, my friend. I have two large photographs on the walls. One shows elegantly dressed men on the steps of the famous St. Paul's Cathedral; the other is of a Collie chasing sheep over a grassy hill in Wales, a part of Britain. I wanted to show the exquisite English suits and where the wool that wove them came from."

"I expect that's why you're here, then." Ožtek wiped the sweat off his face. "Nazis despise the British. So do I, for that matter. They've been the worst fucking capitalists for a hundred years."

Opting out of an unnecessary argument, Willy started on his second sandwich. He was aware people were watching him, and after a few bites, he decided that the only honorable course was to offer what he had to the men positioned around him.

Ožtek grinned approvingly. "You're a capitalist trying to behave like a communist."

When all the food was gone, Willy reread Sophie's note and wept. Thank God, someone loved him.

As the hours passed, guards led the detainees out for interviews, one by one. Most returned later, silent, thoughtful, or dazed. Willy felt too miserable to talk to anyone. Finally, he rolled sideways and pulled up his knees, hoping to doze off using his suitcase and jacket as a pillow. It did not work; he could not sleep, too busy puzzling over the informant Pressburg had mentioned, the person who knew so much about Willy and presumably stood to gain something by hurting him. It had to be someone in frequent contact with Willy and Sophie, perhaps one of the regular guests who came to their apartment. He thought back ten months to the first social luncheon they had put together, based on the idea of a regular get-together for friends and business acquaintances, a strategy for quickly enlarging their circle of friends and promoting Anglotex.

Willy remembered that inaugural lunch clearly. As well as cousins Laci and Janko, the guests had included Hans Lessig, a Sudeten journalist based in Prague; the voluptuous Ruth Eisner from the third floor; Postmaster Molnar, an elegant gray-haired man with a silvery waxed mustache who lived upstairs on the fourth floor; Vlado Unger, an unpublished poet; and Katya Olinová, an attractive blond viola player Willy had met at Svoboda's instrument store.

Willy's mouth watered as he remembered how Elise had surpassed herself with the cooking: *kulajda*, spiced mushroom soup, followed by *svíčková*, marinated sirloin in cream sauce with dumplings and *čočka* lentils on the side. Willy could taste it now. Over generous helpings of food and plenty of Egri Bikavér wine, the lunch guests first discussed the epidemic of Jewish suicides in Germany and then the brutality of Italy's occupation of Abyssinia. The conversation was serious, intelligent and cordial.

However, the atmosphere deteriorated when neighbor Molnar criticized Lessig, a tall, unkempt scarecrow of a man about Willy's age, on the subject of pro-Nazi Sudetenland. He complained that Lessig's articles in *Lidové noviny* about the grievances of the Sudeten population against the Czech government were one-sided and full of lies. Lessig countered with assurances that he was being fair, complaining that German-speaking Sudeten children were being taught in Czech, in Sudetenland, against the wishes of their parents.

Sophie calmed the waters by serving coffee and strudel, but afterward she admitted to Willy that she did not like Lessig. He dressed badly, had unpleasant table manners, and fluttered his eyelashes at her. "Pure lust," she said with a forced laugh. "It was so obvious—and embarrassing. Do we have to have him here?"

"Yes." Willy stroked her hand, surprised that she could be so outspoken about his friend. She was usually enthusiastic about their guests. "Look, strudel. Lessig does me favors. He writes about Anglotex in his gossip column. It's terrific advertising, and free. This is the least we can do in return."

"What about that old grump Molnar? It wasn't very polite of him to pick an argument. I thought these lunches were supposed to be fun and informative, not political shouting matches."

Folding her in his arms, Willy had kissed her ear. "We must take the rough with the smooth. I need Molnar too. He knows Prague inside and out. Most of all, he's cozy with government officials; that way, I get advice and news from a reliable source. Anyway, I like his grumpiness—he reminds me of Father."

∽ ∂ ∽

Before he finally fell asleep under the Novotný conference table, Willy decided that Lessig and perhaps Molnar were the most likely candidates to be Pressburg's informant. They were regulars at the Sunday lunches, and Lessig had to be a suspect, being from pro-German Sudetenland. And Molnar? Well, he was wise and charming but also opaque and indecipherable, always dropping in on the Kohuts to "see how things were progressing." Willy could never decide whose side Molnar was on: pro- or anti-Jewish, pro- or anti-German, for or against the Western powers. Whomever the informant was, Willy knew that when he got out of this Novotný hellhole, he and his cousins would find the scoundrel and beat the hell out of him.

At midnight, the guards burst into the Novotný Offices conference room, yelling and stamping their boots, prodding the sleeping detainees with rifle barrels. "*Alle heraus*, everyone out."

Willy, confused and not fully awake, grabbed his suitcase and lined up to shuffle and squeeze through the doorway. His new acquaintance Ožtek hung on to his jacket sleeve. "Let's stay together, comrade. I have a bad feeling about what is coming next."

"Get downstairs and get into the trucks," shouted one of the soldiers. "And no talking."

∽ ∂ ∽

The next morning, Sophie returned as bidden to the Novotný Legal Offices, this time with a string bag holding another change of underwear, more sandwiches and apples, and a pound cake. She was a few minutes late because the trams were running on a restricted schedule. The streets were almost deserted. Though she had opened Kohut Stoffe for business, many stores had closed to protest the occupation. Huddled in the almost-empty tram, she felt lonely and vulnerable. At the same time, hope sparked through her like an electric current: in a few minutes, she would see Willy. Perhaps they would go home together.

No sentries guarded the entrance of the Novotný chambers. Surprised and uneasy, she knocked and waited. She knocked again—and again. Exasperated, her heart pounding anxiously, she tried the handle; it opened with a squeak of hinges. The hallways were dark and empty. Her steps echoed. No sign of SA troopers or officers. Remembering the way up the stairs, she hurried to the conference room. She knocked, and when there was no answer, she opened the door.

The room was dark and silent. When she switched on the lights, coughing at the acrid farmyard smell, she caught her breath and her heart jumped. It was empty except for crumpled newspapers and cigarette stubs scattered over the parquet floor. Blinking back her tears, angry at being duped, she grimaced at the line of overflowing soil buckets. Nausea swirled up from her stomach. It was then that she thought she recognized Willy's white shirt with blue stripes under the table. Walking unsteadily over to it, she picked it up and found the label: Turnbull and Asser, London. Her breath caught. It was definitely Willy's, with bloodstains on the collar.

Sophie dropped the shirt and pulled a handkerchief over her face to stifle the room's foul odor. She leaned against the table for support. *In God's name! Where have they taken him?* The string bag slipped to the floor, and she ran.

Out on the street, stumbling away from the suffocating emptiness of the building, Sophie saw a stout woman cleaning the windows of a nearby house. "Excuse me, did you see German soldiers in that building today, the law offices?

Face hidden by a voluminous kerchief, the woman did not reply and continued rubbing very hard at the glass pane. She seemed fearful.

Sophie persisted. "My husband was arrested and taken there. I visited him yesterday. Now it's empty."

"I saw what happened, dearie," she said after a long moment. But still did not turn around. "Watched from upstairs.

Big trucks came in the night and took people away."

"Thank you." Sophie turned away, biting her lip, trying to hold herself upright and not break down in front of this stranger.

She could no longer hold back the tears when she realized that, except for the two short army mobilizations last year, she and Willy had never been apart for more than a day. His absence stretched before her like a dark, endless, frightening tunnel. He might be anywhere, in a prison or some requisitioned building in Prague—or God forbid, lying dead in a forest far outside the city. She had to find him.

∽ ∂ ∽

On the way home, Sophie tried to formulate a search plan. When she walked through the door, she summoned enough energy to go through Willy's Kardex in the downstairs office. She needed help. While Pavel played hide and seek with Laci in the storeroom and Janko stayed at the front to greet customers, she made a list of people to telephone. She took the list up to Ruth's apartment and told her what had happened at the Novotný Legal Offices. "Will you help me telephone these people?"

"Of course I'll help." Ruth was dressed to go out in a figure-hugging two-piece suit with a feathery hat. Sophie wrinkled her nose; Ruth's perfume was gardenia, and there was too much of it. "Just as soon as I get back from a lunch appointment. But, here's an idea, darling. Check with *pan* Molnar from upstairs. Get his advice. He's clever; I'm almost certain he's more than just a postmaster. He always seems to know what's going on before the newspapers do."

Ruth stopped at the doorway to pull on her gloves. "Wait a minute, how about this? If Molnar can't help, get hold of that schmuck Lessig. I bet he has already snuggled up to influential Sudetenlanders in the new protectorate administration. He'll definitely help. I've seen how he looks at you—and anyway, he's supposed to be Willy's friend. Call him at the newspaper office. You can use my telephone while I'm out. And distract yourself; amuse Pavel. Forget about what happened today. We'll start on the calling list when I get back."

This is the only woman I know well enough to turn to,

Sophie thought as she walked sadly down the staircase to her apartment. *Lots of fun, but I need someone more sensible and stable. Ruth means well, but she prattles on and on. Willy calls her an empty-headed socialite. If only our mothers were here. Willy's mother is in London and mine is...dead.*

Sophie could not get hold of Havel Molnar when she telephoned. He was not in his apartment or at the Central Post and Telegraph Building, so she looked up Lessig's number on Willy's Kardex.

"I regret that *pan* Lessig has been transferred somewhere else at the request of the occupying forces," said the secretary at the *Lidové noviny* office when Sophie finally got through. "We don't know where he is."

"Oh, God!" Sophie slammed the receiver back on the hook and paced round the apartment, trying to calm herself. She checked Willy's correspondence on the Biedermeier desk and tore up anything she thought might be incriminating. She wrote a message with some instructions for Nanny Ludmila for when she brought Pavel back from his walk. Then she started calling the people on her list. After an hour and a half of sympathetic but unhelpful answers, she gave up, feeling useless and despondent.

That evening, looking at a picture book with Pavel in her lap, Sophie heard President Hácha speak to his fallen nation on the radio. It made her angry. "Rest assured," he said in his doddery voice, "the Third Reich has come to Czechoslovakia to protect the population from external dangers, maintain order, and ensure civil liberties. No harm will come to those who obey and respect the new laws." The president finished his talk with the sentence: "I have entrusted our country to the Führer and have been provided his trust. Good night."

Sophie wanted to shout, "You silly old fool!" Instead, she only murmured the words, not wanting to upset Pavel, running her fingers through his springy curls as she sang his favorite lullaby. He snuggled close against her breast, saying "Again!" each time she finished singing. She did as he asked, herself soothed by the lullaby's verses and refrains, all the while pondering the fact that her telephone calls had not produced a single hopeful lead. She juggled possibilities and questions in her head. *Why did they take him? Why did he minimize what was coming? Why didn't we sell and leave months ago? If only Willy had listened to his father.*

6

GOOD FRIEND LESSIG
MARCH 18, 1939

THE NEXT DAY, an hour before Kohut Stoffe opened, Sophie, Janko, and Laci shared a hurried, silent breakfast of jam pancakes and coffee in the downstairs office. The cousins had spent the night in the store sleeping on makeshift beds of rugs and cushions – neither had washed or shaved. Sophie felt weak and exhausted. Pavel had woken several times in the night needing her attention. During the two restless nights that she had slept alone, she had relived the burning of Willy's files in the stove, the sight of his bruised face, the harsh faces of the German guards, and finding his bloodstained shirt in the empty legal chambers. She now regretted her decision to destroy Willy's business correspondence: too hasty and wrong. She was sure now that the Nazis would interpret it as a clear admission of guilt.

Laci combed thick fingers through his unruly hair, took a final gulp of his coffee, and lit a cigarette. After studying its glow, he gave Sophie a look that she interpreted as curiosity tinged with arrogance. She wondered whether Laci, the older cousin, was expecting to assume Willy's role as the temporary head of the family. She would always defer to her husband but to have the rash and erratic Laci boss her around—that would not do.

"So, Sophie." He blew a stream of smoke out of his nostrils like a horse on a cold morning. "No luck with the telephone calls, eh? What the hell are we going to do to find him? Any ideas? I suppose... He hesitated. "I suppose you're supposed to be the one in charge now; though I'm not sure a housewife dealing with the Nazi bastards will achieve much"

She wanted to tear the cigarette from his mouth. Laci was acting like a boor as well as flouting Willy's strict rules on smoking in the apartment. She waved the smoke away, restraining the impulse to argue with him. She could not afford a resentful cousin just now; the family had to stick together, help one another. Lips compressed, she poured him more coffee from the silver pot.

"No new plan," she said, trying to appear calm. "I have another twenty business acquaintances to contact and then I have an appointment with an official Willy made friends with at the mayor's office. In addition, I would like to get *pan* Molnar's advice on the situation. There's more grocery shopping to be done, but I can send Elena out for that. Pavel needs a walk and time with his *máma*." She sighed, looking pointedly at Laci.

"When you take Pavel, show him the German tanks and soldiers in the streets," Laci said with a laugh. "Kids love soldiers."

Janko punched his brother's biceps. "Shut up, idiot. These are not things to joke about. Anyway, when I stepped round the corner to put out the garbage, the street seemed quiet and safe. I don't think there's any danger for women and children to be out and about. Seems that the Nazis are sticking to their promise to be benign occupiers."

℘ ∂ ℘

By mid-afternoon, Sophie was in tears, disappointed by futile telephone calls. No one knew anything about Willy, and they seemed careful not to offer tangible assistance. She imagined they were afraid of being dragged into the web of her husband's disappearance. In despair and wanting to blot out the fearful images whirling in her head, she took a nap with Pavel.

While she slept, Postmaster Molnar dropped by the store, immaculately dressed as usual He had heard about Willy's arrest from Ruth Eisner. Janko greeted him at the front entrance and showed him into the office. Laci was vacuuming the carpet and removing the stray ashes from around the stove. He waved a greeting to the postmaster.

"A terrible shock, eh?" said Molnar, settling into a chair. "I came to see if there was any news of Willy," he said with a somber face. "Arresting the poor fellow on day one of the occupation; that's shocking. Must be to do with having British suppliers." He shook his head wearily. "These Germans have moved quickly; too well organized by half—and they've got the Czech police eating out of their hands." He sniffed and then coughed, wrinkling his nose. "My heavens, your store smells like the blackened stubble on my papa's farm. What have you been burning?"

Janko raised a warning hand. "Please, *pan* Molnar, not so loud. We have a couple of customers in the showroom looking at samples." He lowered his voice "The stove was going all night burning papers and files. Laci and I slept downstairs, keeping guard."

The postmaster nodded, flicking a speck off his sharply creased trousers before crossing his legs. "That was a difficult decision... to burn. On balance, I'd say it was the wrong one. It will arouse suspicion if the Gestapo comes back. And how is my dear *paní* Kohutová taking her husband's disappearance? She must be devastated."

Janko pulled out a crumpled pack of cigarettes, lit one, and sat on the edge of Willy's desk, in front of Molnar. "She's gone to bed, utterly miserable."

Molnar inserted a thumb into the pocket of his embroidered waistcoat and leaned back in his chair. "Well, Willy's arrest was obviously planned before the invasion. The question is why? As I just suggested, the factor that stands out for me is that he imports British fabrics. Nevertheless, it could all be a terrible misunderstanding—wrong address, wrong name, who knows? Of course, your family is Jewish. That muddies the waters."

"Which means you think they targeted Willy because he's a Jew with English business connections."

"Or perhaps for a reason we don't know. *Pan* Kohut knew loads of people and had his fingers in many pies. He's certainly in good company. The new protectorate administration has arrested nearly a thousand citizens: bankers, journalists, lawyers, doctors, especially communists and prominent Catholics. I suppose they want to control or get rid of influential people who might cause trouble. God knows what panic the prisoner's families are in."

Janko lapsed into silence, stunned by the postmaster's unruffled account of a thousand innocent people thrown into jail. The old man seemed uneasy, uncomfortable. Janko watched Molnar fiddle with his peaked postal cap and wondered if the mysterious fellow was somehow involved in Willy's arrest?

Molnar stood up and put a hand on Janko's shoulder. His face was serious. "Look, I'd like to help you find Willy, but frankly, I've no ideas. Before the Nazis arrived, I had close ties with government officials, but all that has changed. Indeed, I fear the Germans will come for me as they did for Willy. I'm not waiting to find out. In a couple of days, I leave for Poland. That's my farewell advice to all of you: get out. The Nazi honeymoon will be short."

"How can we possibly leave?" said Laci, who had appeared at the office door pushing the now-silent vacuum cleaner. "We've no passports or visas, and we damned well won't leave Prague until Willy is safely home. We have to help Sophie. It's a matter of family loyalty."

Janko nodded. "We owe Willy a great deal. Our father was gassed in the Great War and ended up an invalid. Onkel Emil and Willy kept our family from starving, and then when Papa died and his pension stopped, Willy offered Laci and me work at Kohut Sukno in Košice."

Laci nodded. "Willy's a tough boss, but he can be a generous fellow. To celebrate Pavel's birth in '37, he financed the planting of a whole orange grove at Kibbutz Kvar Masaryk in Palestine."

Molnar shrugged, spreading his hands in apology. "Look, I'm sorry; you're all in a difficult situation, and Willy's arrest is a terrible blow. You must close ranks and trust each other. Willy has intelligence and wiles. Get him home and he'll find a way to get you all out of Prague. For the moment, there's nothing I can do to help. My erstwhile influential contacts in the government have disappeared into the woodwork." He buttoned up his lambs-wool overcoat and pulled on his doeskin gloves.

"Please, give *paní* Kohutové my best wishes. I'll keep my ears flapping for Willy over the next two days...before I leave. If I get a clue of his whereabouts, I'll telephone." He turned for the door. "Perhaps one day we'll meet again."

છ ∂ છ

At six o'clock, as Janko was about to close-up the store, three men swaggered in and stood by the cutting table as if waiting to be served. Two of them were clearly German: a tall, fair-haired, uniformed officer and a small older man. Janko recognized the third man. He had been a guest at Willy and Sophie's lunches: Hans Lessig, the Sudeten journalist.

The officer, who looked to Janko to be in his late twenties, pointed a swagger stick at him. "*Wir sind Sicherheitsdienst*, Security Services. Bring me Frau Kohut, *schnell.*"

Janko, who spoke fragmentary German, nodded and hurried to the back, bounding up the iron staircase to the apartment. Laci watched discreetly from the shelves as he continued removing the canvas covering from a bolt of textured gabardine. Lessig, tall and gawky, stood looking around with his hands in his pockets while the two other men walked methodically around the store, opening drawers, reading fabric labels, and checking the back yard where discarded shipping crates were stacked.

Upstairs, Janko found Sophie in her dressing gown, feeding Pavel yogurt and oatmeal.

"There are two Nazis from the security service in the store," he stuttered as he rushed up to the table. "They want to talk to you. And that strange friend of Willy's, Hans Lessig, is with them."

"Oh, my God." Fear swept into her throat. *Lessig and Germans?* Then she remembered what the secretary at the *Lidové noviny* newspaper had told her: Hans had been transferred to a new project with the occupying forces—and God in heaven; here he was collaborating with the Nazi Sicherheitsdienst. Her heart fluttered, her breathing came fast. Did Lessig have something to do with Willy's arrest? Maybe he knew where Willy was. "Please, Janko. Tell them I'll be down in five minutes. Explain I'm with Pavel."

As she finished cleaning up the food-spattered dining

table, she came up with an idea. When she went downstairs, she would only speak Czech and pretend not to understand German. That way, they might let something slip, a clue about Willy. Of course, Lessig knew she spoke perfect German. If he kept quiet when she pretended not to understand, that would prove he was on her side. If he betrayed her, then she would know where his loyalty lay.

After a few minutes, Sophie came down the back stairs still wearing her brocade dressing gown and slippers, hair unbrushed. She carried Pavel, fragments of oatmeal clinging to the bib she had purposely left round his neck. She wanted to elicit sympathy: a busy, half-dressed mother interrupted by strangers at the very inconvenient moment of feeding her child. At the bottom of the stairs, Laci and Janko positioned themselves behind her facing the three visitors. Sophie gave Lessig a penetrating look, trying to gauge his reaction. He looked away, his narrow face flushed.

"You are Frau Kohut?" asked the smaller man. He wore a badly cut suit with a black leather coat draped over his shoulders. Sophie guessed he was about fifty, noticing that his left eyelid drooped over the iris and part of his left cheek sagged as if he were permanently disgusted with the world. He held a lit cigarette between finger and thumb, the smoke curling around his jacket sleeve like a gray snake.

"*Nicht spricht Deutsch*," she said, noticing Lessig's flash of astonishment. "*Ich bin Tschechin.*"

The man waved his hand in Sophie's direction and turned to Lessig. "*Dummes Weib. Übersetzen*—translate and explain who we are."

Sophie could tell Hans was very nervous, continuously fluttering his eyelashes and jerking his head back to keep strands of unkempt straw hair away from his owl glasses. He bowed to her, awkwardly. "*Servus, pani* Kohutová," he said in Czech. "We apologize for disturbing you. These two gentlemen are from the Gestapo. Allow me to present Obersturmführer Pohl," he indicated the young officer with a polite hand wave, "and this is Herr Altmann."

With a jolt of relief, Sophie realized that Lessig had said nothing about her knowledge of German. She tried not to smile at him, but she felt a surge of gratitude; he was playing along, helping her—for his benefit or hers, she was not sure. It did not matter as long as she found Willy.

Altmann, ignoring a nearby ash stand, crushed his cigarette underfoot and grabbed Lessig's arm. "I can see you know this woman. You only gave us information about her husband, not about her. Explain."

The Sudetenlander offered an uneasy smile. "*Mein Herr*, I hardly know her. I only know her husband, Herr Kohut, because of the two or three short articles I wrote about his new store. We had a mainly professional relationship."

Sophie noticed that Hans had not mentioned his attendance at several of their Sunday lunches over the past year. She was so tense she could not stop herself. "What have you told them?" she demanded in Czech. "Where is Willy?"

Lessig's eyelashes fluttered again as he answered her in the same language. "Stay calm. All I told them was that he imports British cloth and that he's Jewish, plays the piano, and isn't politically active." He twitched his shoulders, shifting his weight from one foot to the other.

Sophie looked down at Pavel, trying to hide her anger. She suspected the journalist was keeping something from her. Pavel reached up, touched her cheek, and smiled. She kissed him, hoping that Lessig had already explained to these men that Willy was his friend, and innocent.

"Come on, Lessig," said Pohl, frowning and slapping his boots with his cane. "Tell the pretty lady why we're here. We want to see everything, down here and upstairs."

Lessig turned back to Sophie. "Please don't show them you're afraid. I'm here to help you. They forced me to act as their translator. Willy's arrest happens to be one of the cases they are working on." He glanced at his companions. "They've come to examine business papers and inspect the upstairs apartment more thoroughly. Herr Altmann says the first search, when Willy was arrested, was very unsatisfactory."

Sophie shifted Pavel on her hip. It had been a terrible shock seeing Hans with these men. What he said sounded plausible enough, but she was not sure. An idea took seed that he and these men knew exactly where Willy was. She tried to appear calm, but inside she was shaking, afraid that they would find something incriminating in the store or discover the passports and money hidden in the apartment. She needed time to think of a way to limit their search and persuade them to reveal Willy's location. "Please, what do you want from us?" she said in Czech. Lessig translated.

"Nice man," said Pavel with a smile on his oatmeal-coated lips. He reached out toward Altmann.

The young officer pushed out his chest and lifted his chin in an accusatory pose. "We suspect your husband is a British spy." Hans translated. Sophie struggled to keep her face blank as if she did not understand him; inside, she trembled. *Willy a spy? How?*

Herr Altmann turned to Lessig. "This woman's husband does most of his business with the British, yes?" The nasal quality of his voice jarred Sophie's ears.

The journalist nodded, glancing at Sophie as if soliciting her approval to reveal more. "Herr Kohut imports British textiles. As you are aware, Czechoslovakia trades with many countries. There is nothing wrong with that, surely."

"All that will change," the shorter man retorted, laying his coat and trilby on the cutting table. With his outer garments off, Sophie noticed how different he was from his taller companions: bandy-legged with powerful arms on a barrel torso. "Tell her this, Lessig: Czechoslovakia no longer exists, and the British will soon be our enemies. We are here to find evidence of his spying." He slipped on white cotton gloves. "Our inspection will take about two hours. We will punish any protest or resistance. Soldiers are on guard outside."

Altmann glanced at the young officer, who was studying Sophie with open admiration. "Pohl, you idiot, stop staring at the Jewess. Put on your gloves and, for God's sake, earn your new promotion. And you, Herr Lessig, take the woman and child upstairs—the two store clerks as well. Keep an eye on them and see they don't move anything." He looked at his watch. "Tell Frau Kohut we'll need refreshments at 19:30. *Kaffee und imbiss.*"

The two Germans pushed past Sophie into the small back office and began opening drawers and rifling through the filing cabinets, stacking anything of interest on the office desk and throwing everything else onto the floor. Sophie and Pavel, followed by Janko, Laci, and Lessig, went upstairs to the apartment where the Elena was waiting, looking ashen.

Laci brought glasses and a quarter-full bottle of *slivovice* to the table. "This will give us courage," he said

When Sophie told her what was going on, Elena's face turned white and she shuddered. "Will the Germans arrest me, *Madám*? I've done nothing wrong. Please, I want to go home. I—I don't think I should come to you anymore."

Sophie put her arm around the girl's shoulders. "You mustn't worry. She tried to calm her own quavering voice. "Nothing will happen to you, I'll make sure of that. They just want to search *pan* Kohut's things, and I want to try to keep an eye on them. Please put Pavel back to bed, sing him a couple of songs. When he's settled, come and sit down with us at the table. I have some other instructions."

☙ ∂ ☙

"In God's name, Hans, are you one of them? A Nazi?" Sophie said in a strangled voice as she and the cousins sat around the dining table, staring at Lessig. "You must know where Willy is." She poured the clear liquor into four glasses.

Looking miserable, Lessig held up his hands in surrender. "I don't know where Willy is, I swear. Look—I didn't volunteer to do this. I was forced. I'm a Sudetenlander. I speak German, Czech, and Slovak—they need me for their work. One doesn't say no to the Gestapo."

Laci leapt up, spilling his glass of *slivovice* on the tablecloth. He grabbed Lessig by the lapels and pulled him up from his chair, thrusting his face close the journalist's beaked nose. "You make me sick, you fucking collaborator." He shoved the cowering journalist back into his chair and began to pace around the room, hands clenched behind his back, muttering and glowering at the walls.

"Control yourself, for God's sake," Janko said to his brother "They'll hear us and think we're going to cause trouble."

Lessig cast an apprehensive glance at the fuming Laci, then took Sophie's hand— his expression as pleading and earnest as a religious supplicant's. "Listen, Sophie, there's a chance I could help you find Willy. Those Gestapo fellows trust me pretty well, and I could try to get a look at their files. Willy has always been good to me. I want to help."

Looking into his pale eyes, Sophie wanted to believe him. She did not like or trust him, but he held the strongest card, his connection to the Nazis. She did not draw back when he gave her a warm, encouraging smile and squeezed her hand.

"Why did you pretend not to speak German?" said Lessig.

"It was a reflex. I just wanted to make everything harder for them, and then I thought acting like a distraught Czech mother would make them feel sorry for me. They might give up on turning my home upside down or at least be nicer to us."

Lessig nodded. "I played along with you, but don't do it again. Altmann, the one in the leather coat, is a clever and dangerous man."

Janko rose from the table and took Laci to the kitchen to help him find more slivovice. From their frowning, tense glances, Sophie guessed that they were as suspicious of Lessig's offer of help as of the way the Sudetenlander was stroking her hand. Although she disliked what he was doing, he was still her husband's friend—and was offering her the chance to find Willy. She had to get to the bottom of Willy's disappearance. "How did you know my husband was arrested?" she said, slowly extricating her hand from his.

He moved his chair closer, as if to give her words more attention. She caught a whiff of pomade, cologne, sweat, and tobacco—not an appetizing combination.

"It was at a planning meeting. I—I saw Willy's name on Altmann's list of detainees. It was a shock, believe me. Altmann is Gestapo. He has about fifty people to investigate. When I saw Willy's name, I asked to be involved, saying that I knew him and because of that could get better information."

"And now you think can you help me? Whose side are you on?"

Lessig grabbed Sophie's hand again and gave her an encouraging smile. "Of course I can help, dear Sophie. I'm a reputable journalist, remember? I have tricks, techniques, contacts. I'm well known in Prague. You're lucky to have me on your side."

Sophie's heart responded with hope, and she gave him a tentative smile. Hans was probably right; he was in a good position to find out the Gestapo secrets. "I'm very grateful, Hans. I suppose it's difficult for you to be walking a tightrope between the Nazis and all your old Czech friends."

Lessig gently squeezed her fingers. "You have no idea how hard. It has been giving me nightmares. It may take me a few more days to gain Altmann's full confidence and trust. I'll telephone you as soon as I find out something important."

Finished dealing with Pavel, Elena set out cold cuts, pickles, and slices of black bread for the Gestapo men, covering them with a linen cloth. The coffee pot was primed with fresh grounds. The cousins returned, Laci with a beer and Janko with a cigarette. "No more *slivovice*," said Laci, disappointed.

Sophie started to tremble as she again disengaged her hand from Lessig's. What if the Nazis came upstairs and found the money hidden inside Willy's sculpture? Even worse, they might discover the passports. Three months earlier, Willy had put the counterfeit Hungarian passports at the bottom of one of the flour bins in the kitchen. He never told her how he had gotten them, only that they were incredibly important, a vital part of their escape should it ever be necessary.

Sophie racked her brain for a way to stop a thorough search of the kitchen. Twisting the strings of her apron nervously, she turned to Elena. "Quick as you can, dear, prepare the schnitzels and vegetables for dinner. Leave everything out on the counter. Make as much of a mess as you can on the counter: flour, breadcrumbs, and vegetable peelings. And leave everything dirty: knives, cutting boards and bowls. Keep water boiling, and fry lots of onions—and don't wipe anything clean."

"But *madám*, don't..." Elena's eyebrows were parachutes on her forehead.

Sophie frowned. "I don't want those Germans turning my kitchen upside down. If they see what a mess it's in, they might only take a quick peek.

಄ ∂ ಄

Twenty minutes later, there was a loud rap on the door. Pohl, the tall officer, entered followed by Altmann. Pohl looked at the food on the table, and pointed his swagger stick at Lessig. "We have finished downstairs. Have the woman bring hot coffee and milk. We haven't eaten since breakfast. Then we search in here."

Sophie walked to the wrecked Biedermeier writing desk, her eyes flashing defiance. "You want me to serve you coffee, you brutes?" she said in Czech, pointing at the desk. "This is what your men did when they took my husband. It's valuable and I want compensation." She turned to Lessig. "Translate *that*."

With a quick intake of breath, Lessig shook his head violently as if warning her to be quiet. His pale cheeks flushed as he translated her request.

Altmann waved a dismissive hand as he sat down at the table. "A stupid demand", he sneered, heaping food on to a plate. "We leave no desk unturned when it comes to rooting out spies. The two store assistants, where are they?"

Lessig excused himself and retrieved Janko and Laci from the kitchen.

"You have been burning papers in the stove downstairs," said Altmann to the two employees who stood in front of him as he ate. "Why?"

"Routine," Laci retorted in passable German. "We burn wrapping paper, packing cloth, and broken packing cases as well. This is what we do with all our discards, especially when the weather is cold." Sophie saw the fury in his eyes and watched him ball his fists behind his back. She prayed that he would not lose his temper. He and Willy were two peas in a pod in the temper department.

Pohl poured his coffee "There was a hell of a lot of ash in that stove pan, "he said with a sardonic laugh "I bet you were burning incriminating materials. Were you?"

"That's enough for the moment, Pohl," said Altmann. He paused to flick a scrap of ham off his jacket lapel on to the floor. "Interrogations are for later. Now, everybody waits downstairs while we finish eating and go through the apartment. Lessig, explain what I said to the woman."

"But—but, my boy is asleep in his room," Sophie said in Czech, eyes widening in alarm after Lessig told her what Altmann had ordered. "He shouldn't be disturbed." She was again regretting her decision to burn the correspondence. It made Willy look guilty when he was not, and now she was terrified that they would find the passports in the flour bin.

"You have to wake the child," said Hans with an apologetic shrug.

Sophie nodded, trying to control the trembling of her

hands. *Please, God, don't let them find the passports.* "I beg you
Hans, tell them not to upset Elena in the kitchen. She's in the
middle of making our supper, and she's very frightened."

"I'll do my best to keep them out of there, or at least hurry
them up."

Altmann prodded a finger into Lessig's chest. "They can
wait downstairs but this time you stay with me. I expect we will
find books and documents in English. I may need you to give me
an idea if they are important. Do you know English?"

Lessig shook his head.

"Idiot."

ത ∂ ര

Just before nine o'clock, the two Germans and Lessig
came downstairs carrying a ledger, several English novels, and
a bundle of documents from the Biedermeier desk. Janko and
Laci stayed close to Sophie, who scanned the Germans' faces for
some sign of the results of their search. She was perspiring and
her pulse raced.

"We have finished." Altmann gave a curt nod to Sophie.
She could not tell from his expression whether he had found
anything or not. "Your kitchen is disgusting. The girl there
needs harsh discipline and training—or throwing out into the
street." He turned to Lessig. "Tell Frau Kohut that her husband
has a fine Bechstein. I tried the Ravel *étude* he had left open
on the music stand—the piano has a beautiful tone, but I pity
his choice of music; French composers are inconsequential and
effete. Brahms, Beethoven, or Wagner—that is music for the
gods." He pulled on his leather gloves. "Tell her also that the
Bechstein family is close friends with the Führer. That you have
such a piano is one positive for you today. Your husband chose
the finest instrument."

"I will tell her," said Lessig in a low voice. "She wants to
know where her husband is and when he is coming home. Do
you know?"

"That is not for me to say."

Sophie watched from inside the store as the two Germans
and Lessig stood talking on the pavement next to the half-track
truck in which they had arrived. She felt as if she had just
emerged from a stinging hot bath, wet with sweat but relaxed

and relieved. All was as well as it could be. She had calmed Elena in the kitchen and then, on her own, checked the flour bin; the passports were still there—and the sculpture holding their money reserve had not been moved. The ordeal was over for the moment.

As she was closing the window blinds, she paused to look out at Lessig talking with Altmann in the street, hoping beyond hope that he would help her find Willy—and that whatever these men had taken away would prove that her husband was innocent.

∾ ∂ ∾

"What do you think, *mein Herr?*" said Obersturmführer Pohl as they stood by the half-track. In the freezing cold, his breath left vapor trails in the light of the street lamp. "Skimpy pickings, eh?"

Altmann dabbed at his nose with a handkerchief. Cold nights made his nose run. "Just focus on the most salient item in this case, Pohl. It was Lessig here who found the codes in the accused's apartment and sent them to Erdaker in Munich. We double-checked those code numbers against the labels on all the fabric bolts in the store. There's no hint of a match-up between the codes from the apartment and any of the fabrics in the store—so what is this treasure that Lessig uncovered for us, eh? A list made to look like fabric inventory numbers. Very cunning. I'm positive we're dealing with British radio transmission codes. You did fine work, Lessig."

"Thank you, *mein Herr.*" Lessig's eyelashes fluttered.

Altmann pulled thoughtfully at his ear. "The directive from the Reichsprotektor says we must be extra gentle with Czech detainees—I find that damned frustrating." He smiled. "We'd save a lot of time on these cases if we flattened these people like the schnitzels that useless girl was preparing, I have always found that pain and fresh blood are wonderful persuaders. Anyway, *der kleiner schwein* Kohut will stay locked up while our people in Munich break his codes. Of course, he denies all of this. As our temporary friend Stalin says, denial is the first sign of a traitor. We will break Kohut soon."

"Pardon me for interrupting," said Lessig tentatively. "I have a suggestion."

The two officials turned and looked at him. "What are you talking about?" Altmann sneered. "A suggestion about what?"

"Look, the Kohut wife trusts me. If I pretend to help her find her husband, I could probably extract some useful information. Let me work on being nice to her. What do you say?"

Pohl guffawed and slapped his thigh. "Lessig, you old stink, I suspected all along you were a sneaky one. I can just imagine what you plan to do with her: extract information after inserting your persuader, eh? Actually, I think she fancied me, not you."

"Shut up, Pohl." Altmann's voice was harsh and cutting. "Keep your brain away from your testicles. Lessig's proposal isn't such a bad one. We'll work out the specifics at my office first thing tomorrow." The Gestapo official turned and looked into Lessig's hollow face. "If your suggestion works, I suppose you'll expect some extra reward other than the chance to bed the Jewess?"

The journalist grinned. "Only that you turn a blind eye, Herr Altmann. Just give me some funds and room to maneuver on my own. As for my specific reward, there are some nice antique pieces in the Kohut flat."

7

PRISON
MARCH 19, 1939

THE BURLY GUARD unlocked the cell door, half-pull-ing, half-shoving Willy inside. He pointed to the lower bunk where a man lay curled up under a blanket. "You're sharing with Károly," he said in Czech. "He's here for strangling his wife. Been inside ten years, but now he's as gentle as a butterfly—too sick to do anything violent. He just smokes, coughs, sleeps, and pees. You're up top."

"What about my suitcase and watch?"

The guard laughed in a deep, musical voice that sounded almost friendly. "That's a stupid question. You get two meals a day. Ten minutes of exercise in the corridor."

"You're Czech," said Willy pointedly. "Why are you doing this?"

"I need to keep my job and my family fed. Keep your nose clean and we'll get along. Right?" He left, clanging the door shut. "Enjoy your time in Pankrác."

Willy's suit, which he had been wearing since the arrest, reeked of sweat and dried urine. Although there was no mirror in the cell, he knew he was on the way to looking like the filthy, degenerate Jew epitomized in Nazi cartoons. It had taken him a surprisingly short time, he thought, to become a humiliated, disgusting wreck.

Does anyone know I'm here? Fear that he would be forgotten, tortured, or even murdered ripped at his guts. He thought of Sophie and Pavel and wanted to weep. He had been taken from them and thrown into a Kafkaesque black hole.

The cell had a round table fixed to the floor, a steel washbasin, and no window. A worn Bible lay on the single bench screwed to the floor. Willy asked Károly if he knew what the time was and got back a terse, "Go fuck yourself." He slumped on the bench. Was this the third or the fourth day he had been cooped up? He was sure more interrogations were coming and, so far, he had told the truth—he was not a British spy. What else could he do?

He drank brackish water from a tin pitcher on the table and climbed up onto his bunk. For a while, he stared at the ceiling, wondering about Havel Molnar. Was he the informant? Probably not, but Willy suspected the man guarded many secrets. Was he good, bad—or both?

They had met the previous year on the day Willy's furniture was being delivered to the empty Masná Street apartment. Willy's new Bechstein piano was the sole piece of furniture in the living room. Workers were hammering and painting in the store below, which was scheduled to open in three weeks. Molnar had appeared at the apartment door while Willy was playing a Bartók piece from the Mikrokosmos series. He had introduced himself as a neighbor from the fourth floor. Willy guessed the man to be in his fifties: elegantly dressed in a fine suit, waistcoat, pocket watch, spats, and a high collar like the one Willy's father wore for business—the style of old Central Europe. The man had a habit, when he spoke, of using two fingers of his left hand to sharpen the point of his silvery-waxed mustache.

"Forgive me for intruding," he had said with a slight bow. "I am Molnar Havel. I just wanted to make sure you had no problems settling in." He had paused. "I heard you playing. You are a fine pianist. It must be a music store you are opening downstairs. There is already a good one, Svoboda, two streets over, and I'm afraid you will have trouble getting customers."

Laughing, Willy had explained that he was a clothier who sold fabrics for men's suits and coats. "We left Košice because we'd had enough of the independence riots in Slovakia. I wanted to start over, fly higher, and supply the best Prague tailors with the finest British fabrics." Willy recalled his boast. "My store, Anglotex, will outshine the elegance of Henry Poole of London, Kníže of Vienna, and Cifonelli of Paris."

Molnar had smiled in a friendly fashion at Willy's exuberance, explaining that he held a senior postmaster position at the Central Post and Telegraph Office. He had offered to introduce Willy to his tailor, Moshe Lemberger, whom he had described as a genius at hiding protruding paunches and bulging buttocks. Molnar had shown Willy the buttonhole of his jacket lapel, a marvel of intricate stitching ending at the top in a curving dragon tail pattern—apparently the master tailor's unique signature. "Moshe is Jewish, of course—chairman of the Prague Tailors' Association," Molnar had added with a knowing smile. "Knows what's going on, like me. I'm guessing you are also Jewish. After all, the rag trade seems to be the purview of the Chosen People. Besides, who but a Jew would give up his business to flee rampant anti-Semitism and Faschismus in Slovakia?"

Molnar had turned to leave, sliding his thumbs into his waistcoat pockets in a gesture that had reminded Willy of his own father when he was about to make an important pronouncement. "By the way, "he said, "don't you think you're taking quite a risk opening a luxury store with so much trouble on our borders? I expect you have invested a great deal of money."

"I'm not sure what you mean by 'quite a risk,'" Willy remembered saying, thinking that *pane* Molnar was congenial but blunt: a little too curious—a man not so different from his own father, who had founded Kohut Fabrics in 1920 in Lučenec, Slovakia...

Molnar had offered a warning. "You may hope for success but mark my words: Hitler will grab Austria soon. Maybe he will come here. Haven't you read about all the terrified refugees flowing into our country? One day you will have only two choices: fight or run. If you run, you won't be able to take Anglotex and the money you invested with you."

Willy remembered thinking that Molnar was far too nosy, and a fear monger; he would let the old postmaster worry about what the Nazis would do next. Willy had a store to open, money to make, a reputation to forge, and debts to pay off.

ళ ∂ ళ

Bored and jittery in the cell, Willy had no idea how many hours had passed. With nothing else to do, he climbed down from his bunk and sat on the bench to skim the well-thumbed Bible. His cellmate watched him impassively through deep-set eyes, smoking cigarette after cigarette, coughing endlessly. Willy repeatedly tried to engage him, to no avail. The guards eventually brought thin soup and bread and a pack of cigarettes for Károly. They changed the slop pail. Willy asked them for the time; there was no answer. He climbed onto his bunk again and counted the stains and cracks in the wall.

He yearned to be at home watching Pavel play with his bricks on the floor, eating Ludmila's cooking, listening to the Ink Spots on the Victrola, practicing on his Bechstein, and holding Sophie close in his arms at night, feeling her smooth body snuggled against his. After counting the 223rd connected crack in the stucco wall, he finally fell asleep.

When the guard opened the door and grunted "Breakfast," Willy knew the long night had passed. He noticed the guard slipping a fresh packet of cigarettes to Károly and cursed. Was this going to be the routine? Between the incessant smoking and coughing of his cellmate and the constant flicker of the light bulb, Willy's sleep had been fitful. He had spent much of the night either reliving happy moments with Pavel and Sophie or chastising himself for being too optimistic, too engaged in his business. He had blinded himself to the warnings of Molnar and his own father. He had let down his wife and son by neglecting the admonitions of those two wise older men to prepare for the worst.

If he was honest with himself, from the time of the Sudeten handover sealed at Munich, Willy had suspected that the Germans would attack Czechoslovakia one day. On the other hand, Molnar had assured him more than once that if it came to hostilities, the large, well prepared, and well-equipped Czech army could actually defeat the Germans. Willy was not sure about that, but he had believed that such a war was far enough in the future for him to sell Anglotex for a princely sum and get his family out of the country. In fact, when he left prison—he was hoping it would not take more than a few days at most—

there was the intriguing possibility of a sale. Before his arrest, his agent friend, Tomáš Motyka, had found a potential buyer from Brno. Would he still want to buy now?

ᔈ ∂ ᔈ

The next time the jailers took Willy to be interrogated, he could not stand still, swaying unsteadily in the harsh light of a single lamp. The room had dark yellow walls and an electric heater glowed and buzzed in a corner. He shivered as the cold ate into his bones.

An interrogator sat in the shadows behind the lamp. Willy made out a drooping eyelid set in an angular, taut face that sagged to the left.

"My name is Altmann, Gestapo." The man spoke in a harsh German monotone. "Be open in your answers and do not hide anything from me. From an informant, we know everything about your family, your business, and your spying. I personally visited and examined your premises, removed documents, and met your wife—a charming woman, by the way. Very attractive. Curious that she doesn't speak German like you."

Willy's mouth was dry and raw. He had missed the midmorning water round. "I already told the truth. I am not a spy. I import British fabrics." He felt dizzy and yearned to lie down, shut his eyes, and drift into unconsciousness.

Altmann flipped a page of his file. "No prevarications, prisoner. Our informant appropriated a document in your apartment purporting to be some kind of stock inventory. At your store, we carefully checked the codes on this document against the numbers on all the bolts of fabric in the storeroom and in the display windows. Almost all your inventory originates in England, isn't that so?"

Willy nodded.

"Well, the numbers on the seized document do not match anything in your store. Thus, the codes must represent something other than bolts of fabric. Our intelligence experts believe these are either secret instructions or links to other agents or sympathizers. Added to this finding is the fact that your father, also an importer of British fabrics, was imprisoned in Slovakia last October by the new Hungarian administration in Lučenec. He bribed the idiots to release him, and seven weeks later, he escaped to London. My guess is that you and he were a duo, working for British intelligence."

As he swayed in the gloom, Willy's usually nimble brain fought to make sense of what this man was saying. The information about his parents was true—they had escaped after losing their house and business—but Altmann's claim about the codes and the inventory was pure fabrication.

"Let's not waste time," the interrogator continued. "Give me the names of your contacts and the key to the codes, and I'll treat you gently. You could be home in a couple of days."

"Prior to my visit to your store," Altmann continued, "your wife and assistants burned many documents. Why did they do that if you're innocent, eh? Well?"

Willy was shocked that Sophie or someone else could have done that. He stuttered. "I-I don't understand any of this. If you show me the document you have with the codes, I can probably explain its significance." He vaguely remembered having mislaid a letter from Kindell & Renfrew at New Year's, after they had held their final Sunday lunch for eight or so guests. Maybe Altmann was referring to *that* document.

Altmann lit a cigarette and looking up at Willy leaned his chair back on two legs. He curled his lip. "I believe your codes were created by MI6 to look like the merchandise numbers you use in your store. An ingenious trick."

"Please show me the document." Willy rubbed his cracked lips in a fruitless attempt to relieve the burning round his mouth. His mind cleared a little. *Perhaps someone in his apartment had found the Kindell & Renfrew shipment list. Why? How?* "This spy accusation is perhaps... a misunderstanding."

Altmann's voice turned to velvet. "Maybe some stimulation will improve you memory?" He pressed a button wired to the desk. The door opened, and two men in dark blue smocks entered.

"Work him over for fifteen minutes and take him back to his cell to think things over," said Altmann, gathering his notes. "Make sure the results are not easily visible. The Reichsprotektor is still publicizing our gentleness toward the Czechs, and I don't want to get into hot water." He walked out.

Willy's heart lurched, his stomach tight with fear. He looked around the room, wondering what these men would use on him, but he saw nothing that looked like torture apparatus. His mind flashed back to 1937 when he was a spectator at the Košice Marathon, caught in the middle of a Vlajka riot, hit by flying stones, and then attacked by thugs. That episode had happened too fast for his body to react with fear or desperation. However, in this room, he had plenty of time to imagine fists and feet, electric shock, or...what?

The men pulled long, bulging socks from a canvas bag. He waited. There was no point in trying to defend himself, and he was not going to throw himself on the floor and beg for mercy. He took off his precious glasses and slid them into the pocket of his jacket, which he folded and placed under his chair. "What do you have for me?" he asked as calmly as he could.

One of the men grinned. "It's only sand, nothing complicated."

"This way it don't show bruises so easy," said the other one, slamming the heavy sock against the wall with one hand, "but it fucking hurts."

He was not lying.

∽ ∂ ∽

Willy could not get up into his bunk. He half-stood in front of Károly, holding on to one of the bunk's metal pillars, the pain coursing through his body "Can you help me climb the ladder?" he mumbled, hoping desperately for some response. He could not bear the thought of lying for hours on the stone floor.

"They really fucked you over," wheezed the older man, staring from under a shelf of gray eyebrows as he rose to his feet. "Get your feet on the first step an' then I'll push on your arse. That's it." The maneuver, accompanied by Willy's groans, took what seemed like several minutes. "You'd better stay up on deck. If you need to pee, give me a shout, sit yourself up on the edge, and I'll bring the bucket."

Through the dim mist of pain, Willy was grateful for Károly's help—and surprised. There was some humanity left in the old curmudgeon. As he turned on the straw mattress trying to get comfortable, the throbbing in Willy's chest and back swamped his every thought and restricted every movement for what seemed like an eternity. Eventually he fell into a deep, exhausted sleep – only to be immediately wakened for supper.

With a moan, he raised himself up enough to eat the cabbage soup and bread that Károly passed up.

Afterwards, Willy passed his hands gently over his torso, wondering if he had any broken ribs. It hurt terribly to breathe. He lay down again, trying to find the least painful position. It seemed the only way he could cope with the pain was to deny it, to try to visualize something beautiful: Sophie in his arms, swan flotillas on the Vltava River, Prague in deep snow, carpets of wild flowers on their hikes in the Tatra Mountains, or watching Sophie dancing the *csárdás* while he accompanied her on the piano.

During the night, he woke Károly twice to get him the slop bucket, banging his tin plate on the frame to wake the old man. The second time, the persistent throbbing in his chest and back prevented him from going back to sleep. He massaged his bruised flesh, wondering about the identity of Altmann's informant. Hans Lessig, the Sudetenlander who had been a frequent guest at their lunches, remained his prime suspect. The man had never uttered a bad word about Hitler, but then he was also a fan of Czech President Beneš. Which side was Hans on?

But what about Havel Molnar, Willy's upstairs neighbor? He was a definite possibility after what happened last September, in the middle of the Czech mobilization. Hitler had threatened war over Sudetenland and Molnar had visited Willy at his machine gun defense post on Křížovnická Street to give him an official note. He, Molnar, was to escort Willy to the Ministry of Foreign Affairs at Černín Palace to meet with the head of Czech security, František Moravec.

Willy was surprised and had angrily refused. What the hell did this Moravec want? Willy had been up half the night, keeping watch, and at eight that morning had received an urgent message from Sophie: Hungarian troops had invaded Southern Slovakia, and his father was in prison. Willy wanted to go to Lučenec to help his parents, not chat with some high and mighty police bureaucrat for some god-forsaken reason

Willy remembered how grim-faced Molnar had hauled him to his feet to show Willy the official order. "This is not an invitation to dinner; it's a military order. You have no option. We take the number 22 tram up Castle Hill."

Half an hour later, in one of the palace's ornate rooms

lined with filing cabinets and cardboard boxes, they had sat opposite Moravec, a broad-shouldered, jowly man clenching a cheroot between his teeth. Willy noted the perfection of the colonel's well-cut pinstripe suit and the trademark button-hole—Moshe Lemberger again.

Moravec had dispensed with the niceties, pushing a stack of files aside to get a clear view of Willy and massaging his chin for a moment. "With the Munich fiasco, we've just lost Sudetenland, one-third of our country, and most of our heavy industries. The new Czech government has cut my budget in half, which is why you are here. *Pane* Molnar tells me you are a resourceful man: reliable, cultured, and a linguist. I need you."

Why does he need me? Willy remembered thinking he had enough complications in his life. He had enough to do trying to sell his business and make escape plans. What was this intelligence chief after? "What do you need me for?"

"You have a friend, Hans Lessig, a Sudetenlander. There are over two hundred Nazi agents, mostly Sudetenlanders, operating in Czechoslovakia and using radio transmitters. We think Lessig might be one of them. In case of a Nazi attack on our soil, we cannot afford to let the details of our military equipment and defense plans be compromised. That's where you come in. I want you to keep an eye on Lessig for me."

Willy recalled how stunned he was that Lessig might be a real Nazi agent, though he realized it was quite feasible. It would be easy enough for a journalist to turn spy, even though Lessig gave the impression of being a disorganized scatterbrain.

"Keep up or even promote your friendship," Moravec had said, slapping his hand on the table in emphasis. "Anything unusual, inform *pane* Molnar—nothing written, mind you. This is a crucial moment for the survival of our democracy. You must help us. A German attack is inevitable, sometime soon. We need to know as much as possible."

It was then that Willy finally understood that there might be no future for him or his family if the Czech army, even though supported by Britain and France, was defeated. To get away, his only chance was to have exit visas or Hungarian passports. The Czech government had stopped issuing exit visas to its citizens, but Hungarians could travel anywhere. If he and Sophie could get out, they would go to his parents in England

or even across the Atlantic to North America. However, it would
not be easy to start a new business unless he had money...and
that meant selling Anglotex.

Willy smiled at the memory of what he did next. "I'll do
what you ask," he had said, "but I want something in return:
counterfeit Hungarian passports and exit visas so that my family
can leave the country quickly if we have to."

Willy recalled how Moravec and Molnar had joked together,
complimenting him on his chutzpah. Jews were the world cham-
pions of bargaining, Moravec had said, and promised to arrange
an appointment with Captain Palaček, his document specialist.
The shock came when he told Willy that fabricating passports
for all the Kohuts would cost in the region of 50,000 korun.
Willy would have to pay.

"I need an answer right now, Kohut," the colonel had said.
"If you watch Lessig for me and come up with the payment,
then you get your passports. Otherwise, forget that this meeting
happened. What do you say?"

Willy had to have the passports, his family's golden keys
to freedom. He'd put out his hand. "Very well, I agree."

8

THE SEARCH
APRIL, 1939

IN THE DAYS following the Gestapo's raid on Kohut Stoffe—she still called it Anglotex—Sophie spent most of her waking hours trying to find Willy. She regularly visited the mayor's office, the central police station, and the Old-New Synagogue, where she asked the rabbi to circulate her plea to the congregation. She asked the Jewish Business Association for help and booked a telephone call to Kindell & Renfrew in London. Willy's friend George Kindell offered to send one of his employees. When she heard the young man did not speak Czech, she declined politely.

She was often on the telephone with acquaintances and with Hans Lessig, who said he was doing his best with the Germans. He told her to be patient. She decided not to inform Willy's parents in London that he was missing; she knew Emil would write at least one scathing I-told-my-son-this-would-happen letter, and she imagined her mother-in-law would expect the worst.

With Postmaster Molnar on his way to Poland, Sophie sought support from Ruth Eisner and kept an eye on Janko and Laci who were running the store—an easy task now, with only two or three customers a day. The usual flow of Prague's commerce had slowed to a trickle as the subjugated inhabitants stayed at home, buying only food and essentials. Besides, the

Czech koruna had lost more than a third of its value. This was not the moment to order fabric for a new suit.

Sophie sent Elena, Elise, and Nanny Ludmila back to their homes. They would be safer with their families outside Prague, and she would save money. She took on the cooking and cleaning and played with Pavel, welcoming the apartment as a haven from the suddenly hostile world outside. Everything reminded her of Willy: the Bechstein strewn with music scores, his favorite coffee cup, the row of suits, his antique silver hairbrush, his gold-plated fountain pen on the broken desk, and the business letters that arrived every day.

Sophie tried distractions to hold back her fear and anxiety, like knitting a scarf for Willy, a symbol of her hope for his return. She listened to records on the phonograph but they made her cry. She attempted to use the Electrolux vacuum cleaner but stopped when it made strange grinding noises. Radio Praha made her angry at its mellifluous propaganda describing the courteous demeanor of the Nazi occupiers. Pavel often asked for his *táta*. Each time, she did her best to reassure him—"*Táta* will be back soon"—and each time, she could not stop her tears.

At night, while her boy slept, Sophie was restless, haunted by fear and loneliness. The cold bed reminded her of sleeping alone as teenager in Berlin. She missed how Willy kept their bed warm with his well-muscled body and lovemaking. Unsettling and often unconnected questions popped into her head: *What if I run out of money? What if Willy never comes back? Should we leave without him? Where would we go? How?* She could not stop reliving the day of Willy's arrest, imagining the fear he must have felt, wondering what privations he was now suffering, what danger threatened him.

જ ∂ જ

Two days later, Lessig telephoned. "Listen, Sophie, good news." Her hopes soared at the sound of his high-pitched, excited voice. "I've made a likely contact at Abwehr headquarters. An officer there is willing to help us find Willy. I have time now. Shall I come and explain?"

"Yes, come."

Half an hour later, he was at Masná Street, sitting close beside her on the couch, a coffee cup and saucer shaking slightly in his spidery fingers. His eyes glittered behind the steel spectacles, and something new, a gold swastika pin, decorated the lapel of his Norfolk jacket. "You must understand, Sophie," he said, throwing back his narrow shoulders as if he deserved a medal, "I've been promoted to a senior editor position at the newspaper. So now, I have a lot of pull. You see, we Sudetenlanders have become essential to greasing the smooth transition of protectorate administration. The Germans respect me."

"Please." Sophie glared, despising him and trying not to look at the swastika pin. "Spare me the boasting. Just tell me what I need to know about Willy."

Lessig's Adam's apple rose and fell; his cheeks looked as though they had been slapped. He removed his glasses and polished them with a napkin from the table. He cleared his throat.

"In the end, I decided that the best thing was to go directly to Abwehr headquarters. That's where I've spent the last two days, bouncing from official to official, asking about Willy."

Sophie clenched her teeth in frustration. "Hans, please. Just give me the essentials. I don't want the long story of how well you managed things."

"Now Sophie, don't get annoyed. You have to understand what I've been through. Receiving under-the-table favors from Nazi administrators requires skill—and some greasing of palms. I found a man, Lieutenant Haeckel, who has access to all the lists of prisoners held in different places in Prague. He is willing to find Willy for twenty thousand korun, about two thousand Reichsmarks. Of course, I'll go with you to headquarters to pay him. I'll smooth the way. Don't worry."

Sophie arched her eyebrows. "You mean...pay him a bribe?"

Hans nodded. Sophie groaned inwardly. What Hans was proposing was absurd, uncertain, and possibly dangerous. Unsure what the reaction would be from Janko and Laci, she thought about rushing upstairs to ask Ruth for advice. How could she decide this on her own? "I would like to think about it overnight."

"No," said Lessig firmly. "This is the only way to get your husband home; it's a gamble, but Lieutenant Haeckel wants to know that the money is available—tonight. He is expecting me to telephone a confirmation. If I cannot guarantee the funds tonight, he will cancel our meeting."

"Oh, God," she muttered, "what else can I do? All right, Hans, I agree. Let's go to see him tomorrow, first thing if possible. I'll have the money ready for him. Can you arrange it?"

He nodded, rubbing his hands with satisfaction. "I think we will work well together." He slipped an arm round her shoulders.

"Why are you doing this for me, Hans?"

"This is what friends are for, Sophie. I'm sure you would do the same for me."

Sophie saw the unmistakable lust in his eyes and wondered for a moment whether intentionally encouraging a flirtation would tie him more closely to her quest for Willy. A cooperative and adoring Hans who worked hand-in-glove with the Nazis could protect her family better than anyone else. However, if she accepted his help, she would be walking a tightrope, using him for her needs while trying to parry his sexual advances. Unlike Ruth, she was reluctant to flirt and string men along, behaviors she had observed as commonplace among the socialite circles since her arrival in Prague. Why tempt fate? She loved Willy.

After Lessig had gone, Sophie got ready for bed. Ruth Eisner had lent her Neruda's *Prague Tales*—she called him the Czech Charles Dickens—and Sophie had found that reading in bed helped bring on the sleep that once had been so easy with a warm husband beside her.

಄ ∂ ಄

The next day in the late afternoon, not 'first thing' as she had wanted, Sophie accompanied Lessig on the tram to Abwehr headquarters in central Prague. As it rumbled through rain-soaked Wenceslas Square and around Wilson Station, she noticed motorized half-tracks, machine gun posts, artillery pieces, and the occasional tank occupying strategic positions at the street intersections. Green-uniformed Wehrmacht soldiers were everywhere and the traffic was slow and chaotic. Cars and buses now had to drive on the right side of the road instead of the left.

Hans had advised Sophie to look matronly and respectful for the Abwehr visit, so she had dressed carefully in a veiled pillbox hat, high-necked silk blouse, dark skirt, coat, and black pumps. At the headquarters gates, Lessig drew a small blue card from his breast pocket and showed it to the guards, who raised the barrier pole. They waited for a few minutes, taking shelter from the biting wind under one of the arches that surrounded the cobbled internal courtyard.

Eventually, a soldier marched up and stamped to attention. "Herr Lessig?" Hans nodded, showing his blue card. "*Kommen Sie mit.*"

The guard escorted them through ironbound doors and along several interconnected corridors. Sophie felt her neck and shoulder blades tighten as they walked. *Is this a trap? What if they arrest me?*

At a half-glassed door guarded by another soldier, Hans turned to Sophie. "You wait here. I will go in first and prepare the officer to receive you and pay him the agreed fee. Give me the money, and then I will come back for you." He rapped firmly on the door.

A voice from inside shouted, "*Herein.*" Lessig took the roll of hundred-korun notes from her and went in, closing the door behind him. The guard began to pace up and down the corridor.

Sophie tried to stay calm, but her heart was racing. *Why did he leave me out here?* She guessed at the answer. Lessig was probably paying himself a commission; that is why he did not want her with him. She plucked up her courage and leaned against the door, straining to catch some words, but she heard only an indistinct murmur of conversation.

After five minutes or so, Lessig came out. He smiled broadly and patted her shoulder. "You can go in now. I'll wait out here. Everything will be fine."

Sophie entered a wood-paneled office that reeked of stale cigars. Two overstuffed leather armchairs and a velvet couch were set against a wall. In the center, a floor lamp shed a pool of light on a desk covered with a jumble of papers and folders. A man in a black uniform with shining silver edging and lapel badges sat in a swivel chair. His eyes flicked up at her as he clamped a lighted cigar between two plump, hairy fingers.

Sophie read USF. HAECKEL stenciled on a wooden holder on the desk. A large swastika flag was unevenly tacked to the wall behind the desk. She decided not to wait for an invitation and sat down in a chair by the desk.

"So, Lessig tells me you speak German," the officer said. "That's good. I hear you are looking for a missing husband?" He sucked at the cigar, and the ash glowed like a furnace.

Sophie tried not to show she was afraid. "Yes, my husband's name is Kohut Willy. Can you help me, please, Herr Haeckel?"

Smoke escaped from his spluttering mouth in little puffs. "I am not just an ordinary *Herr*, woman. I am an officer of the Third Reich, an Untersturmbannführer." His chair rocked back and forth on squeaky hinges.

"Of course you are," she said apologetically, doing her best not to laugh.

"Shut up, woman. You are Jewish, yes? One of the filthy race?"

The words stung like a whiplash. Years back, Sophie had experienced the insinuations of the other girls at her *Hochschule* in Berlin, but never anything so blatant and offensive. She nodded and lowered her gaze, resting clenched fists on knees. *Anivut*—be silent in the face of abuse. That is what her father would have said.

The officer crushed his cigar in the ashtray. He spoke more quietly and opened an empty dossier. "Herr Lessig and I have discussed undertaking a search for your husband's whereabouts. Obviously, he is detained somewhere in Prague."

"Yes, Herr Lessig said you have access to all the prisoner lists."

Haeckel picked another cigar out of the box on his desk and smiled at her. His teeth were yellow. "These lists are always in flux, but now that I have received the requisite financial resources, I will definitely make inquiries. You can come back with Herr Lessig each day at ten to see if I have an answer for you. If it takes longer than a week, I may need more, ah, financing."

"I don't have much." Sophie clutched her purse. *He wants more? Lessig said that 20,000 korun was supposed to cover everything. I can't go on paying this much.*

Haeckel rose from his chair and tossed a small blue pass across the table. "Next time, just show this and ask for me."

Sophie put it in her purse; suspicious that she was being put off, possibly deceived. What else could she do? She tried to hide her relief at remaining unharmed. "Good-bye and thank you. I will do as you say and return tomorrow."

ׂ‎ ∂ ‎ׂ

Lessig was waiting in the corridor. "So, how did it go?" His face was alive with eagerness.

"Haeckel promised to search. You and I must come back at ten tomorrow."

Lessig slid a long arm around her shoulders, and a grin split his thin face. "I think you should be very pleased. We now have official access into the Abwehr—a huge step. If the lieutenant comes up empty-handed, I can find someone else. We'll find Willy, for sure."

She gave him a fleeting smile. Haeckel's visit seemed more like a small but expensive step than a huge one. How many more would there be?

They had a long wait for the tram to Old Town, and as it rattled along, they talked about what had transpired. As they stepped down at the Trida stop, Lessig took her arm. "Perhaps, once I get you home, you would be kind enough to offer me a snack. I'm ravenous—haven't eaten all day."

Sophie nodded assent. "It will be a pleasure." Hans deserved to be fed.

He tucked her arm under his. It was already early evening, and the temperature was dropping fast. A fine, cold rain began to fall, stinging Sophie's face like ice needles. Lessig opened the umbrella for both of them.

Sophie found her previous antipathy toward him waning. Her neck and shoulder muscles relaxed. It felt good to have a man, an advocate and protector, sharing her difficult search, doing something for her. In spite of his odd behaviors and her suspicions about his intentions, Lessig was at least helping to do something for Willy.

Janko, who had been standing in for the absent nanny, had just put Pavel to bed. Sophie gave him an excited but whispered description of what had happened with Lieutenant Haeckel. For once, Janko's narrow face looked happy.

"A good first step, then. Are you sure you will be all right with Lessig on your own?" he murmured. "I don't like him. He's strange. Shall I stay?"

She patted his cheek reassuringly. "Not necessary. He's helping me. What else can I do? She eked out a smile. "Anyway, I've got Pavel to protect me. Off you go."

ↄↄ ∂ ↄↄ

In the kitchen, Sophie put on the kettle for coffee and assembled some bread, cold chicken, and beetroot salad, which she and Hans devoured in hungry silence. Optimistic about finding Willy and pleased to be home, she opened a bottle of Egri Cabernet, and they toasted the success of the day. Lessig explained how Haeckel would investigate and how long it might take.

"I ought to be going." Hans did not attempt to get up. The way he sat so close made her uncomfortable.

Sophie got up at the whistle of the kettle. "We'll finish with coffee. It'll warm you up for the tram home." She went to the kitchen and soon returned with a French press of freshly made coffee. The comforting aroma filled the room, and she noticed he had moved their chairs closer together. After she set the *cafetière* down, he leaned over and slid his hand over hers.

"Sophie, I have to be honest about this. I'm helping with Willy because I'm so very fond of you. I can't bear to see you so desperate and unhappy."

She looked away, not knowing what to say, hoping that what she thought was coming wouldn't come—but she didn't move her hand, fearing he would feel rejected and perhaps refuse to go with her to see Haeckel in the morning.

Lessig took a few sips of his coffee. "Mmm, that's good. Just what I needed. Listen, my dear," he said earnestly. "I'm trying to get Willy back for you at great risk to myself. The Nazis will shoot me if they find out what I'm doing."

Sophie tried to ease her hand away, but Lessig grasped it firmly. Their knees touched under the table. She drew back a little on her chair, trying not to show her anxiety. "Yes, Hans, I know it's terribly dangerous for you. I am grateful, really grateful. I wouldn't have known what to do without you."

He raised her trapped hand to his lips and kissed it several times. "I'm so happy that you are grateful," he murmured. "Of course, we are only at the start of the search, but I will go on helping you until you have Willy home." He edged closer. "But

I need a proper reward for my efforts."

Sophie looked at him, reaching for ways she could extricate herself. She arched an eyebrow. "I was wondering if you took a percentage of Haeckel's bribe, but if not, I could give you some extra koruny for your trouble." She pushed back her chair as if to get up.

Lessig did not let go and shook his head slowly. He reached up with his free hand and began stroke the nape of her neck very gently. "It's not money, dearest Sophie; it's you I want—tonight. Just the one night, making love to you."

Sophie sat stock-still and closed her eyes, panic racing through her mind. *If I refuse, he won't help me. If I agree, I betray Willy.* Her thoughts vacillated: refuse, agree, refuse, agree. One thing was clear: the situation was moving too fast, and the wrong way. She wanted to slow everything down and think through what to do next. *Slap him? Wait and see? Run upstairs to a neighbor for help? Grab a knife off the table? God forgive me, must I betray Willy to save him?*

In the absence of further resistance or protest, Lessig leaned closer and, twisting his head slightly, kissed her gently on the lips. She stayed completely still, not sure what to do. His face was too close to hers; she felt his breath on her cheek. She could smell his cologne, the cigarette fumes on his clothes. Her mind whirled.

"I'm a married woman, Hans," she finally said firmly. "What you ask is not acceptable. You expect me to be unfaithful to Willy while he's a prisoner? Is this why you offered to help me?"

Hans grabbed her and kissed her again, more passionately this time, trying to force his tongue into her mouth. Clenching her teeth, she jerked backwards and slapped him. "That's enough!" she cried out, springing to her feet, grabbing a knife off the table. She looked at his chest, heaving and rasping. Did she have the courage to stab him if he came at her? She felt jittery and weak.

Lessig slammed his hand on the table, making the china clatter. "I have to make love to you, Sophie, I have to." His voice was hoarse. "Goddammit, if you refuse me, I won't help you anymore. If you don't let me fuck you, you'll never see Willy again. They'll kill him for sure."

The words struck her like hammer blows. It was clear now: Hans would have no compunctions about carrying out his threat.

The room vibrated with silence. *No way out.* She dropped the knife and paced about the room, hands clasped together in front of her bosom, and then looked at him with tearful, angry eyes. "Did you mean what you just said?"

"More than ever."

"You were a guest under our roof, you've taken my money, and now you're forcing me to deceive Willy? It's blackmail and rape. Where is your humanity and friendship? Was it you who betrayed Willy to the Nazis?"

Lessig rose from his chair. Like a priest giving benediction, he stretched out his long arms and put his palms together. He smiled and gave a little bow. "If I have to use blackmail, then so be it. Remember, I am the only one who can get Willy back for you. I'm not a brute and I won't force you. You must be willing. If you refuse me now, I will disappear, and you can look for your husband on your own. His fate is in your hands."

For a whole minute, Sophie looked at Lessig, the most despicable man she had ever come across. An idea struck her—a possible way to protect herself or, even better, dampen his desire. "All right," she said in a matter-of-fact tone, stooping to gather up the plates. "We'll make it a business proposition. One night, and if you ever tell Willy or anyone or try again, I'll stick this kitchen knife in your ribs. You have to wear a rubber. Agreed?"

Lessig pulled off his glasses and shook his head as if in wonderment. "Very much agreed—and so practical. I always carry a rubber in my wallet. You're as sensible as you are clever and lovely. Come, let's have a proper kiss now."

Internally cursing that her condom stratagem had failed, she tried but could not stop Lessig from wrapping his arms around her and raining kisses over her face. His erection was beating against her groin. Tears ran down her cheeks. For a moment, she thought again about using the knife, but then dismissed it. *Pavel might wake. The neighbors might hear the protests and struggling. And how would I explain the blood?* It was too late, too hard to resist him.

As Lessig's hands unbuttoned her blouse, she resisted, feebly pushing his wrists away. Everything in her upbringing shouted no. She had been raised to believe that sex was inextricably linked to love and affection—it was not a game or a bargaining chip. If she gave in to Lessig, she would be no better than a whore, and the emotional damage of giving herself to this swine would haunt her forever. Nevertheless, a voice in the back of her mind whispered. *Be realistic, Sophie...one night in a lifetime...easily denied and forgotten. It's to save Willy.*

Sophie shut her eyes, squeezing out the tears as Lessig's hands caressed her naked breasts. Why was she allowing this revolting man do this to her? But at this moment, she thought, *I only have sex as a way to save my family and find my man.*

Hans began to kiss the contours of her breasts, and she felt unwanted wetness between her thighs. A small voice in her head repeated: *I'm doing this for Willy.* She would try to get through the night by imagining it was Willy and not Hans in the bed. *Pretend, pretend... it will be easier to pretend in the dark.*

He laced his fingers into hers. "Where is the bedroom, Sophie?"

She put a finger on his lips, shivering with fear and guilt. "As I said, Hans, this is once only—a reward for finding my husband. We mustn't wake Pavel in the room next door. We must do it quietly, and you must get out before dawn."

He gave a low, triumphant laugh. "Do it quietly? I can try."

9

THE INFORMANT
APRIL, 1939

AS WILLY SLOWLY recovered from the beating, Károly returned to his uncommunicative behavior, characterized by long spells of sleep and stentorous breathing. When the veteran prisoner managed to get up and walk the cell for a few minutes, his eyes would turn red and his face blue. Willy noticed the old man's legs were swollen and the skin bulged out of the slippers he wore with the tops cut open. Willy repeatedly asked what ailed him, and then surprisingly, one morning, he answered. "I get fucking dizzy. Lung trouble. Worked years in the Stráž mines—uranium. Ticker's worn out as well. Blood on the blanket, every morning." He pulled a gilt crucifix from round his neck and kissed it, then winked a rheumy eye at Willy. "You ever seen a man croak? Reckon I don't have long."

Willy knew he had nothing to offer other than sympathy. By now, he had come to appreciate Károly's presence and occasional companionship. "Isn't there a doctor looking after you?" Surely, even in prison, the authorities would look after a dying man.

Károly nodded. "In a way. Before, when I took bad, they got me to the infirmary. The sawbones said he couldn't do nothing for me. He gave me a bottle of tonic and a packet of ciggies. That was the best thing."

"Why did you kill your wife?" Willy had given up on

the niceties of social intercourse. What was the point of being polite? Károly was not a bad sort. What had pushed him to kill?

Shrugging, Károly hauled out another mangled cigarette. "Caught her with a bloke in my bed—the fourth of a string of 'em. Smashed his face an' throttled her."

"Got any advice about how to get out of here?" Willy wanted some insight, a clue to get him working on something. He did not want to give up.

"No."

It was on the day of the seventh breakfast that Willy was returned to the interrogation room, though only after an interminable wait in a bench-filled chamber the guards called 'the refrigerator'. Again, he had missed the water round.

Willy recognized Altmann lounging in his chair. The black-rimmed clock on the wall showed it was close to noon, and Willy's stomach growled at the plate of rolls, sliced salami, and gherkins at the interrogator's elbow. The enticing, almost-forgotten smell of smoked meat and pickles wafted into his nostrils, making his eyes water. He guessed this was all done on purpose... to make him remember what life was like outside, to make him talk.

"Welcome back." Altmann bit into a roll stuffed with the sausage. "I expect, this time, you have decided to give me the truth."

Willy said nothing. He could not take his eyes off the salami or Altmann's jaw working methodically. He could almost taste the succulence of the salami in Altmann's mouth.

"Before we begin on the spying issue," said Altmann, taking a swig from an open bottle of beer on the table, "I'm rather curious about your musical talent. When I examined the musical scores on top of your piano, I was impressed by their complexity: Ravel's *Gaspard de la Nuit*, Brahms' *Klavierstücke*, and the *Goldberg Variations*. You must be good." He sat up straight and jabbed a finger into the middle of his chest. "Once, I myself was headed for a musical career until I realized I would do much better, get further, in the National Socialist Party. Why are you a clothier and not a musician?"

It seemed to Willy that Altmann's face had softened; the German's interest in music offered a glimmer of hope, a possible connection, and a chance to wriggle out of this abysmal situation. He remembered his father's aphorism: *Find a connection*

and you are on the way to getting what you need. Willy raised
his hands, playing pretend scales with his fingers. "When I was
growing up, my parents wanted me to have a concert career. I
was obedient and practiced four hours a day after classes. They
banned rough games: football, gymnastics and cycling. Then
when I was eighteen, a music professor in Bratislava told me
that my hands were too small."

Altmann nodded and his mouth twitched—*maybe a smile,*
thought Willy, *or perhaps a sneer.* "A pathetic turn of events,
indeed. So now, you're just a gifted amateur. It seems you and
I both lost our path through the musical forest. "

He leaned forward and touched a button on his desk. Willy
noticed that a wire from it ran along the floor to the doorway.
He watched the door open, and a tall man with unkempt straw-
colored hair walked in, came to a halt in the shadows close to
the wall, clicked his heels, and made a '*heil*' salute. Even in
the dim light, Willy recognized him: Hans Lessig. His stomach
turned over. Willy knew at once that Hans, dressed in Anglotex
gray pinstripe with a dragon tail buttonhole in his left lapel, had
to be the informant Altmann had talked about. A lacerating fury
tore through Willy's body. *Bastard Sudetener.*

Altmann swallowed the last mouthful of his roll and
washed it down with beer "Now, Herr Kohut... the last time we
met, you asked for evidence for our accusation that you were a
spy. Well, here it is. Herr Lessig will explain how he came upon
the intelligence codes we are in the process of deciphering."

Still in the shadows, Lessig cleared his throat and straightened up. "*Ja,* Herr Altmann. Two or three months ago, I was
a lunch guest at the prisoner's apartment and happened to see,
on his desk, a sheet of paper covered in numbers and letters.
Knowing that he had close ties with the British, I was suspicious. I requisitioned it and passed it on to the Munich authorities."

Willy exploded. "You piece of thieving slime, Lessig—
look at me. Is this what you do to your friends? You know
perfectly well, I'm not a spy. How many times did you enjoy
my hospitality?"

Altmann came round from his desk and calmly smashed
his fist into Willy's left cheekbone, sending his glasses to the
floor. Willy staggered back, a searing pain along his cheek.

"That's a warning. No more impertinence." Altmann slid

a bloodied metal knuckle-duster off his hand, wiped it clean on Willy's jacket, and dropped it on the desk. Then he casually crushed Willy's glasses with the heel of his shoe. He pointed at Lessig. "This man is a reliable witness. We have the document, that's solid evidence."

Altmann stepped closer. "Why are you such an obstinate Jew, Kohut? All I need is information on your contacts and controllers: names and locations. This is what we will do. We will give you pencil and paper. Stew in your cell for a couple of days and write it all down. If you still refuse to cooperate, I will break you, physically. I guarantee it will not be difficult. You are a soft, weak specimen." He waved a hand. "Lessig, you leave now."

As Willy watched Lessig disappear through the door, he finally knew what he was facing. However, a desperate question buzzed in his head. *What about Sophie? And Pavel?* "Where is my wife? Does she know I'm here?"

Altmann slapped Willy's other cheek, a gentle reprimand. "Stupid fool, why should we give prisoners or their families such information? But...this one time I will tell you, she is still at your home. However, if you have not cooperated by our next meeting, I can't guarantee her safety."

Willy shuddered. His mind was not functioning with its usual clarity. "I'll cooperate."

Altmann went back to his desk. "I expect you will. We have set up a court of justice in the prison. Three German judges preside. No lawyers, but defendants have two minutes to plead their case. In the room next to the court, there is a guillotine and a hangman's noose. The sentence is carried out within the hour." He turned to a guard standing by the door. "Get this *dreck* out of here."

Willy felt warm blood trickling down his face onto his lips. He was getting used to tasting its saltiness on his dry tongue. An ironic thought flashed into his mind: at least it was something to drink.

10

WAIT AND SEE
APRIL, 1939

IT WAS AFTER MIDNIGHT. With indescribable relief, Sophie listened to Lessig dress. He had come twice, fumbling assaults that she had found disgusting. "Get out," she hissed. "Just keep your end of the bargain in the morning." He did not say a word.

The next morning, Lessig did not turn up on time to escort her to see Haeckel. She paced round the apartment and went down to check on Janko and Laci in the store, her stomach churning. She regretted what she had done, furious that Lessig had duped her; the swine was not going to turn up. She played half-heartedly with Pavel: hide and seek, building bricks, picture books. His innocent laughter and happiness was such a contrast to the necessary evil she had endured. Somehow, being with Pavel helped make her guilt less of a burden. Self-doubt nagged. *Does the end justify the means? Yes, if what I did gets Willy back.*

By the time she had accepted that the journalist was not going to show up, it was too late to get to the Abwehr by ten o'clock. She cursed Lessig, and she cursed herself for being so trusting. The worst of it was that she still needed him.

Sophie telephoned the *Lidové noviny* newspaper and asked to speak to Hans Lessig; again, no one had seen him. She demanded his home address and took the 58 tram to the Žižkov

district: 4d Seifertova Street. At the run-down apartment building, she rang Lessig's bell several times before finally pushing
the concierge button. A scowling, stout woman in a voluminous
pinafore appeared at the front door. "I've no idea where that
man is," she said in a gruff voice when Sophie asked for Lessig.
"What do you want from him?"

"We had an appointment this morning. He didn't turn
up."

"I'm not surprised. Well—he's not here. Come back later."

At Sophie's insistence, the landlady brought Sophie
upstairs, went through the bundle of keys at her belt, and
unlocked his room. It was in chaos.

"*Zmrd*, asshole. Left in a hurry, the bastard." The landlady
adjusted her headscarf over a crown of paper curlers and pointed
to a scarred wardrobe with its door open. It was empty. "His
suitcase is gone, and so is most of what he calls his treasure, the
trinkets he collected. The swine owes me four months' rent."
She snorted in disgust. "I was about to throw him out."

Sophie gazed in despair at the unmade bed, heaped piles
of clothes, and empty shelves. *Why? He promised me. Maybe
something serious happened to him?* As detestable as he was, she
needed Lessig for her meetings with Haeckel. As she was about
to leave, Sophie recognized her mother's aquamarine glass scent
bottle set between two cut glass tumblers on the mantelpiece.
She put it in her purse, despair turning back to anger.

The landlady rushed over and grabbed at the purse. "You
took something."

"This is mine. He stole it from my apartment."

With a shrug, the landlady released the purse. "What
a thieving bastard," she grumbled. "I don't expect him back,
might as well sell whatever is left."

On the tram ride home, Sophie's disgust deepened. Her
desperation to find Willy and the memory of the nauseating
night with Lessig, gnawed at her mind. The more she thought
about what happened, the more the dangerous consequences
unfolded. She would remember it all of her life. His touch. His
scent. The awful grunts of his pleasure and triumph. Maybe
this was not the end of it. She had read that blackmailers like
Lessig always wanted more. She had a new worry: pregnancy.
Rubbers were not infallible—and God, what if Lessig carried an
infection?

For the rest of the day, Sophie's thoughts shifted back and forth from her fruitless search for Willy to the previous night's terrible mistake. She forced herself to make sure the cousins were paying attention to the store, and she took Pavel for a walk to the Obecní dům, the Art Nouveau Municipal House. The swirling patterns of gold filigree and the dazzling colors in the stained glass helped her forget her troubles for a while. She ordered hot chocolate in the café, and on their way home, Pavel had fun playing with the snowflakes that coated the perambulator. Prague could be so beautiful in the winter. Sophie, her head still whirling with thoughts about Lessig, wished she could share in Pavel's delight.

Late in the afternoon, Ruth Eisner arrived on the doorstep, wrapped in furs and bearing a box of fresh croissants. "I've come to cheer you up, darling." Throwing her hat and coat on the settee, she brought two plates and forks from the kitchen, while Sophie watched from the dining table where she was helping Pavel use crayons on a new coloring book. "I bumped into Janko and Laci on my way," said Ruth. "They were off to meet drinking friends at U Fleků." She gave Sophie a sly smile as she sat down and opened the bakery box. "Janko let slip that Lessig was here last night. You took my advice and hired that peculiar man to be your hunting dog. Is Willy's scent getting hot? Tell me."

Blushing, Sophie turned her face away. "I'm tired, but I'll make some coffee to go with the pastries." She pushed her chair back. She had quickly checked herself that morning for telltale love bites and found nothing, but now she was afraid. Ruth had antennae for things sexual.

Ruth reached out and cupped Sophie's chin, examining moving her features and neck around like a stamp collector using a magnifying lens. "Oh, my God—a love bite. He fucked you, didn't he?"

Sophie jerked away, pulled a mirror from her purse and examined her face. "You're mistaken."

"No, there," Ruth said triumphantly, pointing to the back of Sophie's neck. "Unmistakable."

It was enough to precipitate a flood of tears, an admission of guilt. Ruth lowered Pavel to the floor and put her arms around Sophie, covering her with kisses. "How could you do it—with him?" she breathed in Sophie's ear. "Why don't you tell me about it?"

Glaring at her friend, Sophie tried to disentangle herself. Pavel pulled at her skirt. "*Maminko*, more picture," he said mournfully.

"How could I do it?" Sophie's voice choked as she put Pavel on her lap. "I had no choice. Lessig blackmailed me, said that he would make things worse for Willy unless I gave in to him. Now the bastard has disappeared, taken his suitcase, everything. He was supposed to escort me to the Abwehr this morning. I missed my appointment. The officer there will be angry. I don't know what to do now."

"You poor thing." Ruth stroked Sophie's hand. "Your life gets more complicated by the day. Why the hell did he disappear?"

Sophie pushed her hand away. "I assume he's afraid the Abwehr will be after him. I can't be sure, but I think he pocketed most of the bribe I took on our first visit there. Now I have to deal with the Nazis on my own."

Ruth fitted a cigarette into her holder. "Okay," she said, mimicking an American movie accent. She lit the cigarette and kicked off her high heels with a grateful sigh. "Look, Sophie. I know life only too well. I was married twice, and there was infidelity all over the place. It's not such a disaster. You screwed Lessig for the most honorable of reasons. A woman who really loves a man will do anything to save him. And, let's face it: Willy is in serious danger. Anyway, sex isn't such a big issue—just a biological act, an evanescent, inconsequential moment in the perspective of a person's existence."

Sophie shook her head. "If Willy ever finds out what I did with Lessig, our marriage is finished. Please, never tell, Ruth. You sometimes say things that you shouldn't."

"OK, I promise, it will be our secret." Ruth squeezed Sophie's forearm affectionately. "As to your search, just stick to your guns. Go to Abwehr headquarters on your own. Make an emotional appeal so they feel sympathy and will help you. Be an actress. Dress to persuade. Worth a try."

Ruth could be impractical, Sophie thought, but at least this was a doable suggestion. She racked her brain to think what kind of woman Haeckel might find sympathetic or attractive. Probably someone *zaftig* and subservient. The idea of offering Haeckel a repeat of what she had done with Lessig was out of the question, but she could perhaps be charming enough to make the Nazi officer feel gallant and helpful.

She walked into the kitchen, put on the kettle, and began grinding the coffee beans. "Very well, I'll do what you suggest," she called out through the open door. "There's not much else I can do to tip the scales of his sympathy—if he has any. I want you to help me with the way I present myself. I want to impress him, persuade him to help me."

Ruth puffed on a cigarette. "Absolutely, I will, darling. Now what about something to take your mind off last night's junketings? A change of scene. Let's go to see *Gunga Din* at the Bio Skaut: fabulous actors, Fairbanks and that gorgeous Cary Grant. Late afternoon show. Janko will feed Pavel."

"No, Ruth, I hardly know English and I hate those fuzzy subtitles. Anyway, my mind is all over the place. Just stay and give me some Prague gossip. I know you're not a stay-at-home." Sophie brought the coffee pot, milk, and cups to the dining table.

Ruth poured the coffee and shrugged. "Not much to do except watch the Nazis behave as if they owned the city—which they do. On duty, they're always watching, clicking their heels, and smoking. Off duty, they mob the cafés and stores, buying, buying, and buying—everything is dirt-cheap to them. The koruna has dropped forty percent against the mark. Of course, they chase women. And they can be polite. A charming Nazi officer and his friends at the Weiss Café invited me to a party. I nearly went."

"My God, you are insane. Why the hell get mixed up with them?"

Twirling a lock of hair round her ear, Ruth gave a deep sigh. "My dear, since the master race arrived in Prague, my social life is in tatters. No parties anymore. What Hácha promised is happening. Third Reich peace. The Germans are owls—big, penetrating eyes watching and quietly pulling obedient Czech strings—until they've had too much to drink. Then they're absolutely disgusting, bellowing those ghastly drinking songs."

She opened her compact and repainted her crimson lips. "You know, darling, I have a feeling everything will settle back to the way it was before they turned up. Prague will seduce them."

Sophie raised her eyebrows. "I don't think so. For one

thing, Laci says he has seen plenty of notices on store windows saying 'We don't serve Jews.' That's the opposite of the way it used to be in Prague. Stay away from the Nazis, Ruth. I sampled what they're like when they smashed up my apartment and when I went to see Willy...before he disappeared. If they're so nice, why is Willy in prison somewhere with all those other poor men? Tell me that."

Ruth flicked back her tresses and picked up a chocolate croissant. "Don't worry, my love. I'm sure the Gestapo made a mistake. He'll be back with you soon enough."

cs ∂ cs

The next day, dressed in sensible, dark clothes under a drab supplicant's raincoat, Sophie traveled to Abwehr headquarters. Before leaving the flat, she decided to take some extra banknotes, 5,000 korun, in case Haeckel insisted on squeezing more out of her. She was willing to pay if he had come up with some genuine facts about Willy's whereabouts.

She showed her blue pass and was escorted to Haeckel's messy office. Trying to act the shy, modest housewife, she took a seat and greeted him politely. "Herr Untersturmbannführer, thank you so much for sparing the time to see me this morning. Do you have news of my husband?"

The lieutenant shook his head, but he did smile at her. This was progress, Sophie thought.

"So far, nothing regarding your husband," he said. "Just keep coming back here: three times a week, Tuesday, Thursday, and Friday." He ticked off the days on his fingers. "Punctually, same time as before. My finding fee is fifteen hundred korun per week—or, if you prefer, one hundred fifty Reichsmarks, or seventy-five dollars American. I'm very open to strong currencies."

"But I paid Herr Lessig twenty thousand korun. He promised that would cover everything you are doing in your search."

Haeckel's small eyes were like black currants on top of plump red cheeks. "*Gott im Himmel,* twenty thousand?" he sputtered, his mouth twisting into a snarl. "He gave me five thousand on account and promised to be back later with the rest. *Der Saukerl,* the filthy pig, where is he?" Haeckel's jaw clenched tight, his fingers working together, as if rolling invisible pills.

Sophie shrugged. "He never turned up to escort me yesterday. That's why I couldn't come."

Haeckel scowled. "So—the bastard's taken to his heels. We'll get him. Meantime, you pay me fifteen hundred a week, or you can forget about your husband."

A hot throb of anger flowed into Sophie's neck, and her temples began to pound. For a moment, she was speechless. She hated Lessig for his thieving and rutting, and she hated this *Saukerl* for his greed and insolence. She took a deep breath, opened her handbag, and placed a thousand korun on the desk. "That's the most you get each week, and as soon as you find Lessig, I want to know about it."

He gathered up the banknotes and waved them in the air. "This is not enough."

"As I said." Sophie frowned at him, though inside, her heart was fluttering. "That's my limit. Yes or no?"

Shrugging, Haeckel nodded. "Now get out," he said as she rose from her chair.

ക ∂ ക

On each subsequent visit, she showed her blue card and met briefly with the unpleasant officer. With Ruth's guidance, she tried to dress in ways that might appeal to Haeckel. Each time, he glared at her and told her there was no news. For three consecutive weeks, she paid him 1,000 korun, always hoping that the next time he would have something for her.

Apart from the hours of fruitless travel to the Abwehr, the three weeks without Willy passed slowly and painfully and April was more than halfway over. Sophie took little notice of what was happening in occupied Prague and submerged herself in daily tasks. Ludmila and Elena, reassured by radio reports of the occupiers' benign behavior, wanted to come back to their old jobs. Sophie reluctantly told them that she did not have enough money to pay them, let alone repair the damage to the apartment. Previously, she had never given much thought to the cost of food and clothes; now she was learning to scrimp and save, budget her resources. She made sure the lights in the store and in the apartment above were not left on more than necessary. She bought and cooked less food, and cut back on how often she took clothes to the washerwoman. Money was short, and she had no idea how much more she would have to spend on bribes.

As she worked at Kohut Stoffe with Janko and Laci, she gradually learned how Willy's business was organized. They were patient with her, explaining how they worked with customers and used the till, and they helped her inventory a recent delivery of merchandise from the central customs office. She familiarized herself with those files and accounts that had not been burned and made daily entries into the ledger. It was at times confusing and hard, but she began to enjoy it. As she mastered the intricacies of Kohut Stoffe, she felt happier, more confident. If she could do this, she could find Willy.

Ȅ3 ∂ Ȅ3

At the beginning of April, just two weeks after Willy's arrest on March 15th, a rumpled airmail letter had arrived from London. It was short, written in Czech by Willy's father, Emil. Sophie noticed the postmark was March 18. She had been carrying the letter in her apron pocket and now she pulled it out to read yet again.

Kensington. London. March 18.

Dear Loved Ones,

We heard the terrible news. Nazis in Prague. A pity you did not take my advice last June. Take all your money out of the bank and leave. Contact your cousin, Venter. I gave you his telephone number. He's a Dutch citizen based in Budapest and smuggles valuables to Holland. He knows all the back roads. We hope you are all well. Willy wrote he put the store up for sale. What is happening? How is Pavel? Send us a photo.

Here, we are lucky compared to other refugees. We have to stand in queues for hours to buy food, but we get one English pound a week from the Jewish fund. We also have some money in the Kindell & Renfrew account. We rented a miserable room here in Kensington but we look for a place in the northwest of the city, close to Jewish shops. We heard on the radio that the Germans are behaving relatively well in Prague. This is impossible to believe. Everything else in Germany and Austria proves that the

Nazis are monsters. How is our darling grandson? Come to us as soon as you can.

> A thousand kisses,
> Father and Mother

Tears rolled down Sophie's cheeks as she tucked the letter into her pocket. They were free, but they missed Pavel. She remembered last June when Judita and Emil had visited Prague to celebrate their only grandchild's first birthday. It was the first time they had seen him; when Pavel was born in 1937, Emil had refused to leave his business to come to the bris because of all the fascist and anti-Semitic violence in Lučenec.

Of course, Pavel had not been the only agenda for the visit. Willy had expected Emil would make a thorough inspection of Anglotex and deliver fatherly advice on future commercial strategies.

Knowing that Judita scorned makeup and flashy jewelry, Sophie had put on a respectable mid-calf wool dress, ankle socks, and sandals. When she opened the apartment door with Pavel balanced on her hip, she had been shocked at how Willy's parents had aged. Judita was tinier and plumper, with gray streaks in her wiry hair and the usual mothball vapor clinging to her clothes. Emil was thinner, and his hair had turned white. He smelled of carbolic soap and soused herring.

Sophie remembered how Emil had gently squeezed Pavel's nose with two fingers and squeaked, pretending he had trapped a mouse inside. Willy had laughed. "That's Father's only way of making friends with children." Sophie smiled to herself, remembering that it had worked with Pavel. Judita had grabbed Pavel from her arms, smothering him with kisses, stroking his curls. "I am your *babička*," she had crooned and then pulled a shaggy orange lion with bright button eyes from her carpetbag. "For you, my darling. This is a *Kuscheltier* from your *babička*. It's for snuggling in bed when you go to sleep." Judita had a dazzling smile. Like Willy's.

Later, because Elise the cook was away tending to her sick aunt, Judita had showed Sophie how to cook veal *paprikás* the way Willy liked it: lots of sweet and hot *paprikás* powder with the onions and veal, a touch of wine vinegar, and plenty of cream, served with *halušky* dumplings. For dessert, they had devoured apple compote with chocolate cake, crushed walnuts, and whipped cream.

Later, while Willy played the piano for them, Judita had leaned close to Sophie. "I don't understand how a Hungarian girl like you never learned to cook," she had whispered with her tight, critical smile. "You must hurry up, dear. A woman's beauty fades, but her skill at the stove lasts forever." That was the moment that Sophie knew there might be a barrier between them. Judita was not trying to be bossy; she was just unhappy that she had lost her only son to Sophie.

On their visit to Prague, Willy's parents had brought Sophie a letter from her own father—she called him *Papi*—that had been addressed to Emil's store. It had taken three months to travel from Australia to Lučenec. Ever since then, she had kept the fragile blue airmail letter in her purse. Papi and Sophie's brother, Géza, had left Berlin just in time. Her father had spent five years living in Moscow, working for Siemens, building Soviet power stations, but he was a Jew, and in the summer of 1938 while Sophie's mother, Olga, was dying of cancer in Berlin's Charité Hospital, he was dismissed. The Nazis took everything they owned. Willy sent them money to buy food, and soon after Olga died, her father and brother booked a passage from Marseilles on the SS Strathallan bound for Sydney. Sophie had received only one previous letter in January of 1939, from an Australian internment camp—and then nothing.

Sophie dabbed at the tears on her cheeks. Her mother was dead and all her close family was gone. She and Pavel were trapped, and Willy was a prisoner. Janko and Laci were younger than she, and inexperienced. Molnar had disappeared, and Ruth Eisner was overdramatic and often superficial. There was no one she could turn to in Prague for wisdom and advice. Sophie had only herself to rely on. Somehow, she was holding together, getting things done.

11

PANKRÁC
APRIL, 1939

WILLY STOOD in front of Altmann's desk in the same yellow room. His body still ached from the sand-sock beating by Altmann's thugs, who now stood on either side of him, holding him upright. He was actually grateful for their support; he felt so weak. He was no longer sure of the number of breakfasts he had eaten. Was it twenty...or thirty days in prison?

Willy had the impression that Altmann was angry but without his glasses, he could not be sure. The man's eyes seemed dark and pitiless and his face twisted in irritation. "Those *verdammte* experts in Munich haven't made much progress on your spy codes. "I don't have time to play any more games. Give me the list of contacts I asked for last time."

Willy had made no list, but after what Lessig had said at the previous session, Willy had thought more about the Kindell & Renfrew letter the Sudetenlander had stolen from him. He had a good idea what had transpired at that final Sunday lunch in late December. He, Laci, and Janko had gone out to buy wine, leaving Lessig alone in the sitting room to keep an eye on Pavel in his cot. The Sudetenlander had been "admiring" Willy's recent art acquisitions and taken the opportunity, when he was alone, to skim through the correspondence lying on the Biedermeier desk. The so-called spy codes he stole had to be the inventory numbers of the most recent shipment of British fabrics from England.

"Well," said Altmann. "You've had a taste of our hospitality. Hand over the list."

"Give me some water."

Willy drank as much as the thugs would allow and then stared dully at Altmann, hating him—hating Lessig. He suppressed the urge to launch himself and squeeze the German's eyeballs until they ruptured.

Altmann leaned forward, eyes glittering dangerously. "So, Kohut, give me the damned names, something to work with."

Willy hesitated. He willed himself into another attempt at rational explanation. "Look, I didn't make a list—because I'm not a spy. I can explain what these codes are: inventory numbers from a fabric shipment. I expect you couldn't find them because the delivery of the crate was delayed, probably by the unexpected arrival of the German army in Prague."

Altmann sneered. "That is a pathetic explanation. We checked all the identity numbers in the store, and we questioned your cousins. They knew nothing about a shipment. Neither did your wife. It's no use, Kohut. I want names." He nodded and out of the corner of his eye, Willy saw one of the thugs move. A sledgehammer blow smashed into his right side. He gasped at the sharp, burning pain, that felt as if something inside him had cracked. It was useless telling the truth. He could not go on like this; he had to give Altmann something.

"I... Colonel... Moravec," Willy mumbled, remembering his visit to the government offices with Molnar. He had done what Moravec had asked, kept an eye on Lessig, kept his mouth shut...but now it was every man for himself. "Moravec, the intelligence chief at the Černín palace. He knows about British transmission codes."

"Good." Altmann looked satisfied. "I knew you would help us. It's a start. We'll find him. Give this man more water and take him back to the cell."

෴ ∂ ෴

That evening, as Willy climbed down from his bunk to use the slop pail, he noticed a patch of blood on Károly's pillow. He bent down to check on his cellmate. Károly's face was mottled and dark blue. Willy tried to wake him, but the only response was a groan.

Willy started banging on the barred window with his metal bowl. "This man is very sick," he told the guards who arrived after several minutes. "He needs a doctor, probably a hospital."

One guard bent down and shook Károly's shoulder. "What's the matter, old fellow? You want the prison infirmary again?"

"Fuck off," whispered the gaunt old man, flicking his eyes open. He whistled and groaned as he breathed. "No doctor. I want the fucking priest." He tugged on a leather cord tied round his neck, drew out a crucifix from under his shirt, and kissed it before breaking into a paroxysm of coughing. Willy saw red froth on his lips.

Willy watched the guard give Károly's shoulder a reassuring pat. "We'll get you the priest, but not at this time of night—tomorrow." The guard winked at Willy. "He's done this before. The priest is a soft touch. When he gets here, he always gives the old man cigarettes after pronouncing the last rites."

ღ ∂ ღ

Sometime later, Willy woke from a vivid dream in which he had strangled Lessig on the dining table in his apartment while all his Sunday lunch guests, laughed and applauded. Awakened by pain shooting across his chest, he was struck, after a few minutes by the unexpected silence: his cellmate usually wheezed and coughed all night long.

With some effort, he looked down over the edge of his bunk. Károly was face down and had partly slipped off the lower bunk, his right arm stretched out at an odd angle. Gingerly, grimacing, Willy climbed down the ladder and stood beside the old man, swaying, trying to focus his eyes in the dim light. Willy touched him. Károly was not breathing, and his skin was as cold and clammy as the inside of a window on a frosty morning. He felt for a pulse—nothing.

Willy felt numb, hollowed of emotion. He thought about Károly's futile belief in God and his own desperation to get out of prison. *Poor old fellow, dead. The same could happen to me.*

As he stood there looking at the body, the seed of an idea took root. "Last rites," the guard had said. Well now, Károly would get a Christian burial, be washed and laid out ready for burial—but his corpse could transmit a message asking for help.

Willy untied the leather knot at the back of Károly's neck and removed the heavy metal crucifix. He tried to turn the old man over on to his back but because of his pain, he could not manage it. Pulling up the dead man's shirttail, Willy recoiled for a moment at the grimy, flaking skin and infected pimples. He grasped the gilt crucifix, and using its sharp edge to press hard on the skin between the Károly's shoulder blades, he wrote:

**WILLY IN PANKRÁC
INFORM KOHUT STOFFE
PRAGUE**

He hoped that there existed a person in the outside world who possessed some humanity—who would be moved by his call for help. Willy stuffed the shirttail back into the old man's trousers, retied the crucifix around his neck, and left Károly there, face down. Then he shuffled over to the cell door and started to bang on it with his tin mug.

"He's gone," he said when the night shift guards finally arrived. "Take him away."

"No, we leave him here till morning." They rolled the body back onto the bunk and covered it with a blanket.

Willy climbed on to his bunk and tried to go back to sleep. His mind raced, unnerved by the old man's death and excited by what he had done. He felt a glimmer of hope—and acute fear, what if the wrong people read his message? Probably they would give him a three-minute court hearing inside the prison, followed by execution.

12

MAJOR THÜMMEL
APRIL, 1939

ONE MORNING in late April, Laci called Sophie down to the store to take a telephone call. The caller would not give a name. She ran downstairs exchanging the usual anxious looks with the boys. Every day held the possibility that the call might be about Willy.

"You are the owner of Kohut Stoffe, Masná Street?" The voice was quiet, almost whispering.

She could not tell if it was a man or a woman but whispering strangers equated to danger. "My husband Willy is the owner. I'm his wife. Who is speaking?"

"He is in Pankrác prison."

Sophie's head swam, and she had to sit down and hold the instrument with both hands. "Oh, my God. How do you know this?"

"A message was sent. I can't say any more." The telephone clicked and went dead.

Sophie talked it over with Janko and Laci. She was afraid it was a joke—a hoax, probably dangerous and a trap.

"You have to go to the prison," said Laci squeezing her shoulders in a bear hug. "Why would anyone think up a story like that? It's so strange, it has to be true. What if he's really there?"

She nodded, breathless and excited. "Janko, be a dear. Look

up the telephone number for Pankrác prison. Hurry, please."

ᏖᏑ ᧙ ᏖᏑ

That afternoon, fearful and trembling, Sophie was shown into the Kommandant's office at Pankrác. She noticed something unexpected: a vase of daffodils and narcissus on the desk. The flowers had a miraculous effect on her confidence. They were so natural and innocent. Anyone who had such flowers on his desk had to be a decent human being. She took a deep breath and steadied herself as she looked at the man behind the desk. She read his title on the identification placard next to the vase: MAJOR JOHANN THÜMMEL.

Older, sturdier, and taller than Untersturmbannführer Haeckel from the Abwehr, the major was nearly as ugly but in a paradoxically attractive way. His craggy face was a moonscape of acne scars. What impressed her most were his eyes: malachite green covered by long lashes. He had short gray hair, a lean jawline, and thin lips. Sophie guessed from his stern erect demeanor that he was accustomed to issuing decisive orders, and no doubt reprimands.

Thümmel wore a *feldgrau* officer's uniform with the German state eagle embroidered on his right breast, silver and gold braid shoulder boards, and a Feldgendarmerie cuff on his left arm.

She stood mesmerized, gripping her purse tightly and feeling like a schoolchild in front of a stern teacher. She hoped he would not charge the same exorbitant fee as the fat Abwehr officer had demanded. She had used a good portion of their hidden cash reserves on Lessig and Haeckel.

The officer lit a cigarette and leaned back, blowing smoke rings and studying her with his stony eyes. "I'm Major Thümmel," he said evenly. "You are Frau Kohut. Can you understand me? I don't speak Czech."

She nodded. Her knees trembled. From the multicolored campaign strips and the iron cross hanging at his neck, Sophie realized that this was no plump and lazy bureaucrat. "I speak German, Herr Major."

"Mmm. Describe briefly and exactly what it is you want. I have little time."

"I want to see my husband. They arrested him about four

weeks ago, on the day of the occupation. I've been looking for him all over Prague, and now I know he's here." Her voice faltered. "He's done nothing wrong."

"How did you look for him?"

"An acquaintance, Herr Lessig, introduced me to Lieutenant Haeckel at Abwehr headquarters. He agreed to find my husband for 20,000 korun."

Thümmel frowned and pointed to the chair in front of his desk. Sophie sat down and nervously watched him blow more smoke rings. She waited for his reaction.

"You are accusing Untersturmbannführer Haeckel of taking bribes? That is serious. Officers of the Abwehr do not take bribes."

"Well, it happened. What can I say?"

The major dismissed the subject with a shake of his head and a flick of fingers. "You are from Prague?"

"Yes and no. We moved here from Košice last year."

His lips formed a brief smile. "Ah, so from Slovakia. You are fortunate to be in Prague. A territorial war just started two days ago between the Slovaks and the Hungarians. Those people are no longer sure to which country they belong. But I detect a Berlin accent; you are not Slovak?"

Sophie decided not to hide anything, not to pretend. "I grew up in Berlin. My father worked for Siemens. I'm Jewish. I expect you would find that out sooner or later."

He rose to his feet, came up to her, and inspected her face. "You don't look particularly Jewish. I—"

"Please, where is my husband?" Sophie could not stop herself from interrupting. "I want to see him right now."

He laughed and raised a chiding finger, as if he found her request naïve. "I appreciate your great anxiety, *meine Frau*, but we have many bureaucratic wheels to turn here. For example, we permit relatives to visit prisoners just once a month—and they must register first and pay a fee. Besides, I don't have an updated list for the moment."

Sophie took a deep breath as layer upon layer of anger spread through her. She calmed herself by contemplating her hands, letting the seconds tick by, trying not to show her frustration. If only she could see Willy, just for a minute. It was not too much to ask, surely.

Thümmel returned to his desk. "In any case, I need to see

your papers."

She searched in her bag and pushed her identity booklet across the table. He skimmed the pages.

"Like you, I'm also from Berlin. Where did your family live?"

Sophie shrugged. "A third floor apartment in Uhland-strasse, close to Faisaner Platz."

He took a map out of a side drawer and spread it out on the desk. "I'm looking at the Berlin map. What was the nearest *U-Bahn* station to your apartment?"

"There were two, Spicherstrasse and Augsburgerstrasse. Why do you ask this?"

He nodded, refolding the map and putting it back in the drawer. "I needed a cross-check on your reliability." He leaned forward and stared at her with a penetrating look. "Stories can be invented. So, now - summarize the problem about your husband."

Sophie sensed from the major's composure that, with her Berlin connection validated, she had perhaps made a favorable impression. She still felt nervous, vulnerable. Anything could happen.

"On the day of the occupation, my husband was arrested, and I haven't seen or heard of him since. The Gestapo came to our fabric store accompanied by someone we once thought was a friend, a Sudetenlander, Hans Lessig. They tore the apartment to pieces." In a few more sentences, she described her visits to Untersturmbannführer Haeckel and Lessig's disappearance (though not their night together). The major listened, nodding often and taking notes. "Then I got word that my husband was here."

"You're a persistent woman but, I regret to say, rather too trusting." His mouth twitched in a kindly fashion. "Lessig will be appropriately punished if and when we catch him. In the meantime, I will locate your husband and study his case. Return tomorrow in the late afternoon—say, 1600 hours."

"Can't I see him now?"

"No, but he is somewhere here. I can tell you that." The look on Thümmel's face showed she was close to overstepping the mark.

⁊ ∂ ⁊

The next day, at the agreed time, Sophie again arrived at the major's office. She took off her coat and sat down. Thümmel, smoking and blowing rings again, gazed at her appreciatively.

"Your husband—I've found him. He is being interrogated by Herr Altmann, Gestapo."

She covered her face with gloved hands. Her heart pounded against her ribs. *At last! And he's alive—but in the hands of the Gestapo? Altmann, the detestable man who came to the apartment.* It took her a couple of moments to compose herself and dab away her tears. Thümmel watched her, his ugly face conveying what she thought was a kind of decent sympathy.

"*Das ist wunderbar*," she smiled. "Thank you from the bottom of my heart. Can I see him now?"

"Not yet. He is still suspected of spying for the British."

Sophie's face flamed and she half rose from her seat. "Please, he's not a spy."

Thümmel glanced down at his dossier. "A man called Hans Lessig informed our people in Munich that your husband was communicating with British intelligence. He sent evidence, a list of wireless transmission codes. This is a very serious matter."

"Lessig, my God!" Sophie exclaimed, trying to breathe normally and stay quiet. Inside, she was boiling with fury. At every turn, the Sudeten *Saumensch* pig had betrayed their friendship and generosity. He was the reason Willy was a prisoner, suffering God knows what agonies. Moreover, she had willingly given herself to that *dreck*. She shifted forward, gripping her purse, furious and humiliated at the same time. "What codes do you mean?"

Thümmel paused as if mulling over a decision. He leafed through a couple of pages and then stared at her with penetrating eyes. "Why did you burn the papers at your husband's business? That is a sign of guilt."

Sophie squared her shoulders and looked at him defiantly. "I made a mistake. I thought they detained my husband because there was a problem with his business. Put yourself in my shoes. I just didn't wait to think it through properly."

He stared at her and then shook his head. "I don't believe you. It is not something a sensible wife would do—ruin her husband's business on the off chance. If you want your husband back, you have to tell the truth."

Sophie drew in a long breath. "Yes, of course."

He tapped a forefinger on the manila dossier. "Pay close attention. Here are copies of two pages containing a series of numbers from the documents Lessig acquired from your apartment. Each number is preceded by one or two letters of the alphabet. Our intelligence people are unable to decode this. Because of this, your husband remains under intense interrogation."

Sophie shivered at the words. *Intense? What does that mean?* She remembered Willy's brutalized face at the Novotný legal offices. "I'll do anything you need to have him released."

"Good." The major picked two sheets of paper out of the file. "So—at the top of each page of the document, there is a London address: Kindell & Renfrew, 6 Golden Square. Is this a genuine business address? The truth now."

Sophie put out her hand. "Let me see, please." Thümmel pushed the paper sheets across the desk. When she looked at them, tears of relief ran down her cheeks. She recognized the Kindell & Renfrew order that had disappeared from their writing desk the day of the lunch Lessig had attended. Willy had been furious about losing it—and blamed her. "Yes, the address is that of my husband's fabric supplier in England, a reputable firm." She nodded. "These are the pages that Herr Lessig stole. At the time, he was one of the guests at our lunch." She took a deep breath and exhaled. "These lists of codes have nothing to do with spying. They're inventory numbers. You could telephone the firm in England to check their numbers and authenticity. Didn't your investigators do that?"

He smiled uneasily. "I would guess not. No right-thinking Gestapo man would risk telephoning a hostile country without high-level approval. So, Frau Kohut, why don't you explain these codes to me?"

She took a deep breath. "They are identification numbers for bolts of fabric, with different patterns and colors. Anglotex is my husband's business—although now it's called Kohut Stoffe. Our business acts as the central European distribution agent for Kindell & Renfrew. What Herr Lessig gave your intelligence experts were simply the British shipment details. They would match the numbers on each bolt of fabric in our store."

Thümmel slipped on a pair of steel-rimmed glasses. "Mmm, come here. Show me what you mean."

Sophie walked around the desk and pointed a finger. "On

this first page, most of the numbers are preceded by the letters HT—describing the type of fabric. In this case, HT is Harris Tweed. Here, SW represents Superfine Worsted." Sophie felt a sudden surge of pride; she had learned all this while Willy was a prisoner.

She leaned further forward. "And here, the specific number that follows the letters identifies a certain color or pattern of fabric. We receive the bills of lading separately from delivery of the crate."

"Hmm, interesting."

She straightened up and continued her explanation, frowning as she spoke. "Herr Altmann came to our store with a colleague and Herr Lessig. They spent two hours checking our inventory, and they also made a mess of our apartment, damaging valuable furniture. I want compensation."

Thümmel shook his head, wagging a warning finger "Careful, now. If you want redress for the damage, you will have to see Herr Altmann at the Gestapo offices in the old Petschek palace on Bredovská Street. He was in charge of the inspection of your premises, and he is supervising your husband's interrogation here in Pankrác. But a warning, he has very negative attitudes toward Jews."

Thümmel slipped the papers back into the file.

"I don't understand." She wrung her hands. She had sensed Altmann was a ruthless man when he came to the store. Knowing that he was interrogating Willy made her afraid. "Why didn't he and his men match the fabric codes in the store with the numbers you have in the dossier?"

Thümmel rubbed his forehead, apparently perplexed. "You state the problem exactly, Frau Kohut. They checked thoroughly in your store and found no match. As a consequence, we believe these are British intelligence codes invented to look like the numbers you normally use in your business."

"That's ridiculous." Sophie walked back to her chair, shaking her head. She caught her breath. "Oh, my God, Major! We had a fabric delivery two days ago. It was delayed for weeks at the warehouse, by Protectorate customs. I think this paper that you have in your file may be the invoice for this shipment from England. If my husband's cousins have not yet unpacked them, the codes should still be printed on the wrapping. I beg you, as soon as you can, get one of your people to come to the store and recheck the numbers." A sob caught at her throat. "If they match, then my Willy is innocent. He can go free, yes?"

Thümmel tilted his chair back, avoiding Sophie's earnest gaze. "Possibly. I am willing to arrange for Herr Altmann's assistant, Pohl, to visit your store tomorrow and check again. We can release your husband if the numbers match—but it may take time. This is Herr Altmann's case, and we have protocols to follow. If the numbers don't match—well, I cannot vouch for your husband's future."

Sophie's confidence disintegrated at the major's words. *If they do not match* sounded more like a death sentence than a warning.

He escorted her to the door and, before opening it, laid a hand on her shoulder. His height made him imposing; he was a foot taller than she was. "You are a persistent woman, Frau Kohut. You deserve a chance. Take my advice. If we release your husband, it would be a good idea to leave Prague. The Gestapo will be watching. They have an axiom: once arrested, always guilty. They don't forget people."

Sophie trembled. The major had listened to her and agreed to take action; that was exhilarating. But if it came to nothing, what would they do to Willy? Torture him? Lock him away for a long time?

"Thank you for your advice, Herr Major. Do you and Herr Altmann usually work together on such cases?"

Thümmel's laugh was tinged with a negative overlay—not a sneer, maybe just a little sarcasm. "No we do not. He is Gestapo, whereas I started as a career officer in the Wehrmacht before the rise of National Socialism. Do you know Hitler's book, *Mein Kampf?*"

Sophie nodded, remembering what her father had called it: The Devil's Bible. "I never read it."

"It is his manifesto, written in 1925. He believes the Jews are symbols of evil and that the constant and perpetual use of violence is essential to Germany's success in becoming the world's greatest nation." Thümmel gave her a penetrating look. "I'm sure you understand what that means?"

Sophie looked at him, the words reverberating in her head. She knew all about *Kristallnacht*, the work camps, and the ferocious attacks on Jews in Vienna after the Anschluss. He was telling her the same brutality was coming to the Jews in Prague.

"So, Frau Kohut, I fully expect to see a war with fearsome weapons and much suffering." He opened the door, clicked his heels, and made a slight bow. "I know that many Jewish-owned businesses have been damaged in Prague. If your husband is innocent, I will make sure your store is safe. In addition, I will send you some good customers, brother officers who would like to have suits made for a reasonable price. That may be the only consolation I can offer."

Sophie felt exhausted, shaken, and she could not understand why this man was treating her with such respect. "Thank you. You are very kind," was all she could say, her mind running at full tilt. *Does he have a hidden motive? Is this a trap?*

13

THE VISE
APRIL, 1939

WILLY HAD GIVEN UP counting breakfasts. A new cell-mate had replaced old Károly, František Kohl, a hefty young plumber from Prague, who proudly explained that after the Sudetenland handover, he had turned to burgling Jewish stores and dwellings. It made for an easy living; the authorities ignored such pranks when they involved Jews. The reason he was in prison for a six-month stretch, he told Willy, was that during one robbery he 'defended' himself against the tenant of a luxury apartment. The man had surprised him in the act of break-ing open a desk with a crowbar. The hospitalized old fart was Jewish, which was fine, but he was not a Czech Jew; he was an attaché at the Polish Embassy. The authorities could not ignore the situation this time.

Mortified at sharing the same cell as a homegrown racist, Willy gave František the treatment he had learned from Károly. "Fuck off and don't talk to me."

Two days after the plumber arrived, the prison guards once more took Willy to the interrogation room. Without his glasses, everything was blurred unless he narrowed his eyes almost shut. Altmann sat at the desk, his face thunderous. The same thugs that had beaten him previously leaned silently against the back wall with folded arms. This time, Willy noticed a small table holding a jumble of what looked like woodworking tools. His

stomach churned as he recognized the outline of the socks of
sand hanging from hooks screwed into the edge of the tabletop.
He was ready to say anything to avoid another beating. He had
completely abandoned any moral duty to serve his country and
protect friends and acquaintances. His only purpose was to stay
alive and save himself and his family.

"Today is not a good day, Kohut," said Altmann between
clenched teeth. He tilted his head to examine the glowing
end of his cigarette. "Your erstwhile friend and betrayer has
disappeared. It appears Hans Lessig fooled and swindled the
Abwehr—and between you and me, I have been made to look
stupid for subsidizing his antics with your family. Someone has
to be punished, so it might as well be you."

Willy's heart skittered at the word 'punished', but he
stayed silent, wondering what Altmann meant about Lessig's
'antics with your family'. One thing was certain: when he got
out of Pankrác, he would find Lessig and destroy him, however
long it took. He shuffled forward, pleading with his hands.
"Don't you think Lessig's behavior suggests he concocted the
story that I'm a spy? Lessig is obviously an unreliable witness."

"Another problem." Altmann said, ignoring Willy's appeal.
He blew a long stream of smoke. "At our last encounter, you gave
us the name of Moravec, chief of Czech intelligence. Well, the
day we took Prague, the swine flew out of Kbely Air Base with
six of his staff and a ton of files. We presume he is in France
or England by now." Altmann rose from his desk and sat on the
edge, hands in his pockets. "Of course, after you gave me his
name, I began to wonder how you knew the chief of Czech intelligence—until a compliant secretary at Černín Palace revealed
that you visited Moravec's office last November. Your claim to
be a simple Czech businessman is a blatant lie. What was that
meeting about?"

Willy's courage flickered and disappeared. How much did
Altmann know about the meeting? His nerves stretched and
thrummed like piano wires. He knew that if he held back now
or told more lies, the punishment would be severe, painful, and
possibly even permanent. "Moravec asked me to help keep an
eye on Lessig. He suspected him of being a Nazi agent. As an
ordinary civilian, I was supposed to report anything unusual.
Moravec said he was shorthanded. In fact, over three or so
months, I never noticed any irregularity with Lessig, so I had

nothing to report."

Altmann slapped the table, and his shoulders shook with silent laughter. For a moment he looked like a genial uncle who had dropped in for schnapps and gossip. "*Mein Gott*, Kohut," he said with a residual smile. "What wonderful irony. While you kept an eye on a suspected Nazi informer, he was stealing the British spy codes from under your nose. And you fed and entertained him while this was all happening?"

Willy looked away trying to rein in the expletives threatening to explode from his mouth.

Altmann leaned forward. "As for those codes, our Munich experts are still puzzled. I've spent too long being gentle with you. Today, we will use more persuasive methods to dig out the truth."

"Listen." Willy's insides twisted in terror at the prospect of what Altmann might think up for him. "I'm positive those numbers come from a delayed delivery of fabrics from England. Please check again—with my wife and cousins at the store."

Altmann shook his head. "Just because you say the same thing over and over doesn't mean it's true. There is no point in being brave to protect your network. Your link to Moravec is a very strong piece of evidence against you. He was exceptionally close to British intelligence, and we have circumstantial evidence of your connections to the British legation in Prague. I'm talking about the people who arranged for Jewish children to be transported to England."

Willy shook his head and held up conciliatory palms. "Look, Herr Altmann, I'm not a brave man, and I don't have espionage contacts. You are making a terrible mistake here."

"We shall see." Altmann turned to his two assistants. "Do you know, gentlemen, that Herr Kohut is a fine pianist? We shall persuade him to talk by removing one of his fingers, and if he doesn't cooperate, we'll take off a few more."

Willy looked at the interrogator in horror, unable to believe what he had just heard. "I beg you, don't do this. You are a fine musician yourself. I am innocent. Have pity."

Altmann's face was as impregnable and blank as a concrete wall. "The Third Reich doesn't offer pity to sniveling Jews. Pity is weakness. However, I will give you a choice: cable cutters or the vise. Your digit can be removed whole or just be left as a squashed appendage."

ભ ∂ ભ

A few minutes later, Willy strained vainly against ropes tying down his left arm and both legs. One of Altmann's men forced the little finger of his right hand between the edges of a vise screwed to the workbench. As the flanges tightened, a deep, sickening pain shot up to Willy's shoulder. He gasped, clenched his teeth and with a moan, squeezed his eyes tight. The pain was like an all-encompassing blackness that blew all rational thought out of his head, except for one: *please stop*.

Altmann's silky voice whispered only a few inches away. "Time to give me another name, Kohut." He pointed to the vise handle and nodded to the men. "*Fest machen*."

Willy groaned at the new explosion of pain in his finger. Then he screamed a name: "Molnar Havel." For a split second just before he lost consciousness, he glanced down at his hand: blood, skin, and shredded flesh were clinging to the serrated jaws of the vise.

ભ ∂ ભ

He came to in the cell, slumped on the bench, pain pounding in his right hand. He was hardly aware that the guard was dressing what was left of his finger with Vaseline and a bandage extracted from a black tin box. Plumber František watched the proceedings with what seemed like enjoyment or admiration.

"They really buggered you this time," he said with a gleeful smile.

"Change the mattresses, you pisser," growled the guard, shooting a ferocious look at František. "From now on, Kohut sleeps on the bottom bunk. It's your job to help him open his fly and piss. He can't do it himself."

František nodded and pointed at Willy's wet pants. "He already pissed in his pants."

The guard shrugged. "No, they gave him Altmann's beach special while he was unconscious—sand inside the underwear and then water to make a slurry. Then there's a choice. Do nothing and wait for the sand to rub your skin off as it dries, or take your clothes off and use drinking water to wash it away."

František snarled. "I'm not letting the Jew have any of my water."

As he gingerly levered himself onto the lower bunk, Willy's

mind staggered between clouded pain and clarity *Rethink everything if I get out of here. Tell Laci and Janko about leaving. Show them the counterfeit passports. Get money, work out the best route.* His body began to shake, and a red-hot band of pain plunged up and down his right arm like a steel piston. He closed his eyes and sank into a deep black hole of agony, surrounded by a cloud of hatred.

∾ ∂ ∾

Late the next afternoon, Laci was rearranging the display in the store window when he saw a gray motorcycle and sidecar pull up outside Kohut Stoffe. He could not help but grin as he watched Obersturmführer Pohl struggling to get his long frame out of the sidecar, grabbing onto the windshield, half-upside down with one leg waving in the air.

He welcomed the German at the front door with a frosty look, then went upstairs to find Sophie after informing Janko, who was in the rear storeroom opening the Hessian covering of the most recent shipment. Sophie had been waiting impatiently for this visit. One of Major Thümmel's secretaries had contacted her about it that morning.

Carrying Pavel, she came down the stairs from the flat. The boy's eyes lit up at the uniform. He pointed happily: "Big soldier!" Pavel smiled at his mother as if he wanted her agreement.

Pohl took no notice. "Major Thümmel ordered me to examine the code numbers of recently arrived merchandise." The corners of his mouth arched down in irritation as he rhythmically slapped his leather gloves against an open palm. "I am to check the numbers on the newly delivered bolts of fabric against what I have on this paper. Quickly, woman. I have to be somewhere else in half an hour. Wait over there and do not interfere. "

Sophie sat on the stairs, hands folded in her lap, watching silently as Pohl, aided by Janko, checked the thirty or so recently delivered bolts of textile from Kindell & Renfrew. Pavel disappeared into the storeroom where Janko was working.

She closed her eyes, remembering how, just before their last Sunday lunch three months earlier, Willy had told her he was changing the name of the store from Anglotex to the more

Germanic-sounding Kohut Stoffe— to keep customers coming. He confided that he had arranged Hungarian passports for everyone, including Laci and Janko, but warned her not to tell them yet. They would leave Prague after they had sold the store.

For that final lunch, she had put on a new white embroidered blouse with a dark blue skirt patterned at the hemline in the new, patriotic Svéráz style. Before the guests, Ruth, Laci, Janko, and Lessig arrived, Willy had played her his most recently mastered piece, a Rachmaninoff prelude full of verve and power. At lunch they ate *pörkölt*, a spicy goulash of beef, pork, and *kolbásy* sausage mixed with cream and *kyselé zelí* (sauerkraut), followed by rich desserts from Myšák the confectioners. The conversation had swirled around politics and Hitler's racist speeches, and then switched to which cafés and *Kinos* were changing their names in response to the new government's emphasis on Czech nationalism. Afterwards, with Willy at the Bechstein and Janko on the fiddle, they had played gypsy melodies. She and Ruth had danced to The Swallow Flies—first the slow *lassú* and then the fast 4/4 syncopation.

She knew now that it had been during that lunch that Hans Lessig had stolen her mother's silver perfume bottle from the mantelpiece, and taken the Kindell & Renfrew inventory from Willy's desk. God, how she hated the Sudetenlander.

The click of boot heels brought Sophie back to the present.

"I am leaving now," said Pohl. His face was expressionless.

She followed him to the door with a pleading expression and tremulous voice. "Do the numbers match, Obersturmbannführer? Please, tell me. My husband is innocent, yes?"

He hesitated. "I—they—I am not permitted to disclose, *meine Frau.*"

Sophie's shoulders sagged. Teary-eyed, she opened the door to the street. "*Auf Wiedersehn*, Obersturmbannführer Pohl. When will I hear something?"

"When you hear something."

After she closed the door, Janko held out his arms to embrace her. "Don't worry, I watched him like a hawk, everything he did." His normally sad face was transformed. "The numbers all matched. Willy is free."

14

RELEASE
APRIL, 1939

THE CANVAS-TOPPED German jeep, mockingly known as a *Kübelwagen* or bucket car, screeched to a halt on the corner of Kozí and Dlouhá streets at Old Town Square. At almost the same instant, the carved skeleton of Death atop the medieval tower housing the multi-ringed Astronomical Clock raised his scythe and struck 1800 hours.

"*Hier is gut!*" barked the Wehrmacht sergeant in the front passenger seat, turning his shaved head around to glare at his prisoner. "*Heraus mit ihm*—throw him out."

Propelled by boot jabs and the butt of a machine pistol, Willy tumbled out onto the cobbles. By now, seeing prisoners manhandled into and out of trucks by soldiers was a daily occurrence in the city, and people hurrying home from work or shopping at the nearby stalls either took no notice or were afraid to get involved. Protecting his bandaged finger as best he could, Willy struggled to his feet and picked up the small bag that had been thrown out after him.

In Pankrác, one hour earlier, the guard had helped him roll up his dirty shirt and jacket and pack the bag with an empty wallet, his wedding ring, and a new identity card stamped with a red *J*. No one had told Willy why he was being released or where he was being taken.

He swayed on the sidewalk, confused by the noise and unfocused world around him. He took a breath and tried to take stock. Without his spectacles, he saw only blurred shapes, but he was aware of people walking past and around him. His body and hand throbbed unmercifully. *Where am I?*

He started to make for the fuzzy outlines of what he thought were buildings. With an immense sense of relief, he realized he was in Old Town Square. After more stumbling steps, he recognized the familiar art deco façade of Klíma Books-Antikvariát, his favorite bookstore. His heart surged—not far to Kohut Stoffe. In normal circumstances, it was a ten-minute walk, but now?

He felt a hand grip his shoulder. "What the hell's the matter with you?" Willy looked up at a tall Czech police officer, close enough to see the disgust on the man's face. "*Do prdele*, fuck. You stink worse than a pigsty."

"Masná Street. Number 19," Willy mumbled. "I live there."

"A likely story. What you need is a good hosing down." Willy flinched as a forceful hand pushed him forward along the pavement. The terrible fear of going back into a cell spurred him to draw on his last shreds of energy.

"Please, I'm the owner... Kohut Stoffe fabric store on Masná Street. I've been a prisoner... in Pankrác. The Nazis left me here on the street."

The police officer seemed surprised. "They dumped you?"

Willy tried to respond but it was an effort, his mind still coping with the excruciating burn of wet sand around his groins. "I'm innocent... Please, get me home. It's not far. They broke my glasses, and I can't see well."

"If you want me to take a stink-pot like you home, your folks will have to pay."

Willy nodded.

By the time they reached the store's front entrance, the street was dark. The store window blinds were down, but lights inside showed through the chinks. Willy leaned against one of the entry pillars breathing heavily, his heart pounding. The police officer tried the door; it was locked, so he rapped repeatedly on the reinforced glass.

છ ∂ છ

In the back office, Sophie was adding up the day's takings and updating the inventory. There had been no word from Major Thümmel about Willy's release, and she had been jittery all day and unable to sleep the night before.

Her heart jolted at a repeated knocking at the door, her mind flooding with dreadful possibilities. *Czech police? Vlájka thugs? Gestapo? Pohl again?* She rushed up the stairs to the apartment, where Laci was playing with Pavel and Janko was reheating some stew and sauerkraut in the kitchen. "Quick, Laci. There's someone at the front door. I need you with me."

They ran back down, and she turned out the main lights so they would not be so visible from the street. She took Laci's hand, and they both walked quietly to the front door. Easing back the edge of the blind, she peered out.

"What do you see?" whispered Laci from behind her, holding the poker from the stove in his right hand.

Sophie raised the blind to get a better view. Her heart lurched. Even with a ragged beard and no glasses, she recognized Willy's face and the shape of his balding head.

"What's the cop doing holding up that tramp?" exclaimed Laci, stepping forward, readying his poker.

Sophie pushed him back and scrabbled to unlock the door, sobs of relief bursting from her lungs. "Thank God!" she cried, stepping into the street and throwing her arms around Willy, kissing his cracked lips. Laci turned on the store lights as she drew Willy inside. In her whole life, she had never been so happy—until she saw Willy's bandaged hand and the dried blood all over the front of his pants. "*Bože na nebi*, God in heaven!" she cried out, covering her face.

The police officer handed Willy's bag to Laci. "Found him in the square. Says he was in Pankrác. The bugger needs a damned good bath and maybe a doctor. And he promised me a tip."

Laci dug out his wallet and handed him some koruný notes. "Thanks, friend."

After the police officer vanished into the darkness, Laci locked the door and pulled down the blind. "*Díkybohu!* Thank God, the boss is back." He gave Sophie a huge grin.

Sophie supported Willy as he shuffled slowly toward the back of the store. "Here I am," he said weakly, looking round the store and swaying slightly. "Back in paradise."

"How in God's name did you get here? You're so thin. You need a bath, food, and rest."

Tears flowed down Willy's cheeks. "You don't know how happy I feel," he croaked. "How have you all been? How's my Pavel?"

"We're fine, *miláčku*, but you look terrible." She looked at the bloodstained bandage. "What happened to your hand?" Her heart turned over when she saw him give a little smile. Thank God, he could still smile.

"An injured finger—I'm too exhausted to explain. Every bone aches. My thighs are like raw meat."

Laci stood with Willy on the bottom step of the stairs and threaded his arm round Willy's waist. "Come on, cousin, I'll help you upstairs. It's warm there."

Willy groaned as they maneuvered up the steps. "I know I stink, I'm sorry."

Laci growled at him. "*Kurva drát*, bloody hell, man, how you look and smell isn't your fault. You're home—that's the main thing." When they reached the landing, he kicked the door open and gave a shout. "*Der Gantseh Macher*, the big shot, he's back. Break out the *slivovice*."

At the dining table, they lowered Willy onto a chair covered with an old towel. Laci brought a carafe of water from the kitchen, and Sophie found an old pair of spectacles in the writing desk. "That's much better," Willy murmured as she slid them over his bruised face. "At last, I can see the world clearly. Oh, God, it smells so good in here." He sniffed, squeezing out another smile. "Is that sauerkraut cooking in the kitchen?"

Sophie beckoned to Pavel, who was hiding under the Bechstein. He came out hesitantly and shyly took hold of her skirt.

"*Táto?*" he whispered, staring at Willy. Pavel frowned. He hesitated, then reached up to touch his father's beard.

Tears trickling down his cheeks, Willy tried for a kiss, but Pavel stepped back and hid his face in Sophie's apron. She ran fingers through the boy's hair. "Don't worry, *miláčku*. You look more like an ogre from Grimm's fairy tales than a father. Pavel will recognize you once you've bathed and shaved. It's been such a long time."

Willy gave a slow smile and then grimaced in pain. "Yes, I need a bath most of all."

"I'll help you."

"All right," he muttered, "but it will be an unpleasant sight."

Sophie turned to Janko and Laci. "While I help Willy, you boys eat supper. Then go to your *pension* before curfew. Tomorrow, we'll open the store at eleven—that will give me time to be with him."

"In the prison, I thought so much about you," said Willy slowly. "You must have been shocked when I was arrested. I was terrified they would take you as well. Toward the end, I didn't think I would ever get out." Tears coursed down his cheeks.

"Come on." Sophie gave him a luminous smile. "Cheer up. Bath time. I want to turn you back into an appetizing husband."

She refilled the bath three times, using the first immersion to soak the dirt and feces off his body. After that, she used cotton pads to gently touch and pat the denuded areas on his thighs, groin, and testicles. Her hands trembled as she touched him. "How did all this happen?"

"Sand—a special gift from my interrogator, Altmann."

Sophie looked more closely. "Oh my God, you poor man. I can see the grains still stuck there. How am I going to get them out?"

Willy looked at her, hitching an eyebrow. "Many baths, I suppose, and a soft brush, perhaps?"

The second time, she sat by the bathtub and removed the bandage from his hand, weeping as she inspected the crushed, distorted finger. "*Istenem!* My God," Sophie whispered as she turned both his hands over by the tips of her forefingers, as slowly and delicately as if they were robin's eggs. "Am I hurting you?"

"A little." Willy held his breath. She knew he was in pain and flinched at sight of yellowish fluid oozing from small lacerations on his knuckles and the scratched palms that still showed traces of ingrained dirt. The little finger of his right hand drooped, curving sideways away from the others—squashed red flesh and skin like a piece of butcher's meat.

Her heart broke when she saw him look at the finger. She knew exactly what he was thinking, that he would never again play with the speed and grace that everyone admired so much. "This is horrible," she said in a whisper, gently wrapping his right hand in a clean towel. "The policeman was right about your needing a doctor. When you are clean, I'll call Dr. Pflinz."

During the third bath, she washed Willy's bruised, swollen scrotum and the abraded skin round the upper thighs and lower belly. As she worked on his body and shaved off his beard, she distracted him from the pain by describing what she had done while he was in Pankrác—how she ran the business, about Lessig's bribe and disappearance, about her search for him at the Abwehr, and about Thümmel. As she talked and touched his body, she shivered at the difference between Willy's firm muscular body and Lessig's boniness and scratchy skin. She wanted to admit what she had done with Lessig and why, but she couldn't. She could never tell him; it must remain a secret barrier between them. Dedicating herself to healing him would be a way to pay for her guilt.

Lying in the deep, soapy water, Willy gave her a rueful smile. "So, strudel, you saved my life. You were very brave."

Sophie leaned forward and stroked Willy's arm. "*Miláčku*, Major Thümmel has offered to help us."

"You mean after arranging my release?"

"He said that if you were innocent, he would protect the store and send officers to buy our fabrics. What do you think of that? Our sales have fallen off badly since the occupation. I didn't say no."

For a few moments, Willy looked at her silently, as if troubled by her words. "I hate the idea of Nazi officers buying my fabrics. In prison, I learned to hate. One day, I'll pay them back—and I have an account to settle with that servile bastard Lessig. As soon as I'm fit and we have enough cash, we leave. After that, I'll see about Lessig."

She nodded. "I know you must be very bitter. I can't imagine what you've been through, *miláčku*, but now German customers bring us money. We need it for when we leave. Anyway, they know about us and we can't stop them coming. I'll help you dry and put on pajamas."

After the soothing bath, Willy's pain inched back into his consciousness, aspirin that had made it a little more bearable was wearing off. Sophie put down her copy of Capek's *'An Early Life'* and helped him pull on his dressing gown. In the living room, he eased himself onto the couch beside her and covered her hand with his "So wonderful being back, strudel. Warm and snug with the people I love. I can't describe how free and happy

I feel."

"I feel the same, *miláčku*," she said, kissing his cheek and caressing the back of his neck. "Are you hungry?"

"Yes, very."

"The boys have gone, but they left you a bottle of Zlatý bažant beer to go with the sauerkraut stew. Willy, I have telephoned Dr. Pflinz."

Willy nodded. As he ate—carefully, because his lips were still sore—Willy looked around the living room at the fine furniture, the Bechstein, his newly acquired paintings, and the *objets d'art* they had collected over the previous year. For some inexplicable reason, he felt like a guest in someone else's home.

Sophie watched him closely, content that he was reacquainting himself with all the fine and comfortable things that they had chosen after arriving in Prague. How long would it take him to recover? She remembered Thümmel's advice to get away, but looking at Willy's haggard face and battered body, she wondered if he would get well fast enough. There was a man called Eichmann coming to Prague, Thümmel had said, who would set up a central Jewish Office to register everyone, make a record of their assets, and impose heavy taxes and fines. Travel and commerce for Jews would soon be restricted or even prohibited altogether. "Get away," Thümmel said.

"*Gott behüte.*" Willy stared at the gouged inlays and splintered drawers of the Biedermeier. "What happened to the desk?"

"The Gestapo went through all our things. They were here for nearly three hours with their chisels and hammers and boxes. At least they didn't find the Hungarian passports. I had Elena make a mess in the kitchen, and that put them off."

Willy stared at her in shock, suddenly remembering the passports. "Thank God...I must say, you are very resourceful." He got up and limped to the Bechstein, opened the lid and tried an arpeggio and two chords with his left hand. He sat down on the stool, running his eyes over the pages on the music stand. "Chopin's Prelude #4 in E Minor," he murmured—the piece he had been practicing before his arrest.

Sophie watched him intently. "I'm sorry, *miláčku*. When they came, Altmann played your Chopin. I couldn't stop him. I have to admit, he was quite good."

Willy returned to the dining table and sat down awkwardly, grimacing slightly. He reached across and held Sophie's hand with his good left hand, and they watched Pavel play with his wooden farm animals on the carpet. In the contented silence, Willy studied Sophie's face. Apart from her wistful expression, she was much as he had pictured during the long hours on his bunk: the oval face with a dimple in the chin, fine eyebrows, and the thick black hair curling in crescents around her ears and down onto the neck. He was a lucky man.

"You have a new hairstyle, Sophie."

"Oh! Do you like it? It's called a finger wave; look, a parting on the side. What do you think?"

Willy laughed. "You're the sort of woman who looks lovely with any hairstyle." With his good hand, he tilted her chin and kissed her softly on the mouth. "Thank God, you got to Thümmel before Altmann moved on to my other fingers. I'm proud of you." He pulled her close, trying to blot out the rasping pain that shot through his ribcage and across his shoulders. "Together, we'll beat them."

She looked at him with surprised eyes. "How can we beat them, *miláčku*?"

"First, by not letting them arrest us, and then by leaving the country. I will find an army to join—French, British, I don't know. I have to do something."

"Of course, we'll leave." She stood up abruptly. "But I won't let you abandon us by going off to fight. Pavel and I need you with us, alive."

ℰ∂ℰ

It was past ten in the evening when Sophie showed Dr. Pflinz in to their bedroom. The doctor was a rotund, middle-aged man with reddish side-whiskers that moved up and down as he talked. He wore the high collar, pinstriped suit, and spats favored by upper-echelon city practitioners. He shook Willy's left hand. "Please now, *pan* Kohut, give me some idea of how your injuries were sustained."

Resting on the bed, Willy looked up at the doctor's heavy-lidded eyes, enlarged by his spectacle lenses, hoping that this particular life mechanic was competent.

"Yes, I want to know, too," said Sophie from the doorway. "I gave him a good bath and washed off all the blood and grime. I tried to be gentle; he was in a lot of pain."

"Very well, I'll make it short." Willy sighed, using his good hand to shift and get comfortable. "After they arrested me, I was kept in a room packed with other men, mostly professionals, some Jewish, some not. For two days, they questioned us, one by one. I said I wasn't a spy, but they beat me anyway, mostly fists and kicks around my ribs and face. After that, we were taken in trucks to Pankrác. I was interrogated. Not sure how long all that took, maybe three weeks, maybe more. I counted the days by the number of breakfasts they served."

Dr. Pflinz smiled.

"They beat my chest, back, and lower stomach mostly." Willy paused, watching the doctor's face, which seemed unaffected. Sophie, on the other hand, was breathing fast, staring at him open-mouthed. She clasped her hands together, fingers twisting like twigs in a stream.

Dr. Pflinz reached into the open medical bag at his feet. Willy read the name B. F. PFLINZ, CHEFARZT. BULOVKA HOSPITAL engraved with gold lettering on the black leather. "So, Herr Kohut." The doctor brought out a notebook. "Tell me about the finger."

Willy paused and took a deep breath. "At the end, when I couldn't give them the information they wanted, I said anything that came into my head: names, addresses, stuff like that, about people I knew in Prague. I feel terrible about it now. God knows what will happen to them."

"Don't blame yourself, *miláčku*." Sophie reached over and stroked his arm. "You were being beaten. How could anyone resist?"

Dr. Pflinz patted Willy's knee. "Come, Herr Kohut, what about the finger?"

"They used a vise...I passed out. Later, the guard put iodine on it and bandaged it. Altmann's men also put sand and then water down my front and back. It felt as though my skin was being flayed off with sandpaper. That's it."

Dr. Pflinz stood up. "Slip off your pajamas, young man. I need to inspect everything."

Sophie stood by the bed to watch the examination, wincing whenever Willy groaned or cried out. Large areas of skin around his genitals, thighs, and buttocks were raw and weeping.

"Your testicles are swollen from the beatings," said Pflinz after he had finished, discreetly placing a towel across Willy's groin. "It will take a few weeks for them to settle. I'll check the finger. It will hurt, so roll up this little towel and put it between your teeth."

The doctor pulled on rubber gloves and gently moved the finger this way and that while Willy bit down on the towel, his eyes wide, looking at anything but his hand. "Frau Kohut, please bring a bowl of hot water and two clean towels."

By the time Sophie returned, the doctor had spread his equipment across the bed cover: Vaseline, gauze, iodine, scissors, forceps, bandages, and a U-shaped metal splint. "Please watch carefully, Frau Kohut, because after tonight, this is your daily job. The finger has been crushed, the bones splintered. I cannot predict what will happen. He may never regain much flexion or strength. If the nerve has been destroyed, his finger will be useless. After the first three weeks of rest, you must start to encourage gentle movements many times a day."

Sophie looked at him, surprised, and then at Willy. "I've never done anything like this. Surely this is a nurse's work?"

The doctor nodded. "In normal circumstances, it would be. Unfortunately, the protectorate administration is reorganizing the Prague community health services. So, no nurses."

"I'll do my best then." Sophie smiled encouragingly at Willy, but as she watched Dr. Pflinz work on Willy's floppy finger with iodine swabs and forceps and heard her husband's grunts and moans of pain, she wondered if her best would be enough. "How can it possibly heal? It looks so bad. Doesn't he need an operation?"

The doctor washed his hands in the bowl and dried them on a towel, giving his patient a regretful look. "For the best result, an operation would be ideal. Under anesthetic, the bone would be aligned and then splinted for about five weeks. A Thiersch graft to replace his skin would take six weeks to heal." He looked up with apologetic eyes and shook his head. "The problem is that the Prague hospitals are refusing to take Jewish patients. So you will have to stay at home and hope for the best."

Willy and Sophie stared at the doctor.

Pflinz put on his jacket. "Kept clean and splinted, the finger will heal on its own in four weeks or so. But there's no guarantee what it will look like in the end."

"No need for an operation," said Willy firmly. He

attempted a smile. "We'll take our chances, won't we, strudel?"

Sophie nodded, though she was not sure what was best for Willy. Maybe Dr. Pflinz was wrong about the hospitals. She did not want an argument in front of him, not after he had been so attentive and gentle.

Dr. Pflinz nodded and turned to Sophie. "So change the dressings every two days—very gently, mind you. New skin is as delicate as a spider's web. After you clean the finger, always keep the splint applied so the bone fragments can stabilize and heal. Make sure the bandage goes round the whole hand to keep the finger in the same plane and position as the others."

Sophie nodded. "How long...?"

"In my opinion, the best result you can hope for is a scarred, distorted, but active finger." He began folding up his canvas instrument kit. "But if it gets infected or stays limp and numb, it will have to be amputated."

Sophie looked away and dabbed her nose with a handkerchief. How could her proud pianist ever be happy with a missing finger? He would be a different man.

"Thank you so much, doctor," Willy studied his bandaged hand with an exhausted smile. "It's wrapped up like a birthday gift. If it does heal well, how soon will I be able to play?"

The doctor's cheeks puffed out in a burst of laughter. "Mein Gott, Kohut. Is that what's running through your head? What optimism! If your finger actually learns to move again, then in three or four months' time, you can try to play. The skin could be ultra-sensitive for a long, long time. Do you think you could play if you always had pain?"

Willy nodded.

The doctor looked at Sophie with shrewd eyes. "Here is another task for you, my dear. Make a narrow bag out of fabric, the width and length of two fingers, preferably with a strap—what we call a fingerstall. *Pane* Kohut should wear it over the ring finger and the damaged one. That will help splint the broken finger and prevent it from being caught on doorknobs and furniture. Keep his arm in a sling for at least three weeks."

Sophie nodded. "When will we see you again, doctor?"

"I'm not sure. There is a problem: the Czech Medical Association just banned all Jewish doctors from practicing. Although I'm not a Jew, I am at risk from the Gestapo."

"Why?"

"A long story, better told over good French brandy." Dr. Pflinz pinched his lips together as Sophie handed him his black homburg. "I'm truly sorry the Gestapo did this to you. Not all Germans are as violent and ruthless as Hitler's National Socialists, eh?"

He sat down on the edge of the bed and began to scribble on a small notepad. He tore off a sheet. "Here, Frau Kohut, are two prescriptions. One is for pain: Paracodin, 30 milligrams every four hours, four weeks' supply. The other is for acriflavine tincture to apply to the damaged skin around his thighs and buttocks. First, wash the raw areas with carbolic soap and water and then apply the tincture with a soft sponge, twice daily. After that, spread the Vaseline gently on top. Wear only clothes you can throw away. Acriflavine stains a terrible yellow."

"And what about—those?" Sophie's face turned pink as she gestured toward Willy's swollen testicles.

Chuckling, Pflinz threw up his hands. "Ach, forgive me. I forgot to explain. Bathing is good. Just treat them like precious eggs. Four weeks of complete sexual abstinence and a pillow between the legs at night. It is very probable their function will return completely." He snapped his medical bag shut. "So, *Auf Wiedersehn*. I will submit my bill."

Willy looked anxiously at Sophie when she came back into the bedroom after seeing the doctor out. "Is Pflinz German?"

"Yes, darling. *Pane* Molnar told me about him some time ago. Pflinz is a Catholic, a Social Democrat from Dresden—he resisted Hitler. In 1936, they were going to arrest him, so he came here as a refugee."

"Now I understand. I hope to God he keeps quiet about us. And Sophie, there's something else I didn't tell him about Pankrác, something you should know."

"What?"

"Lessig was there—with Altmann. He was the one who betrayed me to the Gestapo."

"Oh my God, no." Sophie turned away, covering her face with her hands.

15

AN ARRANGEMENT
APRIL, 1939

SOPHIE'S NIGHT was disturbed. She had slept alone for several weeks and now her husband lay beside her restless with pain whenever he moved. When he slept, he cried out and groaned and seemed to be having nightmares. He was still asleep when she got up in the morning. It was close to noon when he woke.

After a cup of coffee, Sophie, his newly appointed nurse, removed the stiff, soiled dressings with a sponge soaked in warm diluted iodine. Striving to cover her repugnance at the sight of Willy's bright red weeping flesh, Sophie mopped the damaged areas with cotton balls and soapy water. She knew it would take many baths and gentle work on her part to remove the tiny particles of sand. She dabbed on acriflavine and Vaseline, then redressed Willy's finger. She took her time, working in a slow and unhurried way, quite unlike her usual tendency to rush through tasks she did not like. At times, she stopped to ease her back.

Finally, she brought a bowl of hot water from the bathroom to help him wash. As she did this, Pavel pushed past her and climbed up on the bed. "*Táta* want play?"

Willy frowned and smiled at the same time. "He shouldn't see me like this."

"Pretty!" Pavel reached out to touch the yellow stains on

his father's lower belly and thighs. Sophie quickly pulled the boy back and slid a towel over Willy's testicles. Willy laughed. "You'd better keep him out of here next time. I expect his hands have been all over the floor."

"How about a paprika omelet for breakfast-lunch?" asked Sophie, taking off her apron and shooing Pavel out of the room.

Willy nodded and gave her a weak smile. "You're a fine nurse."

Her eyes glistened as she bent to give him a long kiss on the lips, reveling in the pleasure of having him home. "Mmm, that's better," she murmured. "Much softer lips today."

He smiled, stroking her hair with his good hand. "It's wonderful to be back with the woman I love." He grimaced as her elbow brushed his ribs.

"Do you want to get out of bed? Laci went out early and bought you a walking stick." Willy squeezed his eyes shut. He had taken his first dose of painkiller on waking, and she could tell it was wearing off.

"Thank you, strudel. I'll stay in the bed; maybe later I'll listen to the radio. Or I could skim the Venkov newspaper; see how things have changed since I was locked up."

Sophie smiled brightly, wanting to cheer him up. "You know *miláčku*, our lives were utterly boring in Prague while you were in prison." She counted on her fingertips. "President Hácha dissolved the Czech Parliament, Hungarian troops occupied poor Košice, Jewish doctors were banned from working in public clinics, cars now drive on the right, causing lots of accidents—and we have curfew at nine every night. Boring!"

Still trying to conceal his pain, Willy grinned back. "As you say, my love, nothing much happened."

Sophie dropped her bloodstained apron on the floor, running a hand through her hair in dismay. "Oh my God, Willy, I just remembered. A letter came a few days ago from your parents in England. I opened it." She hesitated. "I... didn't know when you would be back." She looked ready to cry. "I'll bring it."

When she came back, Willy scanned the text, eager and tight-lipped.

"They want us to leave, don't they?" Sophie sat on the bed, watching the blue airmail paper tremble in her husband's hand. The intense caring for Willy had made her realize that she was tired of running the business, keeping the apartment clean, shopping and cooking, and looking after Pavel and the cousins. With no servants, it had been exhausting. She wanted Willy to get better quickly, but until that happened, she had to be his nurse, a *hausfrau*, the business manager, and Pavel's mother.

Willy nodded. "In prison I thought a lot about how we would get out of the country. I conceived a plan, even made decisions."

"What do you mean?"

"Well, now I want to tell Janko and Laci exactly what's going on. They've been in the dark too long. When I can manage walking a couple of hundred meters, I'll take a taxi to the Dresdner Bank and close the account. We need to work out a travel budget, calculate how much cash we might need as we figure out the route and account for contingencies. If it's still possible, we should pack a crate and send our most valuable things to England."

Sophie eyes shone. "*Nádhera*, wonderful. At last, you are ready. You *want* to leave. I'm happy." She frowned and slapped her thigh in frustration. "Oh, dear, there was also something else. Bad news and good news from Tomáš Motyka, the agent. A week ago, he telephoned saying the buyer interested in Kohut Stoffe backed out when he heard you were arrested, but now he's found someone else. If only we can sell the place quickly."

Willy gave her a sad smile and then stiffened in pain. Sophie adjusted the cushions she had packed between him and the bedhead. "I thought a lot about the store in my cell. Selling it would be a miracle but also cause a new problem; we might end up with nearly a million korun, which is a lot even if it has been devalued. How would we take that much cash to England? Stuffed in a suitcase?" He laughed and shook his head. "I don't have an answer to that."

Willy scooted his bandaged hand further up the pillow; the doctor had said he had to keep it at shoulder height to stop swelling. "And the counterfeit Hungarian passports, are they still in the flour bin?"

Sophie nodded, smiling at the memory of Gestapo search and Altmann's reaction to the mess in the kitchen.

Willy grimaced and again shifted in the bed. "Thank God.

That means we can travel to Budapest but we must behave like true Hungarians on the train and at the borders: talking, reading, toiletries, books, everything must be in Hungarian. We must eliminate everything Czech except the passports; we'll hide those. No one throws away a passport."

Sophie bent down and kissed his head. "In that case, we mustn't forget the clothes labels. I'll unpick the Czech labels and ask Magda to send us Hungarian ones."

"Excellent thinking but where is your Magda going to find clothes tags in Budapest?"

"In her closets, for heaven's sake. She'll cut them off her family's clothes." Sophie got up off the bed. "Willy, I'm worried. Here we are in mid-April and Dr. Pflinz said your skin would heal in about three weeks. The broken bone in your finger will take even longer. Isn't it dangerous to wait so long? Who knows what the Nazis will do next?"

Willy frowned. "Listen. I want to appear normal when we travel. I have to be fit enough to carry a suitcase with ease, pick up Pavel, and walk at least a kilometer. No arm sling or hobbling like a wounded soldier. The police are always alert to something out of the ordinary."

She shrugged her acceptance and handed him a small parcel wrapped in tissue paper. "Here, *milačku*, a present for you: the velvet fingerstall Dr. Pflinz told me to have made. Lemberger's seamstress in Dlouhá Street finished it this morning. See, he even got her to embroider a red dragontail. A gift."

Willy unwrapped the paper and slid the beige velvet pocket over his last two fingers. Sophie helped him tie the strings around his wrist. "That is really kind of the old grump. I'll write him a note. Thank you."

Sophie inspected Willy's face with serious eyes and reached to touch his cheek. "You've said very little about Pankrác, *miláčku*. How do you feel about what happened, what you went through?"

Willy stared down at his bandaged finger. "How do I feel?" he muttered. "What is there to say about pain and hate, about being betrayed and abused? I'm happy to be home; but then I remember the humiliation and the pain." Raising his bandaged hand, he looked up at her with sad eyes. "Will I ever play again?"

၈၃ ∂ ၈၃

Later, using Sophie's silk jacquard scarf as an arm sling, Willy took a slow, limping tour of the apartment, reacquainting himself with the space and furnishings. Pavel followed him, looking up with attentive eyes, repeating "My *táta?*" as if it were a question. Willy yearned to pick up his boy and cover his elfin face with kisses, but knew he could not manage the effort and was afraid of the pain.

Willy inspected the intricate patterns of their antique Persian and Afghan carpets, something he had never studied before, simply taken them for granted. He tried to rearrange some books with his left hand, but two slipped off the lower shelf and fell to the floor. He admired Sophie's iridescent Loetz vases on the top shelf. All these artifacts seemed new and precious, as if Willy had just been invited to someone else's home and was being given a tour of their prized possessions.

He took down the three framed copies of old master paintings embroidered by his mother. Resting on the overstuffed art deco settee, he showed them to Pavel. "Your *babička* made these when I was a little boy. She was clever with her fingers. They will be yours when you are a man."

Pavel was more interested in the sling and the bandage on his father's hand, which he tried to undo. When Willy brushed his hand away to prevent the boy from touching his finger, Pavel scowled and ran off into the kitchen, crying, "*Táta* bad."

For a long time, Willy stood in front of the three oil paintings he had bought months earlier. It had been the start of his new passion for Czech impressionists: one by Novotný, another by Štýrský, and his favorite, a port scene by Reichentahl, a painter from the Bratislava Academy.

A year earlier his now absent neighbor, Havel Molnar, a patron of the arts in Prague, had inspired him to buy the paintings after escorting him on a round of studios and galleries. Willy had enjoyed their outings and conversations. Despite the postmaster's mysterious comings and goings and the way he avoided answering questions, Willy regarded him as a kind of artistic mentor.

According to Sophie, Molnar had gone to Poland permanently. Willy prayed it was true. The guilt of having revealed his mentor's name to Altmann haunted him. His need, during the interrogations, to free himself of the excruciating pain and survive had overwhelmed both loyalty and self-respect. He had also betrayed Moravec, and perhaps others; he could not remember what names he had revealed. He wondered if he could have done more, held out longer, been brave rather than self-serving. Perhaps if he had believed in God, he would have had the strength to resist and be silent. He would never forget this shame.

Willy called Pavel to come back to him. When there was no response, he stroked the smooth curves and jutting angles of the Gutfreund bronze that stood on the windowsill, envying the strong hands and brilliance of the cubist sculptor. Leaving a legacy like that: a physical and beautiful reminder of what one had accomplished was a wonderful achievement. If they managed to escape, all Willy would leave behind were three published piano compositions in the style of Bartók, and the irrelevant ledgers of a merchant.

He stood at the Bechstein, remembering all the frustration he had endured trying to score the notes and chords perfectly. He would probably never play his own compositions again. The piano had become a useless black monster in his living room.

Feeling the return of severe pain, he sank into an armchair and gazed at the vase of daffodils and narcissus on the dining table. Ever since they had arrived in Prague, whatever the season and whatever the cost, Sophie had bought flowers every day... Willy looked around his small kingdom, thinking maybe it was time to believe in God and thank Him for the miracle of being home again. One moment, he had been agonizing within the cold walls of a dank cell, and the next minute, it seemed, he was embracing Sophie and Pavel in his own living room.

಄ ∂ ಄

Mid-morning two days later, there was a rap on the door where the back stairs led down to the store. When Sophie opened it, her eyes widened. "Oh, Major... you..." She thrust her trembling hands into her apron pocket. Why was he here now? Was something wrong?

Thümmel's deep-set eyes crinkled into a smile. He held a briefcase under one arm. "Good day, Frau Kohut, I've come to verify certain facts of Herr Altmann's report when he searched your apartment. Also, I wanted to see if your husband was back. Please, be so kind as to invite me in."

"Of course." She showed the officer into the apartment, talking as they went. "This is the living room, and as you see, my husband is at home. I'm grateful to you. Is there a problem regarding Herr Altmann's search?"

"He asked me to recheck your possessions against his list, and there is a new order. We must record all information from Czech passports. Protectorate citizens can no longer travel with Czech passports. Your husband is still under suspicion, you know."

Sophie tried to suppress the trembling in her legs. *Thank God, Willy got the Hungarian ones.* "I will find the passports for you before you leave."

Willy nodded a greeting from a small table near the piano where he was helping Pavel with a coloring book. The boy looked at Thümmel with interest. "Big soldier," he said in Czech, his eyes glued to the Mauser pistol holstered on the right side of the major's belt. "Gun?"

Willy replied quietly. "Yes, *Pavlíčku*. He has a gun."

"This is Major Thümmel, Willy." Sophie patted her hair nervously as she led the major to the table. "He's the one who ordered your release from Pankrác." She watched as Willy tried to take the measure of the tall officer.

"No need to get up, Herr Kohut." Thümmel raised a gloved hand. "Stay with your boy. Perhaps Frau Kohut will get me some coffee while I look around the apartment and cross-check Herr Altmann's inventory of your belongings. Your wife told me there had been damage." He bent down to remove a dossier from his briefcase.

Willy tried to stay calm. He noticed an Iron Cross, first class, on the breast pocket of the major's tunic, a mark of superior bravery and leadership. The major's uniform had been tailored to the highest quality and carefully pressed. This officer was clearly very particular. "The Gestapo caused considerable damage to our furniture—and they did this." He pulled his arm out of the sling and held out his bandaged hand. Even though he was a wreck, he was still a mensch. Keeping his mouth shut or acting as if nothing had happened was cowardly, unacceptable.

"A pity indeed, Herr Kohut." Thümmel offered a grim smile as he stood with his legs apart and chest out, holding three sheets of paper clipped together. "But I'm from the army and have no control over the actions of the Gestapo. You must complain about this to Altmann. Now I must get to work."

Willy shifted in his chair, watching the visitor tuck gray suede gloves into his tunic belt and begin his inspection, carefully checking the paintings, sculptures, glassware, and decorative china against the list he was carrying. He opened drawers and skimmed the bookshelves.

"What room is this?" Thümmel gestured at the door to Pavel's bedroom.

"My son's crib is in there." Willy was trying hard to control his temper at the man's intrusion into his home.

The officer vanished into the room and closed the door behind him.

Sophie came out from the kitchen with the coffee pot and three cups on a tray. "Where is he?" she asked with a surprised look. Thümmel reappeared and sat down at the table, patting Pavel's curly head—an affectionate, easy gesture, as if he were used to small children. The little boy looked up at Thümmel's pockmarked face. "Not like," he said firmly.

In that moment, Pavel's two Czech words gave Willy sudden insight into the difficulties they might have escaping to Budapest and beyond. Pavel could never pass as a Hungarian toddler. He spoke only Czech. "Not now, *Pavlíčku,*" Willy whispered, holding a finger to his lips. The boy made a face and slid to the floor, where he opened the box of buttons Sophie kept with his other toys under the Bechstein.

Thümmel smiled. Strong-looking teeth and gold fillings flashed in the light. "Your boy has fine blond curls, Frau Kohut, and the bluest eyes I've ever seen. Not at all Jewish. Any self-respecting German mother would be proud of these Aryan traits."

Sophie's face was expressionless as she poured the coffee, but Willy could tell from her blazing eyes that she was incensed. "Why should I be proud that my child looks German, major? Germans tortured my husband and crushed his finger, an innocent man." She pointed at the Bechstein. "He'll never play that piano again."

Willy jerked back in his chair, aghast at Sophie's words. She had never been as blunt as this before—and, for God's sake, this was a Nazi officer. Where had her bravado come from?

Thümmel glanced at the bulky dressing that covered Willy's right hand and calmly surveyed Sophie over his coffee cup. "We are not all devils, Frau Kohut. Altmann and his aides, to whom you refer, live by their own rules. Still, I regret that your husband's finger has been permanently affected. But...*c'est la guerre.*"

Willy massaged his jaw. He was tired of talking. "Is there anything else you need from us before you leave?"

"Yes, Herr Kohut, there is something. I was responsible for your release and now for the stream of officers who now buy fabric for their suits at your store. I think you and your charming wife owe me a small debt of gratitude."

Willy wearily shook his head. "I'm sorry. At the moment, I cannot deal with the ethics of who is indebted to whom. And as for gratitude, my wife has already used up most of our reserve funds bribing German officers."

Thümmel cleared his throat; he seemed embarrassed. "This is not what you think, Kohut. I simply want your help in finding a room to rent by the hour for... for a romantic rendezvous in the daytime. I was hoping you would rent me your boy's room perhaps twice a week, for two to three hours at the most. I noticed a good-sized bed in there."

Willy heard Sophie's sharp intake of breath as he lifted his throbbing hand onto the cushion she had placed for him on the table. *My God, the bastard wants Pavel's room. Maybe it is just a ruse—perhaps to plant or find evidence that proves I'm a spy.* On the other hand, the major's request might be genuine—and renting the room for Reichsmarks would be an excellent way to augment their slim cash reserves and guarantee some protection.

Sophie sipped from her coffee cup, watching Pavel roll a rubber ball to his father, who returned it with his foot, a game they had played earlier that day. Back and forth, back and forth. Willy could tell she was thinking about Thümmel's request. This was risky... collaboration.

He took a deep breath. "I suppose... it is possible. There would be rent, and I would welcome your cooperation on a couple of other matters."

Thümmel nodded and crossed his long legs, the polished jackboots glistening like mercury in the light from the windows. Pavel, now stacking colored blocks on the carpet next to where the officer sat, hesitantly reached up to touch the shiny leather. The major smiled.

"*Přestaň, Pavle,*" hissed Sophie, leaning forward to stop him.

Thümmel waved her away. "Let the boy be, Frau Kohut. He is learning the feel of fine leather. This is excellent coffee, by the way." He looked hard at Willy. "What about my request?"

Willy straightened up, deciding to take Thümmel's request at face value and turn it to his benefit. "Very well, major. You can use that bedroom for your assignations. I presume and hope they will be with the same person. Separate entrances are available. You come through the store and up the back stairs while your lady friend unlocks the front door of the apartment with a key I will give you. There are no other neighbors on this level to see her coming in. When you arrive downstairs, my cousins who staff the store will know about our arrangement. They will keep their mouths shut. My wife and I, and the boy of course, will be out on an errand somewhere. In this way, you will have the free run of the apartment. It will cost you one hundred Reichsmarks for each visit, which will include clean bed linens and towels, a bottle of good wine, coffee, and small pastries."

The major cocked a surprised eyebrow, carefully opened a silver case, and removed a cigarette. He pulled out a lighter and pushed the case across the table. "Do you smoke? Help yourself."

Willy shook his head and rose awkwardly, grimacing. He limped toward the German, who stood up, a full head taller.

"I like your proposal, though it's very expensive." Major Thümmel lit his cigarette as he observed Sophie's dismay with a smile. "I see your wife is not so enthusiastic about having strangers in her home. She will get over it. It's a man's world. When can we start?" He blew a series of smoke rings into the air just above Pavel, who rocked back on his heels, mesmerized.

"I haven't quite finished, Major," said Willy. "The cooperation I mentioned—it would help if the officers you send to buy my fabrics pay in Reichsmarks."

Thümmel gave Willy a sardonic look. "Reichsmarks? Why?

Are you planning to visit Germany? You Czechs are not allowed to leave the protectorate."

"Two reasons, major. Our koruna has plummeted in value while the German Reichsmark remains steady. Why should I make myself poor by trading in koruny? And yes, I admit that we will be traveling once I am better, but obviously not beyond the frontier. After I've sold the store, we'll live with relatives in Slovakia—Ružomberok, to be precise."

Sophie spluttered as she took a mouthful of coffee. Willy could see the alarm and surprise in her eyes. He was pleased his off-the-cuff cover-up of their intentions had worked so smoothly

"*Ganz gut. Festgesetzt.*" Thümmel held out his hand. "I agree to your proposal."

Surprised by the lack of any attempt at bargaining, Willy accepted Thümmel's hand with his uninjured left one.

"One more thing, Major," said Willy wondering if he was going too far with his demands. "I want to be kept up-to-date of the whereabouts of Hans Lessig, the man who informed on me. As you can imagine, he and I have some catching up to do."

Thümmel nodded. "I will do my best for you. Now, the room arrangement... Why not this Thursday at 1400 hours? You have everything ready, and I will leave you an envelope with my payment."

Sophie jumped to her feet. "No, Major. My husband isn't strong enough yet. It must be Thursday next week. For the first time, we'll be here to greet you, just to make sure everything is to your liking."

"Very well." The major held out his hand again. "Please, the apartment key and also your passports. I need another half hour to transcribe all the information into my dossier."

"Give him your key, dear," said Willy.

Sophie glared at him, took the key from a ceramic bowl on a shelf by the table, and with a cheeky curtsy handed it to Thümmel.

∽ ∂ ∽

Willy and Sophie spent most of the evening arguing about the merits and disadvantages of the deal with Thümmel and the evils of collaborating with the occupier and their acolytes. Collaboration had many shades of grey, Sophie agreed. She had

worked with Lessig and his German associates on her search
for Willy—but at least the Sudetenlander was a Czech citizen.
Moreover, was it not true that she and Willy were both equally
guilty of collaborating by selling their fabrics to Nazi officers?

"Most of all," she said, "I'm worried that our agreement
with Thümmel will leak out and we'll end up in the clutches of
the Gestapo. You should have thought more about the possible
consequences."

"For God's sake!" Willy shouted, and then clutched at the
pain in his ribs. "Everyone in this country is a collaborator in
some way. Even doing nothing can be construed as a betrayal.
You want me to close the store now. Throw away the money we
need? Quiver like mice in our apartment?"

Sophie stared at him, amazed. "When I told you that I
had agreed to Thümmel sending us customers, you rolled your
eyes and groused at me. I don't want Nazis in my store, you
grumbled. Now, suddenly, you're happy their money is rolling
into our cash register."

With the two fingers of his left hand, Willy massaged his
nose, something he did when he was very tense. He glared at
her. "Use your brains, strudel. Whatever the morality of our
collaboration, we need the Reichsmarks—especially if we have
to pass through Nazi-occupied territories. We need train tickets, money for taxis, meals, hotel rooms, and to pay for favors."
He gave her a wry smile. "Now, sweetheart, please—I've had
enough excitement, and I don't want to argue. I'm going to
bed."

"Well, I'll come later," she said abruptly, hating that she
had been arguing with her injured husband.

☜ ∂ ☞

Later, unable to sleep at first because of Willy's groans
and sighs, Sophie went over everything that had happened to
them in the past few weeks. Now that he was back, she realized
that Willy expected their relationship to return to its original
groove. That was unlikely; the old record of their marriage was
wearing thin. It was time to put on a new one. Renting the room
to Thümmel was an example of Willy's way of doing things; He
had decided the matter on the spot without asking for her opinion or agreement. She no longer wanted that.

At the beginning of their marriage, following tradition and not knowing any better, Sophie had accepted the role of obedient wife and housekeeper, always backing down when an argument was in the offing. That is what her mother and her mother-in-law had taught her but she was not just a housewife any more. She had astonished herself, running Kohut Stoffe. Hadn't she gotten Willy out of prison? That was a whole lot more than supervising domestics, creating menus and making shopping lists. Sophie did not want her life to revolve around Willy's expectations and orders. She wanted him to respect her capabilities, listen to her, and be more open about his own thoughts. She had earned that.

ᥭ ∂ ᥭ

Willy woke shortly after midnight, and took painkillers for his throbbing hand. He wondered what had gotten into Sophie since his arrest. The way she had spoken to Thümmel had been extraordinary. Willy had to admit she was a wonderful nurse but she also was more argumentative and seemed less willing to accept his direction. Still, apart from the mistake of burning his business correspondence and some of the Anglotex files, she had shown initiative, intelligence, and persistence under great pressure. Maybe that had given her a new kind of confidence. Better to wait, he thought, for things to settle; once he was healed, he was sure their marriage would revert to its old comfortable pattern and he would again be in charge of the family's future.

ᥭ ∂ ᥭ

The following week, Major Thümmel arrived at Kohut Stoffe just before two. He hung his wet military cape on the coat rack, and, nodding to Janko and two customers, strolled round the store interior examining different fabrics. When no one was looking, he took the stairs up to the Kohut apartment and, giving a light knock first, walked in. Sophie had set the table with wine glasses, china, silver, and small pastries.

"You are punctual," said Willy, taking time to put on his coat and hat. He hefted an umbrella with his left hand. "You have three hours. My wife will take Pavel for his usual walk, and I've ordered a taxi to take me to the Café Mánes." He pointed to the bottle on the table. "*Tokaji*, to get you in the mood: it's best quality, six *puttonyos*. A dessert wine. Drink as much as you like."

Thümmel took off his military tunic and slung it over a chair; a few rain droplets dripped onto the polished parquet floor. "I don't like sweet wines."

Willy walked over to a small cabinet and took out a bottle. "Try this instead... *Szamorodni*. It is Hungarian. Much lighter, tastes of nuts and apples."

Thümmel nodded as he accepted the wine. "I feel a little sorry for you, an injured man going outside on such a miserable day. It's windy." He lit a cigarette and gave Willy a crooked smile. "The rough with the smooth, eh?"

Already wearing her hooded blue raincoat, Sophie bent over Pavel to dress him in his outdoor clothes. From her glum expression, Willy guessed she was annoyed at having to take a walk in the rain and regretted the arrangement with Thümmel. He expected she would give him an earful later.

"I hope you don't mind, Major," Sophie said as she straightened up, "we would like to meet your lady friend. We want to make sure she is... you know... respectable. After all, she will be using our things, and our bed."

Thümmel frowned, but after a moment he inclined his head in agreement. "I understand how you feel. Just this once, mark you."

The major ensconced himself in Pavel's room with glasses and the two bottles. The Kohuts finished dressing for the rain and sat around the dining table, umbrellas between their knees, waiting for Thümmel's *amour* to appear. Pavel played on the floor with his toys.

After a few minutes, there was a gentle tap on the door. Sophie opened it and gasped.

"Fani, what a nice surprise." She hesitated. "I'm sorry, we're about to go out." She glanced at Willy, who was frowning. *Talk about an inconvenient visitor.* "It's Fani Ronay, Willy. I met her at one of Ruth's afternoon get-togethers. Her grandfather is the rabbi at the Pinkas Synagogue on Široká." She took the visitor's hand in both of hers. "It's so nice to see you, Fani. You should have telephoned. How did you get into the building?"

"At the front door, someone was leaving and let me in."

Willy got up, fuming, but he forced himself to nod politely. *This woman will ruin the whole Thümmel arrangement.* "A pleasure to meet you. I must apologize; this is not a convenient time to visit. As you see, we are just leaving."

At that moment, the door to Pavel's room opened and Thümmel, his shirt open at the neck and sleeves rolled up, stood framed in the doorway. He had a filled glass in his hand. He raised it and said, "Prost, Fani. Welcome."

Smiling apologetically at the Kohuts, Fani took off her hat and shook free her long, chestnut hair. "*Servus,* Johann." She walked past Thümmel into the bedroom. The major gave the Kohuts a good-humored, conspiratorial look and closed the door.

"Oh, God," groaned Willy as he hobbled down the building's main staircase, holding on to Sophie's arm. "I made a damned mistake renting the room to Thümmel. He cannot do this with a Jewish woman. The Nazis call it *Rassenschande*, racial shame. The granddaughter of a rabbi and a Nazi officer in bed together—who could imagine such a thing?"

"Ruth Eisner could." Sophie shook her head sorrowfully as she fastened Pavel into his perambulator. "She says real life usually outperforms imagination. Perhaps Fani is doing this to protect her family, a sort of insurance policy."

16

THE MAYOR'S LETTER
MAY, 1939

ARRIVING EARLY one morning, Dr. Pflinz pronounced himself satisfied with Willy's progress. Over two weeks, though still delicate, the skin over Willy's groin had begun to crust and re-grow, his testicles had reverted to their normal size, and the crushed finger was clean and healing, though it still looked like chewed meat.

At last, for the first time since his release from prison, Willy was beginning to believe things were going his way. Sales Agent Motyka and the prospective buyer of the store, Hugo Fechin, had just left Kohut Stoffe after a two-hour inspection of the premises, fabric stock, and accounts. The result was an offer of one million korun for the transfer of the store's long-term lease, all furnishings, inventory and assets, and customer goodwill: the equivalent of 55,000 English pounds. It was, Willy estimated, three-quarters of the property's true market value. The apartment was not part of the arrangement, being a straightforward rental.

Willy had been so excited that he wanted to sign the intent to purchase agreement as soon as possible, but Motyka reminded him that he needed to do this in the presence of a lawyer and a witness. After the agent and the buyer had left, Willy lay back against the sofa cushions, shoes off, stockinged feet resting on the footstool his mother had embroidered. His eyes were half closed, face drawn with exhaustion. Maybe waiting to sign the sale document was not such a bad thing; he was not sure he could have even signed his name properly. This time, he would get Sophie's opinion and agreement on the sale. He did not feel strong enough to listen to her growing complaints about being excluded from participating in family decisions.

He had closed Kohut Stoffe that day, not just for the buyer's inspection but because most commercial activity in the city was suspended. The citizens of Prague, and the Czech leadership, were commemorating the re-interment of the remains of the country's greatest poet, Karel Mácha, at the Vyšehrad cemetery. Willy had insisted that Sophie, Pavel, Janko, and Laci join the thousands of citizens who were using the event as a *de facto*, peaceful demonstration against the German occupiers.

"This is going to be a huge symbolic event," Willy had said the day before. "You can't all just sit at home staring at my sling, pretty as it is. Be my proxies. Take photographs. We have to show solidarity."

After a long nap and the Swedish exercises prescribed by Dr. Pflinz, a daily routine to rebuild his strength, Willy shuffled to the kitchen. He made himself some lemon tea, took his third dose of painkiller, and sat down at the dining table for the frustrating task of reading the *Prager Tagblatt* and *České slovo* newspapers with an almost useless right hand.

As usual, the headlines were disturbing. Reichsprotektor von Neurath had implemented more restrictions in Prague: he had ordered that a *J* had to be painted on Jewish stores in the city, the emigration quotas at Prague's foreign embassies were full, and in Switzerland, all male citizens were being mobilized to counter the German threat. Willy's muscles tightened. He was sick of the enforced convalescence that limited their escape plans. Every day brought new difficulties and melodramas. It was only thanks to Thümmel's protection that there was no *J* painted on Kohut Stoffe's store windows. Kohut Stoffe's growing Nazi clientele would have disappeared at the sight of a prominently displayed *J*. When Sophie was asked by neighbors why the store had no *J* on the window, she had no good answer other than, "It's an official waiver...to save embarrassment when our German customers come to buy."

Hoping for something better than the newspapers, Willy

turned to the mail. Apart from several business letters, there was a small parcel from Budapest addressed to Sophie—the Hungarian clothes labels, he guessed, from cousin Magda. Awkwardly, he managed to open each letter, trying to avoid bumping the bandaged finger, which sent an electric shock up his arm that made him gasp and clench his teeth.

There was airmail from his parents in London. Relatively good news, thank God. They were well—as well as could be for refugees reporting every week to the police station in a city preparing for war with food rationing, no heat, sandbags, and gasoline shortages.

The next letter he opened was official, stamped by the Prague mayor's office:

> Honored paní Kohut,
>
> You are required to attend the Dresdner Bank's Prague office on May 19 at 1400 to meet with Assistant Bank Manager Herr Walter Richter. The purpose of the meeting, under the Reichsprotektor Directive Regarding Jewish Property, is the sale and transfer of your property and business, Kohut Stoffe (previously Anglotex), 19 Masná Street, at full market price, to Herr Anton Skovajska.

"Oh, no!" Willy shouted in the empty room. "You damned bastards."

> Be sure to bring with you the property lease, title, last year's tax certificate, a detailed inventory of goods in place, and any other documents relevant to your ownership. This directive legally supersedes any current sale negotiations for the property. Herr Skovajska will also be present.
>
> Your attendance is mandatory. Appeals are forbidden. If you do not appear or fail to deliver the required documents or attempt to sell to an unapproved buyer, the police will immediately be informed and your possessions may be impounded with additional heavy fines.
>
> With the greatest respect,
> Josef Pfitzner, Mayor of the City of Prague

Willy swallowed hard and limped out to the balcony, looking up and down the street without feeling the warm sun or hearing the pigeons cooing amorously on the balustrade next door. Desolation and fury swept over him. A forced sale. The offer of a million korun was about to slip from his fingers. He gripped the balustrade, wanting to scream or smash something and pain flooded up his arm. But with a mounted Nazi soldier guarding the street, he could not draw attention to himself.

Idiot. Why didn't I sign the damned agreement Motyka put in front of me? Shit, shit, and double shit.

∽ ∂ ∽

After the others returned from the cathedral, tired but exhilarated by the dramatic funeral procession with its stirring speeches delivered to a vast crowd, Willy read the mayor's letter to everyone as they snacked at the dining table. For a while, no one said anything.

"How can they do this to us, Willy?" asked Sophie, her eyes shining with tears. "We are the lawful owners. We sell to whoever we want."

"Not anymore. Not if you are a Jew—though it's not clear in the letter if we have to give up the apartment as well. We have twelve days until the meeting at the bank. The letter does say I will get market price, so maybe it won't be so bad. Motyka was here earlier, and his buyer offered me one million korun."

Laci blinked in astonishment. "*Oy vey,* a million," he groaned. "Such a gift."

Sophie fumbled the tray she was carrying. Cups, plates, and cutlery tumbled. Coffee spilled on the polished flooring. Pavel, startled at his mother's reaction and struck by a flying spoon, began to cry and ran to his father. Sophie stared at the floor and then at Willy. He was surprised at the hard set of her face. "So, a few hours ago you had an offer to buy. Why didn't you accept it, for God's sake? Telephone Motyka, right now."

Janko nodded, smiling. "If you sell, Willy, I hope you won't forget your cousins."

Willy raised his left hand, wanting to inspire caution and calm. He had wanted to tell Sophie that he had put off signing so that she could have some say in the decision to sell, but this determined reaction of hers made him hold back. "Not so fast, family. I'm not sure you understand the implications of this letter. If I defy the mayor's order and sell to the new buyer Motyka has found for me, the Dresdner Bank will inform the mayor and the police." He shrugged. "If I do what the mayor's office says, we'll still have enough to get out of the country and start over again, somewhere else."

Laci got up from the table his lips compressed in anger. "Get out of Čzechy? Goddammit, we knew you were thinking of selling, but you could damn well have been more open with us—about leaving. We're your fucking cousins." Brusquely, he walked to the balcony window and looked out, hands locked behind his back.

Willy rubbed at his forehead. "OK, I'm sorry, boys. I meant to talk to you. My time in prison opened my eyes to the danger we're in—not just our family, but also every Jew in Prague. I'm sure the Gestapo still keeps a close eye on me. I don't want them to know we're planning to leave. We have to keep this quiet—just within the family, eh?"

"You may be too late with your travel plans," said Janko, lighting a cigarette and examining the glowing end. "Two weeks ago, all the international express trains from here to Rotterdam were cancelled, and someone at my *pension* told me that passenger traffic on the cross-channel ferries to England will close down in a few days."

Willy's face sagged. "Dammit. Look, I was going to tell you boys after things were more firmed up. Give me some leeway, for God's sake. I'm still recovering from prison. There's a lot to think about and organize."

"You mean like renting out a room to a Nazi officer?" Janko stubbed his cigarette viciously in an ashtray on the table. "You and Sophie have turned into collaborators."

"Stop it." A flush rose up Sophie's neck. "We need the income, and you need your wages."

"Bloody pish," Laci retorted, walking back from the window. "You don't need to make money from Nazis." His face flushed. "In a few days, you'll sell the place and get a pile of shekels from the bank, enough to travel, buy an auto and an apartment, and start a new business in England. And what about us, eh? We get little enough pay now, but with the store gone, we'll have nothing. No work. Is this the way to treat us? Anyway, I can't bear to sell your stuff anymore. Not to those Nazi bastards. Every time they talk to me, I feel like smashing their faces in."

"Stop *gridzing*." Willy slumped back in his chair, hurt by Janko's accusations of collaboration and secrecy. "You are being unfair, boys. My father and I supported your parents for years, pulled you out of dead-end jobs. After what the Gestapo did to me in Pankrác, I could do with a little more sympathy than you have shown. Why not listen to what I have to say?"

Laci reversed a chair and sat on the seat, leaning his chest and powerful arms on top of the ladder-back. "OK, so tell us, cousin."

"While you were at the funeral procession, I did some heavy thinking." Willy's finger was throbbing mercilessly, but he did not want to show his pain, only his determination. He needed to get his agenda on the table. "From today, Kohut Stoffe will be permanently closed, though you will still be paid at the usual rate. You won't have to serve Nazi officers. As soon as I'm fit enough, we'll make a run for it. Get out of here."

Willy looked around at his family. It was time for expediency rather than patriotism. "It's been over five weeks since I came home from Pankrác. I admit I put off thinking about your situation. Trust me; you'll both get a lump sum when this place is sold."

Janko smiled, but Laci turned dark pink. He looked away, seemingly embarrassed. "I see. I'm sorry I got angry. Thanks for including us...but I also have an announcement. I was planning to give you notice."

There was a deathly silence.

Willy's mouth was tight with disapproval. "Explain."

"Well," said Laci, fiddling with the buttons on his jacket sleeve, as if unwilling to look Willy in the eye. "Before you were arrested, I suspected something significant was being planned for the store. For one thing, you kept leaving Janko and me out of the usual business discussions. You didn't ask for our opinions anymore. It was just orders—do this, do that. And then before *pane* Molnar buzzed off to Poland, he offered me a chance, through the Trade Union Association, to join a resistance group."

Willy drew a sharp breath of astonishment. "Isn't that very risky?" asked Sophie, looking up as she cleared up the mess from the dropped tray.

"Well, at least I'll be doing something useful for my country," Laci muttered, rolling his shoulders and bunching his fists. "I would be fighting, not abasing myself in the store, in front of swaggering Wehrmacht officers."

Willy raised a hand. "Okay, I understand, but I've a family to protect, and it's better to fight when you have a decent chance of striking hard and effectively. After two months of occupation, where is our Czech resistance? Nowhere. While the Fascists are flexing their muscles in Prague, bombing cafes and attacking Jews in the street, the police and occupation forces stand around and let it happen. At this stage, you would be better off escaping with us and joining up with the French Legion in North Africa."

Laci scowled. "I've given my word."

"Change your mind. Come with us to Budapest." Sophie smiled encouragingly at him. "Willy is only just recovering. We need your friendship and your muscles."

"Well, I'm coming with you," said Janko, looking at Willy. "Though I don't understand why you didn't send Sophie and Pavel to your parents in London months ago, the same time the Kinder Transport was being organized. You knew some of the British people in charge, didn't you? You could have stayed behind to sell the store and then got out on your own."

Willy sighed, massaging his forehead as if he was trying to keep his thoughts straight. "We considered it, but Sophie said no. She wanted us to stay together."

Sophie put her hand on Willy's shoulder and massaged it gently. She looked tearful. "I was afraid something would happen and we would never see each other again."

"Which reminds me..." Willy gave a deep sigh. "Another letter came from Emil."

"What does the old grump say?" Janko almost smiled, as if remembering the days when he had worked for his autocratic uncle in Lučenec.

"Well, they've resettled in a very small apartment in a neighborhood called Hampstead. The Czech Refugee Trust helps a little with the rent. Mama can't get her tongue around English, and the rationing is getting stricter. Most important of all, he reminded me of the address and telephone number of that courier fellow in Budapest."

"What courier?" asked Laci.

"A sort of courier-smuggler... in fact he's a distant cousin who might take us to Holland in his car. That's why we need plenty of money."

Sophie sat down on the carpet where Pavel lay flat on his stomach tugging on a wooden yellow truck filled with tin soldiers, imitating engine noises. She looked up at Willy, a defiant look in her eyes. "*Miláčku*, I don't like the idea of you going to that meeting at the Dresdner bank. You might not be well enough... I'm sure there'll be soldiers there. What if they stop you, or hurt you? Talk to Karel—you know, Karel Slotnicz, the Polish lawyer from the chess club. He might know a legal way for you to sell to Motyka's buyer before the bank steps in."

Willy smiled at the way she was giving him advice, as if he were still an invalid and could not think straight. However, her suggestion was a good one. "You're right, Sophie. I'll telephone him."

∾ ∂ ∾

Later that day, after several attempts, Willy got hold of Karel Slotnicz. "I'll get straight to the point," Willy said on the telephone. "In twelve days I have to go to the Dresdner Bank to sell my property to some bootlicking businessman, one Anton Skovajska—it's a forced sale by the mayor's office. Do you know about this kind of chicanery?"

"I'm very aware of the new regulations, *pane* Kohut," the lawyer said sympathetically. "The whole Jewish community is in turmoil—forced sales all over the place. These are times when life refuses to cooperate."

"Very well then, listen to me. Today I had a genuine offer for my property from a private buyer. Is there anything I can legally do to prevent the forced sale at the bank?"

Slotnicz coughed and paused. "I'm sorry. There is nothing to be done. If you skip the meeting at the bank, the Gestapo will come to your home and do something unpleasant."

"I can guess," Willy muttered.

"I have one suggestion, Kohut. Go to the bank as soon as you can and take out all your cash. No, not all of it. Leave a small sum behind."

"Why?"

"So as not to draw suspicion. When a Jew empties his bank account, that means he's about to run."

"No, I mean why withdraw now?"

"A rumor, my friend. Karl Rasche, one of the top bank officials in Germany, will soon be here to organize the requisitioning of all the Jewish-held assets—essentially, a repeat of what happened in Austria. When you withdraw the cash, be sure to change it on the spot into Hungarian pengö or German Reichsmarks. Those currencies are keeping their value. Our poor koruna is falling every day."

"Thanks, my friend. Do I owe you anything for this advice?"

"No—well, er, yes. Buy me a pile of *palačinky* crepes at the Café Slávia sometime after the Germans have gone home."

ↄ ∂ ↄ

At ten the next morning, Willy arrived at the Dresdner Bank, where the Kohut family had held an account for 25 years. Sophie, who had come with him in the taxi, waited outside on the marble steps; most women did not have personal accounts or accompany their husbands, so their presence inside a bank often drew suspicious glances.

Carrying a briefcase in his left hand, his right arm in a Jacquard silk sling, Willy walked slowly through the bronze and glass doors, past the gold-braided doorman, and between two helmeted Wehrmacht soldiers carrying machine pistols. More soldiers were stationed at intervals along the hushed main hall. Willy tried to look calm and businesslike, but he was shaking inside. Slowly he approached the long, polished mahogany counter praying that none of Altmann's thugs were hovering in the area. Altmann seemed to have a long reach, a Nazi spider controlling a web of informers.

He greeted the clerk in the customary German and slid a withdrawal slip for 60,000 korun under the art deco brass grille. Following Slotnicz's warning not to raise suspicion with a complete withdrawal, he decided to leave 40,000 korun on deposit. Willy noticed that the sallow-faced teller, who knew him from previous transactions, kept staring at the payment slip.

"I'm sorry, Herr Kohut," said the teller finally, showing gold fillings inside a bleak smile. He glanced down at Willy's sling and raising a questioning eyebrow. "Not too serious, I hope. Do you need assistance?"

Willy shook his head. "An accident."

The teller shifted on his feet, fingering the withdrawal slip. "This is a much larger figure than you usually withdraw, Herr Kohut. I have to check with my superior."

Willy tried to appear casual and noncommittal. "Look, I have a big business deal coming up, buying up bankrupt fabric stock for my store. The seller insists on cash. That's why I need sixty thousand."

The teller nodded, flicking specks of paper off the black covers protecting his shirt cuffs. "I understand what you mean. Everyone likes cash these days."

Willy nodded. "The occupation has turned my business upside down. I'm in a hurry. How long will it take to get the approval?"

The teller put a hand on his telephone but he paused and lowered his voice, looking around as if he might reveal a great secret. "Big changes at the bank, sir. Jewish employees are being replaced with Sudetenlanders. And Dresdner has absorbed two other banks, the Jewish Bohemian Discount and the Petschkův." Turning away, he dialed an extension.

Willy gazed at the man's back. The mention of staff dismissals and Jewish banks being swallowed up was disturbing. Life in Prague was changing too fast. Slotnicz was right about cashing out.

After a murmured conversation, the teller replaced the receiver and turned back with a brief smile. "Everything is, ah, correct, Herr Kohut. Now, may I see your identity card?

With some difficulty, Willy pulled out his wallet and then went through his pockets. *Not here, dammit.* He cursed himself for leaving the card at home, remembering how he had left it by the telephone. "I'm sorry, it's at home. Nevertheless, you know me well and my father has had an account with you for twenty years. How about a visiting card?" Willy shifted on his feet. This was taking too long, and Sophie was waiting outside, probably worried that something had gone wrong.

The teller looked at Willy and shook his head. "New regulations. I must see the required documents."

Willy sucked in a breath and placed his bandaged hand gently on the counter. Exaggeration was necessary. "You see this, my friend? Gestapo handiwork." With his left hand, he undid two buttons of his shirt, exposing faint bluish-yellow bruises covering his chest. "More Gestapo handiwork. Please, I have broken ribs and a damaged hand. I'm too weak to go home and come back again."

The teller's eyes widened and he looked around nervously, clearing his throat. "Please, sir, dress yourself. Ordinarily I shouldn't do this, but between us Czechs, I will make an exception." He keyed open a drawer of stacked banknotes and, after counting out the required amount, pushed the wrapped bundles of korun under the grille.

The teller leaned forward to help Willy stuff the notes into his briefcase. "Between you and me, sir, the Dresdner just got a contract to service all of the Gestapo's banking needs— that covers the Protectorate and perhaps the whole of Germany. I expect the Gestapo will be keeping a close eye on our work. Perhaps you should withdraw everything next time. That is what our Jewish customers are doing. Of course they are watched" He winked.

"Good advice, my friend." *No doubt*, Willy thought, *Altmann would be using this bank and might appear at any moment.* "Now, I must be off. Thank you for helping me."

"A pleasure, Herr Kohut. *Guten Tag.*"

Willy limped the length of the hall to the international counter. His head buzzed, and he staggered a little. He felt weak but managed to ask the teller to change half the 60,000 korun into Reichsmarks and half into Hungarian pengö. Once more, he had to wait while some shadowy bureaucrat in the depths of the bank confirmed the transaction. Willy inserted the fat envelope into his briefcase and slowly made his way along the marble hallway, relieved and elated. He rejoined Sophie outside and slid his arm round her shoulders. He was trembling now.

Willy looked up at the sun-drenched clouds scudding across the sky and kissed Sophie's cheek. "I actually accomplished something important today. I walked into the bank on my own, and it's a beautiful day. I'm getting better by the minute. Do you think we dare celebrate at the Slávia?" The Slávia was Willy's favorite art deco café, where he liked to hold business meetings. It offered coffee, food, billiards, a reading room, and afternoon music—a rendezvous for the well-to-do, the gossips, and the dealmakers.

Sophie nodded and slipped her hand under his good arm. "You're trembling. You need to relax over a coffee. Then we'll take a taxi home."

They took a table by one of the windows overlooking the river. A group of pastry-munching SS officers sat ten feet away. Willy and Sophie restricted their gaze to Prague Castle and Petřín Park, watching the boats pass along the river. "Don't worry about those officers," said Willy in Czech. "We're not on the run yet. As long as we live quietly and don't do anything suspicious, there's no reason for the Gestapo to do anything to us."

A stooped old waiter appeared at their table and bowed. "Good morning, Hugo," said Willy. "Coffee and my favorite pancake, please. Does that suit you, Sophie?"

She smiled her agreement.

The waiter tucked a thumb into his striped waistcoat pocket and closed his eyes for a moment, as if digging into a memory vault. "Ah, yes, *pane* Kohut. I believe you prefer a cream cheese filling with honey, marinated blackberries, caramel, and almonds—for two?"

Sophie laughed. "What a memory he has."

As they ate, Willy absorbed what had just happened at the bank. The bundles of banknotes in his briefcase represented just a fraction of the savings and grinding hard work he and his father had put into the business over the years. He had certainly won a small financial victory, but now he suddenly felt empty and vulnerable. Their situation was precarious, and he was not even close to being ready to escape. Still, the sweetness of the pancake in his mouth made him feel hopeful. He felt that soon his family would be on their way to a safe haven. They would have a future.

As they departed, Sophie said, wistfully looking around the café. "I wonder if we will ever drink coffee at the Slávia again."

17

IT'S JUST BUSINESS
MAY 19, 1939

WILLY TOOK SOPHIE'S ADVICE on how to prepare
for his meeting with the Czech buyer and the Dresdner Bank
official. "I grew up in Berlin, remember?" She smiled as she gave
him a kiss. "If you want to negotiate a price for Kohut Stoffe,
you must impress the Germans—look confident, unbreakable."

She helped him get dressed in a double-breasted pinstriped
broadcloth suit with French facings, a starched white shirt, and
a blue bow tie, with his brown trilby tilted at an angle. She
tucked a lily-of-the valley into the dragontail buttonhole. "That
will distract them from staring at your hand," she said, adjusting his bow tie. "And be firm and precise," Have you got the
mayor's letter? Make sure you get market price."

Willy frowned. Why was she saying this? He was the businessman. "My finger may be damaged, strudel, but my brain is
working perfectly. I know these people want to get the store as
cheaply as they can and I'm not expecting the moon. Whatever
I can negotiate, I'll cash it out on the spot."

Sophie's cheeks turned pink. "I was just trying to help,
you know."

"Do you still want me as your bodyguard?" asked Laci,
putting a big arm round Willy's shoulders. "Stop you from
getting robbed on the way home."

Willy winced with pain. "Yes, but don't hug me like that again. We go together to the bank, and you wait for me outside..."

ꞈ ∂ ꞈ

At the bank, a young woman escorted Willy past a series of glassed-in offices full of serious-looking men writing assiduously at their desks. "Herr Richter's personal secretary will take over from here," she said, opening a carved mahogany door. "She will show you to the meeting room."

A blond woman with her hair pinned up in tight braids advanced toward him with an elegant stride along the patterned carpet. "Good morning, Herr Kohut. Please follow me to Assistant Manager Richter's office."

She showed him into a beech-paneled, windowless room where two men waited at a small table. Both nodded a cursory greeting, and the large, sour-faced one whom Willy took to be the bank official pointed to an empty chair. The usual handshake—always a gesture of respect and courtesy between Czech businessmen—was not offered. Willy vaguely remembered once having met Anton Skovajska at a reception at the Prague Business Club; he was the owner of two mediocre clothing stores in Prague. Maybe Skovajska, who was wearing an ill-fitting suit and unpolished shoes, was just too embarrassed by this charade of a sale to do anything but sit there like a potato dumpling. Willy shuddered at the thought of this man blundering about Kohut Stoffe, alienating the valued customers.

"Herr Kohut? Please sit down." The man who seemed to be in charge wore a high starched collar, black tie, and dark gray jacket, the Dresdner uniform of upper management. "I am Herr Walter Richter, a property loan specialist from the Munich branch. I understand you are fluent in German. As I do not speak Czech, we will conduct business in German."

Willy sat down, depositing his briefcase on the floor. "Agreed."

"Good." Richter rubbed his hands together briskly. "I am here to supervise the Protectorate Property Expropriation Act as it applies to your property. Have you read the mayor's letter?" He looked curiously at Willy's arm in the sling.

Willy nodded, giving the facsimile of a smile, but his fingers were already tight on his lap, thighs twitching, as tense as a sprinter's in the blocks. He tried to tamp down his anger. Far better to show pliability and cooperation at this stage. Losing one's temper was the worst way to get a reasonable price. He was in unexplored territory; he had to be ready for anything.

Richter cleared his throat, squinting at Willy as if he had just found a rat in the pantry. "Dresdner Bank has been officially entrusted by order of the Reichsführer and the German protectorate authorities to facilitate and document all the transactions between Jewish citizens and the new owners of their property. As you are aware, it is illegal for Jews to hold property, collect rent, or run businesses on their own. In this particular instance, we are dealing with Buyer Agreement #2, in which the Jewish property is allocated to a specific non-German buyer. Do you understand?"

Willy nodded as he digested the bureaucratic words that were window dressing for some kind of official thievery.

"Now, I want to be clear, Kohut. In spite of the long history of scandalous and corrupt behavior of Jewish capitalists and moneylenders in Europe, the Third Reich is generously allowing properties such as yours to be sold to new owners." He turned and pointed at the burly man with an uncombed mop of hair. "Herr Skovajska, a Czech citizen, has already deposited at our bank the necessary funds to purchase the recently renamed Kohut Stoffe, 19 Masná Street. You will receive his payment draft of 250,000 korun at the end of this meeting. That is 25,000 Reichsmarks."

"You must be joking." Willy gripped the edge of the table with his left hand as the right one pulsed with pain. "I just had an offer of a million."

Skovajska shifted uncomfortably in his chair and examined his fingernails.

"Do you know what you are buying?" asked Willy in clipped tones, "Kohut Stoffe is a premier importer of luxury men's fabrics. The mayor said in his letter that I would receive market price. I am prepared to let the property go for a million. That's a bargain, gentlemen."

Skovajska went red and opened his mouth to speak. Richter raised a hand to silence him and turned to Willy. His words were precise and sharp, like rapier thrusts. "Past history, Kohut. Under the new regulations, we do not negotiate. The market price is set by the bank. Mr. Anton Skovajska has the necessary funds. It's a reasonable offer."

Willy could not contain himself. "Reasonable? Your damned bank has not even performed an inspection or valuation. Explain how you came up with this laughable figure."

Richter put on pince-nez glasses and glanced at the documents lying in front of him as if he had not heard a word. "The property consists of a sales room, an office and toilet and a small storage area, ten by five and a half meters. Above, there is an apartment connected by stairs. The apartment is rented separately from this transaction. There are business, furniture, and decorative items within the store: several glass display cabinets, a cash register, and a large quantity of merchandise in the form of imported bolts of suiting fabric, all stored on the premises. As I said, Herr Skovajska has agreed to purchase the above for 250,000 korun, a generous offer. The Jew Kohut can keep or dispose of his personal belongings as he sees fit. Both of you must sign this purchase agreement. Are you agreed?"

Willy looked away for a moment. "I don't agree. It's robbery dressed up in legal clothes."

"Don't act the fool." Richter spat out the words like bullets. "If you wish to be difficult, you have a good chance of ending up with nothing."

Willy drew in a deep breath, gripping his knees under the table. He understood that he had to accept. All he would get was a quarter of a million korun—pitiful, but enough to cover food travel, and bribes for their escape, with some left over to help them start again somewhere.

"Get on with it, then," he muttered, drumming the edge of the table with the fingers of his left hand. More than anything, he wanted to fasten them around Richter's neck and squeeze the life out of the bastard.

"Say something, Herr Skovajska—please," said Richter in an irritated tone.

Willy glared at the businessman, concluding that the German bank official did not seem to think much of either of them. He guessed Skovajska, whose name suggested his family originated from outside the republic, had embraced the Protectorate's new social order to feather his own nest. Collaboration came in degrees and shades, Willy thought. Thümmel renting their room was one example. Even if you sat on the fence and kept your mouth shut, some people would regard that arrangement as a form of silent, safe collaboration.

The Czech spoke hesitantly, his words accompanied by fumes of garlic and beer. "Would the Jew Kohut kindly pass me the property titles and the inventory of fabrics, furnishings, and equipment? I wish to review them."

Willy bit his lip to keep from exploding. The juxtaposition of the humiliating phrase "the Jew Kohut" with the word "kindly" was so incongruous that it was almost laughable. Probably Skovajska had rehearsed his part with Richter, Willy thought as he opened his briefcase and handed over the documents. For the next ten minutes, the documents moved back and forth between the bank official and the buyer while they studied the details and Richter made notes in a ledger.

Richter turned to Willy, a smile of satisfaction spreading across his face.

"In conclusion, then... According to the new protectorate regulations, the Dresdner Bank has authorized sale of Kohut Stoffe property to Herr Skovajska for 250,000 Czech korun. Since you already have an account at this bank, I will make out a draft in your name that can be cashed at any time. Now, please, both of you sign the transfer certificate and the sale is complete."

Seeing the title and description of his store at the top of the document proved too much for Willy. He rose to his feet, just able to control his impulse to lash out. "You're an arse-licking worm, Skovajska." He jabbed a finger in the man's face. "You think you've got a cheap deal, but just wait and see what happens when they turn round and do the same to you."

The Czech slid back into his chair, looking at Richter for help. The official laughed and leaned back, lacing his fingers behind his neck. Willy sensed from the gleam in the German's eyes that he was enjoying himself. "Herr Kohut, sit down and sign—and temper your language or I'll have to call the SA guards."

Trapped and defeated, Willy stood, swaying a little, until his anger subsided. He had no wish to suffer more beatings. He sat and signed.

Richter continued. "Good, that's done. The transfer of the store is to take place in four weeks, by the nineteenth of June, in the presence of one of my subordinates. By June fifteenth, Herr Skovajska is required to make an inventory of all pertinent structures and merchandise and present it to me by June nineteenth. He will be in touch with you to arrange a visit to the store."

Richter rang a small brass bell, and the secretary reappeared holding a stick of red wax, matches, and a silvery-looking bank seal.

Richter handed the deed to Skovajska, who wrote a check for 250,000 korun made out to Willy's account. Richter countersigned it and pushed it across the table to Willy. "Fräulein Berger, inform the cashier that the Jew Kohut will deposit a large sum into his account——and that I have witnessed the transaction."

She gave a little curtsy and left the room.

℥ ∂ ℥

Five minutes later, humiliated and angry but relieved to have Skovajska's check in his possession, Willy walked out into the marble banking hall, wondering what he was going to say to Sophie about the so-called "market price." At the teller's counter, he passed Skovajska's check under the grille along with a withdrawal slip for 150,000 korun from his account. He planned to change the money into Reichsmarks as soon as he got the cash. A hundred thousand would stay in Willy's current account to throw the Nazis off the scent - after all, no one in his right mind would leave Czechoslovakia and abandon that amount in a German bank.

A different teller examined the check and the pay-in and withdrawal slips before smiling bleakly at Willy. "Excuse me a moment, Herr Kohut. We have some new changes in procedure. Please wait while I check with my superior."

Willy's instincts and the teller's shifting eyes indicated there was trouble coming. *What the hell will it be this time?*

In five minutes, the teller was back. "I regret we cannot accept any new funds into your account," he said with a poker face, "nor can we allow you to withdraw money." He pushed the bank draft, deposit, and withdrawal slips back to Willy.

"What the hell is this?" Dread cycled through Willy's head. "This note was just countersigned by Herr Richter, one of your officials, after I concluded the sale of my store to Herr Skovajska."

"If you wish to question this policy, I will ask Herr Richter to come out and speak with you." The teller looked away. "I do not think that will change anything."

"You mean my account is frozen?"

The teller nodded. Willy crumpled the useless pieces of paper, suppressing a wild urge to shout and scream. *It was all a fucking charade.* He wanted to run back and smash his fists into both of them, except that he was too weak and only had the use of one fist. As he walked away, head sunk into his shoulders, Willy estimated that he had just under 80,000 korun at home— not much, still enough perhaps to finance their escape, yet far too little to jump-start a new business in another country.

"We're walking home, Laci," said Willy as he came down the broad front steps of the bank. "I need to get the putrid air of hypocrisy out my lungs and work out how to explain what happened to Sophie."

Laci took his arm. "What happened? You don't look so good."

Willy shook off his hand. "Let me be. I have to practice walking on my own, build my stamina."

"So they paid you market price?"

Willy stopped and gave him a reproachful look. "No, Laci—the bastards gave me a check for a quarter of a million and then the bank wouldn't cash or deposit it. New regulations for Jews. They robbed me."

"Holy shit. What are you going to do now?"

Willy swayed a little, and Laci put an arm round his shoulders.

"We should all have left before the Nazis came," Willy muttered gloomily. "Why the hell do the rabbis here keep telling us life here is bearable and that things will settle down? I'm a fool. I thought I could cash my assets and take them with me. Now, please, no more discussion till we get home."

Willy negotiated the streets with his head bowed, inad-

vertently bumping into people, so angry and disappointed that
he did not bother to apologize. Laci held Willy's briefcase and
supported him by the elbow to prevent him from tripping.

Before entering Masná Street, Willy stood for a moment
to wipe the tears from his eyes and dry his glasses. He could not
bear for Sophie to see how miserable and ashamed he was. Tears
were symptoms of sorrow, but easily dried and forgotten. What
really mattered were his family and the future. Willy squared
his shoulders.

The Nazis had won this round. He needed to come up with
a new escape plan.

18

GOODBYES
JUNE, 1939

A FEW DAYS after the evil dispossession—*Zabavení majetku zlem*, as Sophie and the cousins labeled Willy's humiliation at the bank—Skovajska telephoned that he was coming to inventory everything on June 2. The sale of Kohut Stoffe was no longer a unique and private event between buyer and seller; the city authorities had begun to post similar transactions on the bulletin board in the city hall's concourse.

"Skovajska arrives in three days' time," said Willy after lunch. "We must leave before he finds out what we're doing and informs the bank. This afternoon, I'll take a tram to Franz Josef Station to buy tickets and reserve our seats to Budapest."

Sophie clung to him. "*Milačku*, no. Only three days? Do the boys know our plans. Did you give them the travel details you promised? About Budapest?"

"No, I'll tell them at the last minute. Laci swore he wasn't coming but he might change his mind."

"What if Janko changes his mind as well? You are wasting money buying their tickets ahead of time. We need those boys, Willy. You aren't fit enough to travel without their help."

"Well, they're helping pack up the crate. That's a good sign."

Laci had built the crate in the back yard of the store, and Willy and Sophie filled it with clothes, investment bonds, documents, family photograph albums, favorite artwork, and small pieces of furniture, everything wrapped in the thickest fabric from the store. Since the protectorate still allowed international shipping, the crate would be sent to Kindell & Renfrew in London, its contents described in the invoice as returned damaged goods. "An even chance it will reach its destination," Willy said with a shrug as he and Laci affixed the required labels. "It's a gamble, but if anyone decides to take a look inside—well then, goodbye treasures."

∾ ∂ ∾

Everything was moving too fast for Sophie. In the past two weeks, she had lost her appetite, and at night, she slept badly, turning events over and over in her mind. Five weeks of managing Kohut Stoffe without Willy and then caring for him after he got back from Pankrác had worn her down. There were times when she felt listless and numb, and then moments of frantic enthusiasm when she worked on their preparations for departure: removing Czech labels from their clothes and sewing on Hungarian ones sent by Magda, or packing their suitcases. She did the cooking and cleaning and looked after Pavel, taking him for walks every day.

Sophie was proud that she had taken good care of Willy during his rehabilitation. Although passion and sex had been out of the question since his incarceration, she believed that nursing him had helped to strengthen the bond between them. She loved him, and he loved her. Every morning, Sophie would dress Willy's finger and massage sweet oil into the violet streaks of delicate skin around his lower belly and bruised groin. This often produced an erection, which inevitably led to a sorrowful look. "Forgive me," he would say. "I don't think I can give you the pleasure you deserve."

"But it's a hopeful sign." Sophie offered a shy smile. "Soon, I can be a good wife to you again and make you happy. Do you want to try?"

Willy kissed her fingers. "In a day or two, perhaps."

∾ ∂ ∾

When Major Thümmel arrived for the usual rendezvous

with his lady friend, Willy was waiting for him. "After my first visit, you promised you would never be here when I came," said the major, his pockmarked skin suffused a dusky red. "This is incorrect behavior." He looked around and sniffed in disgust, "Why is your apartment in such a mess today? I pay good money. I expect everything to be neat and clean."

Willy uncapped a beer and poured two glasses. "Please forgive us, Major, but we are leaving for Ružomberok...earlier than planned. The Dresdner Bank requisitioned my store and it will be in the hands of someone else very soon. We must terminate our agreement. I waited for you today, to say good-bye and thank you. Join me in a farewell beer?" Sitting this close to a uniformed Nazi made Willy nervous, especially now that he was weaving a false trail.

"When do you leave?"

"After the new owner has made the inventory...two or three days? We will keep the store closed from now on, until he takes over. The apartment key will be with the concierge—and, of course, there is no need to pay after we have gone. If you wish to continue the arrangement with the new owner, *pane* Skovajska, here is his address and telephone number."

Thümmel nodded gravely, taking the note Willy had passed across the table. "I see. Thank you." He swallowed a mouthful of beer and wiped the foam from his mouth. "Actually, now would be a good time for you to get away from Prague. All the old Czech government ordinances are about to be overridden, and the protectorate has just instituted the Nuremberg racial laws. In a few days, a senior officer, Obersturmbannführer Eichmann, will be in Prague to set up a central Jewish Emigration office like the ones in Germany and Vienna."

"Well, that's good news, isn't it?" Willy rubbed at his healing finger. It had become a distracting habit now that the paper-thin skin itched so much. "Finally, the Germans are organizing to help us Jews get out of the country."

The major tapped a cigarette against his silver case, his mouth twisting into a wry smile. "The phrase 'Emigration Office' is more about control than emigration. As has happened in Austria, every Jew here will eventually be registered and required to provide an inventory of family members, possessions, bank accounts, and property. I expect a few of your people will manage to get permission to leave, but they will not be able to take much with them. The rest of Czech Jewry is to be confined to certain geographical areas of the protectorate, their assets frozen, and they will be banned from travel."

Willy stood up, startled at Thümmel's warning. He could almost feel the trap closing in on his family. "We'll leave you here now, but thank you again for your assistance in my release from Pankrác." He put out his left hand for a handshake. Showing gratitude to a Nazi was hard to do. "My wife thanks you also. I doubt we will meet again. Good-bye."

⁊ ∂ ⁊

When Sophie returned from her walk with Pavel late that afternoon, Willy made her sit down beside him on the piano stool where he had been doodling with his left hand. He told her about his conversation with Thümmel. "The major warned me. The Third Reich's honeymoon with Prague is just about over. Life will be much harder, especially for Jews. We will be gone by then, so why don't we make a nice farewell dinner tonight? Impromptu—Janko, Laci, and Ruth. I'll invite them. Janko will bring his violin. I can't play and I want to hear gypsy music before I say goodbye to the Bechstein"

Sophie wearily shook her head. "We have enough to do getting ready to leave. Are you, by any chance, proposing to cook for us? Of course not, you don't even know how to boil an egg. At the same time, you insist we don't have money to spare, so why spend it on an expensive dinner?"

Willy took her arm and drew her toward him, trying to soften her resistance. "Just be a little flexible, strudel. This is a significant moment in our lives. We are leaving our broken country, and we may never come back. Please, do the farewell dinner... for me." Willy took her into his arms and kissed her nose and forehead. "No need to worry about money. We have enough. Come, I'll show you my calculations." He led her to the desk and pulled a sheet of paper out of one of the drawers. "Read it."

Estimates for family voyage, including Janko and Laci
Available funds: 60,000 korun withdrawn from Dresdner Bank, divided into Reichsmarks and pengö. Plus cash in hand. 22,000 korun. TOTAL = 82,000 korun or 7,593 Reichsmarks

Estimated expenses: 5 train tickets Prague-Budapest: 500 korun, 4 nights Budapest lodging for 5 people: 800-900 korun. 5 days food for 5 people: 3,000 korun

Train tickets (Willy, Sophie, Pavel), Budapest to Amsterdam: 4,000 korun (36 Reichsmarks)

Accommodation and food in Amsterdam: 3,500 korun (3–5 days)

3,000 korun/300 Reichsmarks leaving bonus each for Laci and Janko – 6,000 korun

Debts: 25,000 korun to Halač owed for Anglotex construction

20,000 korun owed to Petschek Bank

Shipping crate to London: 2,000 korun

Total expenses: 64,900 korun

Expected funds in hand after arrival and 3-day stay expense in Amsterdam: 17,100 korun/ 1,583 Reichsmarks/3,500 pengö/137 English pounds/792 US dollars

She looked at him, alarmed, and then shook her head as if she could not believe it. "Only seventeen thousand korun after we reach Amsterdam? That's awful, Willy. What if we get stuck there? We have to cross the channel to get to your parents in London and Janko said that would be almost impossible. No more ferries and Nazi U-boats everywhere. Didn't you read the papers?"

"I agree, strudel. Seventeen thousand korun is a very small amount. So I've decided not to repay my debts. That will give us more of a cushion. Of course, I feel bad about the debts, but that would put forty-five thousand korun back into the kitty. Are you still with me?" He was watching and listening to see if she understood the numbers. She nodded.

Willy put his sheet of calculations back in the drawer. "Very well, then. We'll have enough…and when we get to London, Father and Kindell & Renfrew will help us with a loan." He gave her a hug and, very gently kissed her eyelids" I absolutely insist we can afford a farewell dinner. Are you willing to cook for us or not?"

Sophie shrugged. "Yes, I suppose so." Willy could tell from her drawn-in cheeks, downturned mouth that she was unhappy, and feeling put upon.

"Good, then that's settled. So, change Pavel's diaper and

then leave him with me. Go out and buy the food. Dinner at seven o'clock, please."

"Yes, *miláčku*, but under protest."

∞ ∂ ∞

Ruth was the only one who had dressed up: she wore a low-cut sequin-studded silk blouse above a clinging purple skirt. Laci and Janko took Pavel to play hide and seek one last time in the deserted downstairs store where, for once, nothing was shipshape and everything was dusty. Ruth took the little boy to bed and told him stories until he fell asleep.

To Willy's delight, Sophie overcame her annoyance at having to cook, and with Ruth's assistance, she surpassed her limited culinary skills by serving sweet and sour cabbage soup and a creamy veal *pörkölt* stew with *nokkedli* followed by his favorite, a Dobos sponge cake. They ate by candlelight, the warm glow in the dark room insulating them from the sinister sounds of the occupation: the curfew siren, rumbling tanks, and the shouted challenges of German sentries. Afterwards, while Ruth washed the dishes, Willy took out two bottles of Tokay. It was time to drink up what was left in the cupboard.

"So." Janko stretched his long legs and lit a cigarette. "We're having a secular Seder. Goodbye and blessings all round before the exodus to a mystery country. I was expecting some details of what you had in mind for Laci and me..."

"I bless you all, and I wish you bon voyage," Ruth interrupted, somewhat tipsily waving her glass, her painted lips curved into an expression of regret. "I have good news for you, because I'm also leaving. In two days, I will travel first class to Italy with a new admirer, Enrico Falco. Hermann Glessgen, the new protectorate commissioner for Czech film production, introduced me to him at a party. Enrico owns an umbrella factory in Turin, and he's very close to Il Duce."

Sophie gave a nervous laugh. "Don't you feel a little bit ashamed? Leaving Prague under Axis protection?"

Ruth nodded. "Absolutely, I'm ashamed, and I don't care a damn. Who in their right mind wants to stay here? These days each one of us must make the most of our opportunities. But I shall miss you all terribly, especially darling Pavel."

Willy picked at the glossy caramelized top of his Dobos

cake. "Like Ruth, we leave the day after tomorrow: destination London, and then maybe America." He reached across and took Ruth's hand, fixing her with a hard stare. "I know how you like to gossip. You must promise to keep this completely to yourself for the next forty-eight hours."

She bent her head submissively and kissed his fingers, leaving traces of lipstick on them. "I promise—really. Now I'm ready to say good-bye." Sophie and Ruth got up from the table and put their arms around each other for a final embrace.

ᘒ ∂ ᘒ

After Ruth had gone back to her apartment, Sophie cleared the table while the men refilled their glasses with *Tokaji*.

"So what about us, cousin?" Janko paced about the room, his face all frowns. "We have no future here, and we don't have exit visas. We're trapped. How did you get exit visas?"

Willy's eyes twinkled behind his glasses. "Look, I apologize for leaving everything till the last minute. First of all, Sophie and I don't actually have Czech exit visas. For that, we would have had to supply six copies of a sixteen-page application, three identification photos, birth, marriage, and citizenship certificates, a character reference, and municipal proof of residence and then sit waiting three months for approval." Willy took a breath. "So, no exit visas."

"How the devil will you—or we, for that matter—get across the border?" Laci frowned.

Willy arched an eyebrow. "Luckily, your cousin Willy comes galloping to the rescue. Sophie, Pavel, and I are de facto Hungarians—and, as it happens, so are you."

Laci's eyes widened, and then he jabbed a forefinger at Willy's head. "Hungarians! *Meshuganah*. The boss is mad."

"You probably remember that a while back, I asked you to get me passport-style photos because I had to renew your employee identification papers?"

The two young men glanced at each other and nodded.

"I'm sorry, but that was pure deceit. Those photographs are in your new Hungarian passports. You can now travel freely through any place controlled by the Third Reich. No visa necessary. Come with us to Budapest."

A rare, enthusiastic smile spread over Janko's long face.

He rose to his feet and held his glass high. "*Ei, ei*, boss, this is incredible news."

Laci leaned across the table and slapped Willy hard on the back, making him wince. "*Ein guter mensch*. Just like your father, you're a *Macher*; you always keep an eye out for us Kohuts. Now all we need are enough shekels to buy our way out of this shit place."

"Laci, don't say that. Prague is beautiful." Sophie gave him a sad look. "Or was."

"I'll come with you as far as Budapest," Janko told Willy and sat down again, his face twitching with excitement. "I have Zionist friends there who are being smuggled out on a sauerkraut barge on the Danube going to Galati in Romania and then the Black Sea. I'll try and join them, get to Palestine."

Laci smiled apologetically. "Count me out. I'm staying to work with the resistance." He pulled his jacket open to reveal a badge sewn on the left side of his pullover.

Sophie peered at it. "An upside down shield in the national colors? What does NS mean?"

"*Smrt Němcům*, death to the Germans."

Willy gave his cousin's arm an admiring punch. "I envy you, you know. If I didn't have a family, I would be doing the same thing except I wouldn't be rash enough to wear that thing."

Sophie frowned. "That's enough brave talk, gentlemen. Janko, can you bring all your clothes and a suitcase here in the morning? I have to sew Hungarian labels on everything."

Willy pulled two passports and envelopes out of his jacket pocket and slid them across the table. "Time to complete our business, cousins. You need to memorize your new profiles." Laci gave a whistle of surprise as he and Janko examined the documents, raising their eyebrows at each other.

Willy glared. "Concentrate now, boys. Same names but you were both born in Hungary in the town of Szécsény, Nógrád County, close to the Slovak border. The town is in the middle of the Ipoly Valley. The place has five thousand inhabitants, mainly agricultural. It boasts a fine baroque palace, the Forgach, and is the home town of Arnold Schönberg's father. That's probably enough; the rest you have to invent."

Laci shrugged, nonplussed. "Who is Schönberg?"

Janko glared at his brother. "The famous composer, idiot."

"Of course, you fellows are welcome to travel with us to Budapest, but after that, we go our own ways. You talked of needing shekels, Laci. So here, whether you come with us or not, there's money in these envelopes—enough Reichsmarks to keep you out of mischief and hunger for two to three weeks."

"I'm sorry I won't be able to escort you to Budapest," said Laci as he and Janko opened the envelopes and riffled through the banknotes with appreciative nods. "I'm moving to the countryside to be trained in radio transmission and how to handle small arms. No idea where yet."

Janko tucked the banknotes into his wallet and lit a cigarette. "Willy and Sophie, you damned well amaze me. You've just lost your fine business and home, but you both seem almost joyful at leaving Prague. Have you no regrets or bitterness, nostalgia for what might have been?"

"My family is in Australia," said Sophie, massaging her husband's shoulder. "There's nothing left for us here except danger. Why not wipe the slate clean?"

Willy picked an apple out of the fruit bowl and, with a wry smile, held it up by its stalk. "One can look at our life here as a partly spoiled apple. Discard the decayed flesh but the rest is crisp and sweet. That's the part we'll take with us."

Laci stood and began to put on his jacket. "Time for us to say goodbye," he said somberly. His face flushed and his eyes were sad, but he forced a smile at Willy. "Your family has been very good to us. For twenty years, Uncle Emil paid for my father's doctoring and my mother's rent, and then when you opened the business in Košice, you gave Janko and me work— even though the wages were ....well, only just sufficient, ," he added with a rueful grin,

Willy got up. "We did our best for you, you know."

Laci embraced Willy. "Onkel Emil and Tante Judita are in London, and here we are leaving our homeland, off in different directions. Who knows what will happen to us in the end? Somehow, whatever happens, wherever in the world, we must try to stay in touch." He kissed Sophie on both cheeks and paused again by the front door. "Say goodbye to Pavel for me. No more hide-and-seek in the storeroom."

Janko rose from his chair and picked up his coat. "And I will be here in the morning with my suitcase packed."

⋘ ∂ ⋙

In the living room, the leather suitcases were open, await-ing their final layers of clothes. Sophie sat down to make a list in a small notebook of what they were taking. Willy sat at the splintered desk sorting and discarding bills and docu-ments, putting to one side all the letters from Sophie's father in Australia and his parents in London. He wanted to bring them on his journey, precious relics now.

"Later, I'm going to telephone Venter," said Willy, "the fellow Father said smuggles other people's valuables from Budapest to Holland."

Sophie looked up from her list, and the notebook slid from her lap. "How does he do it?"

"He has a car. He drives back and forth between the two countries. People pay him. I think I could persuade him to take us."

Sophie looked alarmed. "You can't be serious. Through Germany? Hungarian Jews traveling among Nazis. I can't think of anything more dangerous and terrifying."

Willy laid a hand on her shoulder. "Very dangerous for Czechs but not for Hungarians—you know, driving on the auto-bahn is the safest way. The train is always risky, patrolled by police— all kinds of people asking for your papers. It's impos-sible to stop a two-year-old like Pavel from speaking Czech. A passenger might inform on us."

"But, for God's sake, *miláčku*, why through Germany? That is madness. There must be other routes from Budapest. We are trying to escape the Nazis, not jump right back into their arms." She shook her head violently. "I don't understand your thinking."

Willy dropped his torn-up correspondence in the waste-basket and twisted round to face her. "Crazy, perhaps, but it's the quickest and probably least dangerous way. Driving through Germany will take only a day or two, and there's less risk of being stopped by the police than if we took the train. The other option is to go north and slip illegally into Poland, then try to board a ship for Scandinavia at Gdansk. Alternatively, we could copy Janko's idea and hide on a barge that takes six weeks to float down the Danube to the Black Sea. At least this Venter fellow will take us on a route he knows. He'll be our driver and guide. That's a huge advantage, worth every Reichsmark we pay him."

Willy looked at his watch. Eleven o'clock—good chance of Venter being home. He got up from the settee, walked to the wall phone, dialed the Prague exchange, and was soon connected to the Budapest number he requested.

"Here is Martha Harsanyi. Who is this?" A harsh, smoker's voice; the tone was hesitant, suspicious, almost antagonistic.

"Good evening, Mrs. Harsanyi," he said firmly, not liking the hostile tone of her voice. "Forgive the lateness, but this is an urgent matter. I am calling from Prague. I believe that Mr. Andreas Venter is staying with you. My name is Kohut Willy. I am a distant relative of his from Lučenec in Slovakia. Andreas will know who I am."

"Kohut Willy, you say?" She sounded reassured by the explanation of family connections.

"Yes, yes. I'm calling from Prague."

"Please wait a minute."

Willy heard conversation and music in the background and recognized a familiar violin concerto. A gramophone? Or the radio? Was it Mendelssohn? Somehow, the charm of the music made him feel hopeful.

"Yes?" A male voice, brisk and guttural. "Venter here. What do you want?"

"Hullo, my name is Kohut Willy. I am from Lučenec in Slovakia and more recently Prague. My father, Emil Kohut, gave me your number. He told me you are a distant relative."

"Maybe. I do not care much for relatives. What do you want?"

"My father said you convey valuable merchandise and people to Holland... for a fee."

"Merchandise, yes. People, no. Why should I help you?"

"Well, for a start, I'm a relative. I want to take my family to Holland. What if I paid you a lot of money?" There was a long pause, and then Willy heard the man clear his throat.

"You are calling from Prague. So you're Czech, not Slovak."

Willy heard a cynical chuckle but could not understand the man's logic. The fear of being rejected and losing this chance clutched at Willy's throat. "When could we meet—somewhere in Budapest?"

"You're fucking crazy, Kohut. Czechs cannot leave the country. You're trying to set me up for something."

"This is no setup, Venter. Whatever it takes to meet you in Budapest, I'll do it. Guaranteed."

There was a pause. "Maybe. Anyway, I leave for Holland tomorrow. I'll be back Saturday."

"Three days' time, then. That's good. Where can we meet?" Willy's mind was whirring with logistics. Everything was ready for the journey: train tickets, clothes almost packed, and Sophie had put aside canned food just in case. He had wrapped a silk scarf around the Czech passports, their birth and marriage certificates, and the proof of his ownership of Anglotex, and Sophie had sewn it all into the lining of one of the smaller suitcases. Willy had locked Kohut Stoffe store tight. The chaos inside was waiting for the unsuspecting new owner. As for their apartment, the concierge at 19 Masna Street told Sophie that a new tenant was moving in: a wealthy Jewish doctor, Erwin Froehlich by name, and his family.

There was a long pause on the line, with just music in the background. Willy recognized it now: Mendelssohn's *Violin Concerto in E Minor*. The violin had such a pure tone; he reasoned it had to be Jascha Heifetz.

"Are you still there, Kohut? OK, we can meet. You buy me dinner at Gundel on Saturday night at eight. Come alone, mind. When you get there, ask Alexi, the *maître d'hôtel*, for my table. He knows me. Bring the equivalent of thirty thousand korun in Reichsmarks or Hungarian pengö. If I like you and everything looks correct, I'll take you and your family to Holland."

Willy winced and sucked in a deep breath. His guess had been 20,000 korun, tops. His war chest was not big enough for this, and his calculations were off. There and then, he decided to keep this information from Sophie until he was forced to reveal it. Telling her now would only add to her anxiety about their journey to Budapest—and anyway, he might find a way to lower Venter's price.

"Very well," he said hesitantly. "Eight o'clock then, but I'll only bring half the amount: a deposit, fifteen thousand." Willy now realized that he would definitely have to leave his outstanding debts unpaid, perhaps for a long time; he felt bad for the good-natured Halač, who had done such a nice job remodeling

Anglotex, and the defunct Petschek Bank, which had put its trust in his business. *Unpaid debts are worms that rot the soul,* his father would have said. Perhaps that was true in the old days, Willy thought, but in a crisis you did what was necessary—and now that the Petschek was owned by the Dresdner Bank, his soul rejoiced at the thought that he was indirectly screwing the Nazis.

After a pause, the voice grunted. "Very well, we meet. And I want to see your documentation at the restaurant: passports and correspondence, preferably from your father, to make sure you are you."

"Certainly." The receiver shook with the tension in Willy's fingers. He tried to inject some levity into his voice. "In the same vein, I expect to see your passport, to make sure you are you. By the way, I'm curious. What's the violin concerto I heard playing in the background?"

"Ah, so you like classical?" Venter's voice gave a hint of warmth. "Wait a minute..." There was a moment of muffled talk away from the line. "It's Mendelssohn, in E minor."

"Good, I was right. Well, thanks, Venter. Gundel at eight, Saturday." Willy felt a surge of hope as he put down the telephone. Even though he did not believe in God, miracles or magical thinking, he could not help wondering whether his recognition of the Mendelssohn concerto might be a lucky sign. Come hell or high water, he was determined that Andreas Venter was going to be their way out of Hungary.

19

LEAVING PRAGUE
JUNE, 1939

THE TAXI DEPOSITED the family at the great stone and
steel Secessionist structure of Franz Josef Station, crowned by
its glass cupola. They were dressed unremarkably in well-worn
clothes…nothing gaudy or too fashionable. Everyone except
Pavel wore a hat to hide their faces as much as possible; Willy
had his black Homburg, Janko a battered trilby and Sophie had
made herself a wide brim felt cloche, securely fastened with
a long hatpin. Surrounded by travelers streaming toward the
ticket counters and platforms, Willy looked for someone with a
cart to help them, but he saw only one or two porters, and they
were busy. He studied the clicking departure board." Ah, there
is the Bratislava train. See, platform 4A."

"Come on," Janko shouted above the blaring loudspeaker
announcements and the clatter and hissing of locomotives. He
was frowning. "Let's get to the train. We don't have much time."

Willy shook his head and grimaced at their luggage. "Get
us a cart, Janko; I won't be able to carry much."

It took Janko a good five minutes to locate a spare trolley, and after he had stacked the suitcases, he lifted a smiling
Pavel on top. As Willy started pulling the cart, Janko followed
with a suitcase in either hand, and the boy, wearing a toy-filled
khaki pack on his shoulders, began sliding and slipping, unable
to find a stable spot.

"Pavel, hold on tight to those string bags," said Sophie, with an anxious look. She was carrying her purse and the food basket. "Don't let go, whatever you do."

As they approached the platform and began the search for their assigned carriage, Pavel clung to his suitcase throne, seemingly hypnotized by the clanking and the bursts of steam from the locomotive.

"Here we are." Willy smiled, but his heart gave a sudden lurch. Ten meters away, half hidden by the crowd, he spotted two Nazi officers in dark uniforms. They were talking to a small man in a black leather coat who had his back half-turned. It was Altmann. Willy could tell from Sophie's wide eyes and trembling chin that she had recognized him as well. "Don't look round," he said grimly as he lifted Pavel down from the cart, wincing as he caught his fingerstall in the netting of a string bag. He tilted the homburg to hide more of his face, while at the same time keeping an eye out for Altmann. "Come on, Janko, fast as you can, get on the train and help me lift the luggage up the steps. Sophie, you go first with Pavel and find our seats."

In the compartment, Janko, being the tallest, took on the job of pushing the suitcases onto the overhead racks and organizing the space to accommodate the hand luggage, bags, and coats. To give him room, Willy, holding Pavel in his arms, stood in the corridor along the side of the carriage overlooking the platform.

Sophie stood beside him. "Why is Altmann here?"

"God knows. Best get inside the compartment," Willy murmured. "Tell Janko to keep his head down, and nobody look out of the windows." He wondered whether Altmann's presence on the platform was a coincidence or if it presaged some horrible setback. He looked at his watch. "Ten minutes before we leave. I hope to God he didn't see us."

When he looked up, Altmann had disappeared—and Janko as well.

Pavel jabbed a finger into Willy's cheek. "Bad men, *táto*," he said, pointing to a couple of soldiers with rifles slung on their shoulders chatting among the milling passengers.

"*Guten Tag*, Herr Kohut."

Willy jerked around. Just two meters away, Herr Altmann stood in the carriage corridor, a cigarette between his gloved fingers. They stared at each other as passengers with suitcases and bags squeezed by, murmuring excuses.

Willy tried his best to appear calm, but his bones had turned to jelly. "This is a surprise, Herr Altmann. Are you here because of us, or is this just a coincidence?"

The Gestapo official drew closer to Willy, flattening himself against the side to let other passengers in the corridor ease past. Altmann squeezed up on the other side. "Molnar Havel, the Post Office official you told me about. Remember? Have you seen him?"

At that moment, Sophie appeared at the compartment door. She froze when she saw the Gestapo officer, and Altmann gave her an appreciative smile. "A pleasure to renew your acquaintance Frau Kohut. You are well I trust. You look quite charming today."

Willy watched as she tried to speak, but nothing came from her half-open mouth.

Altmann swiveled his gaze back to Willy. "I understand you just sold your store."

Willy nodded. He yearned to make some acid comment about what had happened to him at the bank, but held back.

Altmann stepped forward to scan the compartment. "This is the Bratislava train, isn't it? I was informed that you were leaving for a long stay in Ružomberok. You are taking a very roundabout route to get there, wouldn't you say?"

"First we visit friends in Bratislava," said Sophie quickly, edging forward to fill the doorway. "My husband studied piano there."

"Ah, yes, the lovely Bechstein." Altmann looked down at Willy's fingerstall and grabbed Willy's lapel, pulling him close. Willy reflexively jerked back. It revolted him to be so close to his tormentor. "Now that you will be away for a while, Herr Kohut, I'm sure you won't mind lending it to me. I do rather miss making music. With your permission, I will arrange its transfer to my apartment. When should I expect to return it?"

Willy tried to suppress the hot rage that almost choked him. He was unlikely to see his precious Bechstein again. "In three or four months," he muttered, looking away, keeping up the pretense of traveling to Ružomberok.

By the way," Altmann said with a sneer. "I have some news

of your erstwhile friend, the criminal, Hans Lessig."

Willy stiffened. He yearned to knee the German in the groin and stamp on his twisted face. Altmann laughed. "He was identified by our people in Lichtenstein, close to the Swiss frontier, making travel inquiries about trains...obviously trying to get into to France or Holland. A very slippery customer, your Lessig. He swindled the Third Reich out of a lot of money. Don't worry, we'll get him."

Sophie shuddered and turned away at the mention of Lessig. "Going to Ružomberok, are you?" Altmann dabbed a glove at his wasted cheek where wetness oozed from the drooping eyelid. "Wise decision. You will avoid the many problems Prague Jews will soon be facing." He clicked his heels and lifted his wrist in a limited Nazi salute.

As the German walked away, Sophie slid her arms around Willy and burrowed her face into his neck with a muffled, "Thank God."

There were shouts on the platform. A whistle blew, followed by the audible blast of steam from the engine. Groups of people on the platform began to wave goodbye.

"We're off." Willy's eyes glowed with relief as he kissed Pavel's cheek. He was sweating profusely. "Janko has to be on the damned train somewhere. He gave Sophie's shoulders a reassuring squeeze. "Go and sit down, strudel, dear," he said. "Pavel and I will stay in the corridor and watch the outskirts of Prague go by." He needed the comfort of the boy in his arms to come down from the cage of fear erected by Altmann.

Just then, murmuring a greeting, an elegant, small woman, a lavender straw hat perched atop bobbed hair and a silk scarf wound round her neck, pushed past Willy into the compartment. She carried a soft leather suitcase. Nodding a greeting to Sophie, she sat down in one corner and lifted up a fine black veil to remove her hat. Willy glanced back at Sophie. He knew what she was thinking: the woman was probably harmless, but with false passports, they would have to be careful what they said or did. No one could be taken for granted, not even Janko, who had disappeared. *Where the hell is he?*

As the train shuddered and began to gather speed, Willy put Pavel down and gazed back at the families on the diminishing platform waving colored handkerchiefs and hats of all shapes and sizes. He wondered who would be safer or better off in a year's time: the passengers on this train or their loved ones on the platform.

Just as Willy was about to follow Pavel back into the compartment, a breathless Janko came lurching along the corridor, weaving in and out between passengers, a smile on his face. In his hands, he held a stack of pancakes, double-wrapped in wax paper. The heavenly smell of hot pancake and apricot jam filled the compartment. Pavel reached up, eyes flaring with anticipation. "Please," he said in Czech. "I want..."

"Oh, *palacsinta*, so delicious," Sophie said in Hungarian, clapping her hands.

Willy laughed at the incongruity—the seesaw of evil and good, Altmann to pancakes. "A brilliant last-minute idea, Janko."

Janko sat down, putting a small suitcase on his knees to make a stable surface. He spread apricot jam on the top pancake with a wooden spatula, rolled it up and handed it to Pavel. The boy stuffed it into his mouth, smearing apricot jam all over his face and on his shirt. Janko offered a pancake to the elegant stranger, but she smilingly shook her head.

"Very kind, but too messy for me," she said in Hungarian, looking around at the Kohuts. "You have a lovely little boy. Even though he's so messy." Her laugh was like tinkling bells.

For four uneventful hours, the train passed through rolling countryside, and then industrial Brno as it rattled toward Bratislava. Lulled by the train's regular sway and clatter and exhausted by the rushed packing, the travelers slept much of the time.

Sophie opened her eyes and noticed that the stranger, who looked to be in her fifties, was awake. Sophie's offer of some cake and a peach was accepted and, as they ate, they chatted in Hungarian. Sophie commented on the elegance of the woman's fringed dress and charming felt hat. "You have such exquisite taste, *madám*. Where did you buy your clothes, in Prague or Budapest?"

"In Vienna, actually," the woman said with a smile. "If you like, I could give you the address of a wonderful dressmaker there. She gives discounts for beautiful women who are willing to be photographed for magazines. You are pretty enough to qualify, I think."

Sophie blushed, happy for the compliment. "You are too kind. I do not think we will be going to Vienna any time soon. Allow me to introduce myself. I'm Kohut Sophie." They shook hands.

"Well, my dear, I'm delighted. My name is Horváth Ilse. Are you all going as far as Budapest? Is it business or pleasure?"

Sophie flushed, remembering the cover story she had rehearsed with Willy many times in the last few days. *If you tell a lie,* her mother used to say, *always keep close to the truth.* Sophie looked down at her hands, not wanting her face to betray any deception. "My husband has a store in Prague. He sells luxury fabrics for men's clothes. We're visiting friends in Budapest for a funeral."

Madám Horváth's eyes widened and she covered her mouth with a gloved hand. "Oh dear, I am sorry. How sad. My husband and I are from Salgótarján, on the eastern border with Slovakia. Egon is a career officer in the Honvédség—you know, the Homeland Defense Force. We have lived there for a long time. Have you heard of the town?"

Sophie gulped in astonishment. "Know it, Madám Horváth? I was born there. My father, Ligeti Zoltan, was an engineer at the coalmines until Siemens in Berlin hired him. They sent him to Moscow but I grew up in Berlin." Madám Horvath's eyes glowed with interest. She nodded. "How is it then that your lovely boy speaks only Czech?"

Sophie felt her pulse racing. This woman seemed so very nice, but she was inquisitive. Would she say anything that might endanger them when the police made their inspection at the frontier? "Pavel, yes, he was born in Czechoslovakia... We've been in Prague quite a while."

"Tsk, tsk." Madám Horváth frowned a little. "Isn't it time he started learning his mother's tongue as well?"

"You're absolutely right. Well past time."

ඏ ∂ ඏ

In Bratislava, they changed trains to catch the Vienna express on its way to Budapest. Madám Horváth invited herself to share the next phase of their journey, and after receiving signals from Willy that they should not object, Sophie told her they would be honored to have her company.

The older lady turned out to be a cultured and entertaining travel companion who spoke easily about subjects ranging from the art of breeding Vizsla hunting dogs to the books of Dezsö Kosztolányi and the hot jazz of Django Reinhardt. Here was a woman to be admired, thought Sophie: elegant, clever, and worldly in her own right, not necessarily because of her husband's high position. Sophie wondered how Madám Horváth had risen to this pinnacle, the self-assured wife of a senior military officer. It was a pity they would part ways soon. She would have welcomed a chance to learn the secret of carving out a rewarding life within the constraints of what was probably a traditional Hungarian marriage.

ⅭⅩ ∂ ⅭⅩ

The train stopped close to the border at Esztergom, and they waited in their seats for customs and passport control. An overweight, blue-uniformed customs official entered the compartment, whistling some tune under his breath. He asked some harmless questions and then for a long moment focused his eyes on the two attractive women. He resumed his whistling and departed without examining anything.

He was followed by two *csendörs* with impassive expressions. The Hungarian gendarmes in uniform and plumed black hats carried Mannlicher carbines slung on their shoulders. They spent some time examining the Kohuts' passports. "These passports," one of them said, looking suspiciously at Willy. "How long have you had them?"

"I don't know the exact date, but it was sometime last November." Willy felt pleased that he had reviewed the passports in detail while sitting in the rail car toilet just an hour earlier. All the same, the fear he had felt with Altmann wormed its way back into his head.

The *csendör* nodded and was handing back the passports when Pavel spoke. "*Krásný vojak.*" He pointed at the one of the officials with a melting smile. "Beautiful soldier."

The more senior *csendör* standing at the compartment door stiffened, raising his gloved hand—a stop gesture. He glanced at his colleague. "Wait a minute, Kornél. This child speaks Czech. Take another look at their passports."

The other officer studied the passports carefully in the silent compartment before pointing a finger at Willy. "Except for this older lady, you must all descend from the train while we examine your luggage."

Willy sent Sophie a desperate now-it's-your-turn glance. This was something they had talked about; with her perfect accent and Hungarian origins, she would be the one to respond if they were challenged on the train. He noticed that Madám Horváth was looking at him with eyebrows raised, her head tilted to one side. His stomach knotted. She knows the truth.

"Excuse me, sir," Sophie said. "We live in Prague. That is why the child speaks Czech. I am from Salgótarján. My husband took Hungarian citizenship when we married. We are attending a funeral in Budapest and we must stay on this train. A delay would be terrible. Please, please, let us go on."

The *csendőr* looked at her with narrowed eyes and then questioningly at his older comrade.

Madám Horváth rose from her seat. Willy scrutinized her face for some clue of what she might be about to say, praying she would not inadvertently betray them.

"Pardon me, officer," she said calmly, showing him her passport again. "You will see that I am married to Major-General Horváth of the Second Motorized Brigade. A war hero. You have heard of him, yes? We live in Salgótarján, the same town this young woman is from. Why do you think we are sitting here together, eh?"

The second *csendőr*, looking nervous, nudged the older officer. "Come on, Miklós, let's leave them be. I don't want unnecessary trouble."

For what seemed like an age, the two *csendőrs* stood awkwardly at the compartment door, looking at each other and then at the seated passengers. Finally, the older gendarme saluted and they left.

Two long minutes later, the train began to move. Madám Horváth smiled at Sophie, hands folded on her lap. "Now we are in Hungary, my dear. Everything will be all right." Sophie mouthed a silent 'thank you', and then closed her eyes in gratitude and relief.

Leaning across from his seat, Willy gently took Madám Horváth's hand and kissed it. "Thank you very much. You helped us avoid a difficult moment."

"Why not? I was glad to do it. Why should they ruin your journey and make a mess of your luggage? It's so unnecessary."

As the express rattled its way to Budapest, Willy took Sophie out into the corridor and gave her a long embrace of relief. She wrinkled her nose. "You are perspiring too much, *miláčku*. Please, do not sit close to Madám Horváth. She won't enjoy talking to you."

"What do you expect?" He gave an apologetic shrug. "After what we've just been through? My congratulations, strudel. With your presence of mind and that kind woman's help, we squeezed through the first hurdle. Obviously, we need to get better at presenting ourselves as Hungarians. We can't rely on luck and a stranger's help."

Sophie nodded, twiddling a curl, looking distracted. "Yes, we can practice in the hotel. Oh dear, I forgot. Where did you say we're staying?"

"In the rush to leave Masná Street, I forgot to book a room," said Willy, shamefaced, "but Madám Horváth mentioned the Rákóczi Hotel on Szép utca. We'll try that tonight. If it's nice, we'll make that our headquarters. Anyway, tomorrow I have a full agenda: checking routes to the west, train schedules, visa requirements, and I want to change koruny at the bank before that dinner meeting with Venter at Gundel."

"Well, I want to take Pavel to see Magda and her children. It might be our only chance to get together, but Pavel and I could help you with errands in the morning."

"Maybe." Willy nodded, cupped her cheek and nuzzled her ear. Now that the dangerous part of their journey was over, the desire he had felt in the last two weeks had returned. He found himself admiring the way she moved, her breasts and shapely legs. They had tried to make love a couple of times in the previous week but his pain and Sophie's apparent reluctance had aborted the attempt. He wondered if she found his injuries unappetizing. Understandable of course, and a difficult thing to talk about. That night in the Rákóczi Hotel, he would try again, hoping that it would for once be successful.

For the past month, the delicacy and tenderness of the newly grown skin around his belly and genitals had consistently sabotaged his desire and performance. The inadequacy and shame he felt had begun to spill over into his daytime thoughts. In bed, Sophie always seemed worried that sex would damage him in some way, whispering as she caressed him, "Are you all right, *miláčku*? Don't force yourself, darling. Maybe we should wait longer?" For this disgrace, Willy could thank Altmann and his thugs. It was high time he proved he could be a proper husband again.

Later, Madám Horváth shared a small bottle of peach brandy from her capacious bag to celebrate their impending arrival in Budapest. When the train finally slowed at the edges of the city, Sophie and Willy embraced her and once again thanked her for helping them.

"Goodbye, nice people," she smiled, putting on her hat and pulling its fine veil down over her elfin face. Janko had taken her small suitcase down from the rack. "I must catch my train to Salgótarján. This was a most interesting and entertaining journey. What a pity you have to attend a funeral in Budapest. The city is a place to have fun. At least you won't be in Prague looking over your shoulder for Nazis."

20

BUDAPEST
JUNE, 1939

SATURDAY, THE KOHUTS' first day in Budapest, began with an emotional breakfast at the Rákóczi Hotel. "Time for me to leave you," Janko said, his face even more mournful than usual. "My 'sauerkraut' barge is being loaded at Százhalombatta, a few miles downriver; it leaves late this afternoon." He tucked a couple of sweet breakfast rolls into his jacket pocket and circled the table to kiss everyone. Sophie wept and Pavel looked anxious, unsure of what was going on.

As Janko bent to pick up his suitcase in the reception area, Willy hooked the strap of the battered fiddle case over his cousin's shoulder. "Don't be shy about playing, Janko. Music is as good as money at getting you out of scrapes. Good luck, anyway. I think it will be a while before we meet again. Maybe in London. You have Father's address?"

Janko nodded, and then he was gone.

Willy went back into the dining area to rejoin Sophie, who still held Pavel on her lap. She was dabbing at her eyes with his jam-stained napkin. "Such a sweet man," she said. "Always quiet and gentle. I'll miss him."

"Especially his music." Willy sat down beside her, and Pavel reached out to touch his father's face, as if he were not quite sure whether his father would be leaving like Janko. "Bye-bye, *táta*." There was silence for a moment.

"So," said Sophie, smiling and wiping away her tears. "I'm going to telephone Magda. We have a lot to catch up on, and I'm sure Pavel will love playing with her brood. What about you? Come and meet us at Magda's this afternoon."

Willy consulted a scrap of paper he had pulled from his breast pocket. "Okay, I've got some errands to do: change money into Reichsmarks and Swiss Francs, go to the library, and check the German road maps so I know what route I'm negotiating about with Venter. Also, in the event that my meeting with him does not work out, I will check the train schedules to Paris and Amsterdam. In addition, I want to find out if there is still a chance that the Dutch and French Embassies here are issuing transit visas. We'll need them at the frontiers." He paused to catch his breath. "I should be able to come to Magda's by four."

"I wish I could help you with something."

Willy put a comforting hand on her knee. "You are helping. You're doing what a mother is best at."

⁂ ∂ ⁂

By the time Willy arrived at Magda's apartments, he had changed his koruny into Reichsmarks and a few French and Swiss francs, discovered that it was no longer possible to change money at railway stations, and experienced how slow and complicated banks were making financial transactions for foreigners.

At Ravelstein & Son, a numismatic and philatelic dealer near Gerbeaud's café, Willy bought two gold coins, an Emperor Franz Joseph gold crown, and a twenty-franc gold French Rooster for 500 Reichsmarks each. "Just in case, a hidden reserve, eh? In case you get robbed" the talkative, sharp-faced Mr. Ravelstein said, "These days most of my customers are refugees: buying or selling, usually selling."

Willy asked Mr. Ravelstein, who professed himself as Budapest's expert on refugee matters, for guidance on the easiest, least dangerous route out of Hungary. "If you have an official visa," said the dealer, mopping his brow— the dark clouds and humid air threatened a thunderstorm—"it's simple. Jump on a train north to the Baltic and then on to Scandinavia." He spread his hands sorrowfully. "But you probably know that the foreign embassies here have stopped issuing visas."

"But what if I wanted to get to the Low Countries or

France—through Germany?"

Ravelstein frowned. "Certainly foolish and damned risky. The trains are full of Wehrmacht troops, and the French and German borders teem with *Geheimstadt Polizei*. Jews are being arrested all along the German borders."

Willy's spirits sank. With Hungarian passports, they were free to enter and travel through Austria and Germany, but with no entry visa into France or Holland, they would probably have to scramble across the border illegally—probably at night, carrying their suitcases. It would be a hard and dangerous journey, beyond his experience. As he took the tram to Magda's apartment, he realized that his meeting with Venter was going to be crucial. Venter was the one who knew how to get them to Holland.

৵ ∂ ৵

At four, Willy collected Sophie and Pavel from Magda's. It was clear that they had enjoyed themselves and Pavel showed him a jointed soldier puppet. "Mine," he said proudly. Willy politely refused a coffee. From past experience, he could not cope with Magda for more than ten minutes; she was a well-meaning, overwhelming chatterbox who showered food on her guests, and was offended if they refused even the smallest pastry.

By seven thirty, they were in a pub around the corner from their hotel. Willy had ordered a beer and smiled as he watched Sophie and Pavel eat veal schnitzel, apple dumplings and a *puszta* salad of cabbage and red pepper pickles. Pavel played with his wooden puppet making more than the usual mess of his food." Mine," he said, bouncing the soldier's flexible legs across the table surface.

Willy nodded. "Very fine. Where did you get it?"

"Dav…dav…id."

Sophie smiled. "Magda's boy. He is eleven, too grown up to play with puppets."

Willy chuckled. "A wonderful gift, Pavel. You're a lucky boy."

"How did everything go for you today?" Sophie spooned more meat and vegetables on to her plate.

"A mixed bag. I got some depressing information about visas and trains. Foreign embassies in Budapest have stopped giving out visas, and nearly all the international train services have been cut back. I hope I can work something out with Venter this evening. The good news is that I changed most of the Czech money, though the exchange rate was awful. Still, we should have enough cash for most eventualities. All the same, if we're pushed, I might have to sell your jewelry."

Sophie's cheeks reddened as she gave him a sharp look. "I don't like your idea. Don't you think I deserve a say in what happens to my jewelry? Especially the pieces from my mother and grandmother."

Willy stared at her, rubbing the itch on his injured finger. "Don't be so contrary. I said 'if we're pushed.' I'm trying to deal with a lot of uncertainty here. We have to be flexible."

She gave him an imperceptible shake of the head. "I'm not being contrary. I just want to be more involved in your decisions. Do not forget, I had Pavel with me all day, and in the back of my mind, I kept wondering what you had managed to accomplish, whether you had found a way for us to get out. Am I supposed to be the only person who looks after Pavel? Couldn't you help out a little?"

Willy took her hand, trying not to show his irritation. Admittedly, a maid or a nanny had always looked after his son. Now that she was on her own, Sophie was probably feeling overwhelmed. All the same, Willy felt that his authority was being eroded. "Listen to me, strudel. Our life has changed drastically, and I suppose that applies to how we behave and deal with each other. I've done my best to make the right decisions for you and Pavel to be safe, but I have a strong impression that you don't think that's enough."

"That's right." She fixed him with a steady gaze, her chin defiantly tilted upwards. "Not so long ago I was an obedient housewife and mother from a bourgeois Prague family. Now everything has changed, and we are refugees about to run terrible risks; think of what nearly happened with those officials on the train from Prague. I need to be part of what's decided, before it's decided."

Willy cupped her chin affectionately with his good hand. What she said made sense, but he wondered whether in a real crisis, an emergency, he could trust her to act sensibly and bravely. "Well," he sighed, "except for keeping our home tick-ing over and supervising Pavel's needs, which were within your domain, I admit that I have always made the decisions for our family. I am the man of the household. That's what I learned growing up. So far, the arrangement has worked well. But I promise I'll try to involve you more in deciding what we do next."

"I'd like that."

"But just you be ready to take on a lot more active responsibility—I don't want you turning to me in every crisis, saying, 'Willy, what should we do now?'"

Sophie's lips parted in surprise. "I... I'm not sure what you mean about a lot more responsibility. Look, I am afraid of what is in store for us. I have nothing to hold on to except you and Pavel. I'm not proposing to take equal responsibility. I just want to know what you are thinking so we can talk things over. That's all."

Willy took her hand and kissed her fingers. "Thank you, dear. I think I understand now. We have cleared the air a little. And I will commit myself to look after Pavel if you ask me to." He looked at his watch. "Look, it's time I went back to the hotel to get dressed. I want to be punctual for my meeting at Gundel."

Sophie stopped in the middle of cutting her schnitzel and gave him a sharp look of reprimand. "There you are, exactly what I was getting at about being involved. You never asked me what I thought about your rendezvous with this Venter man and your crazy idea of escaping through Germany. Remember when you showed me your estimates of the money needed for our escape? You said we would only have enough if you did not pay off your debts, but I saw nothing written down about the estimated cost of a fancy dinner at Gundel's. Who is paying for that? How much does this Venter want from us?"

Willy shrugged. He was suddenly tired of the discussion, which seemed to be sliding into an argument, again. He was already regretting his willingness to involve Sophie in his decisions. It felt as though he had given in too easily and weakened his position in the family. Unlike him, Sophie was still young and inexperienced, and perhaps too self-centered. She was still learning her role as his wife. "Look, this meeting with Venter is delicate and crucial. I'm the one who made contact with him, and I'm making the deal for him to drive us, not you. I'll give you the details when I get back."

Saying nothing, Sophie began to cut up more food for Pavel.

Willy stood up and said, coldly, "Please, this is not the time or place to start to fight. There's something useful you could do while I'm out. I am sure you will have the time to do it. Have everything packed, just in case Venter agrees to take us. What if he wants to leave tomorrow?"

She nodded stiffly without looking at him.

∾ ∂ ∾

An hour later, Willy took a taxi to Állatkert Street. He was dressed in his double-breasted coal-gray pinstripe, a white silk shirt, and a tie. His leather briefcase carried 3,000 Reichsmarks, the two counterfeit Hungarian passports, his marriage certificate, and a letter from his father.

As the streets of Budapest sped by, he reflected on the altercation with Sophie and mulled over the recent changes in his marriage. When he had been down—physically weak, humiliated, and dispossessed—Sophie had shown strength, sprung him from jail, been a good mother to Pavel, and run Anglotex for a while. Now he was taking charge again. Marriage was like that, he concluded: an up-and-down system that stayed intact only if the partners worked at it. His parents' marriage had never been a seesaw like this. It had been more like a rope ladder where Emil always sat at the top, stopping Judita from climbing up to his level. Willy had always found his parent's situation objectionable; he hated watching his mother being ground down, but he was sure he was not replicating his father's attitudes. He would give Sophie her head when the time was right.

As Willy wound down the window to get more air, his thoughts turned to his meeting with Venter at Gundel, the expensive art deco restaurant. Everyone in Europe knew of Károly Gundel, the creator of dishes rivaling those of the greatest French chefs, and Willy was looking forward to something special. He had brought the agreed-upon deposit, but he knew his budget would not cover the amount Venter had quoted over the telephone. The prospect of failure gnawed at his stomach. The alternative destinations he had considered, Poland, Romania and Istanbul involved complicated and daunting routes by train and autobus and they were all places he had never visited.

The taxi stopped outside Gundel's wrought iron gates, and the driver opened the door, grinning. "It's a warm night, boss. If you are lucky enough to get a terrace table, you'll hear the elephants trumpeting at the zoo next door." The driver held out his hand. "That will be forty pengö."

Wincing at the amount, Willy paid and walked along the short gravel driveway, buoyed by the anticipation of an interesting meal at a famous restaurant. In front of him, gas *torchères* in the form of voluptuous nymphs illuminated the fan-roofed entryway. He pushed through glass-paneled doors engraved with the outline of an elephant and entered baroque splendor: elaborate gilt wall brackets, a dark blue plush carpet, and wainscoting covered in red and silver moiré satin.

He stood aside to let a group of jocular guests depart and caught the scent of expensive perfume, cigars, and rich food. *Hungarian bastards*, he thought bitterly, recalling how the previous November, Hungary, with Hitler's backing, had swallowed up his birthplace, southern Slovakia. Thank God, he had left Košice for Prague in time.

The concierge, a tall man in black tie and tails standing behind a high desk, looked up. "Good evening, sir."

"I'm meeting someone. Mr. Andreas Venter. My name is Kohut."

The concierge checked his roster. "Ah, yes, sir. You are expected. Please follow me to the *maître d'hôtel*."

Willy entered the ballroom-sized restaurant, his gaze drawn to the three majestic chandeliers suspended from a white coffered ceiling decorated with gilded plasterwork. The lower walls were paneled in polished rosewood. He surveyed the tables filled with well-dressed men and bejeweled women. Passing a table occupied by several men in high-collared, gray-green tunics, he felt another surge of anger: German officers. What were these bastards doing in Budapest?

"Good evening. I am Alexi, the *maître d'hôtel*. I will take you to Mr. Venter." The pear-shaped maître d' was surprisingly agile, avoiding the tray-balancing waiters in rustling, starched white aprons. Willy followed, taking note of the gaily dressed gypsy band playing on a small dais in one corner. *A mediocre violinist*, thought Willy, unlike Janko, who could make your heart shiver with joy or shatter with sadness. *Bon voyage with the sauerkraut, Janko.*

The maître d' directed Willy toward a small table set in an alcove partially hidden behind a tall, potted fern where Venter, an elongated man who looked to be in his early thirties, contemplated the crowded room. His stretched-out legs ended in a pair of black-and-white patent leather shoes. He wore a charcoal gray suit, a red silk shirt, and a spotted bowtie and he smoked a cigarillo. Venter seemed quite the opposite of what Willy had imagined when his father had described him as a crook.

Willy bowed. "How do you do?" he said in Hungarian. "I am Willy Kohut."

"Ah, Kohut, good to see you. But let's speak Czech." Venter blew out a stream of smoke. "I don't much like Hungarians or the way they talk. They are fascists. Always have been." He refilled his glass from a nearly empty wine bottle. "There are plenty of spies and fellow travelers here in Budapest, but at least the Nazis here aren't here pressing their boots on our necks."

"Very well, we talk in Czech." Willy took a seat. Venter was clearly opinionated and blunt.

For a moment, there was silence, and Willy was struck by Venter's odd physical appearance. Even seated, he appeared unnaturally tall, probably over two meters. Translucent skin, tight as a drum, covered his gaunt face. Scanty brown hair, slick with brilliantine, was parted in the middle and plastered over his collar at the back.

With one arm hooked over the back of his chair, Venter lifted up a glass of wine. "I was just about to order dinner. Join me in a glass of this excellent Egri Bikavér. Wine is the one item in which the Hungarians far outdo the Czechs." Venter's voice contrasted with his elegant appearance. It was hoarse, like a saw scraping on metal.

"Yes, I'm familiar with the wine. It is good. Thank you."

A waiter approached, bowed low, and with a flourish placed a menu embossed with a golden elephant in front of each man. "I will be back to take your order shortly."

"Bring another bottle," Venter called after the waiter. He turned his protuberant eyes to Willy. "You have the identification documents for me?"

Willy nodded and reached for his briefcase, still analyzing

his companion's odd appearance. The muscles of the Dutchman's temples and cheeks were thin and wasted, and his yellow skin stretched as tightly as parchment over the bones. How could he ever smile with skin as tight as that? What was this? A disease? Something inherited?

Willy handed over the passports, his marriage certificate, and the old letter from his father.

"Nice-looking passports," Venter grunted as he leafed through them. His wrists and skinny hands poked out like crab legs from his embroidered shirt cuffs. "They're forged, of course, but the technique is pretty good. Probably from Lugosi's workshop here in Budapest, but they should get you through most checkpoints. Oh, yes—and the child, Pavel, is on your wife's passport. Overall, everything looks acceptable. It appears you are who you say you are. By the way, why do you have that velvet covering on your right hand?"

Willy thought it best not to reveal any details about his time with the Gestapo. "I damaged my finger, that's all. It will heal in time."

Venter nodded. "Intricate little bit of embroidery on it—something medieval, I suppose? A dragon, perhaps? Now, let's order." He handed the documents back.

"Excuse me," said Willy, suddenly remembering what he needed to do. "I should like to see your passport now—and your Dutch driver's permit." Venter reached into his jacket and slid the documents across the table. Willy scanned them, nodded, and passed them back. "Why are you called Venter? My father said you came from my mother's side, the Waldmann family."

Venter winked. "The name has more of a Dutch sound. Better for the business I'm in."

The waiter returned and hovered expectantly beside the table, gloved hands clasped behind his back while Willy flipped the menu pages. "Your order, gentlemen?"

"They never write anything down," said Venter from behind his menu, and Willy wondered if the slurred way he spoke was the result of his unusual physical condition or too much wine. "I'll choose what Gundel does best. The smoked goose liver braised in *Tokaji Azsu* with truffles—a brioche on the side—and after that, fish. Lake Balaton Fogas, with all my usual accompaniments. What about you, Kohut? Remember, this is your treat."

Willy smiled. Just looking at the menu made his mouth water. "Please, the grilled goose liver with baked apple and sour cherries for the first course. Yes, then it will be... er... um." He looked up at the waiter. "Tell me more about the pork loin with morels?"

"That would be a good choice, sir." The waiter picked up the empty wine bottle. "The chef grills two substantial cuts of pork that have been marinated for twenty-four hours in raspberry vinegar. A cream sauce made with braised wild morels. We pour red wine over the meat just before serving. The dish comes with sauerkraut and lyonnaise potatoes."

"Sounds delicious. That would suit me fine."

The waiter smiled his approval and departed.

Venter rubbed his hands together expectantly and smiled. "So, Kohut, now that our dinner plans are set—to business. Tell me what you're after."

Willy forced a smile back. He looked around to make sure no one could overhear them and was reassured by the playing of the band and the privacy of the alcove. "As you know from my passports, I have a wife and a small child just under two years old. We want to get to England quickly. Holland first."

"That's possible." Venter scratched his chin with a long finger. "But first, you should know something about me. Officially, I am a buyer of antique timepieces, and I travel Central and Western Europe at the behest of important British and American collectors. The reality is that for select customers, I also transport valuables or money across borders. I hardly ever transport people."

The waiter appeared and opened another bottle of wine, pouring a glass for each guest.

Venter paused for an instant, allowing time for the waiter to get out of earshot. "My fee for taking you is forty thousand korun or four thousand Reichsmarks, give or take—and you also must pay for my food and lodging on the way."

Willy's stomach did a somersault. The fee was exorbitant; all he had was 7,000 Reichsmarks. He sucked in a long breath, thinking what paying out 4,000 Reichsmarks would do to his budget. After settling the Budapest hotel bill and paying Venter, there would not be much left when they reached Holland—

maybe 600 Reichsmarks apart from the gold coins he had just bought... and Sophie's jewelry. Her reddening face flashed into his mind, angry about her jewels and arguing about their relationship. What would she say when he told her about Venter's fee? He had to temporize, work something out to lower the fee. "On the telephone you quoted me thirty thousand korun; that's about three thousand Reichsmarks. Why has your fee gone up?"

Venter shook his head wearily, as if disappointed at his companion's lack of comprehension. "Kohut, my friend, have you looked at a map recently? It's a hellish long way to Amsterdam—over a thousand kilometers. It will take us two days or so to get there, more if we have to use the back roads to avoid police patrols. The main reason is that the price of petrol has gone up twenty percent."

In spite of the prospect of a large financial hole in his war chest, Willy still considered Venter's offer to have a key advantage: they would make a straight, short run from Budapest to Amsterdam, where they would end up very poor but safe. He sighed. "Very well, I'll pay what you ask. We would bring three suitcases and some hand luggage. Do you agree?"

Venter nodded, his smile stretching like an elastic band.

The waiter reappeared and set down a basket of warm rolls sprinkled with poppy seeds. A younger assistant placed a covered warming dish in front of the Dutchman. On a finely decorated Herend china plate, the waiter served Willy a fan of foie gras slices, nestled on a bed of caramelized apples and covered with dark cherry sauce.

"Let's eat." Venter rubbed his spindly hands together. "*Bon appétit.*"

Venter removed the lid of his dish. A whole foie gras was floating in *Tokaji* sauce. Willy watched his companion carve off a generous slice, place it with great care on a piece of brioche, and slide it into his mouth. The Dutchman's eyes dilated. "Superb," he sighed.

As he savored the bittersweet taste of foie gras mingled with the tartness of apples and sour cherries, Willy decided to focus on checking Venter's competence and trustworthiness rather than be drawn into a culinary discussion of sophisticated Hungarian cuisine.

"Listen, Venter, I need some details about your plan for

getting us into Holland. Give me an idea of the route you'll take."

Venter grimaced. He put his knife and fork down with clatter and jabbed a forefinger into Willy's face.

"*Do prdele*, shit, Kohut, you don't trust me, do you? Look, I have done this trip maybe thirty or forty times. I can drive it with my eyes shut. We travel from here to Vienna and then on to Munich. From there we take the new autobahn to Würzburg, on through Wiesbaden toward Koblenz and Köln. North of Aachen, we turn off toward the little towns—Alsdorf, Hillensberg, or Gangelt. Those last two are right on the Dutch border. The checkpoints there are sloppily managed, and their telephones are often out of order, which means the German police may have trouble checking with Berlin to see if your visas and papers are in order. You'll just have to trust me."

Willy nodded, reassured. That morning, he had visited the Szabo library at the Wenckheim Palace and pored over detailed maps of Europe, checking the most practical options for driving through Germany, crossing the frontier, and going on to Amsterdam. The route he worked out was close enough to Venter's description. It made sense.

"You have Dutch entry visas, I presume," said Venter as he resumed eating.

Willy shook his head. "The Dutch embassy has stopped issuing visas here in Budapest."

Venter threw down his silverware again, frowning. "Ei, ei, not a good fucking situation. With valid entry visas, crossing the German-Dutch frontier would be as easy as slicing soft butter. Without a visa, different story." He paused to dab his lips with a napkin. "I happen to know that the Dutch embassy in Munich is still doling out visas. We could stop for you to get visas in Munich on our way. Of course, that would lengthen our trip, to maybe two nights in Germany. In which case my fee rises to six thousand Reichsmarks plus lodging and expenses."

The pit of Willy's stomach felt like a deep hole. He grabbed the smuggler's arm. "Be a mensch, Venter. You just upped your price by two thousand Reichsmarks. That is big money. Too much. We are related, you and I, remember? Doesn't that count for something?"

Venter waved a long, denying forefinger. "Why should I

do favors for family people I don't even know? It's six thousand Reichsmarks for going via Munich to get visas. Take it or leave it. If you don't like my offer, go find yourself another courier."

Willy sipped his wine in silence, desperately thinking of a way to persuade his companion to take less. His mind went blank. It was hopeless. He rose from his chair. "Listen, Venter, six thousand Reichsmarks is ridiculous. We would be left with the barest margin, hardly enough to survive. This has been a waste of time. I'll pay for the meal and go home."

Venter grabbed his arm and pulled him back down with a smile. "Listen, distant cousin, it's a crime to leave in the middle of a fine dinner. Our dealing is over but I am enjoying your company. Why not make things interesting and fun? A wager, for instance? If you win, I'll drop my fee. What do you say?"

Willy sat down, mind whirring. *What is this fellow up to? Some trick?* "What's the wager?"

Venter waved his glass in the direction of the gypsy violinist who was serenading guests at their tables while his band played on the stage. "Let's bet on music. I remember you spotted Mendelssohn on the telephone. Myself, I am a lover of operettas. You may know your classics, but I'm willing to bet you don't know the gypsy repertoire."

"So, what's the wager?" Willy repeated, feeling a morsel of hope. He had played the piano for Janko's fiddling many a time, but he only knew the names of a handful of gypsy tunes.

"Give me the title of the next song the gypsy band plays, and I'll take you to Holland for only three thousand Reichsmarks. If you get it wrong, you pay me six thousand Reichsmarks, unless you want to cancel and stay in Budapest." He started a laugh that ended in a spasmodic coughing fit. "I'm betting that a man who can identify Mendelssohn by hearing just a few bars on the telephone will not also be an expert on gypsy music."

Willy shrugged. If he lost the wager, he and Sophie would have to come up with a new escape plan. "So be it—let's play your game. At least you're giving me a chance."

Venter pulled a pen from his pocket. "When the band plays the next tune, you write down the title on my napkin. After they're done, I'll call the fiddler over and ask him the title."

Willy nodded. Restaurant gypsy bands tended to repeat

old favorites night after night, so he had a chance. He had listened to Janko playing often enough.

When the band launched into its next number, with a flood of relief, Willy quickly recognized the melody. But what was the damned tune's title? He stared down at the table and closed his eyes, trying to concentrate, shutting everything else out. He had Venter's pen and the napkin, but he had no words to write down.

Venter waved a come-hither hand, and the swarthy, black-haired fiddler approached their table, sawing away at his instrument.

Venter turned to Willy. "So, my dear relative, what is the name of this tune? I see you haven't written anything down yet." He tucked a banknote into the man's waist sash. The fiddler bowed and smiled through a droopy mustache.

"No, wait. I...I think this song is called... *Csavargók*—Tramps." Willy gasped out, writing the word on his napkin.

"So, my friend," said Venter to the fiddler when the tune ended. He winked at Willy. "What is the name of the melody your band just played?"

The gypsy bowed. "*Csavargók*, your honor."

Feeling a surge of triumph, Willy opened his wallet and stuffed two banknotes into the folds of the gypsy's red sash. "*Köszönöm*, thank you, your honor." The fiddler moved on to another table as the band started up again.

Venter grunted and took a mouthful of wine. "I'm impressed, Kohut. You win—and I will take you and your family to Munich and Holland for three thousand Reichsmarks. Now give me fifteen hundred as a first installment, nonreturnable."

Willy nodded and reached for his wallet.

"Not in here," the Dutchman said in a low voice, pulling a cigarillo out of a shiny leather case. He bit off the end and spat it on the floor. "When we're outside. At least, you have shown me you have the guts to gamble. But are you willing to gamble on taking the trip?" Venter looked at Willy expectantly, amusement playing around his mouth.

Willy wondered how much he could trust this man. Not one hundred percent, for sure. Images swirled in his head: Venter handing them over to the *Staatspolizei*; Venter crashing through a fence into a ravine, Venter driving them to an isolated spot, pulling a gun, and robbing them. All Willy had to defend himself and Sophie, was the clasp knife in his briefcase. He would keep it in his pocket from now on. Perhaps he could buy a gun illegally the next day. "For a Jew like me", Willy said with a shrug, "the idea of driving through Nazi Germany is completely counterintuitive, not to mention crazy. Nevertheless, we'll come. When do we start?"

Venter was cleaning his teeth with a Gundel silver toothpick. "First thing tomorrow. Five o'clock."

Willy swallowed hard. *Gott behüte*. No time to do anything but pack and sleep a little—and Sophie would be outraged, even though he had prepared her for something like this.

"Write down your hotel address. I will pick you up. We will drive straight to Munich and try for your Dutch visas at the embassy. Listen. I do not want to be calling you *pane* Kohut all the time. Not if you're a relative."

"I'm Willy. Look, Venter, five in the morning seems very early. We've got to pack, get the child ready..."

Venter's face darkened into a frown.

"You pay, I organize. I am the boss on this journey. You and your family must do what I say, jump when I say, and pay when I say. Otherwise, there is no deal. At five o'clock, there's less stuff that tends to clutter the road: farm wagons, stray cows, geese and goats. If you are not there at the hotel on the dot, I will be gone. With your deposit."

After this outburst, the meal continued in relative silence, and Willy reflected on the suddenly revealed tough side of his dining companion. The man was unpredictable, a seemingly well-educated ex-Czech Dutch Jew who liked to take risks, gamble, and make easy money. Did that make him a liability, or just the fellow they needed? As long as he got them to safety, that was all that mattered.

The meal ended with Gundel's classic dessert: thin, flambéed pancakes flavored with raisins and lemon rind, stuffed with walnut purée, and covered in chocolate sauce.

Willy showed his Hungarian passport to the maître d' and wrote a Dresdner Bank check for the 380 Reichsmark bill, which he knew would bounce. He could not afford to part with any more of his ready cash. For the time being, the honorable way of treating his creditors had to be put aside. Swindling the Gundel restaurant was the fault of the Nazis and anyway, the Hungarian government was fascist.

Outside, in the warm, sticky night, they shook hands on the restaurant steps. Willy was pleased. He had gambled and won. He had a solid plan: drive with Venter through Germany to Holland—though there was no telling how the journey might turn out. He and Sophie would just have to work with the hand they had been dealt.

"Deposit time, friend," said Venter, towering over Willy as they shook hands. "I prefer Reichsmarks—fifteen hundred, if you please."

In the taxi on the way home, feeling overfed, slightly drunk, and sleepy, Willy reflected on the strong possibility that he might never see the unlikeable, spindly beanpole or his money again. He hoped luck would stay on their side.

Climbing the hotel stairs to their second floor room, Willy cursed at the thought of waking Sophie up and telling her that they were leaving at five in the morning in Venter's Mercedes. He had left her in a bad mood. What if she hadn't packed as he had asked?

No, it would be done. No reason to doubt her.

21

THE BLACK MERCEDES
JULY, 1939

AT DAYBREAK, dark clouds hung low over Budapest, their edges tinged with pink. Apart from street cleaners and the horse-drawn milk carts clattering along the cobbled streets, the city was still asleep. Surrounded by luggage in the hotel lobby, coats over their arms, Willy, Sophie, and Pavel were ready and waiting for Venter's Mercedes to arrive.

Willy paced the marble floor, trying not to reveal how tense he was, fearful that the Dutchman might not appear. He had hosted a lavish dinner with a bad check and turned over 1,500 precious Reichsmarks to Venter. If the man did not turn up, Sophie would be justifiably infuriated and, worst of all, they would have to find another way to leave Hungary. Willy circled the potted palm in the center of the small lobby, cursing at the vulnerability of their situation, with or without Venter.

They had not slept much that night. Pavel had woken a couple of times, frightened by something he could not or would not explain. It was not the first time. Pavel's night terrors had begun a month after Willy's arrest and had become more frequent. The boy had changed from a placid, happy child who ate and slept soundly to a two year-old who threw his food on the floor, often refused to obey or cooperate, and sometimes exploded into leg-kicking tantrums.

"I took him to the doctor while you were in Pankrác,"

Sophie had told Willy on his return from prison. "He said Pavel was physically quite normal and he explained the tantrums as not unusual for a two year-old. I suppose we'll just have to put up with it and try not to get too angry with him."

Willy stopped pacing the lobby and glanced at Pavel, who was crouched on his haunches, happily marching his toy soldier round the plant pots. "I have a feeling Venter's not used to kids, especially temperamental ones," he said to Sophie, who sat on an upholstered bench with her eyes closed. "We'll be on the road for many hours, and it won't be easy keeping the boy quiet. You'll be in the back with him. I want to keep a close eye on our driver."

Sophie jerked awake and glared at him.

Willy gave a fatalistic shrug; his woman was out of sorts at having to be dressed and packed by five in the morning. To be expected.

"I heard what you said." Her mouth twitched angrily. "But don't you think we could change places from time to time, to give me some relief from Pavel?" She looked at her watch. "Your man is late. Is this why we had to wake up at four?"

Willy shrugged again. He could not be responsible for everything. Since the dinner at Gundel, his thoughts had snagged on every little catch that might happen on this trip: an accident, a car breakdown, police checkpoints. What if Sophie could not tolerate the long hours and strain in the car journey? How would she react if something unforeseen occurred—or if Venter betrayed them? For the moment, Sophie's irritation at having to leave so early was the least of his worries. *Why the hell isn't Venter here?*

"Is that him?" Through the glass entry door, Sophie had spotted Andreas Venter getting out of his car. She looked away. "That face," she whispered. "He looks like one of those gargoyles from St. Vitus Cathedral in Prague... And he's so long and thin."

"I warned you," said Willy as they ferried their luggage— two large leather cases, one small cardboard suitcase, and string bags—to the bottom of the hotel steps where Venter was waiting. Willy was flabbergasted at the Dutchman's clothes: a blue linen jacket with gold buttons, a red silk scarf wound around his neck, slim dark blue pants, and suede boots. He wore a black fedora tilted to one side. The contrast between Venter's appearance and his warnings of danger the previous evening was inexplicable; the man had dressed like a Hollywood star. Willy glanced at Sophie, who was holding Pavel firmly in her arms, a look of incredulity on her face. He put a finger to his lips and shook his head: a warning to keep silent.

As they came down the steps, Venter swept off his hat in greeting and patted the hood of the Mercedes. "How do you like my lovely machine?" He paid no attention to Sophie and with a beaming smile opened the driver's door to show them the leather interior and gleaming woodwork. "Beautiful, eh? 260D model: the first diesel with upright headlamps and a vertical spare tire between the bonnet and running board. Usually she gleams, but I dirtied the bodywork so we wouldn't attract attention on the road." Hands on hips, he looked askance at the pile of luggage on the pavement. "My God, Kohut," he grumbled, picking up a suitcase, moving as awkwardly as a heron. "Are you are trying to escape from the Nazis, or planning an African safari with a retinue?"

"Didn't you tell him what we were bringing?" Sophie narrowed her eyes at Willy as if daring him to argue. "This man has no manners."

"I mentioned how much luggage we had last night," said Willy gruffly. *This is not a good start*, he thought.

The trunk of the Mercedes was not large enough to take all the cases, so they had to stack the small one and the string bags inside, in one corner of the back seat. Two old brass clocks lay on towels on the rear windowsill, as if to substantiate Venter's claim to be an antiques dealer.

Sophie got into the rear and lowered Pavel down onto a small blanket with a pillow under his head, between the small case and her seat in the other corner. He was quiet, holding his furry lion against his face, a sign he would soon be asleep. "I wish we had more room here, but we will manage, I suppose."

Venter switched on the diesel starter. "Here we go, friends," he said lightly, glancing back at Sophie as the engine coughed into a rumble. He handed Willy a paper bag. "Some sweet rolls—your breakfast."

As Willy passed the bag to Sophie in the back, Venter kept his hand held out over Willy's lap, palm open. "Time to pay the remaining fifteen hundred Reichsmarks, my friend."

Forcing a smile, Willy shook his head. "Come on, we haven't even started. Let's wait till after we have the visas and are well on our way to the Dutch frontier."

Venter's thin mouth turned down, and then he shrugged. "As you wish. I'm going to stop in an hour to store some valuables in a special place in the trunk—yours as well—and then we're off to Munich for the visas." He adjusted his hat and scarf, gunned the engine, and turned on the headlights.

☙ ∂ ☙

They left the sleeping city far behind. With the warmth of dawn breaking up low-lying wreaths of mist, Venter, his long frame hunched over the dashboard, pushed the Mercedes mercilessly. As the car rushed on, Willy kept looking back over his shoulder to see how Sophie and Pavel were taking the speed, which he noticed was close to 65 kph. Sophie smiled reassuringly back at him, indicating with a nod that Pavel was asleep.

After an hour and a half, beyond the small town of Tatabánya, Venter slowed as they came abreast of a derelict farmhouse. He turned into a lane and passed on through an open farm gate. On either side lay green fields of half-grown maize. Woodlands formed a dark line in the distance. By now the sun was up, a silver-orange disc, showing through layers of gauzy clouds. For half a kilometer, the car bumped along a narrow rutted track lined by dilapidated wood-and-wire fencing, finally stopping in a small clearing surrounded by a palisade of birch trees. Six glum cows chewing cud stared at them from over the fence.

Pavel, woken by the lurching, looked around sleepily. "Want drink, *Maminko*," he said, looking at the back of Venter's head with interest. He sat up, leaned forward, and touched the curtain of greasy hair that lay on the Dutchman's collar. "Who is man?"

"That's Mr. Venter," said Willy hastily after the Dutchman took a hand off the steering wheel and flapped at the hair on his neck. "A nice man. You saw him before you went to sleep."

Venter got out, leaving his door ajar. He had a small leather bag in his hand. At the back of the car, he crooked a finger at Willy through the rear window. "Come on, Kohut," he shouted. "Help me take out the suitcases. It's time to stash our treasures."

During their dinner at Gundel, Venter had mentioned how he had created hidden spaces inside the car for the valuables he smuggled.

Sophie helped Pavel push through the lush mixture of grass, dandelions, and white flower heads of Queen Anne's lace. It was her chance to go to the bathroom and entertain Pavel by admiring the cows. At the fence, Pavel bounced up and down in excitement. "I like cows, *Maminko.*" Sophie pulled up a handful of long grass and pushed it through the wire squares to the nearest beast. With a cry of delight, Pavel followed suit.

"You see those bags under the cow's back legs?" she said. "That's where the cow makes her milk. We drink the same milk for breakfast every day. The farmer sends it in a barrel to town, and the milkman brings it to us every morning." Pavel gave her a certain look with his serious eyes, and she was pleased he had absorbed everything she had said. He resumed pulling up grass.

Handing a flashlight to Willy, Venter stooped down into the empty trunk, holding a screwdriver. "Point here," he commanded as he pulled back the rubber flooring and unscrewed two metal plates, each one revealing a small recess. After a moment of groping, he extracted two cigar boxes fastened by rubber bands, one larger than the other. "My favorite smoke, Dutch Willem II. These two are empty. Now, show me what you have. I want to be sure everything fits."

Willy drew an envelope containing Hungarian bonds from his jacket pocket and called Sophie to come back and bring her jewels. While Pavel stayed to feed the cows through the wire fence, Sophie brought a blue velvet bag from her purse. Willy frowned at her hesitation. "Go on. It's safe. He knows what he's doing."

With a smile, Venter released the ribbon around the bag's neck and looked inside. "Abracadabra!" he chuckled. "Nice stuff. Now cup your hands, dear. Let's have a look-see." He tipped everything into Sophie's hands.

Sophie stared at him in horror and then at the glittering pile in her hands.

"Don't be nervous, lady." Venter pulled a small loupe from his pocket and began to examine the stones, returning each one to the bag as he finished. "I'm doing you a favor. I will give you an estimate of what your gems might sell for. Amsterdam, where

I live, has the world's best diamond cutters and dealers. This stuff isn't too bad, three to four thousand Reichsmarks' worth if you sell to De Groot, the dealer I usually work with. You can put everything back in the bag now."

Venter put another leather bag he had brought from the car into the large cigar box and placed Sophie's bag and the Hungarian bonds in the smaller one. Each box fitted into a recessed cavity. He stuffed rags around them and bolted on the covering metal plates.

"Couldn't we just hide the valuables under the seats?" asked Sophie as Venter stretched out his long back with a groan.

Venter sneered. "That's the first place the cops look. My way, if we are stopped, all they will find is luggage. If they discovered contraband or jewels under the seats like you suggested, they would pocket them and you would get..." He drew a dramatic finger across his neck and grinned. "Be grateful, lady. I'm looking out for you."

Willy had watched Venter with increasing apprehension, feeling his control of the situation was slipping away. With hardly any warning or discussion, Venter had locked their valuables into the frame of the Mercedes. If getting them back meant an argument or a fight, all Willy had was the small clasp knife in his pocket. "When do we get these back?" he asked.

"After we cross into Holland."

They rejoined the road and traveled another hour to Mosonmagyaróvár, where they stopped for coffee and a snack. At the Austro-Hungarian frontier, which lay just beyond the town, Venter greeted the police and customs agents like old friends. No one bothered to check the Mercedes or their luggage. Willy and Sophie watched him from the car as he transferred two bottles of what looked like brandy into the supervisor's hands. They were soon on their way again.

"Just over an hour to Vienna, and after that we stop in Linz for a break," said Venter. "Then another six hours to Munich." They headed west under a cloudless sky, passing through a rolling landscape of small towns, neat farms, dairy herds, and scattered forests.

Barreling along at 70 kph, Venter lit up a cigarillo from a Willem II box set beside him and began telling fanciful stories about his smuggling adventures: marvelous escapes, horrible dangers, clever deals he had completed—none of which Willy believed. In between stories, he sang out-of-tune snatches of Viennese operetta hits, proudly announcing the titles and composers like *"The Merry Widow"* by Franz Lehar and *"Black Forest Girl"* by Leon Jessel. Venter apparently suffered an irresistible compulsion to fill the car with tobacco smoke and the sound of his hoarse voice.

"Please," Willy said, having calculated that they had tolerated Venter's antics for over two hours. "Could we have some peace and quiet? We were up at five this morning. One hour without cigar smoke or a song is all we ask. "

Venter spat cigarillo fragments out of his half-open window. "Look, Kohut, this is the way I travel. Driving is boring, so I entertain myself. You paid for transportation, not for personal convenience or pleasure. If you and your bad-tempered wife can't put up with me, it will be no trouble to dump you and your kid at the roadside for the police to find."

❦ ∂ ❦

In the back, Sophie tried to keep Pavel entertained, reading and telling stories, playing games, spotting and describing the animals they saw in the fields. With the car full of smoke, he began to cough and after another hour, he could not keep still. He became restless and whiny, climbing all over the back seat, kicking his feet against the front seats. "Don't like, *Maminko*," he kept saying, pointing to the back of Venter's head. "*Táta* drive."

She leaned forward. From the start, she had disliked this strange, erratic man, and now she feared him as well. He was so unpredictable and unappetizing. She had seen the warning signs that Pavel was getting close to one of his tantrums. If that happened, Venter might throw them out. She forced herself to be polite, hoping that he would be more considerate. "Please, Mr. Venter, could you stop smoking for a while? Pavel is coughing and getting very agitated. He needs to pee and get a breath of fresh air."

"Yes, yes, I can hear and see what the kid's doing, *madám* high and mighty." Venter stubbed out his cigar in the overflowing ashtray on the dash. "He's a damned fucking pain, crawling all over the place. I'll find you a place to stop, but after that, you'd better make sure he behaves."

Venter stopped for a toilet break, turning off onto a side road near a wood. Willy and Sophie took Pavel to a group of large rocks and let him explore the nooks and crannies while they made the most of the sunshine and the clean air. Willy put his arms around Sophie. "I wasn't expecting Venter would be like this. We have to stick it out somehow."

"I know, but he's so... awful. My patience is paper thin." There was a tired, almost hopeless look in her eyes. "You grabbed at Venter's offer without thinking of the consequences. I don't know if I can keep Pavel calm in the car, and I'm afraid I'll do or say something that will make that crook do something unexpected."

Willy's face turned beet red, and he took her firmly by the elbow. "Look, Father recommended him, and now he's our only chance. I know the man's unpredictable—a *khazer*, a pig—but you have to try to be pleasant. We can't afford to offend him - he has our valuables and he is our ticket to safety. We're stuck with him."

The twenty-minute break was enough to improve Pavel's mood, and when they reached Wels at a quarter to nine, Venter drew up at a *Konditorei* where Willy bought pastries, milk for Pavel, and coffee for the adults. Sophie decided to put Pavel back into diapers—she could not risk an accident, and this way they would not have to stop. She took him for a stroll in a nearby handkerchief park. It had a swing, a climbing frame, and several large, flat rocks set out like stepping-stones. He clambered about poking sticks into the damp earth, looking for earthworms and insects while she exercised her arms and legs, wondering whether she had the strength to keep suppressing her anger toward Venter—and concerned that she might lose control of Pavel during what seemed more and more like an endless journey.

As he lit up another cigar, Venter called out to them through his window. "Hurry up, Kohuts. Munich ahead. The Dutch Embassy awaits you, and there will be refreshments and relaxation for me. Shouldn't take more than five hours or so to get there."

"We should get there about two o'clock," Willy said in a low voice to Sophie as they all climbed back into the car. "Just grit your teeth and hope that Pavel goes to sleep."

ↄ ∂ ↄ

Even from the smeared back window of the Mercedes, Sophie could see that Munich was awash with military personnel. The main thoroughfares fluttered with red and black Nazi flags. Willy turned to her, shaking his head. "Difficult to believe we are doing this. Munich is the belly of the beast, frightening and exciting at the same time."

"I feel cold all over," she said. "I can't bear it. I'm going to close my eyes until we stop."

Venter seemed to know his way around the city, and it was two-thirty when he dropped the Kohuts off at the Dutch immigration office in Marsstrasse. "Shouldn't take you more than a couple of hours. I will wait for you at the Holz Bierstube on Nymphenberger Strasse. Take a taxi when you've finished."

In the anteroom of the consulate, they waited patiently for their turn. It was very hot and a ceiling fan whirred in the humid air, chirping like a little bird. It seemed to Sophie as if every man, woman, and child from central and eastern Europe was trying to get a visa into Holland. All the benches and chairs were occupied, the spaces filling up as soon as somebody left, which seemed to be happening at a very fast pace. Thick cigarette smoke, the smell of sweaty bodies, and the pervading odor of onion and sausage sandwiches made Sophie feel as if she were in some refugee detention center rather than an embassy.

Nevertheless, she was glad to be out of the Mercedes and on her feet. She took short walks up and down the corridor. After first enjoying the hustle and bustle and watching other children running around, Pavel quickly tired of waiting and launched a tantrum, lying on the floor and kicking his legs and shrieking. Sophie tried to pacify him, picking him up, murmuring soothing words. Everyone was looking at her; she felt desperately ashamed and frightened. An angry-looking plump woman, an embassy employee, strode into waiting area and stood there accusingly, hands on hips. Red-faced, and exasperated, Willy gave Pavel a hard slap on the leg. The tantrum shuddered to a halt.

"You never did that before," Sophie whispered, tears rolling down her cheeks.

Willy glared. "I had to do something. She was going to throw us out."

∾ ∂ ∾

Finally, they sat in front of Mr. van der Straat, a Dutch consular official who wearily flipped through their application forms. Pavel, wandering around the room, found a dilapidated teddy bear tucked away behind a cabinet. Smiling, he ran to Sophie to show it to her.

"I'm sorry, Mr. Kohut," the official said, benignly nodding permission for Pavel to keep the treasure. "Our consulate will be permanently closed from tomorrow. All our diplomatic staff in Germany are being repatriated. We are not issuing visas until the political situation with Germany is resolved and we can reopen the consulate. Who knows when that will be?"

Willy ground his teeth. They had waited nearly two hours for this. "So, please, what is meant by these words, 'political situation'? Why didn't you announce this decision in the waiting room?"

The official sighed and shrugged. "Sometime in the next two days, the Dutch frontier will be closed to non-nationals. It may be sealed altogether. I fear Hitler intends to invade Holland soon. Alternatively, he might attack Poland first. Who knows?"

Willy shifted forward in his chair. "Listen, I'm sorry for you Dutch people. The same thing happened to Czechoslovakia, but my family has to get into Holland. You see, my wife's uncle is dying in Amsterdam." He pulled out his wallet. "I have Reichsmarks, pengö, and Swiss francs. How much would it take for you to break the rules and give us visas?" Sophie raised her eyebrows at both the lie and the bribe, but she stayed silent.

"I appreciate your offer," said Mr. van der Straat, dabbing the sweat from his forehead with a handkerchief, "but issuing a visa is impossible. As Hungarians, you cannot enter Holland—legally." He pushed the passports and applications back across the table. "Of course, there are other ways. You can hire local people to guide you. The frontier is very porous at the moment, but also very dangerous."

Willy felt his spirit wilting, a sense of helplessness and of being trapped. "What do you suggest I do?"

"Find yourself someone who knows the frontier well."

Willy looked sideways at Sophie, holding a tear-stained Pavel on her lap. Her lips were trembling. "Venter, I suppose" she whispered. He put a reassuring hand on her shoulder. *Venter knows the frontier*, he thought. *We have to stick with him, whatever the bastard does.*

Mr. Van der Straat leaned across the desk and proffered his hand. "Good-bye, Mr. Kohut. Good luck."

Willy sighed deeply. His plan was wearing thin and he was tired of needing luck. He wanted to be sure they would get into Holland.

22

A CHANGE OF PLAN
JULY, 1939

AT THE HOLZ BIERSTUBE, Sophie and Willy found Venter at a table cluttered with empty beer and schnapps glasses. He was finishing off a caraway seed roll from which protruded the charred ends of a *Wurst* laced with mustard. He glared up at them, jabbing a finger at his watch. "Just after five. I've been here nearly three fucking hours. What happened?"

They sat down at the table. "Nothing," Willy said, with a glum look. "Precisely nothing." Sophie nudged Willy's arm, letting Pavel go. "Tell him how we wasted two hours."

Willy shook his head and studied his hands, the picture of gloom.

Pavel wandered off, and Sophie watched him explore the intricacies of the beamed room with its antler lamps and colored glass windows. Articulated, painted gnomes and creatures hung from hooks on the walls. "*Mami, Maminko*, come see," he called out, laughing as he yanked on the string that hung down from most of the puppets. "They walk."

Sophie nudged Willy again. "At least that one's happy."

When Willy finally explained what had transpired at the embassy, Venter slammed his beer glass on the table. "Damned Nazis!" He took a draught of beer and wiped his mouth with back of his hand. "This is fucking bad, Willy. I bet things are chaotic at the frontier. Maybe it's too difficult, going on. We're stuck in Germany." He swigged schnapps from a line of waiting shot glasses.

Willy grabbed the Dutchman's arm. Staying in Germany was not an option. Better to overcome the odds, take a chance. "Don't tell me you're backing out, Venter. What kind of pathetic smuggler are you? What about all that bragging in the car about how you always fooled the police and were so brave? Remember what you said at Gundel? 'I know the Dutch border like the back of my hand,' you said. Well prove it, damn you."

Venter shook his head. "It's too damned risky, Kohut. The fact that the Dutch are closing the frontier posts means they are expecting Nazi aggression. If we don't get there in a few hours, there'll be troops everywhere."

Willy glanced at Sophie, trying not to let her see his anger rising. If he lost control now, their trip with Venter would be over. He took hold of the Dutchman's lapel and pulled him close. "Last night you said you liked to gamble. If you don't take us, you'll lose fifteen hundred Reichsmarks, and I'll make sure your reputation stinks."

Venter pushed Willy's hand away. "Look, bigmouth. I could just as easily leave you people in Munich. Wouldn't be long before they strung you up. Now, shut up. I'm off to have a piss." He got up and wobbled away, steadying himself by holding on to the backs of chairs.

Willy looked at Sophie and shook his head. "If he agrees we can go, I'll have to do the driving."

Pavel, back from his explorations, insinuated himself between Sophie's knees and shyly showed her what he had acquired: the carved leg of one of the wooden puppets. He looked at her as if he was not quite sure if he had done something wrong.

"Where did you get this?" she whispered, pulling him onto her lap.

"Hope he didn't twist it off one of those puppets," said Willy with the trace of a smile, half-annoyed and half-amused.

Clutching the leg tightly, Pavel pointed to a large armchair tucked into a dark corner of the *Stube*. "Pavel keep."

Sophie shrugged at his pleading look and turned to Willy. "He's collecting puppets."

"All right, let him keep it," Willy muttered. "I don't want any screaming and yelling in here."

Venter returned and sat down again. Willy noticed the unfocused look in the Dutchman's eyes. The idiot was drunk. "We leave—now." Venter's voice was thicker than usual. "You pay my bill, as agreed."

"OK, but if the frontier is closed when we get there, what's your plan? Where do we cross?" Willy pulled out his wallet with a frosty stare.

"Jesus Christ, Kohut. I told you at Gundel. We take farm roads... Bypass the frontier post; just as long as we're there before the Dutch troops decide to shut down the whole border."

"What if we don't get there in time?" said Sophie.

Venter put both hands on his forehead and rocked in his seat, knocking over an empty beer bottle. "God, I don't know. I will have to think of something. I'm good at that." He shrugged, hiccupped, and then guffawed; pointing a wavering finger at her, "You're regretting your husband's decision to ride with me, hunh?"

 ℣ ∂ ℣

It was five o'clock and the *Bierstube* was filling up with workers. The streets were busy with people heading home. Venter, sweating profusely and muttering curses stood by the Mercedes searching his pockets for the key. He seemed agitated, and his words were even more slurred than in the *Bierstube*. "We must drive fast, nonstop, all through the night if necessary. We take turns napping, *ja?*" The Dutchman jabbed a finger in to Willy's arm. "I drive first."

With a smile of befuddled triumph he produced the car key, fumbled the door open and slid sideways with his knees on the pavement.

Sophie, holding on to Pavel, clamped a hand over her mouth and began to laugh, shoulders shaking. "The *saukerl* is completely soused." She looked at Willy with anxious eyes. "Please, *miláčku*, you have to drive us. Later, it will be dark. Do you think you can do it?"

Willy gave her reassuring smile as he pushed Venter into the passenger seat. "I have to, strudel. It's many years since I drove Father's Fiat. We will manage. Meantime, it's nap time for smugglers."

Venter nodded agreement, and ten minutes after they left the city limits and joined the new autobahn to Würzburg, he had folded himself into the passenger seat and was snoring. He woke an hour later and took over from Willy, driving at top speed as he tried to loosen up his body and long legs, straightening out his neck and shoulders to get comfortable. Muttering curses and glancing frequently in the rearview mirror, he lit the first of many cigarillos. Willy and Sophie exchanged panicked frowns as they realized he was about to reprise his earlier performance.

Sophie and Willy had not eaten since their early morning stop at Wels, and Sophie gave Pavel the last of the food and milk from her bag. Soon after, she could tell he needed to be changed, a tough challenge in the fast Mercedes. The worst part was the pungent smell of the soiled diaper mixed with cigar smoke. She solved half the problem by throwing the diaper out the window.

"Can we stop and buy something to eat?" she asked as they entered the town of Fürsten-Feldbruck. "Pavel needs fresh milk, and we're hungry."

"No," said Venter fiercely. "No time for that. You will have to stay hungry for another four hours or so until we get to Wiesbaden. You have water. That should be enough."

"For God's sake," said Willy, "we go past Würzburg and Nuremberg before that. Surely we can stop for twenty minutes to get something to eat?"

"Maybe."

For nearly an hour as Venter smoked and sang his operettas, Sophie showed Pavel picture books, told him stories, and practiced saying nursery rhymes together. When she ran out of ideas, he played with his new toys, the broken puppet and the teddy bear from the Dutch embassy. Finally, his eyes drooped. Sophie covered him with a knitted blanket in the small space beside her. She looked pleadingly at Willy as she lowered the window partway to let the acrid tobacco fumes blow out. "My stomach's aching for food. Can't you make him stop?"

He turned, putting a warning finger to his lips.

"Shut the fucking window, woman," Venter said after a few moments. "I can't concentrate on the road with cold air blasting down my neck. And we don't have time to stop for food."

She noticed Willy balling his fists. Then he turned and stretching out a calming hand to touch her knee. "Close the window, dear. I expect it will be all right with Venter if you open it from time to time."

She shook her head violently, mouthing the words at him. "I have to breathe."

They were on the A3, a new autobahn running north from Munich. Their journey was proceeding smoothly and efficiently, with sparse traffic due to gasoline shortages, according to Venter. Willy's fear that the empty roads were yet another sign of an impending attack on Holland began to subside. Only Venter's singing and smoking and what was turning into a tug-of-war about Sophie's open window made the drive endlessly unpleasant. On only one occasion, a car marked *POLIZEI* drove past in the opposite direction; its occupants did not even look at them.

Willy and Sophie tamped down their hunger, gazing at the flat, uninteresting countryside until Venter overtook a string of horse-drawn military wagons full of helmeted troops and then a two-kilometer convoy of camouflaged trucks.

"Fucking Nazis going north," said Venter grimly, looking at his watch. "Seven thirty. They're on their way to gobble up Holland."

"I can't believe they still use horses," Willy said. "The Wehrmacht is supposed to be modern and efficient. Even before we capitulated, the Czech Army had given up on using horses."

"Saving gasoline for combat operations, friend. Most of the heavy equipment, like tanks and guns, goes by train."

They passed through Nuremberg and Würzburg without stopping, and soon blustery clouds were coalescing and darkening the sky. Warning raindrops spattered, smearing the windshield. The Mercedes, traveling at its top speed of 80 kph, hit a curtain of gray rain and started into a sideways skid that Venter mastered, swearing copiously. He dropped the speed to 50 kph, but even so, the wipers' hiccupping sweep was hopelessly inadequate. "I told you before, woman, close the damned window," he shouted. "The fucking rain will spoil my leather seats."

"For God's sake, Sophie, do as he says," said Willy, gripping the sides of his seat as the car veered toward the edge of the road. Venter wrenched at the steering wheel.

As she wound up the window, the rain mixed with her tears, soaking the front of her dress.

മ ∂ മ

A sudden lurching of the Mercedes woke Pavel and he looked around wildly, unsure where he was. His face had the feral, uncomprehending expression that Sophie recognized as preliminary to one of his explosions. She tried to calm him. "Don't want car, don't want car," he shouted, starting to climb all over her—and then, burrowing like a dog into the clothes and bags in the back seat, pushed them out behind him with his feet. "*Maminko*," he whined, turning the string bags upside down so that their contents fell on the floor. "No like car."

She held one arm and tried to stroke his head, hoping to quiet him down. "We can't stop, darling. It's raining out there. Let's stay dry in the car."

"Don't want car," Pavel shouted, screwing up his face. "Don't want car." He repeated the words over and over, banging his hand against the back of Venter's seat, each thump coinciding with the word 'car'. Afraid he was going to hurt himself, Sophie wrapped her arms round him, trying to shush him.

Willy turned with a look that conveyed both annoyance and anxiety. "Be quiet, Pavel," he growled, but his son took no notice.

"Don't want car."

Venter banged the palm of his hand on the steering wheel. "Fuck it. Shut the brat up or I'll whack his *tuches*."

"Pavel!" Willy yelled. "Stop it." The boy suddenly stopped, eyes afire, and pointed at the back of the Dutchman's head. "Don't like. No, NO."

Sophie massaged the boy's back and arms, crooning endearments to him, afraid that Venter might put his physical threat into action if Pavel started again. "Be quiet, *miláčku*. Come, I've found a nice piece of chocolate for you, and then we'll sing a song." Pavel grabbed the chocolate and stuffed it into his mouth. "Don't like," he mumbled repeatedly. Chocolate stained his chin. "I want go home."

Venter glanced in the rearview mirror. "Knock the kid out with something, can't you? I have a flask of brandy. There, Willy, somewhere on the floor by your feet. Put some in his milk, for God's sake."

Sophie jerked the top of Venter's seat as hard as she could, wishing she was actually pulling his head backwards. She boiled inside, wanting to scream and lash out at the man in front of her—and her bladder was full. Summoning all her reserves of

self-control, she swallowed her anger and crossed her legs, leaning forward in the hopes of relieving her urge to urinate. This
awful man was also their salvation; she was going to beg for
what she needed. "Please, *pane* Venter, we have no milk. We
need to buy some more, and food as well. You cannot expect a
boy of two to put up with traveling like this for hours on end.
If you stop, I promise he will settle down. Anyway, I desperately
need to go to the toilet. Please."

"Absolutely not!" Venter shouted through the cigar smoke.
"Are you stupid or what? It's fucking raining and we're in a
hurry. Just shut the kid up. You people are nothing but trouble.
Fucking Jews. I was crazy to take you on."

"You're a fucking Jew yourself," Willy shouted, slamming
his fist against the side of his door. "My wife is doing the best
for our boy in a very difficult situation. Be a mensch, Venter."
Sophie watched Willy's face go beet red; she was afraid that he
might go crazy and grab the steering wheel or haul on the brake.

"Holy shit, Kohut," the Dutchman yelled as he swung the
Mercedes to overtake a white van and two motorcyclists. "I'm
having a hard enough time keeping this crate straight without
you and your kid distracting me."

Pavel began to sob. Sophie could tell the shouting had
frightened him, and she tried to console him, cuddling him to
her breast, but the boy's tears kept flowing. Gradually, like a
hurricane gathering force, his sobs and heaves multiplied until he
finally exploded into a back-arching, leg-kicking, arm-thrashing
tantrum on the car floor. She tried to keep him pinned down.

"For God's sake, woman," yelled Venter, as he passed a
swaying farm truck loaded with hay bales. "Shut the little fucker
up. I've got to concentrate."

From the back, Sophie watched the spray from the truck's
tires opacify the windshield. For a moment, she could not see
anything, and the vise of fear added greater urgency to the painful fullness of her bladder. She was sure they would crash.

"Calm down, Andreas," Willy exclaimed as the wipers
cleared their view. Sophie saw he was gripping the dashboard,
pale and shaking. "Yelling and swearing only makes things
worse."

Venter's drawn, pale face turned livid, his mouth a red
gash across the taut, shiny skin. "Shut the fuck up, pisser."

Pavel's crying grew louder and more piercing. He writhed

around in the back seat, striking out with arms and legs and scratching at his mother. As Sophie tried to contain him, she noticed brown liquid running down his leg onto the seat. A powerful, acrid smell pervaded the car's interior. She banged on the back of Willy's seat. "Make Venter stop, please," she begged. "Pavel has diarrhea."

"*Kurva drát*, bloody hell," Venter yelled, looking in the rear mirror. "I smell shit. If your fucking kid has crapped on my leather seats, I will kill you. Clean it up." He wound down his window a little but kept on driving. Raindrops spattered inside.

Pavel, who had stopped in mid-tantrum at the sight of the brown liquid covering his legs, began to cry and kick again. Drops of brown spattered the back of the front seats, some landing on Venter's collar. Sophie desperately tried to control Pavel's legs and stem the flow, pushing a couple of scarves under him, but failed. "I've had enough!" she screamed out, banging her fists repeatedly on the front seats. She grabbed at Willy's shoulder. "Willy, make Venter stop. You don't expect me to sit in this revolting mess for another three hours?"

Willy looked down between the seats and shook his head in disgust. "There's *kacke* on the seat and on the floor."

Venter's face and clenched hands had gone white. "OK. We're going to stop soon, and precious Frau Kohut is going to clean the shit out of my car." He leaned forward to clear the misted windshield with his handkerchief.

"Look out!" Willy gasped, reaching out to the dashboard as if readying for a collision. "There's something on the road."

"*Allmächtige Christus!*" Venter yelled, slamming on the brakes. The Mercedes fishtailed and began to skid. Through the windscreen, Sophie watched a merry-go-round of road, trees, and fields. She opened her mouth to scream, but the sound stayed inside until the moment the car came to rest against a copse of small trees.

In the back, Pavel shrieked, his legs still covered in brown slime. Her breath coming in great gulps, Sophie scrabbled to dig him out of the jumble of baggage that had fallen on top of them. During the skid, her face had struck the back of Willy's seat. She tasted blood in her mouth, but she was in one piece—and so was Pavel, thank God.

Over Venter's shoulders, she watched his long, white fingers massaging the rim of the steering wheel as he sucked in deep breaths. With a groan of dismay, the Dutchman levered himself out of his seat and went out in the rain to check the front of the car. After a few moments, he climbed back in, shaking his head. "Damned lucky. Not a scratch, just mud and grass everywhere." He reversed the Mercedes a few feet and drove it back onto edge of the hardtop. "Some metal object was in the middle of the road."

"I think it was a steel drum; must have fallen off a truck." Willy mopped his face.

Venter sniffed as he restarted the engine. "Now, *paní* Kohutová, you clean the kid up as best you can. Soon we stop to eat something." He gave Willy a hard look. "I expect we both need a double schnapps to celebrate a lucky escape, eh?"

Willy took off his glasses and demisted them with a flap of his shirt. "You don't make sense, Venter. What was all the panic? First, you said we had to go nonstop to the frontier. Now, suddenly, there's time for food and drink."

Sophie leaned forward, close to tears again. "Thank you for stopping."

Venter glanced at his watch and pointed a long, bony finger back at Pavel. "He's the fucking reason. Him and his mother made us late. Now, if we keep going, it will be close to midnight when we get to the Dutch border. The farm lights will be off—tougher to get my bearings. Easy to get lost and picked up by the *Grenzpolizei*. So, why bother to rush? If we are stopped, too bad. Meantime, we will eat at a country place I know, and you can concentrate on cleaning up my car. You take the wheel, Kohut. I'm frazzled."

∽ ∂ ∽

The sky cleared, and an hour later, Venter guided Willy to the Drei Bären Gasthaus, an oak-beamed chalet set back among a cluster of beeches and oaks a kilometer off the autobahn. He parked beside a small paved terrace surrounded by geranium-filled boxes that glowed in the evening sun. A billboard of three cavorting black bears on a light blue background swung above long tables and benches set out on the forecourt.

A tall, muscular man wearing a leather apron came to the door and greeted them as they got out of the Mercedes. He obviously knew Venter, and they walked into the empty Stube, chat-

ting and glancing back at the Kohuts. Willy wondered what they
were saying. Was Venter just explaining their circumstances,
or was something more sinister being plotted? "One of us has
to stay close to Venter," he said to Sophie as they waited at
the main door, a massive oak-planked structure with elaborate
hinges. "No telling what he might do."

"You mean he might leave us?" Sophie looked sorrowfully
down at her stained and bedraggled son. "Like this?"

Willy gave her a grim smile. "I don't think so. I kept the
keys to the Mercedes, and I also haven't paid him the second
half of his fee."

The innkeeper gave Sophie permission to use an upstairs
bathroom, where she washed Pavel and dressed him in clothes
from one of the suitcases in the car. Venter sat in the bar, drinking.

While Willy took Pavel exploring in the damp woods
behind the inn, Sophie borrowed a pail of water, soap, and
some rags and spent half an hour cleaning the seats and floor in
the back of Venter's car as best she could. After the Dutchman
had inspected the back seat and grudgingly approved, they ate in
the inn's kitchen, watching Venter gorge himself on meatballs,
dumplings, potato salad, beer, and schnapps.

"Come on, Venter." Willy moved the bottle of Doppelkorn
to another table. "That's enough schnapps for one day. I'm sure
you're over your scare on the road."

The Dutchman wiped his bowl clean with hunks of black
bread and let out an explosive burp. "Much better now. We go
on now. But first, I want the rest of my money." He held out a
hand. "Come on, pay up."

"I said I would only pay you after we crossed the Dutch
border." Willy shook his head as he rose from the table. From
the way Venter was looking at him, he sensed that some crisis
was brewing. Willy believed he had enough strength to over-
power the Dutchman if it came to a fight, and he had a clasp
knife in his pocket. The man was spindly and taller than Willy,
but he seemed physically fragile—and he was tipsy again.

Venter frowned, the skin taut on his gaunt face. "Come
on, friend. The way your kid behaved has changed the situation.
I want compensation for damage to my car. God knows how
much it will cost to have the interior properly cleaned—maybe
even new seat covers. If you don't cough up, well, we can just

hang around this nice inn until you change your mind."

"We can leave without you." Willy gestured for Sophie and Pavel to follow and began moving toward the door. "I have your car keys."

Venter erupted into laughter. "I can just see you pissing about on the Dutch border driving my car, the middle of the night. Anyway, take a look outside."

Willy looked through the doorway into the forecourt. The innkeeper and another burly man were smoking and leaning against the Mercedes. They waved a salutation, the kind of gesture that meant, 'If you make trouble, we can make trouble.' Willy pulled out his wallet and counted 750 Reichsmarks onto the table. "Half now and half when we get there. What do you say?"

Venter grunted, tucking the wad of notes into his jacket pocket. He got up, swaying a little. "You drive again, Kohut." He leered at Sophie. "Just be sure your kid doesn't annoy me anymore. Meet you at the car. I'm off for a piss."

Eyes widening in anger, Sophie opened her mouth to say something; Willy touched her shoulder and shook his head.

℘ ∂ ℘

Back on the road, they passed through a series of brief squalls, arriving after three-quarters of an hour at the town of Wiesbaden. It was late evening and the spa town was quiet, just a few cars trundling by and almost no pedestrians. Venter directed Willy through wet streets along the Bismarckring.

"Stop—over there," said Venter suddenly, "and turn off the engine."

"Why? Where are we?" Willy asked, complying. "What's wrong? Why did we stop?"

"What is that big building?" Sophie peered out of the car's rear window as she turned to check on Pavel, who was waking up, rubbing his eyes.

"We are on the southern edge of the city," said Venter. "That's the Hauptbahnhof, the main train station."

Willy wound down his window and looked up at the monumental sandstone façade faintly illuminated by streetlights that cast cones of light onto the wet pavement. He was uneasy. What were they doing here? Apart from a few cars and a van parked in the low-walled forecourt, the place looked forbidding and deserted.

"Wedding-cake spa architecture." Venter gave a scornful laugh, winding down his window. "I've never been inside the damned place; it's supposed to be remarkably ugly."

"So why did we stop?" Willy rubbed nervously at his injured finger. "Do you want to switch drivers now? Koblenz is the next city, I think." Around them, a fine mist rose from the road surface. Apart from the gas lamps, everything on the streets was dark and silent.

Venter shifted in his seat, clearing his throat with a great rasp of mucus that he spat out his open window. "We say good-bye here." In a swift motion, he pulled a short-barreled pistol from beneath his seat and shoved it against Willy's right temple. "I'm going on alone. You stay here in Wiesbaden. I want nothing more to do with you people. Hand over the other 750 Reichsmarks and then get out."

In the back seat, Sophie gasped and pulled Pavel close while Willy, shrinking from the cold metal ring pressing into his skin, fumbled for his wallet and said nothing. His mind raced. As he handed the money over, he slid his fingers into his pocket and curled them round the clasp knife. The end of the pistol barrel wavered and moved close to his right eye. Heart pounding, Willy raised his hands in the air. "All right, all right, we'll get out. For God's sake, put down the gun. Be sensible, Venter. If you shoot me, what will you do with my wife and child? Shoot them as well? We are relatives, remember? Jews just like you."

With a swift flick of his arm, Venter struck Willy's cheek with the barrel of his gun. "Get out."

Sophie, who had been sitting on the edge of her seat, gasped and buried her face in her hands. Pavel stared at the blood coursing down his father's cheek. "*Táto,*" he said in a thin, choked voice. "*Maminko?*"

Willy pulled a handkerchief from his pocket and tried to stanch the flow of blood. His voice shook. "God, Venter. Why did you do that?"

"To show you I mean business."

"So we get out. Then what? What are you going to do? Leave us here in the dark. Shoot us? The police patrols will find us. They'll find you too."

Venter waved his pistol at Sophie and Pavel in the back. "Don't be so fucking dramatic, Kohut. I did you a favor bringing you to the station. Take the damned train to wherever you want. Everything out of the trunk... *Honem voorhuit*, quick."

As Willy opened his door, Venter leaned forward and pocketed the car keys. He got out, checked that no one was around, and opened the trunk, holding the pistol loosely by his right knee. Sophie helped Pavel scramble out at the back while Willy unloaded and stacked their belongings on the sidewalk.

Sophie, her face white with fear, darted glances at the Dutchman and said nothing.

The sky began to spit fine rain droplets. Venter shrugged on a thin rain jacket and closed the lid of the trunk. He pointed toward the station. "Get your skates on, people. It's getting late."

However, Willy had not given up. "Not until you give our valuables back."

Venter rubbed at his chin with his gun-free hand. The tight parchment of his grinning face shone yellow in the lamplight. He seemed to be turning things over in his mind. "Ah well, I suppose so," he sighed, handing Willy a flashlight from his pocket. He opened the trunk again. "Stay here. I'll get a wrench for the bolts." He walked toward the front of the Mercedes and slid into the driver's seat, bending down as if looking for something. The engine coughed and burst into life.

"What the—" yelled Willy, clutching at the upper edge of the fender.

"*Au revoir!*" the Dutchman shouted, slamming his door. The car accelerated away on squealing tires, spraying dirty water from the gutter before disappearing round a corner, its trunk cover bouncing crazily. Willy lay sprawled on the wet ground.

Sophie and Pavel, in tears, stood by the luggage looking at him, immobilized by the vicious suddenness of Venter's actions.

"Don't cry, *Pavlíčku*," Willy stammered as he struggled to his feet, a searing pain above his right eye. He touched his temple. Even in the dim light, he could see the blood smears on his velvet fingerstall. "Don't cry."

23

WIESBADEN
JULY, 1939

BLEEDING AND LIMPING, Willy carried the two mid-sized suitcases toward the arched station entrance while Sophie, trailed by Pavel, carried the smallest one with one hand and two packed string bags and her purse with the other. They had left the largest suitcase behind hidden in the shadow of a parked van. Lights glowed from inside the building, and through the entrance-door glass, they glimpsed a uniformed man talking to an elderly woman wearing a headscarf, a knapsack on her shoulders.

"Still open, thank God." Willy opened one of the swinging doors with his backside. "I'll go back for the big case if we have time. We were mad to bring so much stuff." His head throbbed and rage clawed at his insides—rage at his ignominious sprawl on the wet road, rage at his own blunders, rage at Venter for stealing their valuables, and rage at everything that had conspired to bring them to this. In the brightly lit forecourt, he looked at Sophie, gauging her reaction to their new situation. Her eyes were squeezed shut, and tears rolled down her cheeks as if she were trying to forget everything that had just happened.

Halfway across the tiled concourse, Willy set the suitcases down and took a deep breath. The place where he had cracked his head on the road pounded like a blacksmith's hammer, but it seemed like a small price to pay for seeing the last of Venter. Willy was just grateful to be alive with his family unhurt.

"You're still bleeding," said Sophie gently. "Press this against your cheek." It was the last of Pavel's diapers.

"We look like gypsy rabble." He stared dejectedly at his torn jacket and muddy trousers, thinking how conspicuous and vulnerable they were. "Thank God, this place is almost empty." Hoping that his pain would soon subside, Willy glanced around the large main hall. Smooth sandstone walls separated fluted columns bearing the carved heads of important citizens. So, this was the famous neo-baroque Wiesbaden station that his father said had been built to receive the Kaiser on his annual spa cure. Now it had a forlorn, uncared-for look: unswept floors, cigarette butts, and chipped floor tiles.

"May I assist you?" asked a voice behind them. They turned to face a small bearded official in a black uniform marked with the insignia RBD Wiesbaden. He stepped back in surprise at the sight of Willy's bloodied face, his gaze slowly traversing all aspects of the Kohut family. *"Ich habe hier die Aufsicht.* I am the supervisor. What happened to you? It looks serious. Shall I call the police for you?"

Sophie had enough presence of mind to speak first, in her Berlin accent. "No need, *mein Herr.* We were traveling in a car from Munich. As we were entering Wiesbaden, there was an accident in the rainstorm. Nothing serious. However, we need to get the train to Amsterdam. Can you help us find the right platform? Is there a direct connection?"

The official shrugged his silver epaulettes. "Unfortunately you are too late for a train tonight, but tomorrow morning at six there is an express to Aachen; change there for Amsterdam." He shook his head, rolling expressive eyes in sympathy. "Why don't you stay in a hotel? Otherwise, you must wait in the station all night. I can telephone for a taxi."

Still holding the diaper against his face, Willy half-shook his head, sending a no signal to Sophie. The idea of a soft hotel bed was wonderful, but it would have meant showing their passports and repeating their Hungarian story again. It was too risky. Too much had gone wrong already. "You are very thoughtful," she said to the official in German, "but we stay here." She gently removed the diaper from Willy's head and dabbed at the raw skin. "Not too bad," she muttered. "It's just a scrape."

The official reached out for one of the suitcases Willy had put down. "I am Herr Gruber. If you permit me, I will carry this and show you the way. Perhaps you wish to buy your tickets to Aachen, before the office closes. That way you will be ready in the morning."

"Thank you," said Sophie.

After they bought three tickets, Herr Gruber led them slowly down a corridor and then out onto a dimly lit platform past a scattering of perhaps twenty waiting passengers. Further along they stopped in front of the doors of the Wartezimmer.

"Not very welcoming." Sophie looked at the waiting room's cracked windowpanes and peeling paint. Such a contrast to the stations she knew: Berlin, Prague, and Budapest. She put down her case and the bags and looked at Willy in despair. Seven hours to wait in this miserable place?

Gruber, seeing her gloomy face, shrugged, raising small hands as if in self-defense. "Ah, *meine Frau*, this station was once a glory, but with the Great Depression..." He shrugged again, giving her a weak, asymmetrical smile and pointed to a tall, brass-faced wall clock hung on the outside wall, its hands stuck at 16.00. "Nothing works properly, except perhaps the trains."

Willy glanced at his watch. "It will be midnight soon."

Pavel looked up and down the empty platform, disappointment on his face. "No train, *mami*," he said. "Where is train?" He wandered over to an empty four-wheeled luggage trolley parked against the wall and fiddled with the handle resting on the ground. He pulled on it, and the trolley shifted a little. Sophie nudged Willy's arm, managing a smile as she watched the determination on her son's face. Pavel turned and grinned at them hopefully.

The official went up to Pavel and ruffled his hair. "You are a strong boy," he said, nodding his permission at Sophie. "How old?"

She smiled. "Just under two."

"If you give him a hand, he can have some fun pushing the trolley before I go home. After that, Georg is on duty. Keep away from that one; he is a bad-tempered fellow. Remember now, the Aachen train leaves from this platform at six. *Auf Wiedersehn.*"

Willy put a restraining hand on Gruber's shoulder. "Please, tell this night watchman we really must get some sleep. We

would be grateful if he didn't disturb us." He handed Herr
Gruber a five-Reichsmark silver coin. Herr Gruber saluted, gave
a little bow, and walked off.

While Pavel played with the trolley, Sophie and Willy took
off their coats and hats and moved their cases and belongings
to one of the old-fashioned slatted benches that lined the waiting room. "This place must have been really pretty once," said
Sophie, admiring the faded depictions of country fairs and idyl-
lic landscapes painted on the walls between wooden columns. A
marble fireplace was partly obscured by stacked wooden boxes
filled with empty beer bottles. A brass chandelier with bulb
holders shaped like foxes' heads hung down from the coved ceiling. Only three light bulbs were working.

"Perhaps it was the old Kaiser's waiting room?" said Willy,
looking round.

Inside the waiting room, Pavel created a new game, taking
beer bottles out of the boxes, setting them out on the linoleum
floor in irregular lines, and then knocking them over.

Willy, grumbling, moved to discipline the boy, but Sophie
forestalled him. "*Miláčku*, Let him do it for a few minutes. The
poor mite needs some fun for a change. Maybe he'll forget what
he's been through. Anyway, thank God, we're settled. Time to
look at what Venter did to your face." She pulled him toward
the light and searched his face. "Your cheek and chin have the
worst scrapes. If I can find some running water, I'll clean it up."

He held up a hand. "Not yet, strudel. I'm going back to
get our big suitcase before the night watchman comes on."

"Are you sure you can manage on your own? In the rain?
With your bad finger?"

He gave her a resigned but proud look. "I can manage.
One thing is for sure: now that we're taking the train, we have
to rethink what we are able to carry."

When he got back with the large dripping suitcase, Willy
slumped on the bench, pale and breathing heavily. Sophie wiped
his wet face gently with a fresh handkerchief she had wrung out
in the sink of the women's toilet. She gave him an encouraging
smile, alarmed that he suddenly seemed so fragile. "Not so bad,
miláčku." She and Pavel needed him to be strong. "Nothing
deep, but you ought to have some antiseptic and Vaseline."

Willy shrugged and walked to the faded mirror over the
fireplace to examine his face. "Well, we don't have any. It'll do."

He came back, offered a wry smile and kissed the tip of her nose. "As I said before, you would have made a good nurse. A shame I always seem to need patching up. Let's get to work before we settle Pavel down." With a grunt, he lifted the large suitcase onto the bench and snapped it open. "All we will take on the train are essential clothes and toiletries packed in one case, the one where you hid the documents and Czech passports. We can take your string bags and some of Pavel's toys. Nothing else. We have to be light on our feet."

Sophie's face flushed with a mixture of surprise and disappointment. "You mean... We're leaving three suitcases behind? I want to decide what we leave behind as well as you."

Willy took a deep breath and gave Sophie a patient look. "It's not a question of who decides. I'm being logical, that is all. We can talk as we go through the suitcases and repack. Look, I know it was an effort for you to choose what to bring, but we have to be ready for the worst. When we're safe and finally get hold of some money, then we can think about having nice things." He flipped through his wallet. "I think we have just about enough to buy train tickets in Aachen, stay a couple of days in Amsterdam, and then get a boat to London. Once we get on the train to Aachen, I'm sure we can make it to Holland."

Sophie looked at him, unconvinced. His expression did not display his usual confidence. "You paid him good money, Willy, and you made the decision to travel with him. That filthy *Saumensch* deceived and hurt us." She pulled something from her dress pocket, and held out a hand, which glittered in the dim light. "I kept some diamonds back before Venter hid the jewels... couldn't bring myself to trust him. I've stopped trusting people...except you," she muttered.

Willy beamed, stroked her cheek and kissed her. "You clever, wonderful strudel. You've saved us and taken a huge worry off my mind. Amsterdam is the perfect place to turn diamonds into cash. Thank you from the bottom of my heart."

Sophie looked down at all their belongings and sighed. "Enough compliments for now, *milačku*. Pavel looks exhausted and needs to sleep. Give him his furry lion and soldier and lie him down on the bench, tucked inside our overcoats. As soon as he's asleep, we'll deal with the suitcases."

To keep him from getting out onto the platform while they slept, Willy blocked the waiting room door from the inside by piling up their luggage against it.

Once Pavel was asleep, Willy and Sophie opened the cases and changed into dry clothes, hoping no one would see them. Then they removed everything from the suitcases and piled all the clothes on another bench.

"I'm exhausted and my face hurts. Let's take a break." Willy sank down beside Pavel and skimmed *Der Angriff*, a two-day-old Nazi newspaper he found in a corner.

Simultaneously tired and alert, Sophie stood looking out through the waiting room windows, moodily studying the rain bouncing off the edge of the platform into darkness. Black thoughts in a run-down station in the middle of Nazi Germany—in just a few months her whole life had become a mess. She smiled, remembering how wonderfully their marriage had started after she eloped with Willy in 1936. They had two happy, exciting years and then, everything turned sour very quickly. As soon as her mother died of cancer in Berlin her gentle father and brother had sailed for Australia.

They were now interned, prisoners really, in a camp near Melbourne, while she and Willy were trapped and hopeless in this grimy waiting room, afraid that they would be arrested at any moment. She was especially anxious since Willy seemed so unsure of what to do. After the horrible fiasco with Venter, he was cowed and without confidence.

Sometime later—it was one in the morning when Willy looked at his watch—there was a noise at the door. He saw a pudgy face staring at him through the glass. The swing door moved slightly inwards, and one of the suitcases toppled over. Willy put a finger to his lips, pointing to Pavel sleeping on the bench, and tiptoed to the door.

"*Alles in Ordnung?* Everything all right?" said the night watchman through the crack in the door.

"Yes, we are trying to sleep," Willy whispered. "I put the suitcases here to stop the boy from getting out. Didn't Herr Gruber tell you about us?"

The night watchman pushed harder, shifting the suitcases enough to slide his head and shoulders inside the door. "I don't care about Gruber," he grumbled. "My orders are to lock the waiting room till five. You better come out and wait on the platform."

Holding a ten-mark note between his thumb and forefinger, Willy gave the man a modified Nazi salute and winked. Not a word was said, but the night watchman took the note and disappeared. Willy silently repositioned the suitcases. He returned to the bench, drenched in self-recrimination for having saluted the Führer. He rolled up a coat for a pillow and stared at the ceiling massaging and flexing his damaged finger, something he tried to do several times a day. For a while, his mind wandered, wondering what fear-provoking challenges the morning would bring. Then he slept.

It seemed like only moments later when Willy woke to the sound of snapping locks. Cuffing his weary eyes, he saw that it was still dark outside. Pavel was asleep, but Sophie was crouched beside the large suitcase, pulling out clothes. "What are you doing?"

"You said you wanted to go through the suitcases." She frowned at him. "It's half past three. We do not have much time. I already washed."

He stretched and yawned. "Remember, we'll only take the medium-sized case with us."

"That means I have to leave most of my clothes behind." Sophie gave him a sullen look. "Pavel is short on diapers. I might as well cut up the dresses into squares." She unzipped a toilet bag and pulled out nail scissors."

"Clever idea." Willy bent to caress her hair. "I'm sorry. It will be hard to destroy your nice blouses and dresses. I'd better get washed before we wake Pavel."

Later, at the sound of boots and shoes clumping on the platform outside Willy checked his watch again: 5:00 a.m. After Sophie washed and dressed Pavel, they gathered up their possessions and joined the crowd of passengers on the platform, leaving behind a jumble of clothes and suitcases scattered over the floor of the waiting room. The loudspeaker was blaring information about the Aachen train.

"Pavel like," Pavel shouted above the din, pointing at the steam coming from the black and silver locomotive.

Willy nodded. "Very big and fast. An express. Look at the back of it - do you see the men who drive it?"

Pavel nodded, and then pointed to the insignia painted on the side of the closest carriage. "What is picture?"

"It's an eagle on top of a black circle, Pavlíčku. It's called a swastika."

Pavel smiled. He repeated *swa-stika, swa-stika*, over and over.

In a previously agreed strategy for making sure they got seats, Sophie, carrying Pavel and the two coats, wearing the cloche hat to hide her unwashed hair, clambered up the carriage steps and found an empty compartment. She spread the coats on the two opposing window seats and positioned her beret to reserve a third.

Willy fought his way through the milling crowd, needing all his strength to get the suitcase and bags up on the lower step, taking care to protect his little finger. He hauled the suitcase over the upper steps, and in a few moments, they were settled. Willy placed the suitcase and bags in the overhead rack, and with sighs of relief, they sat down in the window seats. "Much better than the Kaiser's waiting room." He ran a hand over the velvet moquette. "Very sensuous."

Sophie laughed. "What a husband. You manage to find pleasure even in the most difficult situations." She pulled Pavel toward her. "Listen, *Pavlíčku*. If someone else, a stranger, sits with us, I want you to be very quiet. If you want to say something, whisper it in my ear. Do you understand?"

Pavel looked gravely at his mother. "Why, *Maminko*?"

"Just because. We don't want people to hear what we say. It's very important."

As Willy rose to open the small ventilation window to the outside, a ruddy face topped by a gray field cap peered through the compartment window. The door slid open, and five Wehrmacht soldiers in gray uniforms and caps trooped into the compartment, smoking and talking. "*Guten Morgen*," they chorused, stashing their equipment and rifles in the nooks and crannies of the overhead racks. After some pushing and arguing about where to sit, they flopped onto the seats.

Sophie could feel the sweat running down the back of her neck and under her arms. She tried a smile of greeting, but fear froze her lips. *Almighty God, what is going to happen with these soldiers?*

"*Guten Morgen*," said Willy in a monotone, glancing at Sophie in a way that conveyed great danger. This was worse than imaginable. The German army had surrounded them.

Pavel sat close to his mother holding her hand, studying each of the soldiers carefully. At first, he was silent, but after a few minutes, he frowned. "Táta says soldiers bad."

"Shush." Sophie put a finger to her lips. The young men talking and joking kept stealing glances at her. She had become used to the 'wandering eye', as Ruth Eisner called it, and the boys did not look unkind or evil. However, she was also aware that these nice boys were trained to kill and had been taught that Jews were to be despised and disposed of.

She could see Pavel was intrigued. Apart from Major Thümmel, he had never been so close to soldiers before. How would he react? In the past month or so, in parallel with his frequent tempers, he had become more inquisitive and sociable—endearing qualities at any other time. She was afraid that after he got over his shyness, he would start talking to them. She was confident that their own clothes, passports, books, and documents were all solidly Hungarian, but if by some bizarre chance one of these soldiers recognized that Pavel was speaking Czech, the masquerade could turn into a nightmare.

In the station waiting room, she and Willy had rehearsed what to do if they fell into conversation with German travelers. They would speak German and say that they were on their way to visit cousins in Aachen, not even mentioning Holland or Amsterdam. Her accent would clearly show she was from Berlin. Willy would be the Hungarian husband in the clothing business. They would have to gamble that the locals in this part of Germany would not know the difference between Czech and Hungarian.

She could see that Willy was trying to appear preoccupied, but the unshaven soldiers launched into friendly queries about who the Kohuts were and where they were headed. They explained they were local boys, traveling after a few days leave to rejoin their infantry regiment in Aachen and still recovering from joyous and schnapps-laden family reunions.

"Your kid keeps starin' at us," said the smiling, pink-cheeked, round-faced soldier who sat opposite Sophie, looking her up and down. Pavel had suddenly backed himself in between her knees, exposing the lower part of her thighs, toward which young male eyes flickered like hummingbirds drawn to nectar. Blushing, she quickly pushed Pavel forward and pulled down her skirt.

"He's a walking advertisement for the Reich," said another soldier. "Gold curls and blue eyes. Pure Aryan, eh? You ought to have a photograph made and send it in to someone high up in the Propaganda Ministry. My little cousin Helga's got lovely braids, same color as his. A photographer paid my auntie to use Helga's picture for a government poster."

One of the other soldiers, tall and long-nosed with a dark forelock over his ferrety eyes, kept switching his gaze from Sophie's thick, unkempt hair to the thin brown layers on Willy's prematurely balding head. "Don't get me wrong," he said in a mocking tone, "but I was wondering where your boy gets his blond hair from. Not from his dad, surely?" He chuckled, looking round at his mates as if expecting their approval. Sophie and Willy stared at him, saying nothing.

The soldier's face colored and he laughed. "Oops! Maybe I said the wrong thing?" He pointed at Willy's cheek. "That's a nasty new scrape on your face. What happened?"

Sophie replied quickly. "It's not as bad as it looks. He tripped over a luggage cart outside the station at Wiesbaden."

"Bad luck. Are you people from around here? You don't look from around here," said the ferret. "Different cut to your clothes."

"We're Hungarian," Willy interjected in German, jingling coins nervously inside his trouser pocket.

This young soldier not only looked like a ferret, Sophie thought, he acted like one, poking his nose into other people's affairs.

"We're on our way to Aachen," said Willy. "I'm from Budapest, and my wife grew up in Berlin. The little one, he speaks only Hungarian."

"Your German isn't too bad. What's in Aachen?"

Sophie twisted Pavel's curls between her fingers, looking from one soldier to the other, hoping the questions would stop. "A family get-together. I have a cousin there."

"We're rejoining our units in Herzogenrath," said another soldier, "close enough to the border to shake apples off the Dutch orchards." The other soldiers laughed.

"Holland will make a nice change," said the ferret. "I spent two weeks there on a school trip; all those canals, windmills, and funny old houses. I got to taste the gin too—*Oude Genever*, they called it. Had four shots. Luckily, my dad didn't find out."

There was more laughter.

After a while, two or three of the men began asking Pavel

questions. How old was he, and did he like chocolate? He shook his head, just stared at them with his wide blue eyes. Sophie could feel the heat of Willy's anxiety. He put a hand over hers. There was a moment of stillness and silence in the compartment.

"Not worth talking to the nipper—he only talks Hungarian," said the ferret.

"Too bad," retorted a scruffy, dark-faced soldier. His tunic was undone, showing a sweat-stained undershirt and curls of black chest hair. "What if I tried one of my tricks? He might like that."

"Go on, then, Manfred," someone called out.

Manfred pulled a silver coin from his pocket, popped it into his mouth, gulped it dramatically down, and then, after rolling his eyes, pulled it from his ear. Pavel giggled. "*Ještě*, again," he said.

"He wants you to do it again," said Willy.

After three more repeats, the soldier performed the same routine with a hard-boiled egg he got out of his knapsack. Pavel clapped his hands and shrieked in pleasure. "*Ještě jednou*, more," he chortled.

"He wants more tricks," Sophie spoke in German, offering her most enchanting smile. It was obvious to her that the soldiers had no idea what language Pavel spoke. Relief washed over her as Willy, squeezing her hand in reassurance, leaned back into his seat, the tense, anxious look gone from his face.

The next entertainer had a shaved head and an unshaven chin. In what Willy thought was a pleasant baritone with concert potential, he sang a bawdy country song and bounced Pavel on his knees. The others joined in the raucous, vulgar choruses. He passed the boy round to the others, who did the same thing with the songs and nursery rhymes they knew. Pavel babbled away to them in Czech.

"*Schöne blaue Augen*," said one of them. "Beautiful blue eyes."

Ridiculously, Willy wished for a camera. Once they were safe, he would send a photo of this scene direct to Herr Altmann at Gestapo headquarters in Prague – Nazi soldiers playing with the little Jewish boy, helping his family escape.

Best defense against prying is attack, Willy thought and began to ask the soldiers about their lives and families. Sophie caught on to the idea and soon the carriage was buzzing with laughter and conversation. Time and the countryside passed pleasantly by until an instantly recognizable smell invaded the compartment. One of the soldiers jumped to his feet and pried open the small upper window. Someone else muttered "*Kacke*" and the rest, with shy smiles, rubbed or covered their noses, looking at the sleeping Pavel.

Sophie flushed, feeling embarrassed and worried as she groped in the string bag where she kept the cut-up squares of her dresses and a small moist towel. She nudged Pavel awake. "High time to get you changed," she said in Czech. She stared at Willy and he nodded agreement.

"Take him to the washroom," he said in the same language. "No one will see his circumcision. If these boys get one glimpse of Pavel's penis, we're done for."

"I apologize for the smell." Sophie rose from her seat. "I'll take him to the washroom."

"Certainly, *gnädige* Frau," said one of the soldiers, rising to his feet, "but why don't you just do it in here? The corridor is packed with passengers and luggage, and there is a queue for the washroom. I don't think you want to wait there for twenty minutes holding a stinky kid. It's no place for a nice lady like you, and there is nowhere to put the kid down except on the dirty floor or the toilet seat. Why not change him here?"

"*Ja, ja, viel besser hier,*" the others echoed with nods and grins. "Better here."

Sophie stood still with Pavel in her arms, swaying to the train's rhythm, as if transfixed by indecision. The young man was right about how difficult it would be at the washroom, but she was terrified they would see Pavel's penis if she cleaned him in the compartment.

"Excuse the trouble," Willy said to the soldiers as he reached out to take her arm. "You see, my wife is very embarrassed to do this in front of a bunch of young men. Perhaps if you could give her some privacy? Wait outside?"

"Don't you fret, Frau Kohut," said the hirsute coin and egg juggler, patting her on the shoulder. "We won't be looking, will we, lads? We'll be out in the corridor with our backs to the door—and stop people spying on you. Guaranteed." The others nodded and grunted agreement.

Sophie gave them a brief, shy smile as she delved once

again into the bags to find the items she needed. "Thank you so much. You are very helpful."

The soldiers filed out and aligned their backs across the compartment door and windows, pushing other passengers out of the way. Sophie turned her back, blocking their view of Pavel's buttocks and legs. Willy, in the guise of helping her, placed himself as well as he could between Sophie and corridor. In a few minutes, she finished the task, and Willy slid open the door to recall the grinning soldiers back to their seats. One of them, tall and floppy-haired, peering through wire-rimmed glasses, volunteered to dispose of the soiled diaper, now tightly wrapped up in pages of *Der Angriff* newspaper.

"I'm an expert," he said with a wink. "I've got a little girl at home about his age." He left the compartment and returned five minutes later. "Had to throw it out of the window," he said with a shake of the head. "Toilet's blocked."

Once the unpleasant smell had dissipated, the soldiers broke out their packs, producing hard-boiled eggs, Braunschweiger sausage, ham, pickled gherkins, and hunks of black bread. "Good, solid home food," said the ferret, "not like the usual army shit. Please, share some with us, if you like."

As the men ate, the entertainment and horseplay continued. The corporal with the shaved head kept tossing a gherkin in the air, trying to spear it with his clasp knife. After more than 10 attempts, he at last succeeded in hitting it, and fragments of gherkin showered onto the floor to hoots of laughter.

Pavel moved from one soldier to the next, sampling their food. He sat on their laps, asked questions in Czech, and fingered the embroidered labels on their shoulder straps and insignias on their lapels. He pulled the metal badges off their field caps and shoved a hand into their pockets, looking for coins. He even tried to unbutton the holster of a soldier's pistol. As a finale to the lunchtime show, another soldier took his rifle down from the luggage rack, disengaged the razor-sharp bayonet, and used it to slice up an apple strudel. Using his knapsack as a tray, he laid out the portions on wax paper. "Please, *Herr und Frau* Kohut, you must try some," he said with a proud grin. "My mother made this for my unit brothers. She's a fine cook."

Pavel gobbled up his serving. "I want more," he said, with hopeful look.

Sophie shook her head. "That's enough, darling." She

smiled at the soldier. "This strudel is absolutely wonderful. So light. My compliments to your mother."

When the train arrived at the station in Aachen, the soldiers carried the Kohuts' luggage down to the platform, saying goodbye with friendly pats and ruffling Pavel's blond curls. Only the ferret soldier lingered close to Willy. "I thought you might like to know, Herr Hungarian," he said with an amused gleam in his eyes. "My mother is Czech, from Brno. I was wondering why your little boy was speaking Czech. Perhaps all is not as it seems? *Na shledanou*, see you later." He winked and walked away.

Pavel looked up at Willy. "Me like soldiers."

"Yes." Willy took Sophie's arm, anxiety eating at his guts. "Nice soldiers, Pavel, but they're gone now, and we must hurry to find the train."

24

TRAIN TO NOWHERE
JULY, 1939

"I JUST HOPE those soldier fellows won't be around when we buy our tickets to Amsterdam—we told them we were staying here in Aachen."

They walked along the platform toward the stairs of the iron-beamed gangway that crossed the tracks and led to the arrivals and departures hall. Shading his eyes against the sun shimmering through the glass of the iron lattice roof, Willy noticed a burly policeman standing beside the ticket collector at the foot of the stairs and on the opposite platform, a couple of armed soldiers accompanied by a leashed Alsatian dog. "We must appear calm and orderly. The police are everywhere."

"So, pull...pull your hat down, Willy," Sophie murmured, adjusting her cloche forwards. "If someone notices the mess your face is in, we might be stopped."

Willy paused to tilt his homburg down on one side and grinned at her. "So I look like Humphrey Bogart, you mean?"

She crinkled her eyes at him. "Yes, but he's a lot more handsome than you at this particular moment."

They passed the policeman, handed in their tickets without even a glance from the railway official, and crossed the gangway. After 50 meters, they entered a large, busy stone-walled concourse with high-arched Romanesque windows. Wehrmacht soldiers sat in groups on the tiled floor, smoking and fiddling with their packs as if they were bored with waiting. Willy heard them complaining about their lack of orders.

He looked up at the suspended timetable, clicking out platform numbers, destinations, and arrival and departure times. "Look," he said. "We've two options. In an hour's time, there is a train for Amsterdam. Gets there at two." He pointed to the lower part of the board. "But there's also a train to Paris, though it doesn't leave until six and gets in at ten tonight. If we choose the Paris train, we will have to wait here another nine hours and run the risk of the police or Gestapo stopping us. We don't much look like respectable travelers anymore."

"I'm hungry," Pavel said, pulling at Sophie's sleeve.

She unwrapped her last chocolate pastille and watched him eat it. "I don't think I can manage nine hours more on a hard bench, trying to keep Pavel happy and quiet. I want to get somewhere safe, quickly. Let's go to Amsterdam."

Willy put his arm around her. "Amsterdam is tempting, but there's the chance they might close the border. Perhaps we should just wait for the Paris express. "

Pavel, an oval of chocolate smeared round his lips, was studying his parents' faces closely, as if he understood that they were talking about something important.

She pursed her lips. "I vote for Amsterdam. We could be there by early this afternoon and then find a way to get to England. That's what you want, isn't it? If we take the French express tonight, I'm afraid we'll be stuck in Paris. Didn't Janko say the Channel ferries had stopped working?"

Willy straightened his shoulders. "Amsterdam it is." It was good to have made a joint decision. Sophie's smile showed relief and satisfaction.

When the dirt-streaked International Express, destination Amsterdam, arrived at Platform 3, the Kohuts had no trouble finding an empty compartment. After stowing their belongings, Willy surveyed the platform from the top of the carriage steps, wanting to be sure that if their previous soldier acquaintances turned up, he would spot them first so they could take evasive action.

"Why are so few people traveling today?" he asked the railway supervisor, who was holding a green flag. "Are there any problems at the border?"

"*Ich weiss nicht.*" The man shrugged his epaulettes and

walked away. Willy felt a trickle of fear, though it seemed understandable that people would shelve their travel plans if there were increasing tension on the border.

Their compartment was empty and clean, though it smelled of cheap perfume and recently smoked cigarettes. As was usual on international trains, it had a sliding door giving access to a windowed corridor that ran the length of the train. Willy and Sophie sat opposite each other on the bench seats. While they waited for the guard's whistle, and to calm his own impatience, Willy showed Pavel the sepia tourist photographs posted above the headrests, each titled in white cursive: the Zugspitze and Hochwanner Mountains in Bavaria, a Berchtesgaden winter scene with skiers, Heidelberg castle, and a beer garden full of jolly people cavorting to an oompah band.

Finally, the guard blew his whistle and the train moved away. Willy's face split into a wide smile, and he slid his arms round Pavel and Sophie, kissing them both. "This is almost the last lap, my darlings, and we're alone here... No need to pretend. We can make ourselves comfortable, spread out."

Sophie kicked off her heeled pumps and put her sock-covered feet on the edge of the opposite seat. "*Gott sei Dank*, this is so much better." She heaved a sigh of relief, mopping her face with a handkerchief. "Sitting with those soldiers was nerve-racking, but we got through it."

Willy leaned forward and gave her toes an affectionate squeeze. "It was touch and go. Most of the time, my stomach was churning like a coffee grinder. You did so well with Pavel. You were calm and practical. Superb."

Sophie laughed. "It helped that they were good boys, just ordinary soldiers. But what if they had seen Pavel's circumcision? I can't believe they wouldn't have reported us."

Willy looked at his watch. "That ferret-faced one knew we were Czech. He was giving us a chance. Anyway, don't let us be too sure yet. At the Dutch frontier, we'll play the Hungarian story again, but with a new twist. We're on the way to visit my cousin Andreas Venter who lives in the town of Zaandam, Schansend Street."

Sophie raised her eyebrows. "For heaven's sake. I didn't know you had his address."

Willy shook his head and handed her the wrapper from Pavel's chocolate pastille. "I don't—just took it from this.

Zandaam is where Verkade make their chocolate. Which reminds me... We should eat something. I saw a vendor getting on the train with a tray full of sausages and rolls."

ↀ ∂ ↀ

Half an hour after passing the town of Gangelt, still on the German side of the Dutch frontier, the train clanked to a halt. Willy looked out of the window. Woods with an understory of straggly shrubs surrounded them. He could not see any station, just a huddle of wooden sheds with corrugated roofs. They waited a quarter of an hour, growing more and more anxious, until two *Grenzpolizei* officials slid open the door and saluted with perfunctory '*heils*'. With calm, impenetrable faces and polite efficiency, they examined and stamped the Hungarian passports.

"Why do we stop here?" Willy asked tentatively.

One official shrugged, staring at Sophie. "*Alles in Ordnung*," said the other with a brief smile. "*Gute Reise*. Safe journey." They clicked their heels and left.

Willy leaned back, hands locked behind his head. He puffed out a sigh of relief. "You see? Everything is fine—just like that. Very polite and no questions. They even smiled at us."

"Police don't smile. Something's got to be wrong." Sophie ran her fingers through her tangled hair, scratching her scalp; she desperately needed a hair wash and a good bath. "Why aren't we moving?" She got up to peer out of the window.

"Stop agitating and sit down." Willy frowned. "We'll find out soon enough."

Five minutes later, the train shunted forward 50 meters and stopped again. Willy and Sophie looked at each other. Willy eyes shone with anticipation and he clapped his hands happily, trying to get Pavel to do the same. "This must mean we've moved to the Dutch side. Dutch customs next. We're nearly free."

Pavel climbed from the seat onto the D-shaped table at the windowsill and peered out. Sophie held on to his legs. "Why train stop? Lokomo go sleep?"

At that moment, the compartment door slid open and a tall, fair-haired man in a blue uniform with leather belt and cross straps stepped in. "*Paspoorten, alstublieft*." Willy dug into his jacket pocket and handed him the documents. With a quick look and a shake of his flaxen hair, the Dutch customs agent handed them back to Willy. "*Tot onze spijt is de grens voor buitenlanders gesloten.*"

They give him a blank stare. What was he saying?

"*Sie sprechen Deutsch?*"

"*Nein,*" said Willy, sticking to his role as a Hungarian businessman. He knew the Dutch disliked Germans and hated speaking their language even more.

"Speak English?"

Willy nodded, holding up his thumb and forefinger to show a limited command of English, which, in reality, he spoke fluently.

"Nederlands and Germany no longer cooperate," said the official. "Today, only Dutch citizens enter. For you, frontier is closed, *gesloten*. We stopped this train. No more travel." He pointed through the compartment window. "Road transport takes you back to Gangelt. From there, you go where you want. It is an order."

The police officer left, slamming the door shut.

His hopes stymied, Willy made a great effort to explain, quietly, what the official had said. Sophie's face turned ashen and she began to sob. Pavel leaned against her, looking as though he was ready to follow suit. At that moment, they heard the loudspeaker. "*Achtung*, attention. All passengers who are not Dutch citizens must immediately proceed with their luggage to the trucks. You will be transported to Gangelt by road. No exceptions."

Trucks! Willy looked out and saw what looked like farm trucks lined up in a clearing on the other side of the tracks. He turned and saw Sophie's face filled with alarm. She grabbed his arm. "Must we obey?"

Willy could not bear the thought of staying in Germany to wait for yet another train that went nowhere. There had to be a way out of this for them. Maybe they could hide in the woods and then follow the railway tracks toward the Dutch border?

"Wait here a minute. I'll go into the corridor and check the other side of the train," he said. "We might be able to slip out unnoticed and hide."

A minute later, he was back, rubbing his unshaved chin, shoulders drooping. "They've got armed guards all along both sides of the track. I saw another train further down the line loaded with tanks, soldiers all over the place. We must do what they say." Feeling disheartened and impotent, he pulled their suitcase down from the rack.

"We get off the train now, Pavel," said Sophie, looking at their shabby possessions as if she could not stand them anymore. "This train is stuck."

Willy could not bear to tell Sophie what he was thinking. *What if those trucks are not headed for Gangelt?*

25

Doubling Back
July, 1939

A **GLIMMER OF SUN** filtered through the diminishing rain clouds as Willy, carrying the suitcase followed the other passengers squelching along a narrow, muddy path that meandered across a lush meadow dotted with flowering elderberry bushes. Sophie followed just behind him, Pavel in her arms. Several armed soldiers stood at intervals on either side of the path, knee-deep in wildflowers, pointing encouragingly toward the line of trucks. *"Schnell machen."*

Sophie slipped repeatedly on the mud and finally put Pavel down. He pulled away and plunged into the grass to blow the parachute heads off dandelions and chase vaulting grasshoppers, covering his clothes with wet seed heads. "Come here, Pavel," she shouted in Hungarian when he had fallen about twenty meters behind. Though he spoke only Czech, she knew he understood simple Magyar commands. He took no notice, crisscrossing the path and getting in the way of other straggling passengers. A sour-faced woman shook her fist at him, but he did not react, just hopped off into the grass again.

"Hurry up, Pavel, we'll miss the truck," Willy shouted angrily, turning to Sophie. "You should have kept him with you."

Pavel looked up at the sound of his father's voice but stopped in front of a stack of moss-covered logs and began to peer into the crevices.

"Damned brat," Willy said abruptly. "I'll go back for him. You go ahead and snag us a decent place on the truck—somewhere we can rest our backs against something." Carrying the suitcase, he strode back along the path past the last few stragglers.

The path widened to a graveled area where several farm trucks were parked. Sophie passed a couple of soldiers with machine pistols hanging from their shoulders. Beside each vehicle, an official with a Nazi armband was directing the passengers to step up onto a battered wooden box and then scramble into the truck. As the waiting line edged closer, Sophie noticed that all the suitcases were being stacked in the center of the truck bed, while most passengers fitted themselves on low narrow benches round the sides.

After some pushing, shoving, and arguing, Sophie claimed a corner space big enough for herself and Willy with Pavel on his lap. She unpinned her cloche hat, sat down and turned to a well-dressed man she guessed was in his fifties who seemed very calm as if he knew what was going on. "Excuse me, please." she said in German Why are all the soldiers here? Are you sure they are taking us to Gangelt?"

He patted her knee reassuringly as more passengers found space on the floor around the pile of suitcases "The soldiers are here because the frontier has closed and they have to take us back—it's because our boys are getting ready to thump the Dutch."

By the time Willy had dragged Pavel away from the log pile, the truck engines were revving up and acrid diesel fumes swirled into the air. With Pavel struggling and yelling protests in Czech, they reached the back of the truck as the last passengers were climbing up over the tailgate.

A young soldier stepped forward and put a hand on Willy's chest. "Full. Understand? Take your screaming kid to that last one, over there."

Willy saw Sophie sitting in the corner, looking at him with desperation on her face. "My wife is on this one. See, over there. The boy needs her. Please let us on."

"Full," the soldier shouted in Willy's face, slipping the machine pistol off his shoulder. "Go to that other truck." He shoved the pistol barrel into Willy's chest.

Suddenly fearful the young soldier might lose control, Willy tucked his wriggling, shrieking son under one arm and ran awkwardly with the suitcase to the last truck. A young man helped them clamber up into the back, Pavel was swinging his arms wildly, bumping against passengers, shouting, "I want *Maminka*, where is *Maminka*?"

Willy, terrified that Pavel's tantrum and Czech words would bring serious trouble did the only thing he could think of that had worked fast before...he slapped Pavel hard on each buttock and sat him on the floor. With a few residual, jagged sobs, Pavel turned quiet, staring at Willy with reproachful blue eyes. "Where *Maminka*? I want *Maminka*."

"She's on another truck, the one behind us. We will see her at the end of this journey. Now be quiet."

"*Dieser Kerl hat gut gemacht*, he did the right thing," said a thin, sandy-haired man pointing Willy out to the woman beside him. In her lap, she held a little girl wearing a blue headscarf, perhaps two years older than Pavel. He pointed his feathered trilby hat at Pavel. "That's the right way to discipline a bumptious kid." His wife nodded her approval.

The rattletrap truck was open to the sky, its sides constructed of a lattice of rough-sawn wood. The passengers shouted at each other above the whine of the engine noise and the harsh bounce of the springs. As the truck convoy trundled along the country roads, Pavel gradually lost his sullen look and the corners of his mouth turned up. Swaying between Willy's arms, he looked out through spaces in the wooden framework.

Willy watched his boy gaze at the passing countryside and smiled. This bumpy ride was not so bad. They were in the open air, and there were no soldiers. He thought about Sophie sitting in one of the other trucks ahead, sure that she found it uncomfortable and alarming to be by herself among strangers. This was their first separation since his release from prison, and he hoped she had the strength to stay calm and keep conversation to a minimum. Anyway, there was nothing more he could do until the trucks reached their destination.

A young woman in a flowered dress and clogs sitting next to Willy offered him a cigarette, which he politely refused. "I saw how you controlled your boy," she said with admiring eyes. "How old is he?"

"Just over two."

"And still in diapers? What language were you speaking with him?"

"Czech," he replied, and then, cursing his mistake, came up with another deceptive explanation. "We were on our way to Amsterdam. With the frontier blocked, we must go back to Bonn and then home to Sudetenland."

"Ach, so, Sudetenland—now I understand where your accent comes from. It is a year now since we liberated your land from the Czechs and annexed Austria. Everyone is proud of what we did. I just do not understand why Germany needs to have rationing, shortages of everything, and so much rudeness from officials. I wish the old days were back."

"Shush." Willy frowned, putting a finger to his lips. "It's not wise to complain in public." He turned his shoulder and looked away, not wanting to talk anymore.

℘ ∂ ℘

Sophie managed to slide off her coat and fold it to sit on. The bench corner she was sitting on was uneven and had a split in the wood. Where were Willy and Pavel? Panic grabbed at her...had they been left behind? She summoned up her common-sense. It was almost guaranteed that Willy and Pavel were on another truck, probably the one just behind them in the convoy. She stood up and looked back, holding herself steady against the wood framing, in the hope she might at least recognize Willy's homburg as they rounded a bend. As she was sitting down, the truck rocked and the man she had spoken to put a hand on her thigh, as if to steady her. He did not remove it until she was sitting on the bench. She looked at him; he was clean-shaven and well dressed, with dark eyes and close-cut brownish hair... respectable.

"Thank you."

"A pleasure, Fraulein."

Concern flashed through her mind at his smiling response. She had sensed danger in the long pressure of his fingers.

Half an hour later, her anxiety about her neighbor abated. He had not made eye contact again. Now she thought about how Willy was coping with Pavel in whatever truck they were riding. She prayed that Pavel had settled, after his tantrum. We must not draw attention to ourselves, Willy had said. She sighed.

This was their journey's first separation, but soon they would be re-united.

It was then that she felt a hand slide up under her dress and rest on her thigh, nothing subtle about it. She grabbed his wrist and glared. "Stop this, now."

He shook his head, a smile playing on his lips. "Surely, you wouldn't want to cause a scene, pretty Fraulein. Not with soldiers here. I won't hurt you and you will enjoy it. I'm an expert."

Sophie looked to see if the passengers close by had seen what was happening. Most were dozing, no one had noticed. She wanted to call out for help, but was afraid.

Her neighbor was strong and, in spite of her efforts, his hand advanced toward her groin, as he massaged her flesh. She twisted her body away from him, feeling trapped and nauseated.

"Come on now, my dear. I do not want to force you. Just let yourself go and enjoy it." His voice was hoarse in her ear.

She could not look at him. She held her breath, her mind racing. *Whatever you do, Sophie, don't make a fuss.* A fuss would attract shameful attention, and the soldiers... what would they do? God knows what might happen when they reached Gangelt: questions, identity checks, detention...their journey would be over. And Willy? How would he react? She had to fight back, somehow.

She plunged her hands into her bag, momentarily leaving the man's fingers creeping up her inner thigh. In almost the same instant, she felt the handle of the long hatpin pinned in her hat. She grabbed the ivory handle and drove its five-inch spike into the man's upper arm...twice. She felt the hatpin grate on bone and shuddered.

The man's grip on her skin loosened. With a groan, he pulled his arm away, at the same time exposing the whole of her bare leg. "Bitch," he shouted, holding his arms across his heaving chest, rocking back and forth. "Bitch." He began to shake and touched the wet patch on his upper sleeve. He was breathing fast, his face crunched in pain.

Sophie straightened her dress as a handful of nearby passengers, jerked awake from their doze and stared at her. "*Was ist los?* What happened?"

"Nothing," Sophie replied calmly, though her heart thudded like a steam hammer. In a minute or two, everyone either nodded off again, or no longer paid her attention. She leaned close to her attacker who was looking down at his knees, muttering "Shit, shit, and shit."

She considered trying to move away, squeeze into a spot somewhere else, but she was afraid of provoking anger, causing trouble. She decided she would have to stay next to this schmuck however long it took. Just to be on the safe side she waved the hatpin in front of his face and whispered. "If you even look at me again I'll blind you with this."

⁖ ∂ ⁖

In the bare waiting room at Gangelt, surrounded by noisy, arguing passengers, Sophie sat down and studied her face in a hand mirror trying to repair the truck journey's ravages with what remained of her lipstick and powder. Her heart was still pounding. Not because of the would-be rapist but because, for the first few minutes as the crowd dispersed and thinned out, she had not seen Willy and Pavel. Fear gripped her heart.

Then Pavel appeared out of nowhere and climbed into her lap, laughing and throwing his arms around her neck. Willy appeared at the waiting room door, holding the suitcase. He sat down beside her and they hugged and kissed, all three of them.

Willy stroked Sophie's hair, caressing her with his eyes. "I hope you weren't too worried about us, strudel? Pavel and I had fun; how was it for you?"

"I was afraid we wouldn't find each other." Sophie tried to hold back the tears of relief. "A man tried to be fresh with me, but I stopped him." What was the point of giving Willy the gory details? The man was gone and her husband had enough to contend with.

"Good for you, strudel."

They sat on another hard bench waiting for a local train to take them back to Aachen so that, this time, they could catch the express to Paris. She looked up at Willy with disheartened eyes. "When will this nightmare journey stop?"

Willy gave her an encouraging look. "Cheer up sweetheart. We'll keep trying."

"How can you stay so optimistic, *miláčku*? After what we've been through." Sophie put her face in her hands. Pavel clung to her skirt, looking anxious.

"Could be a lot worse?" Willy said with a bright smile. "We're still together and we still have hope and some money. You seem shaken. "

She lowered her hands and looked at him through glistening tears, her happiness mixed up with residual anger from her journey on the truck "Wouldn't you be? My bottom is bruised, an unpleasant man pestered me and I haven't bathed or changed clothes for three days." She took a deep breath. "And I'm ravenous. "

Seeing the despair and weariness on Sophie's face, Willy wanted to comfort her, take her in his arms, but the presence of the other people in the waiting room stopped him. Displays of emotion drew people's attention and suspicions.

He squeezed her hand to reassure her and then stood up. Hands in pockets, he walked across the floor to study a vast railway map that filled one entire wall of the waiting room. With the reverses they had suffered and Sophie feeling down, his own self-confidence was ebbing, though he was determined not to show it.

"Listen, Sophie," he muttered after sitting down again. "I looked at the railway map and timetable. It's still only midday. When we get back to Aachen, we'll take the evening Paris train. It goes through Liège. It'll take us about four hours from Aachen, including passport control."

"Liège? Where's that? Why don't we get off there? "

"Liège is in Belgium, and the train only stops there for five minutes before going on to Paris. Who do we know in Liège? I've never been there. Paris I know, and there is a Czech legation there. What about your cousin Feri? Doesn't his family live in Paris?"

Sophie nodded vigorously. "Yes, of course. Feri is at the Sorbonne. We could look his family up in the telephone directory. I seem to remember they have a carpet store."

Willy put his hand on her forearm, giving her a congratulatory squeeze. "Excellent. I had forgotten about him. At least we have someone to fall back on."

She smiled. "Already I can imagine sleeping in a nice French bed."

He looked at his watch. "We have another forty-five minutes till the Gangelt-Aachen train arrives. I noticed a café opposite the station entrance. Let's see if we can get something to eat."

ରେ ∂ ରେ

The local train was on time, and after a short, uneventful journey, the Kohuts were returned to the Aachen station at two in the afternoon. After a morning storm, the sky had cleared, and it was now sweltering, even in the shade of the platform overhangs. For a minute or two, they were not sure where to go amid the confusion of signs. After consulting with a porter, they followed a stream of travelers to the footbridge that led to the international platform.

Gazing around at the bustling, noisy crowd rushing past them, Pavel suddenly pointed ahead. "*Táto, táto*, look! I see bad car man."

"My God," gasped Willy. "Look."

Andreas Venter was slumped against an iron stanchion near the bottom of the footbridge stairs, his hands manacled behind him. A police officer stood close by, idly smoking a cigarette and looking across the tracks.

Sophie, startled, grabbed hold of Willy's hand. "Venter? Why is he here?"

"Arrested it seems. Not too surprising though. He was traveling north like us."

"He looks awful. He seems to be in pain."

"Well, they probably beat him up." Willy was breathing heavily as he carried the bulging suitcase up the steps. He felt the sweat on his back. "Don't look—keep going. He's trouble."

"But the money you paid him...my jewels. Can't we ask him where they are? Still in his car, do you think? He is your relative. We should help him."

"Absolutely not with that policeman hovering over him. We will make do without jewels. Ignore him, the past is the past. We cannot risk tangling with the police."

Slowing her pace, Sophie watched Venter raise his head, and she shuddered at the bruises and blood smears on his face. Their glances met and he cracked a smile. Closing his eyes, he slumped his shoulders and turned his head away.

26

Anything to Declare
July, 1939

ON THE PARIS EXPRESS, the Kohuts shared their compartment with an older couple, the man occupying a window seat, his wife seated beside him. As the train pulled out of Aachen, Willy and Sophie offered a nod and a faint *Guten Tag* and then lapsed into silence, still shocked by seeing Venter again. With polite smiles, the couple nodded back. Pavel sat on Sophie's lap with his face glued to the window, silently watching the flat countryside go by.

Willy picked up a folded newspaper that someone had left tucked into a crevice in the cushions—that day's *Kölnischer Westdeutscher Beobachter*, well respected and not prone to exaggerated propaganda. Skimming the front page, he felt a surge of panic. An editorial praised the newly established Jewish Registration Center in Berlin for its efficiency in requisitioning thousands of Jewish properties and businesses and reported that a flood of Polish and German Jews were trying to flee to the west. The frontier in northwest Germany was on high alert because of the tensions with France, Belgium, and Holland.

He decided to keep the news to himself—Sophie had been through enough already. He glanced at his watch. Soon they would reach Kelmis, a small town on the German-Belgian frontier. According to the newspaper, that was exactly where the German guards would be on high alert for Jews. He thrust the newspaper away, took off his sweaty jacket, and leaned toward Sophie. "I'm sure you realize these friendly-looking people in the window seats are French. I don't think we have to be afraid of them," he said quietly in Hungarian.

Sophie smiled at him, and he felt her body relax against his. "Yes, they sounded just like my French teacher in *Hochschule*. I am so relieved. I've had enough of worrying about Pavel speaking Czech and covering up who we are."

Willy pulled out the front of his shirt and polished his glasses with it. He did not have a handkerchief anymore, and he was past caring about polite behavior. He was trying hard to suppress the fear of what was waiting for them at Kelmis, imagining something similar to what had happened at the Dutch frontier near Gangelt: heavily armed soldiers, personnel carriers, and barbed wire rolled out along the tracks. He was not sure Sophie could manage another round of reverses and fear.

"You will adore Paris," said Willy, trying to put her at ease. "Pavel will love it as well. I'll take you up the Eiffel Tower, and we'll have a boat ride on the Seine. They call them *Bateaux Mouches*—fly boats because they glide on top of the water like insects." He laughed, stroking Pavel's knee and ruffling his curls. "I have a good feeling about this train. Today, we'll be lucky." Slipping an arm around Sophie's shoulders, he kissed her cheek.

Sophie leaned in and gently squeezed the fingers of his good hand. "In Paris, we can be happy again. First, I will have a wonderful bath. Then we'll go to museums and eat delicious food, and you will learn to play the piano again." She touched the scrapes and bruises on his face. "No more of these."

Willy could not help preparing her a little for what was coming. "In forty-five minutes, we will be at the border—our last hurdle. I'm praying that the *Grenzpolizei* will just take a quick look at our passports and let us through."

Sophie's dreamy smile vanished. "Oh God, me too."

Trying to keep from imagining the harrowing scenarios that might play out at the frontier, Willy decided to engage the older French couple. The man was small and grizzled with a mobile face that twitched when he spoke. A weather-beaten black beret clung to his bald head. His chubby wife, who wore a short-sleeved flowered dress with a frilly collar, could not stop fiddling with the flashing rings and bracelets that adorned her wrists and fingers. Willy swallowed his prejudice against the Frenchman's rumpled, badly cut serge suit and, in fluent French, introduced his family

M. and Mme. Panasse responded in kind; they were Frédéric and Jeanine, proud parents of three children and one new grandchild. Madame had a tendency to giggle at everything, whatever the subject. Whenever her husband made the smallest comment, her eyes would gleam with admiration and pleasure, as if she were married to the most entertaining man in the world.

"We are Hungarians," said Willy. "Regretfully, my wife, Sophie, speaks very little French, though she knows German well—and our Pavel here, he's just over two and speaks a mixture of languages. We all do. That's how it is where we're from—the center of Europe."

M. Panasse pressed his hands together in delight. "Ah, *mon Dieu*, Sophie—a French name, and so appropriate for your charming wife. And you, monsieur, your French—*vous parlez bien*. Where did you learn to speak so fluently?"

"In Paris, at the time of the Great Exhibition. I was a student at the Dufour Business College in the sixth arrondissement."

"Aha, *un étudiant sérieux*."

Willy shook his head and laughed somewhat shamefacedly. "I must admit I skimmed my studies. I was too busy guiding central Europeans around the sights and playing piano in night clubs to cover my rent."

"*Ah, bon? Très intéressant*."

Willy translated for Sophie as the conversation rolled along while Pavel slumbered in his mother's lap. "Why were you in Germany? You French have no love for *les Boches*."

M. Panasse nodded. "*C'est simple*: My family originated from the part of Germany that used to belong to France—Aix-la-Chapelle, now called Aachen. My cousin's family still lives there, and of course, they all speak German. My wife doesn't."

"Lucky for me, his relatives wheeled their rusty French out of the garage." Mme Panasse collapsed into peals of laughter, her meaty arms trembling with the effort.

Her husband frowned. "*Assez de plaisanteries, chérie, le comedien c'est moi*. Enough with the jokes my dear. I'm the funny one."

She dutifully lowered her eyes, carefully straightening the rumpled pleats of her dress over dimpled knees. Looking at Willy, she laid a hand over her ample bosom. "Me, I'm from the port of Boulogne. My family runs a sailors hostel near the docks."

M. Panasse looked at Sophie, apparently disregarding his wife's contribution to the conversation. "Do you know Aix-la-Chapelle, Madame? We have the oldest cathedral in northern Europe. The great King of the Franks, Charlemagne, is buried there. A wonderful place."

Mme. Panasse crossed herself, fingering the jeweled crucifix hanging from her neck. "They have incredible relics there." She rolled her eyes skyward. "*Incroyable*. Everything genuine. Jesus' swaddling clothes—his loincloth from the cross, the blessed virgin's cloak, and the cloth that lay under John the Baptist's severed head, all in the famous chapel. You must make a pilgrimage." She closed her eyes and crossed herself again, lips moving in silent prayer.

"Impossible to believe they dragged all that paraphernalia from Palestine to Aachen more than a thousand years ago." M. Panasse waved his smoky Gauloise in a figure-eight pattern. "My wife is very religious. Boring, but she means no harm."

A typical French husband, Willy surmised, domineering, but entertaining.

Pavel woke up still clutching his furry lion. He looked intently at the French couple, perhaps bewildered, Willy thought, by their conversation. "What do they say, *Táto?*"

"These people speak French, Pavel. We are traveling with them to a new country, France."

"What's France, *Táto?*"

"A new country. You and *maminka* will have to learn to speak like they do."

"Why, *Táto?*" Like a dog sniffing out a rabbit, Pavel wrinkled his nose, turning his face into Willy's chest. "That man smells."

Willy shared an amused look with Sophie. "Garlic."

Pavel unburied his face. "What is garlic, *Táto?*"

Sophie took over. "A sort of vegetable, like an onion. People use it to make food taste good."

Willy ran his hands through Pavel's curls. "In France, they cook with garlic all the time."

"Cigarette?" M. Panasse took out a rumpled pack of cigarettes and offered it to both Sophie and Willy. After they declined, he extracted a floppy one and lit it with a high-flame gold lighter. Pavel sat forward, eyes wide with wonder.

"I knew your boy would be interested," said M. Panasse with a proud smile, leaning forward, flicking the flame on and off. "*Très spéciale*. It's a lighter made by Myon in the shape of the Eiffel Tower."

At that moment, the train began to slow. Sophie wrapped her arms round the boy, nuzzling his neck and face as if she thought it would strengthen him for any ordeal that might be coming. Willy noticed that she was pale, and her eyes were wide with anxiety. He patted her knee. "Everything will be fine. We are almost out of Germany."

The train screeched and clattered, jerking to a stop after what seemed an interminably long five minutes. Mme. Panasse kicked off her shoes, sprang up onto the corner seat, and stuck her head out of the small central window. "*Enfin, la frontière!* I see a little station."

Willy translated for Sophie. "It's the German-Belgian frontier..." The blast from a loudspeaker drowned his voice. "*Kelmis. Alle aussteigen. Heraus. Alle aussteigen.*"

"We all get out here." The Frenchman patted his wife's hand reassuringly.

Seeing the fear pulling at Sophie's face, Willy laced his fingers with hers. "We must keep calm, strudel."

Their carriage jerked forward once more and then stopped. A whistle blew. Willy looked out and saw a narrow platform in front of the three square stucco buildings with barred windows that made up Kelmis Station. Armed men—SS, dressed in black, others in *feldgrau* with dogs on leashes—walked up and down the platform, some waving and shouting for passengers to get out with their luggage. Other men in civilian garb and leather coats on their shoulders stood close to the entry doors of the main building. With a jolt, Willy realized they were Gestapo.

A train conductor slid open the compartment door. "This is Kelmis. Bring your luggage," he said in a curt, barking voice. "After you pass through German passport and customs control, the train will move to the Belgian section. Passengers who have been cleared can then re-board. Belgian control is on the train. Departure for Paris in ninety minutes."

Willy and Sophie looked at each other, too tense and fearful to speak. Despite the embarrassment of having M. and Mme. Panasse observe their distress, Willy took Sophie's hand and slid a bundle of Reichsmark bills and a slip of paper into it. "Here... three hundred marks or so—enough for a couple of days of food and lodging in Paris. Also my parents' address in London. If we are somehow separated or I am detained, you must not wait or look for me inside Germany. You must get on the train to Paris—save yourself and Pavel, reach England."

She gasped and looked at him, terror-stricken. "I couldn't do that—not without knowing what was happening to you."

"Just take the money. What did you do with the diamonds you saved from Venter?"

"In my brassiere."

"Good. Let's hope they don't make us strip."

Within fifteen minutes, the passengers were standing in lines supervised by armed soldiers at thirty-meter intervals. Willy and the others from their compartment had disembarked and were now squeezed together as if they were all one family. The sun beat down on the tin roof and the passengers, shuffling slowly forward, began to complain about the heat.

After twenty minutes had passed, worry began to ripple along the line. With only seventy minutes before the train left for Paris, how could everyone get through in time? Some passengers began to protest and break ranks; the soldiers responded with shouts, readying their guns and encouraging their dogs to snarl and strain on the leashes.

Willy looked around for a possible way out in case things went wrong, but he could see that escape would be impossible with a small child in tow. Solid-looking storm troopers guarded both sides of the tracks for at least two hundred meters. Far down the track beyond the train, he could make out the shape of an armored car topped by a soldier operating a machine gun.

The loudspeaker blared again. "Passengers will be escorted in batches of ten to German customs and passport control hall. Re-boarding of the train must be completed one hour from now."

At the entrance to the station hall, SS troopers supervised the formation of a single-file queue. With each blast of a whistle, a soldier funneled a group of ten passengers forward into the adjacent building. Willy, Sophie, and Pavel, still on the platform, watched as an engine shunted the empty train to the Belgian side of the station. Willy wistfully imagined his family on that train, having passed through German control with flying colors. That triggered an idea. "The officials might ask who we know in Paris or where we plan to stay," he said in a low tone to Sophie. "You have your cousin's full name and address, I suppose?" Sophie, looking miserable, shook her head. "I made a note, *miláčku*, but I lost it. All I know is that Feri is a medical student at the Sorbonne and his parents have a carpet store."

Willy racked his brain to invent a believable Paris address but all he came up with was Rue Monge on the Left Bank. Maybe that would suffice. He grew more and more afraid of what was coming. He took off his jacket; his shirt was soaked with perspiration, and his little finger itched uncontrollably inside its velvet fingerstall. There was nothing more to say or do. *Will we ever get back on the train?*

In the passport control office, two immigration men were checking passenger documents briskly and efficiently—assembly-line stuff, Willy realized with a sudden wave of relief. There were no seats. Everyone had to stand in line, shuffling along and then stopping with their luggage. When it was their turn, he handed their passports to the heavy-set older official.

"Aha," he grunted to his coworker as he flipped the pages. "Hungarians—we don't get many at this border." He stepped back and, with his hands on his hips, slowly looked the Kohuts up and down. Willy went cold. He had an inkling of what the man was thinking: "These are sweaty, nervous, unwashed people in wrinkled clothes, and the male has healing scars on his face— very suspicious." Perhaps, thought Willy hopefully, Pavel's Aryan blond curls and blue eyes might help them get through.

The official hooked a finger. "*Komm mit uns.*" Two soldiers escorted the Kohuts to another room and made them sit down in front of the desk of a small, fat man in a rumpled brown suit.

Sophie sat still, looking down at her hands, while Pavel stood between her knees looking around confused. "Where is train gone, *Táto?*"

"Kohut Willy," the man read aloud from the passport. "A Czech name, *ja?*"

Willy noticed Sophie catch her breath and shook his head, trying to warn her to stay calm. "No, we're Hungarian from close to the Slovak border. Kohuts live on both sides of the

Czech-Hungarian border."

The official drilled them with gimlet eyes. "Hunnh! You have come all the way from Hungary. Why?"

"To visit family and have a holiday," said Willy in as bad a German accent as he could muster.

The night before in the Wiesbaden waiting room, as they whiled away the hours, Willy and Sophie had again practiced giving limited and stupid replies to questions in German or Hungarian. The idea was to frustrate the officials enough to just let them go.

"What is the name of your family in France and say where they live?"

"Lihčet. They live in Paris, the Bois de Boulogne," said Sophie quickly, two red spots burning on her cheeks. She had remembered. "They sell carpets."

"Hmm. With all the shit going on around here, I cannot believe you people are stupid enough to go to Paris on holiday Don't you read the papers? Listen to the radio?"

Willy shrugged his shoulders helplessly. "We bought our train tickets long ago and couldn't get refunds. We thought we would chance it."

The man's eyes flickered to Sophie, settling on her bosom, as if he was a snake sizing up a delectable mouse. He turned and, prodding a finger into Willy's chest, peered into his face. "Your story is weak and it looks like someone beat you up. Besides, people going on holiday don't dress like tramps and get beaten up," he said in a slow, acid voice. "You can't fool me. You are refugees. Admit it"

Willy shook his head and tried to blink away the sweat that dripped from his eyebrows. A hammer pulsed inside his skull. What if they were separated again? He leaned toward Sophie, who was staring fixedly at the floor, and murmured in Hungarian, "Remember, Sophie, I love you."

The other official, a thinly built man with sloping shoulders, a blue chin, and broken veins on his cheeks, mopped his face and took their passports. "Hungarians, you say?" He switched on a desk lamp, pulling it down close to examine each page with a magnifying glass. Then he held the pages up against the light and grunted.

Massaging his itchy finger, Willy studied the official's face, desperately hoping for a sign that he would be satisfied with their passports. There were no signs.

"Nice forgeries, these." The official curled his upper lip. "But not good enough." He jabbed his coworker in the ribs, pointing to one of the pages. "Look at this, Jürgen. See the slight smudging on the typeface?"

Willy's stomach turned. He gripped the arms of his chair, trying desperately to keep his mind calm and agile as weariness and dread flooded his body. Denial was probably useless, but for the moment, he would go on pretending to be a Hungarian. There was a ghost of a chance the officials might overlook the deceit and allow them through. He put on a puzzled face and shrugged, as if he did not quite understand.

"Fucking idiots," the heavily built official muttered. He pointed a stubby finger. "You, Kohut—*Jude, ja?* Your boy has blonde hair. Maybe you dyed it. I have a nose for Jews, you see. Admit who you are...it will make things much easier for everyone."

Willy shook his head. "*Wir sind Hungarisch. Turisten.*"

The official waved a commanding hand. "Get the woman to pull down the kid's pants. If he's circumcised, their game is over."

The man who had checked the Kohuts' passports tugged on Pavel's waistband. He looked at Sophie, and mimed removing the boy's pants. "*Hose aus—und schnell.*"

Seeing the alarm on Pavel's face, Willy gave up the pretense. "Yes, we are Jews," he said, trying to keep his voice strong. He heaved a sigh, looking at Sophie. Her clenched lips were white as snow, and he guessed she was thinking the worst was about to happen.

The heavy official grunted as he sat down again. He placed a rubber band round the passports after making quick notes on a sheet of paper and then looked up at the Kohuts. "We don't tolerate Jews who weasel their way out of Germany—especially if they have false papers." They should be working for the Fatherland. He shook the passports threateningly at Willy. "Counterfeit passports are illegal; the penalties are severe—fines, prison or worse."

Willy and Sophie said nothing. Pavel looked anxiously from face to face. Willy saw the boy's lips quivering as if he knew something was very wrong. Was this going to be the prelude to a tantrum? That would be a disaster.

"Put your watches, trinkets, coins, and wallet in this basket. After we go through your suitcase and bags, we decide what to do with you."

Even though he had admitted to being Jewish, Willy kept up trying to convey a lack of understanding. "Not good speak Deutsch," he said in German, as he watched Sophie running her fingers through Pavel's curls and stroking his face and arms to reassure him. Willy understood why—it was a mother's reflex, in case they took Pavel away from her. She was trying to memorize every molecule of her only child. He envied her the chance to hold his boy close.

The official picked up a battered telephone. "*Kriminalrat* Klemper here. Get me the *Reichszentrale für jüdische Auswanderung* in Berlin." He paused and cleared his throat. "So, *gut*. I am *Kriminalrat* Rudi Klemper, Kelmis Border post, near Aachen." He paused, frowning and raised his voice. "*Gott verdammt, dummer kerl*. Kelmis is on the Belgian frontier. Just stop asking questions and put me through to your senior officer." As he waited, his eyes roved over the Kohuts, finally resting on Sophie again. "Listen, I have a name for you to check—Kohut, Willy Kohut. Jewish, Hungarian, Czech, or maybe Austrian, we are not sure yet. I'll wait."

Still holding the receiver, he pressed a button on his desk, and two armed SS guards entered the room. "Take all their stuff apart," said Klemper, turning toward them. "Check the shoes and the suitcase lining as well. I will join you in a few minutes— and for a change, do a thorough job, you lazy buggers. These people are probably Hungarian Jews—hardly speak German. Off with you, now."

He turned back to the telephone. "What's that? You will telephone back? Twenty minutes? Good."

Carrying their one suitcase and other possessions, Willy, Sophie, and Pavel were marched by the guards into a window-less, stifling room furnished only with a long, metal table. As soon as they had closed and bolted the door, each guard unbuttoned his tunic and dropped it on the table. They rolled up their sleeves. For a moment, Willy's brain blazed with fear: he remembered Pankrác...these were preparations for a beating.

"*Gott ist das heiß*, too damned hot in here," one of them complained, spitting into a corner.

"*Schlussel*, key," the other one ordered, thrusting a hand

at Willy. He was pudgy, with wiry, red hair and protuberant eyes. The guard pantomimed the twisting of a key in the suitcase lock; Willy untied it from the string around his neck and handed it over.

They emptied out Sophie's bags and tipped the contents of the suitcase onto the table, sorting through the pile, feeling and examining each item before grouping them in piles using some system Willy could not fathom. "Shit," said the small, thinner guard, "there's fuck-all but clothes here."

"Pickings have been lean the last few days," snarled the carrot top.

The other guard examined the soles of Willy and Sophie's shoes, shaking the heels close to his ear. He laughed. "Relax, comrade. At least we get to keep all we find. As long as we keep quiet about his strange fun and games, Oberführer Heizinger does not care what we do with the confiscated stuff. All right, you two, put your shoes back on."

The carrot-top guard smirked. "More and more, Heizinger is turning into a head case. Did you hear how he bought a weasel from some local farmer and feeds it live mice in his bedroom?

Both guards laughed.

"Fun and games"—what did they mean? Willy caught his breath, his mind racing as he tied his laces. His Pankrác interrogators had used a similar phrase to mean torture of some kind. Was it going to happen here? At least these guards had not found the coins in his shoe heels—a small but promising success in a sea of possible catastrophes.

With a malicious laugh, the carrot top guard bent down and pulled the furry lion out of Pavel's arms. He poked and prodded it, slammed it on the tabletop and threw it on the floor. "Nothing in that. Just a stuffed toy," he said.

Pavel began to cry and grabbed it back. "Nasty soldier," he sobbed, scuttling to his mother's side.

Willy glared. "Leave my boy alone."

"Shut up," said the smaller guard, turning the empty suitcase upside down and shaking it close to his ear. With deft fingers, he began probing its sides and lining.

The door opened and *Kriminalrat* Klemper stepped in. "*Gott behüte*, it's a steam bath in here." He mopped his forehead with his handkerchief again. "Have you fellows found anything?"

"There's something sewn into the lining of the suitcase."

The guard pulled out a long-bladed knife, ripped open the moiré satin, and fumbled around. With a grunt of satisfaction, he drew out a flat beige envelope. "*Da ist es.* Here it is."

Klemper tore open the envelope and thumbed through the contents with a triumphant smile. "As I suspected, boys: Czech passports and some other documents. I don't read Czech, but this parchment one with a wax seal looks like a property transaction." He turned to the guards. "Enough foraging for now. Time for a strip search."

Anxiety churned through Willy's guts, and he and Sophie exchanged frightened, apprehensive glances. *Strip search? Sophie stripped by men?* What he feared more than anything now was what they might do to her, especially if they found the hidden diamonds. Anything was possible—rape, or even murder. Would this end up as another Pankrác but with Sophie and Pavel included? He boiled with rage and helplessness.

"Fetch Bruch to search the woman and child," said Klemper. "Keep the man locked in here until Heizinger is ready for him."

"Please," said Willy, looking at each of the three men in turn. "Don't separate us."

"Shut up, filth," said Klemper calmly.

27

STRIP SEARCH
JULY, 1939

SOPHIE AND PAVEL were thrust out into the corridor and told to stand against the wall, where a fair-haired teenage boy, dressed in the brown shirt and the black lederhosen of Hitler Youth, watched them. Within a few minutes, a heavily built female guard arrived. She wore a *feldgrau* jacket, and her flared pencil skirt bulged round the waist and even more so over her large hips. A long, narrow truncheon dangled from a wide leather belt.

"You can leave, my little shrimp." She patted the teenager's cheek. He gave her a murderous look and vanished as she turned to Sophie. "We wait here," she said in what seemed a kindly tone.

Sophie guessed the woman to be in her forties, tall and broad-beamed with no trace of makeup on her coarse but amiable face. Double braids of thick blond hair were pinned on the top of her head. *A stolid peasant type*, Sophie thought, hoping that this peasant was as good-hearted as she appeared.

Klemper came out of the inspection room, and Sophie noticed that he walked with an obvious limp. The woman clicked her heavy shoes together and gave a '*heil*' salute.

"Fräulein Bruch," he barked. "Strip-search this Jewish woman—and no holding back this time. The child also."

She nodded, licking her lips nervously. "Yes, Herr

Kriminalrat. I have a small request because of what happened to
me last week. If the boy soils himself this woman will need to
clean him. She must have suitable items for this in her luggage.
The condition of the cell is my responsibility, and I won't clean
up after stinking Jews."

Frowning, Klemper shrugged acceptance and jerked his
head, indicating the room that still housed the Kohuts' belongings. "*Schnell machen.* Hurry..." He stared contemptuously at
the female guard. "Don't stand there like an old heifer. Help the
fucking woman get the stuff she needs."

Five minutes later, Sophie walked along the corridor holding a paper bag containing squares of her cut-up skirts. She was
close to tears, but she wanted to appear calm for Pavel's sake. He
trotted along beside her, holding his lion. She prayed he would
not end up in one of his tantrums. There was no knowing what
the woman guard would do if Pavel transformed himself into a
miniature dervish.

Fräulein Bruch took them into a white-tiled cubicle fitted
with a metal bench. A central light bulb glared from the ceiling, and a black-rimmed clock on one wall was the only decora-
tion. A grated drain was set in the center of the floor, and the
single small barred window showed some blue sky and the tops
of distant trees. The place was stifling and smelled of sweat and
stale farts.

"Don't like," Pavel said in a tremulous voice, looking
around. "I want *Tátu.* I want train."

"What's he saying?" said the blond-haired woman, putting
on orange rubber gloves.

"He's afraid. He is only just over two, but he is a good
talker. "

Bruch stared at Pavel. "Tell him if he behaves proper, he
won't get hurt. Now, Sarah, let's get this over. Everything off,
clothes folded on the bench."

Sophie's nostrils flared. "My name is Kohut Sophie, not
Sarah." She spit the words out in Berliner dialect; she was done
with pretending to be someone else. Besides, she had already
discarded her initial impression that Fräulein Bruch was a
reasonably humane woman doing difficult work in unpleasant
circumstances.

"Shut up," the guard grunted. "Your man's a Yid, isn't he?
So, you must be called Sarah. Now, let's get on with it: front

and back—no screaming, mind you."

As Sophie started to undress, she saw Fräulein Bruch glance at Pavel, who had retreated to the wall by the bench. He was staring at her, his toy lion dangling from one hand. The guard pointed at the bench. "Sit, kid, and keep your mouth shut. *Sit*."

Sophie could tell Pavel was confused and frightened. "Sit on the bench, darling," she said in Czech, undoing her blouse. "There's nothing to be afraid of. She won't hurt you, or me."

Pavel climbed on the bench, perching like a terrified bird, staring at the two women with tears smearing his cheeks.

Sophie stood in front of him with her back to the guard. She held his gaze as she slipped off her dress and her unwashed underthings, surreptitiously letting the diamonds slide down inside his shirt collar. She put a finger to her lips, willing him to understand he had to be quiet.

Sophie, ashamed of her total nakedness in front of a stranger turned towards Fräulein Bruch gritting her teeth, determined to beat down her fear. If what the guard did to her were painful or despicable, she would not show it. She covered her breasts with her right arm, her privates with her left hand, at the same time, trying, to avoid the gaze of the guard's ice-blue eyes. Her body was coiled tight as a spring, ready to comfort Pavel if he broke down. The poor darling had been through too much already.

Sophie knew this was the first time Pavel had seen her completely naked. He was looking at her with wide, unblinking eyes, as silent and frozen as a garden gnome. She felt the guard's hands in her hair, pulling on the roots—and then rubber-covered fingers were roughly exploring her armpits and squeezing her breasts.

"Breasts a little small," said the guard with a smug expression, readjusting her gloves. Sophie jerked her head away from the smell of Bruch's cheap scent and sweat, nauseated by the woman's vulgarity. "Now, save yourself trouble and tell me if you have any treasures hidden in your lusthole: little bags of diamonds or gold—I have to look, you know. If you tell me what you are hiding, I will be more gentle."

"Please, please, I beg you, not in front of the child," Sophie pleaded, glancing at Pavel again. "I have nothing hidden. Have some sympathy for us."

"Sympathy?" Fräulein Bruch gave a cynical laugh. "*Gott im*

Himmel, was fur ein Dummheit."

Pavel looked away, making a pathetic, whimpering noise. "Your little fucker looks as if he's going to be difficult." Fräulein Bruch turned her beer-barrel body to look at the boy. "His face is all red."

Sophie shook her head vigorously. "A red face means he's done a big job. He needs to be changed."

Fräulein Bruch sniffed. "Shit! You're right."

Sophie made a move toward Pavel, but the guard grabbed her arm. "No, no, *no*. I do you first. Stand with your legs apart, hands on top of your head. Lock the fingers. Yes, like that."

"I just started my monthly." Sophie shut her eyes tight, hating this coarse woman, desperately hoping that she would stop what she was doing because of the bleeding. She rotated her hips, hoping that this would limit Pavel seeing what was happening.

"I don't care a damn about that." Fräulein Bruch pulled a bundle of bloodstained fabric squares out of Sophie's vagina, then bent down and thrust her fingers deep into Sophie's body, twisting them this way and that. Sophie winced, grunting in pain, and she tried to push the guard's hand away. They struggled briefly.

"Hands back on your head, or I'll beat you black and blue," Fräulein Bruch growled.

Sophie's determination to hide her feelings evaporated. "Stop it, for God's sake. Please. You are hurting me terribly. No, no... "

Fräulein Bruch jerked her hand out, and Sophie looked down; blood was trickling down the inside of her right thigh. Panicked, she looked at Pavel. He sat frozen on the bench, whispering over and over, *"Maminko* hurt."

"Clean as a whistle," said the guard with satisfaction. "Now, squat down on your heels and cough."

Sophie took a deep breath. She would not obey; it was time to stand her ground.

The simultaneous thwack of Bruch's truncheon and the searing pain along the side of her hipbone shattered her resistance. "Squat, bitch," yelled Bruch, grabbing Sophie's hair and forcing her to her knees. "Stay down there and give me a big cough, five times."

Pavel was whimpering, his mouth working. *"Mami, mami,*

Maminko."

"Aaagh—my God—aagh," Sophie groaned, trying to cough at the same time. "How can you do this to another woman?"

"Shut up, Sarah. Stand up, bend over and touch your toes."

Ready for another blow, Sophie obeyed and felt the guard's fingers digging painfully in her rectum, a sharp-toothed animal clawing to get inside her body.

"Good—that's over." Fräulein Bruch ripped off her gloves and threw them into a metal bucket in the corner. "At least you're not hiding anything."

"Can I dress now?" Sophie gasped, desperate to finish the nightmare but terrified that the officials would take her and Pavel somewhere else where other bad things might happen—or, worse, that they might never see Willy again.

"Yes, dress. I'll get you some rags to clean yourself up."

"Could you bring some extra ones so I can change my boy? I can't leave him all dirty."

Fräulein Bruch grunted and clumped out of the room. Moments later, she returned and threw what looked like torn-up clothes and sheets into a corner. "Use those." She pulled out a cigarette and lit it. "The stink is awful. Clean him up. I'll be back in five minutes," she said as she left the room again."

Sophie wiped the blood off her thighs and dressed herself, trying to ignore the insistent throbbing somewhere between her hips. She could not focus properly; her head swirled, and she wanted nothing more than to sink to the floor and close her eyes, obliterate everything. Somehow, for Pavel's sake, she had to pull herself out of the shame of violation and suppress the pain. She wanted to show strength and resistance, somehow fight back at this woman.

Taking a deep breath, she retrieved the handful of diamonds from under the back of Pavel's shirt, unfastened the belt of his pants, and transferred the stones back into her brassiere. More than anything she, wanted to pay Bruch back for making Pavel watch her pain and humiliation.

Fräulein Bruch came back into the room and stood watching, hands hitched on her hips as Sophie slipped off Pavel's pants and, as well as she could, use the rest of the rags to clean him. She took a fresh square from her bag, folded it into a triangle and secured it around him. He got off the bench and stood scratching at his hair, staring at the stout blond woman.

Bruch suddenly bent down and picked up something from under the bench. She straightened, grinning, two stones glittering on the palm of her plump hand. "Clever Sarah, but not clever enough. Where is the rest of your treasure?"

Sophie felt her stomach twist into knots, fear washed through her body.

Within moments, the guard had culled the rest of the diamonds from Sophie's brassiere and with a crafty look slipped them inside her own blouse. "Smuggling diamonds is a serious crime. However, I will not say anything about this if you don't. Agreed?"

Sophie, still trembling, understood and nodded

"Get the boy dressed. There's an empty bucket under the bench for the dirty stuff. When you're finished, I'll be waiting outside in the corridor" She left abruptly, buttocks seesawing like sacks of potatoes.

Sophie turned to finish dressing Pavel, furious with herself for her carelessness. She dreaded telling Willy what had happened. The wall clock showed that Paris train would be leaving in 40 minutes. Depending on what happened to Willy, she knew they would soon be either under official arrest or miraculously on the train to France. One way or other, she hoped Bruch would not come back to check on her. She had a handful of minutes to leave a small token of 'appreciation' for Fräulein Bruch

"Stay there, *Pavlíčku*, and wait."

Sophie removed the soiled diaper from bucket and rubbed a thin layer of the brown contents back and forth along the underside of the bench. Then she walked to the window and daubed the dark iron bars. Pavel, clutching his lion, watched her. When she had finished, she threw the rags and diaper back into the bucket. Shuddering but feeling triumphant, Sophie looked at her brown, bloodstained hands and rubbed them with more rags as the rich scent of her son's poop permeated the room.

They walked down the corridor toward Fräulein Bruch, her back half-turned as she conferred with a male guard and puffed on a cigarette. Half to Pavel and half to herself, Sophie muttered, "I hope to God it's Fräulein Bruch's job to clean the cell."

"*Komm mit*," said Bruch, turning to face Sophie.

"*Kriminalrat* Klemper wants you."

Back in the interview room, Sophie and Pavel again stood in front of Klemper's desk. Fräulein Bruch stood at attention in one corner, her face blank.

A brown cigarette drooping from his lips, Klemper indicated a bench set along one wall. "Wait here," he said wearily.

Sophie pulled Pavel to her and sat down. With one ordeal over, another fear took hold of her. "*Bitte*, where is my husband?"

"*Gottverdammt*. Just wait."

"We have to wait for *Tátu*, darling," she told Pavel, feeling a trickle of warm stickiness under her dress. She raised her smeared hands, eschewing all politeness and delicacy. "Look, *mein Herr*, *Blut und Kot*, they're revolting." She nodded toward Bruch. "It was her fault. I need to wash my hands."

Klemper looked at her smeared hands and sniffed in disgust. He crooked his finger at Bruch. "Take them to the washroom. Stay with them all the time."

"Where is *Táta?*" Pavel asked as they followed the blond guard's heaving buttocks.

Sophie tried to hold back the tears. *What if they don't give Willy back to me?*

28

THE BUTTONHOLE
JULY, 1939

STOMACH CHURNING in apprehension, Willy followed the armed guard along a bare corridor until they stopped at a half-glass door with OBERFÜHRER M. HEIZINGER, KOMMANDANT stenciled in gothic black script on the opaque glass. Willy hoped the interview would be short and pain-free, but he had his doubts. He took a deep breath as the guard knocked on the door.

"*Herein.*"

The escort propelled Willy forward and saluted from the doorway. "Detainee Jew Kohut, Oberführer Heizinger," he said. "Do you wish me to assist you during the interrogation?" Willy flinched. In his situation, he knew 'Assist' would translate into the use of violence.

"No, Sternbach. Just put all the man's documents and paraphernalia on my desk and wait outside."

Willy stood at the desk, hardly absorbing the appearance of the man sitting there. His thoughts tumbled round and round—Sophie, Pavel, memories of Pankrác, the train to Paris, which passports they would be allowed to keep. He racked his brain for some plan or idea to solve his family's predicament, his senses on high alert, but he could not think of anything. To curb the wave of panic that threatened to destabilize him, Willy offered what he thought was a respectful smile to the gray-suited

man seated in a chrome chair behind the desk. He took stock of
the room: the musty smell, the linoleum, a stuffed velvet settee,
two easy chairs, and several filing cabinets. On a side table
by the wall, a wood-encased radio glowed, broadcasting barely
audible dance music. High up on one of the walls, too small for
any escape, a window let in a javelin of sunshine.

The clean-shaven SS official—Willy spied the SS light-
ning-bolt pin on his lapel—looked to be in his late twenties. He
had deep-set, lead-gray eyes, a high forehead half hidden by a
curtain of black hair, and wide, thick lips. He was athletic-look-
ing and perfectly dressed—nothing like Altmann in Pankrác.

"So, you are Herr Willy Kohut," said Oberführer Heizinger,
lazily picking up a glowing black cigarette from his ashtray. His
surprisingly soft, gentle voice somehow made Willy feel even
more tense, as if he were listening to the purring of a predator.
"It's quite obvious you and your family are traveling without
official approval. In Germany, Jews cannot travel as they please.
What are you doing here?"

"We're visiting family in Paris, not deporting ourselves."

"How is it that you and your family look so bedraggled
and carry just one small suitcase? Not very suitable for a holiday
in Paris, is it?"

Willy inclined his head and spread his hands, struggling to
keep his poise. "A friend was driving us through Germany, and
near Wiesbaden we had an accident. Our luggage was damaged.
We had to spend the night in the station and travel by train. You
could check this with the station supervisor, a Herr Gruber."

The Oberführer stroked his chin and stared at Willy, then
began going through the small pile of documents and papers the
guard had placed on his desk. Willy watched him leaf through
his business documents and then examine the false Hungarian
and genuine Czech passports that the guards had extracted from
the suitcase lining. "*Ach*, so, you are from Prague," Heizinger
muttered as he flipped the pages.

Willy's courage and strength began to leach away.

"Take everything off," the man said suddenly, pointing at
a nearby chair. "Shoes, clothes—over there."

Willy quickly obeyed, folding his things carefully. He
knew he was in for a body search but found it inexplicable that
a senior official would demean himself with such a task.

Oberführer Heizinger got up and came toward Willy, pull-

ing on rubber gloves. "Stand still, Israel." While Willy stood
naked, hands at his sides, the German went to the chair and
carefully examined each article of clothing before coming back
to face him.

"What are you looking for?" Willy wanted to show that
he was docile and collaborating. "Maybe I can save you time?"

"Just look straight ahead, don't talk, and don't move." The
official circled Willy, prodding his shoulders, thighs, buttocks,
chest, and belly, humming as he moved. Finally, he took Willy's
penis in his gloved hand and, bending over it like a praying
mantis, squeezed. Willy groaned and lurched forward. Releasing
and squeezing as Willy writhed in pain, the man smiled. "I see
you are somewhat different from the other Jewish men who have
arrived at this godforsaken hole. More intelligent, cleaner...and
you tell lies very smoothly. I must say you have a finely sculpted
penis." Heizinger giggled. "I have surprised you, yes? With all
you Jews trying to cross the border, I have become something
of an expert on circumcised penises. Quite a variety. I must say.
Let's have a look at the rest of you."

Eyes half closed in a futile attempt to suppress his agony,
Willy saw Heizinger's eyebrows arch inquiringly as if he expected
some sign of submission. He was not going to give the German
that victory.

The official kept his gloved hand clamped on Willy's
penis, using it as a handle to jerk Willy around while he made
his inspection. "I see you have quite a few scars and bruises—
recent ones on your face. Did you get into a tussle on your trav-
els, with the police, perhaps?"

Willy stared up at the ceiling, fixing his eyes on the lamp,
hoping to distance himself from what was happening.

"And that velvet bag around the fingers of your hand.
What is it for?"

"Protection. Injured little finger. The bones were broken."
Willy had an almost irresistible urge to lash out, retaliate. He
fought it down, digging his fingers into the sides of his thighs,
willing himself to stay still.

"Interesting embroidery on the bag," said the Oberführer
with a puzzled look. "Almost like the tail of a dragon. I've seen
that design somewhere."

Willy was still bent over from the throbbing that spread
throughout his pelvis and thighs. Sweat ran down on his face.

He felt as though he were suffocating. *What the hell is this bastard going to do to me?* "Yes, it's a dragon tail," he gasped, pointing at the lapel of Heizinger's suit. "Same pattern as your buttonhole."

Heizinger stepped back, eyes wide, released Willy's penis and turned his lapel. He looked at it for a moment. "*Hunhh, das ist richtig.*"

Willy nodded, seeing an opening. "You had the suit made in Prague, in the Old Town. Moshe Lemberger, the tailor. He sews buttonholes like that."

"How the devil did you know I was in Prague?" the official exclaimed. He picked up one of the passports and flicked over a page or two. "*Ach, du lieber Gott.* I see now—the name... You are that Kohut. Your store sold English suit fabrics, *ja?*"

"Yes," said Willy, breathing more easily. His pain had diminished leaving a nauseating, dull ache in his testicles. He reached out hesitantly, not quite touching the lapel. "Your suit is made of superfine merino wool from England—it came from my store, Kohut Stoffe."

Heizinger tested the flap of his jacket between two fingers, as if confirming the soft texture for himself, and then burst into laughter.

"So, what a strange twist of fate, eh?" He punched Willy amicably on the naked shoulder. "I remember, now. Heinrich Thümmel brought me to your store. I had three suits made by that tailor, beautiful and dirt-cheap. Then, *in Gottes Namen*, I was transferred to this dump."

Willy straightened up and attempted to smile. "Oberführer Heizinger, I would very much appreciate it if you let my family get back on the train. In memory of the cloth you bought from me to create your fine suits, surely you could bend the rules a little. We worked closely with Major Thümmel, your brother officer. "

Heizinger did not smile as Willy had hoped.

"Please," Willy said, spreading his hands. "I would like to get dressed so we can catch the train." He looked at the clock. "It leaves very soon."

"Wait," barked Heizinger. He walked to the door, opened it, and spoke to the guard outside before turning the key in the lock. He winked at Willy. "I sent the guard away. Best not to have snoopers close by for our fun and games." He retrieved the passports and documents from his desk and slipped them under Willy's clothes on the chair.

Willy felt his skin flush and his pulse race. A flood of relief swept over him. "So you are letting us go?"

Heizinger half smiled. He approached Willy and grasped his elbow. "Yes and no. I have a dilemma: you see, if your name is on the list at the *Reich Centrale* in Berlin, it means the Jewish registration office in Prague has already identified you for detention—in which case I am bound to arrest your family."

Willy's heart sank. "Am I on that list?"

"We are still waiting to hear. It takes a while." Heizinger moved closer.

"I wish to get dressed." Willy backed away from Heizinger, fearing some kind of renewed assault. His penis and testicles throbbed. If there was going to be more brutality, he would beg for mercy, do anything, to get out of there and find Sophie.

"On the other hand, my dear Israel, today's coincidence does bring back the good times I spent in Prague. In fact, in the last few minutes, I have developed a soft spot for you even though you are a Jew. So why don't we play a little pleasure game before you catch the train."

"A pleasure game? There isn't time." Willy made as if to move toward his clothes on the chair, but a knife blade had appeared in Heizinger's hand, the sharp point pressed against Willy's skin above his left nipple, just enough to release a small rose of blood. He felt the German's other hand grab his hair, pulling the roots. The pain spread like lava over his scalp

Willy took hold of the man's wrist desperately trying to restrain him. Heizinger smiled and pressed the blade more deeply. "If you resist, Jew, this will go straight into your heart. Let go of my wrist."

Willy, clenching his teeth in pain, complied. Heizinger was dangerous...was he also unpredictable?

You see, I am in total command here in Kelmis. I do what I enjoy."

Willy, the roots of his hair screaming, stared into the official's eyes. He was afraid and in despair. His attempt to generate sympathy had failed. Possibly his life hung by a thread. It only needed a quick thrust from Heizinger's blade.

"Which one of your family will play sex with me?" Heizinger whispered huskily into Willy's ear still pulling on his hair. The knife moved across and around his skin. He felt the blood running. "Choose: you, your pretty wife, or your charming little boy? When we've finished the game, you can all go to the train."

Willy's heart plummeted and skipped a beat. He was trapped, with no recourse, in the coils of a sexual pervert. Anything could happen. Like oil and water, despair and hope roiled together as he inched his hands up to touch Heizinger's wrist where he held the knife against his chest. There was still time to get the train... he gasped with pain as the knife moved around his skin, cutting deeper. The pain was agonizing. "What do I have to do?"

Heizinger slid the knife into a leather sheath attached to his belt and dropped his trousers. Pulling out his engorged penis, he lifted it toward Willy. "You Jews have no self-respect or courage," he said disdainfully. "Anything to avoid pain, eh? So, get fucking started, Israel. Your train leaves in half an hour."

Blood dripping down his chest and on to the floor, Willy got down on his knees.

29

THE LAST HURDLE
JULY, 1939

WILLY WAS STILL struggling to remove Heizinger's bitter slime from his mouth as the guard pushed him through the door into *Kriminalrat* Klemper's office. His relief at seeing Sophie and Pavel was short-lived. They were slumped on the bench, disheveled and red-eyed from crying. Sophie's face was white and drawn and she looked as if she had aged ten years. Nevertheless, they were there, waiting for him.

Sophie gave him a weak smile and pulled him down next to her. He wrapped an arm round Pavel's thin chest and held him close. He felt the boy's heart pounding. His own throbbed in time with the pain from the cut on his chest. He used his other hand to compress his shirt and jacket over the wound.

"Thank God, you're back," she said in a low voice. "What happened? There's blood on you."

He wanted to ask her the same question, but the gluey sensation of Heizinger's semen in his throat made him gag. God, if only he could get a drink of water. The room was like a steam bath.

She stroked his cheek. He rocked back and forth holding his chest. "You're so pale, Willy. Did they hurt you? For God's sake tell me what happened."

"Later." Willy swallowed hard, trying to hide the extensive bloodstains under his jacket. "What about you and Pavel?"

Sophie shook her head. "Later," She echoed with a bleak smile.

Willy looked up, noticing that Klemper and Heizinger were in animated conversation on the other side of the room. The *Kriminalrat* glanced at them, shaking his head and banging the back of his right hand angrily against a sheaf of papers.

A moment later, Max Heizinger, stood in front of them wiping his bloodstained hands with a towel. He dropped it on the floor and gave Willy an enigmatic smile as he lit a cigarette. "So. Your names do not appear in the central Berlin registry and consequently we have no official reason to hold you. Of course, possession of false passports is a serious criminal offense."

Willy caught his breath. The swine! The bastard had fooled him—played with him...as promised. His chest pain vanished as a gush of angry strength poured into his arms and fists. "You agreed to let us go," he shouted, jumping to his feet, jostling Pavel sideways against Sophie.

Sophie grabbed Willy's forearm. "No," she cried out, eyes wide with fear. Out of the corner of her eye, she had seen Klemper unholster his pistol.

"Behave yourself, Israel," Heizinger continued, taking a pull on his cigarette. "Or you will ruin everything for your family. Our orders are to detain officially registered Jews or travelers carrying seditious materials. You are not Germans, and apart from the false passports, we found nothing against the Third Reich in your belongings. You should be glad."

Willy raised his arms in a hopeless gesture, as if unsure of what to do, and then dropped them by his sides. Drops of blood spattered on the floor. "Why do you tell me this? Are you arresting us or not?" He wondered bitterly if this was another part of Heizinger's fun and games.

Kriminalrat Klemper, holding a cardboard box, appeared at Heizinger's side, the sheen of sweat on his plump cheeks. "There is a fine for possessing false papers," he said to Willy, looking at Heizinger, who nodded approval. "One thousand Reichsmarks."

"You have my wallet," said Willy with a helpless shrug. He had to have some cash if they managed to get out of this mess. "And you took the fifteen hundred Reichsmarks hidden in my suitcase. You say the fine is one thousand, so give me five hundred back."

Klemper shook his head with a look of pure innocence. "Amazing how easily you Jews manipulate and tell lies. My men found absolutely no money in the suitcase. We will keep your valuables and your wallet, but you cannot continue your journey unless you pay the full fine. You must return to Aachen."

Willy compressed his lips. He was not ready to give up. They were so close to France. He had to take the risk of angering the men who held his family's fate in their hands. "This is not correct. There were definitely fifteen hundred Reichsmarks in my suitcase." Still pressing a hand against his chest, he turned to Heizinger. "This fellow is lining his pockets under your nose. Why do you allow this? You gave me a Nazi officer's promise. Are you a man of your word or not?"

Heizinger's neck flushed and he looked away. "All right, then go," he muttered.

Sophie straightened up, her face transformed. "You mean we can board the train?"

Klemper looking angrily at the Oberführer, spat on the floor, and walked away muttering under his breath.

Heizinger looked at his watch. "Ignore him. The train leaves at any moment. Get your things from the inspection room and get the hell out of here."

With a surge of energy, Willy scooped Pavel up and rushed with Sophie to the room where their ripped suitcase lay on the table. Sophie grabbed a handful of clothes and stuffed them into the two string bags. Willy picked up Pavel's bag of toys and his furry lion. It was at that moment that Sophie saw his blood-soaked shirt. She stood stock-still and opened her mouth to say something.

"Not now!" he admonished. "I've got passports and tickets. That's all we need."

They ran out of the building, stumbling past two startled Nazi soldiers, who unshouldered their weapons. As they ran toward the train, Heizinger called after the Kohuts from the building's doorway. "Don't run, idiots. These men will shoot." He waved and shouted at the soldiers, "*Nicht schiessen.*"

Willy slowed to a quick walk. In his arms Pavel, eyes dilated with fear, took great breaths and sobbed "*Maminko...Maminko...Maminko.*" Sophie followed behind them.

On the platform, the train dispatcher, green flag tucked under his armpit, was looking up and down the platform, a silver whistle between his lips. Seeing the Kohuts hurrying toward him, he waved an angry hurry-it-up hand. The loudspeaker's voice boomed a warning of departure in French. Curious faces peered out of open carriage windows as the Kohuts slowed to a fast walk. Willy, trying to hang on to a wriggling Pavel, noticed with alarm that Sophie was limping and breathing heavily. He said nothing. He was limping too.

∽ ∂ ∽

M. and Mme. Panasse were waiting for them in the same compartment. "For a while we were very, very worried," said Mme Panasse, her face glowing with pleasure as Sophie walked in with Pavel. "Other people wanted to come in, but we kept your reserved seats for you." She embraced the tearful Sophie and kissed Pavel who tried to wriggle free.

The Frenchman, smiling, looked at Willy's right hand with its velvet fingerstall and then shook the left one, vigorously. "*Mon Dieu*, we thought you had been arrested. *Quelle horreur!* There is blood on your shirt and jacket. You have been wounded."

Willy sat down and lay back against the seat, pressing his hand to his left breast.

"What in God's name happened, monsieur? Did they...? We know *les Boches* do dreadful things to people.'"

Willy could not say anything. His body ached, his head was spinning, and he was in no condition to maintain any pretense. His chest throbbed and he could not get rid of the shameful feeling of Heizinger's swollen member in his mouth, as nauseating as a putrid sausage. He tried to smile his thanks to M. and Mme. Panasse, but disgust swamped his thoughts.

M. Panasse lit a battered Gauloise and studied the glowing end as if it were helping him think. He stuck it between his lips. "Please, M. Kohut, you must at least wash off the blood and put on a clean shirt. Or are you still bleeding?"

"Where is your suitcase?" Mme. Panasse patted Sophie's hand sympathetically.

"They destroyed it," Willy mumbled. "They kept everything: our money, my wallet, my wife's purse and our watches. We have nothing now except our passports. And what we have left in these string bags."

"*C'est affreux! Les pauvres gens.*" With a shake of the silver bracelets on her wrists, Mme Panasse entwined her fingers in prayer. "You poor people. Do not despair. Lord Jesus redeems those who have suffered. He will guide and protect your journey. Praise Him and you shall be rewarded."

The train began to move forward with a jerk. With great gentleness, Willy kissed the palm of Sophie's hand. "So, my love," he whispered, gazing into her eyes, his heart surging with love and joy. "We got through. We left those foul Nazis behind."

"The train is going, *Maminko!*" Pavel was bouncing on his seat. "I want drink."

Sophie gave his back a reassuring rub and turned back to Willy. "He's thirsty. Do you have any money?"

Willy groaned and with one hand searched through his pockets. With bloodstained fingers, he triumphantly held up three Reichsmarks. "This may be enough to get something from the vendor. I expect we can drink from the tap in the toilet. I'll take him and clean myself up as well."

M. Panasse was digging around in a suitcase he had pulled down from the stringed rack. He handed some handkerchiefs and a folded blue shirt to Sophie. "What did they do to him?"

She shrugged, as if she did not understand, tears streaming down her face.

"They cut me with a knife." Willy said in French.

"Patch yourself up with these, monsieur. My shirt may be a little too small for you, but too bad, eh? You repay me later."

Mme Panasse unwound a long chiffon scarf from her neck and handed it to Willy. "Use this, monsieur, to hold everything in place."

Willy rose from his seat holding the French couples' gifts, tears in his eyes. "I can't thank you enough. You are very generous. Come, Pavel. Let me get washed and then we'll find something to drink."

∾ ∂ ∾

"We are well into in Belgium now," said M. Panasse half an hour later. "Time to celebrate." Like a magician pulling a pigeon from a hat, he delved into a large canvas haversack and produced a bottle and a corkscrew. "*Allons, mes amis*, with *les Boches* far behind us, we'll drink some Touraine Sauvignon. I'm glad you managed to get the boy lemonade; he can join in the toast."

Willy nodded. Now that he had cleaned out his mouth and stanched the cut with the Frenchman's handkerchiefs, he was light-headed: restored and almost joyful. In the toilet's small mirror, he had washed the curving laceration on his chest. As he redressed it, Pavel gazing at him in fascination, he wondered why Heizinger had cut him like that. No matter, the worst was over.

Wine was exactly what he and Sophie needed: healing, uplifting soothing... a harbinger of the new life they would find in Paris.

"I have no wine glasses," said M. Panasse with an apologetic shrug of the shoulders, "but as we are already friends, we drink straight from the bottle like drunks, no?"

His wife chuckled, her cheeks quivering like jelly. "With wine, we also need food." She dug through a lidded basket and brought out a loaf of black bread, a length of thick sausage, and a dishcloth. She broke the bread into chunks and sliced the sausage with a penknife. "*Avez-vous faim?* You are hungry? *Saucisson lyonnais. C'est bon.*"

"Tell them they are very kind people," Sophie murmured to Willy as she ate, smiling her thanks. She put rounds of sausage on small chunks of bread for Pavel.

He smiled in between mouthfuls. "Pavel like sausage," he said as the breadcrumbs tumbled down his chest.

Willy took a large swig of wine, using it to rinse his mouth thoroughly. By the third mouthful, he could finally discern that it was dry and fruity; the taste of Heizinger had gone. He wondered if he would find the courage to tell Sophie everything that had happened to him at the *Grenze Kontrol*—probably a bad idea. From the way she trembled and twisted her hands, she seemed in a very fragile state. She, of course, would want to know how he had been cut and how he had finagled their release. When the time came to tell her, he would gloss over his humiliation by Heizinger. He did not know if he could ever manage to forget. Perhaps, some things were best left unsaid.

30

FRANCE
JULY, 1939

As THE TRAIN RATTLED along, Sophie began to feel stronger and more composed despite a diffuse ache deep and low in her belly and a feeling of stickiness between her thighs. Was it possible that the woman guard had damaged her? Pavel had seen everything, but he was too little to say anything. Most of all, she was afraid of how would Willy react if she told him about the frontier guard's assault. Would he give her love and sympathy or keep her at arm's length—and then never forget? No, she could not tell him. Like the awful night with Lessig, here was another burden she would bear on her own.

The squeaking noise of the compartment door sliding open interrupted her thoughts. She looked up. Four uniformed men crowded round the entrance: two Belgians in beige uniforms and helmets and two French gendarmes in dark blue, with cockaded *képis* and white gloves. The Belgian frontier police quickly scanned everyone's passport and left with curt nods. The mustachioed Frenchmen tarried, chatting with everyone as they ogled Sophie. At first, she felt embarrassed, even afraid, at the frank way they looked her. However, she soon realized that they behaved more like handsome, charming Frenchmen from a romantic film than any police officers she had encountered. She felt flattered by the thought that they admired her, even in her bedraggled state.

The gendarme who was looking at the passports shook his head. "This is not correct. You have no German frontier stamp. We cannot allow an unofficial entry into France."

Willy's face turned ghost-white, and he slowly got to his feet. "*Soyez aimables, Messieurs*," he said, opening his jacket. He unbuttoned the too-small shirt and slid the make-do dressing aside to show the cut on his chest, still oozing watery blood. "This is just one of the abominable things they did to me at the frontier."

Mme Panasse covered her eyes, M. Panasse nodded. "He's telling the truth. Be kind and welcome them into our country."

The smaller gendarme took a closer look at Willy's wound and exchanged a meaningful glance with his companion. "*Sâles Boches*," he exclaimed, stepping back. "Those filthy Germans need a taste of their own medicine." He touched his cap in an elegant salute. "*Messieurs et Mesdames, tout est en ordre. Bienvenue en France.*" Just as he was closing the compartment door, the taller of the two officials looked back, twirled his handlebar mustache, and winked at Pavel.

"Me like soldiers," said the boy, bouncing up and down on his seat, suddenly full of energy. He began marching up and down the small compartment space, practicing salutes and bumping against knees and feet.

"They're called gendarmes, Pavel." Willy smiled as he buttoned up his new shirt. "Can you say 'gendarmes'?"

Pavel looked around shyly: "Jundahm." Mme. Panasse beamed.

Forty-five minutes later, Willy and Pavel huddled together asleep. The Panasses had followed suit and were snoring like metronomes. Only Sophie remained awake, her head in turmoil, her lower belly throbbing. She shivered, afraid that something was wrong; the cramps were much worse than usual. She felt the warm stickiness again. If she needed a doctor in Paris, Willy would have to translate—and then he would know the humiliation she had endured.

As she looked out at the passing fields of cabbages and beets, her thoughts gelled in a single conclusion. Willy's plan to get to London immediately was a fantasy. They needed time to recover; they needed money, and she had no idea if they could find her cousin Feri in Paris. Earlier, M. Panasse had said that getting to England was not possible. U-boats infested the Channel, and ferry crossings to England had been cancelled. According to the ticket collector who had come by after the gendarmes had left, they had another four hours on the train. Tears rolled down her cheeks as she realized the irony—they would arrive in Paris safe and free, but homeless and destitute.

"I imagine this journey has been very hard for you." M. Panasse was gazing at her with sympathetic eyes. He spoke in halting German.

He must have woken and has been watching me, Sophie thought, doing her best to raise a smile. The Frenchman slid an arm into his backpack. "Be assured, Mme. Sophie, I have another bottle of the Touraine—and a nice red Cahors also. It will bring color to your cheeks."

"Thank you," she whispered as Willy opened his eyes. "You are most generous, but my husband and I cannot arrive in Paris drunk. We must be alert."

Willy stretched, grimacing as his forearm brushed the cut on his chest. "Perhaps," he said, his face reddening with embarrassment. "You can help us with some advice, *m'sieu. Les Boches* took everything. We have just the clothes we are wearing, and we need a place to stay. Tomorrow, I will ask the Czech Embassy for help, maybe find some work."

Mme. Panasse, woken by the conversation, clutched her cheeks in alarm. "*Ah, mon Dieu.* You do not have enough money for a hotel?"

"They took everything."

M. Panasse leaned forward and patted Willy's knee. "Listen, *mon ami*, I'll gladly lend you something to tide you over. You would do the same for me if I were in your place, *n'est-ce pas?*"

Willy's eyes widened in surprise. "Oh no, please. You have already been very generous to us, M. Panasse. Food, drink, great kindness—and a clean shirt. As I said, there is a Czech legation in Paris, and my wife has distant relatives there. We just have to find them. We'll manage."

The Frenchman drew a wallet from his jacket and handed Willy a 500-franc note. "*Voilà.* This should do for food and three nights at a hotel."

Willy's cheeks turned deep red. He shook his head ruefully, glancing at Sophie as if he could not bear her to see him taking a handout from a stranger. "You are too good-hearted." He leaned forward and pumped M. Panasse's hand vigorously. "Of course, I will repay you."

"No need," said M. Panasse with a dismissive flourish of his hand. "But if you wish to do so, come to my office when you are settled: 2 Quai de Grenelle."

Relieved that they had just avoided another night in a station waiting room, Sophie watched Willy write the address on a slip of paper. She could tell how ashamed he felt. She reached out to him, and he put the palm of her hand against his unshaven cheek. "This gift feels worse than a beating," he murmured in Czech. "Thank God, there are good-hearted people in this world."

ಐ ∂ ಐ

When the train steamed into the Gare de l'Est, the sky outside the station was still light and the air was warm. Walking along the platform, Willy recalled the smell of French stations from his student days: coal dust, Gauloise cigarettes, cheap perfume, and open urinals. When they passed the food stalls, the aroma of *pommes frites* made him salivate. He was hungry. At least they could pay for food now.

The two families handed in their tickets at the barrier where a young couple with three children stood waving and shouting, "*Bonjour, Grandpapa! Bienvenue, Grandmaman!*" Smiling at the sight of the welcoming party, Willy and Sophie stopped for a moment to say thank you and receive garlicky goodbye kisses. Madame gave Pavel's cheek a friendly caress even though he tried to cover his face in his mother's skirt.

As the couple trotted away, Sophie put down her bags and leaned wearily against Willy's chest. "So, *miláčku*—what now?" She was shivering in spite of the warm air.

He put an arm round her. "Before anything, I want to give thanks—to any and every God who might live up in the heavens, for watching over us. I am a lucky man to have you and Pavel with me. Now tell me what you want first. Food or bed?"

Sophie closed her eyes, as if undecided. "I'm tired, but my stomach says we eat before anything else. After that, I want a decent mattress."

"I'm hungry too, *Maminko*," said Pavel, trotting around

their string bags, waving his furry lion. He growled and pawed the air. "Me, hungry lion. Eat sausage."

Laughing, Willy patted his son's head affectionately. "Me too, *Pavlíčku*. Now if I remember correctly from the old times, there are a couple of bistros close by." Outside on the sidewalk, he waved a hand at the speeding cars and buses and smiled. "I wasn't expecting so much traffic. The French must still have plenty of gasoline."

"This neighborhood is grimy." Sophie gazed around hesitantly at the poorly lit, shuttered buildings. "I haven't seen one decently painted house, and everything needs repair. This isn't the Paris you told me about." She pointed down the street at some old men and women who sat outside their doorways smoking, fanning themselves, and chatting. "You wouldn't see that in Prague." A drunk in tatters, propped up against a nearby water fountain, put his hand out and said something she did not understand. She turned to Willy with a disappointed look. "Or that."

He laughed, sliding an affectionate arm around her, squeezing her tight. "Oh, come, Sophie, the neighborhood around a train station is never the best part of the city. We're safe, and we'll soon have some good food." His gaze roved over the familiar sights of the quarter: cyclists with baguettes strapped across their baskets, the *tabac* across the street next to a butcher, delivery carts parked around a bar where a group of old men propped up the zinc counter, arguing and waving their hands in the air. It was just as he remembered it. "What do you think of this place, Pavel?" he said, tousling the boy's hair.

Pavel did not answer; he was watching the low-slung automobiles dodging around buses, klaxons blaring. Willy bent down. "Look, *Pavlíčku*. Those cars are all French: they're called Citroën, Peugeot, and Renault—and those are French buses." He pointed at the snout-nosed buses: green with beige tops and yellow wheels, the open balcony at the back of each one filled with standing passengers. "Tomorrow we'll ride on one of those."

"Perhaps we should look for a hotel first?" Sophie sighed anxiously. "It's getting late; we might not be able to get a room."

Willy pointed down the street. His chest throbbed unmercifully but he could not let Sophie see his pain. "Look, three hotel signs just in this street. They stay open late to catch people off the train. Come on; make one last effort. We eat first."

With Pavel twisting and turning to look at the honking cars, they crossed the street at the traffic lights. Willy led them past overflowing dustbins, a blind man playing an accordion, and a bakery with pastries and *gateaux* temptingly displayed in the lighted window. At the next intersection, they turned right, walked along the Rue du Faubourg-Saint-Denis, turned left, and there it was, just as he remembered: a café terrace under a multicolored awning. On the terrace, a party of noisy, laughing people clustered around one table while a solitary man in a corner sipped at a tall lager.

The café owner's wife listened patiently to Willy's apology for their scarecrow appearance. She nodded sympathetically, raising her eyebrows when she noticed Willy's bloody jacket. "I understand, *m'sieu*. Life is hard for refugees, and we have too many here. However, you are welcome in my café just as long as you have money to pay. Are you injured *m'sieu?*"

"A little, nothing serious. Do not be concerned. We just got off the train," Willy said.

He ordered fish soup, country *pâté*, ham, and *salade Niçoise*, accompanied by a basket of bread, a bowl of matchstick *frites*, and a carafe of the house red. There was milk for Pavel. They ate in silence, watching the other guests, while Sophie tried to understand what they were saying. She quickly gave up. Her mind was too full of hunger, exhaustion, and belly pain.

For dessert, they ate slices of caramelized lemon tart topped with cream and thin spirals of lemon peel. After he had finished half of his slice, Pavel climbed onto his father's lap and closed his eyes. Willy stroked his curls and then reached across to take Sophie's hand. He smiled at her—that brilliant, heart-stopping smile he used to give her in the months and years before his arrest. "You're looking much better after some food. You were so pale and exhausted on the train, I worried that you were getting ill. Do you feel up to a kiss?"

"Yes, but I'm too sleepy for a really big kiss," she murmured, putting her lips to his ear to make him shiver and remind him that she loved him.

"I've been wondering ever since we left the German border. What happened—when the woman guard went off with you and Pavel?"

Sophie hesitated, trying to blink her tears away, hoping the dam would not burst. She tried to straighten her unkempt hair, her mind rolling back to the feel of Bruch's rubber gloves penetrating deep inside her. "I made the Nazis pay for what they did to us. I smeared Pavel's *kacke* all over the cell."

"God in heaven!" Willy gazed at her, his hands clenching the edge of the table. "Didn't you think of the consequences of getting caught? For you, or Pavel, or me?"

"You're right. I was too outraged to think straight. Do not talk so loudly, *milačku*. People will hear us."

Willy exploded into laughter and raised his glass to her. "They don't understand Czech here, and it's a free country, not Germany. You can shout it out if you like. All the same, I wish I had seen Pavel's *kacke* all over your cell. You showed guts."

Sophie took a deep breath. She was afraid of what to say next, but she had to ask. "It's my turn now. What happened to you? Why did they let us go so easily? We were Jews with false passports, for God's sake. I was sure they would arrest us."

Willy's gaze shifted around the room. She guessed he was trying to marshal his thoughts. "They stripped me. Cut me with a knife... to show who was boss, I suppose. Then I had a touch of luck. The Oberführer who interrogated me, a fellow called Heizinger, was Gestapo, a dandy. Unbelievably, I recognized his suit—Anglotex fabric with Lemberger's tailoring. It had a dragon tail buttonhole."

Sophie's eyes grew as large as turtle eggs. Her mouth dropped open. "You're joking with me. The Gestapo man had been to Prague?"

Willy nodded. "Turned out Heizinger was there with our friend Thümmel, who brought him to our store. When Heizinger said he remembered me from the store, we talked more amicably—and he gave us a break."

Sophie could not believe her ears. "That was it? He let us go for just knowing you?"

Willy started to smile—an uneasy smile, Sophie thought.

"He cut me, part of his interrogation. But my name wasn't on any wanted list in Berlin—of course, he took all our money."

Sophie's face fell. "I'm sorry, Willy. They found my diamonds."

Willy winked and put a forefinger against the side of his nose. "Don't worry, strudel. I'm a magician and I've conjured up a reserve fund."

Sophie gave him a frosty stare. "This is not a time for joking, Willy."

"No, really. I have a couple of valuable gold coins inside the heels of my shoes. Had it done in Budapest. We'll sell them here, I'll repay my debt to M. Panasse, and we can rent a decent room."

Sophie smiled, applauding him silently. Pavel was fast asleep on his father's knees. "I'm so proud of you, Willy. *Du bist ein echter Macher.*"

Willy sipped his coffee and gave her a wistful look. "Not really, strudel, a Macher is someone who gets things done by insights or devising clever solutions. We are here because I broke rules; I lied, bribed, and betrayed people. I'm no longer the honorable person you married."

She took a swallow of Perrier water. "That's ridiculous. You did it for us, didn't you? I don't understand why you didn't tell me about the coins. It's what I said before: you make decisions without me and keep secrets."

"It was one less burden for you to carry in your head, my dear, one less thing to be forced out of you if we were detained."

Sophie shook her head. She wanted to share burdens, not ignore or deny them. She leaned back with a resigned sigh. "So, tomorrow. What happens, and the day after?"

Willy took a long sip of wine and, in spite of the somnolent Pavel slung over his lap, tapped out a quiet left-handed arpeggio along the edge of the table. "Tomorrow, we'll send a telegram to my parents in London that we're safe. After that, you contact your cousin Feri, and I will try to sell the coins. Of course, we must find somewhere cheap and nice to stay, and I will go to the Czech legation. They give advice for newly arrived refugees. Maybe I'll even find work."

Sophie laughed. "Not until your wound is taken care of. Besides, I don't see you taking orders from anyone. You've always been your own boss."

Willy waved a correcting finger at her. "I could use my languages, offer my skills to the French security service, or work for the Czech consulate. Selling the coins should buy me enough time to scout for a decent job. In Budapest, the dealer told me they were worth around four hundred American dollars. That's probably enough to cover our food and lodging for a while." Wincing, Willy stiffly pushed back his chair. "Listen, I'll get us a room at the Hôtel de Metz across the street. You stay here with Pavel. It shouldn't take long." Solemnly, he handed her the five-hundred-franc note donated by M. Panasse. "Never too early to start. This will be your first important task in France. Pay the bill and give the friendly lady a five-franc tip." Grinning at her alarm, he kissed the tip of her nose and shuffled away.

When Willy returned ten minutes later, he put his right arm around her shoulders and hugged her. "You paid? Everything fine?"

She nodded and handed him a bundle of notes and coins.

"Good girl. We have a room—a small double bed, and there's a washbasin in the corner."

They walked out of the café with the sleeping Pavel draped over Willy's right shoulder. Sophie followed behind, carrying the string bags. They crossed the street, both limping; the sounds of conversation and laughter from the café terrace faded.

As they waited in the somber hotel lobby for someone to respond to the reception bell, Willy pointed to a poster on the wall opposite the desk. Gazing imperiously into the distance, a golden-haired woman in a voluminous white dress held the French tricolor flag aloft with one arm. Her other hand held an outsized bar of chocolate. The words CHOCOLAT BONNART formed a semi-circular banner over her head.

"That's Marianne, selling chocolate," Willy said with a sardonic glint in his eye. "She's the symbol and spirit of the French Republic. You see what is written underneath. LIBERTÉ, EGALITÉ, FRATERNITÉ—that's the motto of the French Revolution." He turned to Sophie, eyebrows raised. "Impressive, don't you think? A woman in charge of the soul of France."

Giving her husband a skeptical look, Sophie cocked her head. "She might be in charge of France's soul, but what about the other French women? I heard they don't even have the vote—Slovak women do."

Surprised at Sophie's knowledge, Willy gave her a quizzical look. "Well, no, but I don't think we should argue about that now." He shifted Pavel's position on his shoulder and winced.

"I—"

The velvet curtain behind the reception desk swished open and a short, elderly woman in a dark purple dress appeared at the desk. "*Ah, oui, c'est vous, m'sieu.* You came by earlier." She opened a ledger, her tongue massaging her lips with effort of writing. "I give you Room 17, fifth floor." She dropped a large black key attached to a short section of plumber's lead piping on the countertop. "It's heavy. You will hear if this falls from your pocket. The room is one hundred and five francs for the night. No breakfast. Pay now." She looked hard at Willy's jacket and then back at Sophie. "You speak good French, *m'sieu.* From the look of you, you have had a painful journey. Do you need medical attention?"

"No thank you."

"Excuse me for asking but are you by any chance Jewish refugees? So many come to Paris these days."

Willy hesitated for a moment. "No," he said firmly, putting the correct money in bills next to the key. "We are not Jews." His heart thumped with anger and shame at the indignity of having to lie. He could not allow his family to be thrown out on the street, not now. They were all too tired. Thank God, Sophie and Pavel did not understand French.

The woman dabbed her drippy nose with a handkerchief. "You see, *m'sieu,* I ask because my son forbids Jews in his hotel."

Willy looked directly into her eyes. He was ready for a fight, but this was neither the time nor place to make a stand. "We are refugees, *madame,* not Jews," he said, cursing her for making him lie again.

She nodded. "Remember, number 17, fifth floor. Through the courtyard. The stairs are on your right. *Bonne nuit, m'sieu, madame.*"

As they walked through the dimly lit courtyard, Willy noticed another poster fastened to the concrete wall above a cluster of dustbins. He checked his step for a moment to peer at it—and sucked in a breath. It was crudely done. A misshapen, wolfish-looking man with a Star of David hanging from his neck crouched on his hands and knees. With rotting teeth, he snarled up at a fresh-faced French couple standing with their arms around a little girl's shoulders in front of a neat cottage. At the bottom were the words:

DON'T LET THEM DESTROY YOUR COUNTRY
EJECT THE JEWS
JOIN LA LIGUE FRANÇAISE

Willy clasped Pavel more tightly as anger swept through his body. Years ago as a student in Paris, he had never come across anything as blatant as this. Anti-Semitism had become a contagion in Europe.

He started up the stairs, but Sophie stayed back to look at the poster. She put her finger on the Star of David and looked round at Willy with startled eyes. "I may not understand the words, but I know what this means." Her face was inexpressibly sad. "After all the hardships we've been through, the same hatred is here in France."

He paused on the stairs and shrugged. "It's everywhere."

On the way up to the room, they stopped to wash in the small bathroom. Sophie made use of her last squares of dress for her period, wondering how she would manage in the morning. She waited outside with Pavel while Willy examined the extent of his cut and washed off the crusted blood. He covered it again with the Frenchman's bloody handkerchiefs, fastening everything with Madame's chiffon scarf around his upper chest.

They undressed in the hot room, too tired to notice the shredded wallpaper and torn lace curtains. Willy opened the window wide and lay down on the lumpy mattress beside Sophie, with Pavel between them, his feet by their faces, the moonlight shining on his chubby nakedness.

After a while, Willy turned to face Sophie and saw she was still awake. "I thought you were exhausted. What are you thinking about?"

"So many things. Too many things. That poster as well. I saw how they pictured the Jew."

His heart turned over at the sight of tears glistening on her cheek. Tears were sad but also good. Tears meant she had not been completely numbed by the harshness of their journey. He watched her wipe them away with the edge of the coverlet. "I was thinking how lucky we are to be safe and have Pavel with us," she whispered, "and how sad I am to lose the things I loved.

I want us to be happy. Do you think we can be happy again like we used to be—even if we have to stay here?"

Willy reached over Pavel's sleeping form to trace her lips with his fingers. He smiled at her in the half-light. "I still love you just as much, strudel. As for happiness, I am sure it will come, but only after we have the essentials: food, a place to sleep, and a feeling of security. What we've been through these past few days has blown away the life we knew, probably changed us in ways we don't yet know."

Sophie nodded. Her voice was low but intense. "I think you have hardened, become angry at life."

Willy sighed. He was intensely aware of the thirst to revenge himself on everything represented by Altmann, Lessig, and Heizinger— the Nazis and the country that nursed them to power. He could think of only one way to do that, join the forces opposing them. Fight with the French or British army, even though their politicians had betrayed Czechoslovakia and handed her to the Nazis. How could he do that and protect his family at the same time? That was the conundrum.

In prison, he had been afraid only for himself, had almost forgotten his family and betrayed others. He still felt the tug of his past life, but the dreams of success were gone. He had no country now. Maybe one day there would be a better future.

"You are right, strudel. I see the world as a dangerous place, and every time we run up against some crisis my smashed finger works as a signal. Any wrong or sudden movement sends shocks up my arm, and like a reflex, my anger boils up from deep inside me." His face molded into a dark expression of exasperation and determination. "Even here we will meet obstacles and reversals. We just have to hope. One way or another, we will find a way to Britain and join my parents. We can catch our breath here and work on ways of getting to London. If we are blocked, I will show you Paris, and you and Pavel will learn French. We'll get through this together."

Sophie raised herself on an elbow, and Willy caught his breath as the moonlight suffused her hair and high cheeks with delicate, silvery light. Worn out, bedraggled and disheveled, she was still beautiful.

Gazing at him across the pillows, Sophie grew nostalgic for the passion of their marriage. Somehow, Willy suffering in prison had diminished their love, first physically, and then a distance had grown between them. Making love again when they were ready, she thought, would repair their closeness. In the meantime, she was glad Willy had kept some optimism. She and Pavel needed it.

I have become hard, too, she thought. *I hate the country I grew up in. Like Willy, I will do anything to help bring Germany down.*

Looking back on her contented, soft life in Prague, Sophie understood that the difficult journey had tested her, tempered her mind and body. For the moment, she was exhausted, but she was also ready for the future. She shifted closer to Willy, Pavel's legs pressing against her breasts. The boy did not stir. "You were always such an optimist," she whispered. "Remember in Budapest, you said our escape would be an adventure. Well, you were right. It was an adventure—but a horrible one without any fun. Even so, we were lucky—and you made the right decisions at the right times."

"Thank you, strudel." Willy lifted his injured hand level with his shoulder and tucked a pillow under it—Dr. Pflinz's orders. "In Paris, we will have the same: luck, chutzpah, and strategic thinking, but with a French flair this time."

Sophie smiled and stifled a yawn. "That will be fine, *miláčku*. I don't want to talk about our escape anymore. I am very tired. Nevertheless, there is one last thing I want to get straight: no more calling me 'strudel.' I am not a dessert; I'm a woman."

Willy nodded and laughing softly, kissed her, his face just above hers. "It's a little bit different for women in France, you know. Husbands here call their wives '*mon petit chou*,' 'my little cabbage.' What if I called you that?"

Sophie's face registered horror. "Horrible. From now on, I just want to be me, Sophie."

"So be it. You will be just you."

"I'm afraid of the future, Willy."

Willy smiled "I'm not. Hitler will never defeat France, and Britain rules the seas. We paid a price for getting here in one piece. Tomorrow we start over."

"Your dressing has shifted." Sophie raised herself on her elbow. "Now I can see what he did to you." She put a tentative finger on his skin, close to the cut. "It looks like a snake."

Willy fell back on his pillow and looked out at the moon, through the lace curtain. "No, it's not a snake. Heizinger said he would give me a memento. I think he was trying to carve a dragon tail."

NOTES AND ACKNOWLEDGEMENTS

I have relied heavily on certain published resources:

MASTER OF SPIES by General Frantisek Moravec, Sphere Books Ltd. 1975.

PRAGUE IN DANGER by Peter Demetz, Farrar, Strauss and Giroux, 2008.

ON ALL FRONTS: CZECHS AND SLOVAKS IN WORLD WAR 2, Editor Lewis M. White.

EAST EUROPEAN MONOGRAPHS, Boulder CO. 1991 (Vols 1, 2)

CZECHOSLOVAKIA IN WW2, EAST EUROPEAN MONOGRAPHS, Boulder CO. 2000. Ed, Lewis M. White.

PRAGUE IN THE SHADOW OF THE SWASTIKA, Collum MacDonald and Jan Kaplan, Facultas Verlags-und Buchhandels AG. 2001 Wien.

EAST CENTRAL EUROPE BETWEEN THE TWO WORLD WARS, Joseph Rothschild, University of Washington Press, 1974.

Letters from Prague, 1939-1945, compiled by Raya Czener Schapiro and Helga Czerner Weinberg. Academy Chicago Publishers, 2006.

The Jews of Bohemia and Moravia: Facing the Holocaust, 2005. University of Nebraska Press.

The Rescue of the Prague Refugees, 1938-1939 by William Chadwick, Matador Press, 2010.

The Jews of Czechoslovakia: Historical Studies and Surveys, volume 3. Eds. Avigdor Dagan, Gertrude Hirschler, and Lewis Weiner, 1984.

The Jewish Publication Society of America, Philadelphia.

Society for the History of Czechoslovak Jews, New York.

Memoirs of a Volunteer, Henry Baumgarten, The Book Guild Ltd. Lewes. Sussex, UK. 1990.

Escape to England, Karel A. Machachek, 1988. The Book Guild Ltd. Lewes, Sussex, UK.

There are also digital sources, specifically www.Chaverim.sk/English/history.php and the Lučenec Encyclopedia of Jewish Communities, Slovakia at www.jewishgen.org/yizkor/pinkas_slovakia.

യ ∂ യ

To my publisher and editor David Blixt of Sordelet Ink, thank you for enthusiastically taking a chance on me. Thanks also to Marlin Greene of 3Hats, an extraordinary photographer responsible for my website and book cover design.

I am indebted to the vociferous critiques and energizing encouragement of two writer groups in Seattle. Vios Writers: Lynn Knight, Lauren Basson, Brita Butler-Wall, Gary Bloxham and Scott

Wyatt. Third Place Writers: Teresa Hayden, Teri Howatt, Elizabeth Gage, Brian Schuessler and Bob Macalister.

I am also grateful to book doctor Jason Black for his incisive diagnosis and recommendations and to Peter Demetz, David Laskin, Helen Szablyahj for their reviews.

Thanks also to Victoria Gardner, Larry Smith, Jacqueline Williams, Goldie Silverman, Lynn and George Guttman and Elisabeth Krijgsman for critical reading of the manuscript.

My thanks to Lisa Poisso, copy editor and to Nina Marcussen of the Václav Havel Czech School of Dallas for language authenticity.

ᔉ ∂ ᔉ

For more information on my historical research and this book, please visit www.petercurtisauthor. com.

Discussion Questions / Reading Group Guide
The Dragontail Buttonhole
by Peter Curtis

Synopsis

Willy and Sophie Kohut (and their toddler Pavel) own a store in Prague, selling men's suiting fabrics imported from Britain and Italy. On March 15th 1939 the Nazis occupy Czechoslovakia. Willy is arrested as a British spy and tortured. After his release the family, posing as Hungarians, escapes through Hungary and Germany paying a small time smuggler to drive them. Their journey is fraught with dangerous incidents, but they battle through. Finally, at the German frontier with Belgium they are unmasked as Jewish and detained. Through a strange coincidence involving the recognition of a dragontail buttonhole on the senior German official's jacket, they are allowed to regain the train to Paris and safety.

Dispossessed, nearly penniless and changed by events beyond their control, Willy and his wife Sophie now have different ideas about what they want from life.

Reading Group Questions

1. The Dragontail Buttonhole takes place in three different European countries as WW2 is about to start. How does the atmosphere of the three countries differ and affect the story?

2. Did the author provide enough background information for you to understand the story's narrative?

3. What motivates Willy Kohut's actions? Are they justified, understandable, realistic?

4. What motivates Sophie Kohut's actions? Are they justified, understandable, realistic?

5. What was your reaction to the actions of characters who seemed to change allegiance or attitudes?

6. Who were the villains in the story? What motives drove them?

7. The Kohuts come into contact with friends, acquaintances and enemies. Which ones did you find the most memorable or vivid?

8. In the course of the story the two protagonists come face to face with danger and adversity. How do they change by the end of the novel?

9. What was most important in this novel, the characters or the plot? Was the action believable?

10. Did you find yourself on the edge of your seat during any of the scenes? Did the plot twists hold your interest? Explain.

11. How did Willy and Sophie's flashbacks affect the story and your appreciation of it?

12. What did you think of the ending?

13. Little Pavel plays an increasing role in the story as it progresses. Does his character and behavior fit his age?

14. What was your favorite scene or passage in The Dragontail Buttonhole. Was there anything unique about the writing style?

15. Did you find the author's use of foreign words enhanced or detracted from the story.

16. In this novel the author explores how a family under severe stress and fear reacts.... as individuals and working together. How successfully does he show this?

17. Can you identify the central message of The

Dragontail Buttonhole. What do Willy and Sophie think about the world and their role in it?

18. What statement is Peter Curtis making about human nature in his novel?

19. Now that you've read The Dragontail Buttonhole, are you interested in the sequel that follows their lives in France and escape to Britain?

FOR MORE, PLEASE VISIT
WWW.PETERCURTISAUTHOR.COM

CPSIA information can be obtained
at www.ICGtesting.com
Printed in the USA
LVOW12s2256180717

541841LV00001B/43/P